The

SAGA TREE

The
SAGA TREE

Hugh Noble

LITTLE, BROWN AND COMPANY

A *Little, Brown* Book

First published in Great Britain in 1994
by Little, Brown and Company

Copyright © Hugh Noble 1994

A CIP catalogue record for this book is
available from the British Library

ISBN 0 316 90675 1

Typeset by M Rules
Printed and bound in Great Britain by
BPC Hazell Books Ltd.
A member of
The British Printing Company Ltd.

Little, Brown and Company (UK) Limited
Brettenham House
Lancaster Place
London WC2E 7EN

To Frances

Best friend and love, my true contemporary,
She taught me how to live, then how to die,
And I curate her dreams and gallery.

Douglas Dunn, *Writing with Light*

Acknowledgements

I would like to thank my agent Robin Denniston for much encouragement and very good advice. I would also like to thank my son David for not being as critical as I thought he would be and for pointing out some mistakes. (All errors and omissions are, of course, my own.) My main thanks, however, must go to my late wife Frances who, despite her desperate and painful illness, gave some bits a thumbs up, others a thumbs down, gave everything a smile and told me that women do not behave like that. Above all, she gave me unstinting encouragement and love.

PROLOGUE

'Why's it called Yggdrasil?' said Ian.

They were moving up hard, steep snow in the corrie below the climb. They paused and leaned backwards to look at the precipice above them.

'Because it's shaped like a tree,' said Allan. 'The Yggdrasil was a kind of tree.'

The cliff above them was foreshortened by the angle but they could see the way the groove branched and branched again as the narrow band of green ice, trapped between the white crusted rocks, soared upwards.

'Never seen one. Where does it grow?'

'It's a mythical tree. It's in the old Norse Sagas. Its branches, trunk and roots are supposed to hold together Heaven, Earth and Hell. But it got all burned up on the Day of Ragnarok – that was a sort of Twilight of the Gods.'

The axes gave purchase. They had two each. The downwardly curved blades bit solidly. Hamish in the lead kept up a steady rhythm. The snow accepted the bite of their crampons with a squeal like harvest mice.

Hamish said, 'That must be a hell of a tree. Which is which?'

'Which is what?'

'Are the branches Hell or are the roots Hell or what?'

'The branches are Heaven and the trunk is Earth or ordinary life and the roots are in Hell. They dip into a spring which is the "Spring of all Knowledge".'

Ian paused and considered that, leaning forward on his axe. His breath hung white in the still air. Their mouths tasted the coldness of it. 'Useful for examination purposes,' he said.

'Aye,' said Allan. He paused below Ian and buried the shaft of his axe deep. 'But there's a price to pay if you drink there.'

'Knew there'd be a catch. What's the price?'

'Odin had to sacrifice an eye.'

1

Thirteen Months Earlier:
JANUARY

They sat by the summit cairn, sheltering under balaclavas and anorak hoods while the wind lifted ice-particles off the surface and drove them against their backs like grape-shot. The sandwiches they ate with clumsy mittened hands were frozen and tasteless and the chocolate bars were as brittle as glass. The snow-bound peaks around them were named and argued over and reminisced about and then they moved on, descending the western ridge and taking the wind head on. Lower down the snow was wet and the spindrift lost its sting. A long plod came next through wet snow, then bog and mud to the glen and the tents. Thermal clothing was dank with perspiration, cold crept into the bones and thoughts turned wearily to hot soup.

The camp site was a flat piece of grass beside the river at a point where the flood burst through a narrow gap in a natural dyke. Water, the colour of muddy custard, surged and roared. A small sidestream from which they drew their drinking water had risen during the day and had turned the flat area of grass into a pond, leaving the tents above water level, but only just. There was another tent nearby and a camper van had arrived during the day. The people inside drank tea and watched with amusement the efforts of the trio to get out of their wet clothes and into something dry without getting their tents soaked in the process.

That was when the stranger arrived. He was young, his climbing gear was split new and he was totally exhausted. He flopped down beside them, ashen faced. The story was punctuated by pauses as he sucked air.

They had been trying to climb the Dearg slabs.

'In these conditions?' Ian rolled his eyes and spread his palms in supplication to the heavens.

Avalanche. Windslab had swept three of them off the rock face. Two companions were buried in snow at the base of the cliff. He had landed in deep powder. A third friend was stranded high on the rock.

It was Allan, the quiet one, who gave the orders. He pushed the exhausted climber into the camper van. He sent the van and its occupants up the glen for help. He dragged the couple out of the other tent and used them as beasts of burden for ropes, axes, pegs, torches, sleeping bags, stove, cans, chocolate bars. He attacked their own tents and stripped them of the long, flexible, carbon fibre poles which held them up. For a moment Hamish watched him open-mouthed as the tents collapsed into a sodden heap. Then he began to help. They thrust complaining limbs back into their cold, sodden clothing.

It was darkening. There was a lurid orange patch in the western sky and the black ragged clouds were beginning to disperse. The wind was dropping. A star or two twinkled through chinks.

They walked fast, stumbling occasionally into a jog trot and then dropping back to walking pace. Legs, stiff at first, settled back into harness. They stuffed chocolate bars as they walked.

Gradually the group began to straggle. Each took rests, dropping out of the group when lungs or legs or heart would do no more. They rested where they were, on hands and knees, eyes shut, head down into the mud, open-mouthed and gasping. Mud and bog came first, then snow, soft and dragging at their limbs, then hard and slippery as the temperature dropped, then dry and powdery above the melt line.

It was black when Allan reached the corrie. The wind had

gone and the sky was clear. The mountain stood wedge-shaped and jet against prickly stars. By torchlight he found the tracks made by the exhausted climber. They led to a steep bank of snow below the crags. He knew the climb. A shallow scoop running up the slabs – easy enough in summer but a natural avalanche chute in these conditions. The beam of his head-lamp torch shafted through the darkness. The lower half of the slabs had been swept clean but a weight of snow still clung to the upper half, threatening to bury them all. There was a cry from somewhere above. The climber was there, to the right of the groove, a splodge of coloured windproofs clinging to bare rock six hundred feet up.

Hamish and Ian arrived and began quartering the snow drift, prodding, prodding, prodding with the long carbon fibre poles. Allan extracted pegs and a hammer from his rucksack, clipped them to his waistline and started up the slabs. He was a hundred feet up and going rhythmically, legs working like a paddle-steamer, when he heard other voices below him. More lights were flicking along the base of the cliff.

There was a great stillness. The noise of falling water echoed in the huge rock amphitheatre like the rustle of an expectant audience. The slabs were not vertical but it was dark, and powder snow, packed hard by the force of the avalanche, stuck to the holds. The pool of light from his head torch illuminated a holographic image of the changing seasons. Looking upwards there seemed to be no snow but looking downwards all was white. And all the time he was conscious of the big bank of snow sitting high above him on the slabs, waiting to slide.

He heard a shout from below. The voice rang out, echoing among the black crags. Then there was more shouting and Ian's voice came floating up the face to him.

'We've got one of them!/them! He's still alive!/alive!' The words had a double beat in the hollow blackness.

He wished he had taken time to put on crampons. They would have been awkward no doubt since there was no depth of snow for them to bite into – it would have been like walking on stilts – but at least they would have sunk through the thin layer of snow on the holds. He scraped each hold clear with the adze of his axe. The noise of it, a hollow drain-pipe sound, echoed round the corrie. Gloved hands were sopping wet and growing numb as he fumbled for a purchase. His breath wheezed. A hundred feet higher the holds became smaller and he had difficulty making progress. Quiet whimpering noises came to him from the trapped climber, not too far above now. That helped. He did not have to waste time looking for him. He moved towards the sound, conscious of a great, black empty space around and below.

And then the climber was there just above him, crouching, half lying against the rock face. A huddle of anorak, red snow-gaiters and a small patch of white which might have been a face. A bit of rope was tied to the man's waist. It was severed and splayed on the rock, unravelling like long, white silky hair.

Allan moved to the left, afraid that the man would try to move and fall before he could get to him. He climbed past him. Allan now needed to get the rucksack off but there was nowhere to stop. He went a few feet higher and heard a stran-gled cry of despair from the trapped climber.

He tried to be reassuring. 'Just hang on – I need a belay.' He kept his voice quiet and undramatic.

At last! A ledge half the width of his boots where he could stand without handholds. He selected a short steel peg and tried it for size in several cracks near him. Blind cracks going nowhere. He moved sideways a couple of yards and found one which took the peg. Legs splayed, he leant forwards, stomach against the cliff, hammer in his right hand, peg in his left, left arm across his chest threatening to topple him backwards. At first he could do little more than tap the peg with the hammer. Then as the peg bit into the rock he could take his left hand away and take a proper swing. The sound of it changed from a dull clatter to a musical ping, rising in pitch as the exposed length of the peg shortened. The clear ringing tones rang round the mountain.

'It's the bells! It's the bells!' The words from far below were scrambled by the echo but were cheerful in the darkness. Ian doing his Henry Irving impersonation.

Another shout floated up.

'We've got the other one, Allan!/Allan! Do you need help?/help?'

The peg was in. He clipped himself to it and could relax. He needed more rope but it was too complicated to explain while the trapped climber was still clinging to the cliff. The man would be deathly cold, perhaps barely conscious. Allan ignored the shouts and concentrated on getting a rope out of the pack.

'Do/do . . . you/you . . . need/need . . . help?/help?'

Slowly, with his chest against the rock, he disengaged the straps of the rucksack from his shoulders and eased them down past his elbows. The straps, damp and stiff, were reluctant to move. For a moment his arms were pinned at his sides. He shook himself until the pack dropped a little further. Then it was free and he had it in one hand.

From out of the blackness came the throb of helicopter blades.

Still he leant forwards with chest on the rock, feet spread widely and sideways. He swung the pack up and clipped it to the peg. Numbed hands fumbled at the quick release buckles. The rope came out and dragged a couple of pegs with it. They clattered down the cliff.

'Ya!/Ya! . . . missed me!/missed me!' That was Hamish's voice.

Damn! he could have used these pegs. From the darkness below came the drain-pipe gargle of an axe scraping on rock. He clipped the rope to the peg and threw the coil down the slabs. It tangled and landed in a heap but at least it had got past the climber. He unclipped himself from the peg and reclipped his harness to the rope. With straddled legs he gripped the rope and walked backwards down the cliff until he stood astride the trapped man. He had him now. He pinned the man against the rock with his weight.

'Get this round you.'

Just a youth still in his teens. He was too frightened or too cold to let go of the indifferent handholds. Allan thrust a loop of nylon tape round the boy's waist and round his thighs to form a makeshift harness. They were clipped together. The boy could not fall now.

'I've got him on the rope/rope but I need more rope!/rope!' He heard his own words converted into a staccato double beat.

'What?/What?'

'Need/need . . . more/more . . . rope/rope!!'

'Broke?/broke?'

'Rrrope!/rope!'

The scraping noise started again. Ian and Hamish were discussing something. He heard a laugh. Lights were flicking about at the base of the cliff and another pair of lights were nearer on the rock itself and getting closer. The other bunch of lights were moving away from the cliff. The noise of the chopper was also closer, thrumming like drumbeats. There was a light in the sky – close above – moving inside the corrie.

Allan spread his legs again and began to ease himself and his bundle down the rope. The boy cried out in fear as he lost his grip and slid downwards until the harness held him. They slid down the cliff together. When they reached the tangle they had to stop while Allan tried with one hand to free it. He got it clear. Ian and Hamish were closer.

By the time Allan reached the end of his rope Hamish was beside him.

'How're you doing, lad?'

'OK, but I've got no more rope and this one is fixed. I'll have to leave it behind or go up for it.' Hamish climbed past him and found a place to drive a peg. The bell tone rang again and then Allan was able to transfer himself and his bundle to the second rope. This time the rope was doubled so that they could bring it down after them. They repeated the operation before they reached the base of the cliff. Ian and Hamish took turns at shepherding him and rearranging the ropes. As they neared the base of the cliff they were caught in a brilliant spotlight from high above them. The beat of chopper blades was very loud and the down-draught caught them. Dazzled, they dropped down on to the snow cone and half fell, half slid to the foot of the avalanche debris.

The couple from the camp site were a short distance away. The chopper was directly overhead. Deafening. The two avalanche victims were in sleeping bags. Suddenly there was another man with them, two men. Helmets. Flying suits. And a stretcher with straps and flaps. A primus stove was going and someone thrust a mug of soup into Allan's hands. Someone held a mug to the boy's lips. The men from the chopper took over, carrying the avalanche victims to a spot where the chopper could hover. Hamish was talking to them. He shouted into the ear of one of them, 'We need our sleeping bags!' and the man nodded and pointed up at the chopper with his thumb.

The three victims were hoisted aboard and a bundle of wet sleeping bags thudded down on to the rocks.

And then the chopper was gone in a great downrush of air. Darkness and silence settled back into the corrie.

It was dawn before they reached the tents. On the way down, cold as they were, they stopped every few yards for rest, legs plastered in mud, boots full of bog water. The tents were flat on the ground. A sheep was standing in the middle of a crumpled heap of canvas. The burn had risen a little further. The tents were awash.

'Fucking hell,' said Ian, sinking to his knees. 'We left the fucking tent poles up in that fucking avalanche cone.'

2

APRIL

'It's the Tunnocks y' want then.'

The taxi driver had a rasping, nicotine-laden voice. He eyed the suitcase cautiously, held the boot open, and stood well back as Allan lifted it in, large and as heavy as a gravestone.

'The Tunnocks? No, the MCI building.'

'Aye, the MCI place – we ca' it the Tunnocks here.'

In the back seat Allan extracted his letter of appointment from an inside pocket and studied it. At the top were the letters MCI in tan with a gold lightning flash superimposed. Underneath was the address of the local Gairnock Plant, 'Scottish Director, Wensley Halpern BSc FBCS'. At the bottom of the page were more addresses in tiny lettering – the company headquarters in Ocean Springs, Chile, 'President, J. Norman Marble', the New York Office – more names, the London Office. There was no reference to 'Tunnocks'.

The rain had started again. Water was sluicing across the windscreen, and the wipers, swishing like curling brooms, were being overwhelmed. The driver, however, seemed to be operating on radar. He pointed right in the direction of the sea where only a few yards of white froth were visible in the murk. 'Over there y've got the Cloch lighthouse. Doon there . . .' – he pointed ahead and to the right – ' . . . y've got the

Gantocks. An' doon here where the MCI plant is, y've got the Tunnocks.' He laughed. Allan was not sure if he was the source of mirth. The driver extracted a fag from his mouth and coughed heavily. ' . . . where,' he went on, 'if they don't like you they don't sack you, they just call in the Mafia and bump you off.' He laughed again. Allan had seen the bill posters on the station news-stands –

SECOND MCI BOFFIN DEAD
SILICON GLEN MYSTERY DEEPENS

'You going to work for them, lad?'

'Aye.'

'Whadya make of it then?' He lifted a tabloid newspaper from the seat beside him and held it so that Allan could see the front page. For a moment Allan was transfixed by the road ahead as the car veered towards oncoming traffic. With difficulty he looked at the page before him. It had a large picture of the Prime Minister with mouth open and finger wagging. Underneath it were the words:

BIMBO'S BOOBS WORTH £1M

Allan blinked and tried to connect the two.

Beside the picture it said:

CID PROBE COMPUTER PLANT

'I don't know. I haven't read about it.'

'That's the second one. The first guy is supposed to have driven his car off a cliff and now this one.'

'What do you think?'

'Something dead fishy about it. Dead fishy, I reckon . . . dead . . .' Belatedly the driver saw his own pun and began a laugh which developed into a choking cough.

The rain stopped as suddenly as it had begun. Unnaturally bright sunlight glinted on the wet road. There were railings to the right, a sea wall, a strip of grass or two and the occasional house. On the left, a phalanx of sandstone houses with bay windows hid their impoverished gentility behind privet hedges. Rooms to let signs and lots of cars and motorcycles wedged in each front drive suggested multiple down-market occupation.

The sea had turned slate blue with white caps dancing. You could see right across the water to the hills of Cowal, grey-blue and sharp edged.

They passed a sign pointing left to a factory plant and further on there was a second notice, this time pointing to MCI. They swung off the main road away from the sea, climbed a hill, and passed some concrete pillars and a noticeboard with the MCI logo. Under the logo was a minor legal document threatening dire consequences stopping just short of summary execution for illegal parking. Lawns stretched out on both sides. It looked like a modern university campus, or a crematorium. The driver pulled up on the gravel in the visitors' car park in front of a large, low-rise rectangular building in biscuit-coloured concrete. It had a continuous band of chocolate-tinted plate glass windows running right round it.

'There y'are,' said the taxi driver. 'D'ye no think it looks just like a Tunnock's Caramel Wafer?'

Three white police cars with flame pink side-bands were prominent in the visitors' car park. They were parked awkwardly – careless of the disciplined order of the other cars. A dark blue police van was parked bang in front of the main door. Any employee who parked there, Allan suspected, would have had his car sent to the crusher.

The taxi driver lifted the lid of the boot and again stood aside while Allan hefted the suitcase. He wished now that he had left it at the station. It hung leaden against his knees, threatening to drag his arms out of their sockets. For a moment he considered swinging it on to his shoulder but he had on his good suit and anyway someone might think it an uncouth way to deal with the problem. This was a very couth place.

A young policeman was sheltering from the wind and rain under the concrete canopy by the front door. He watched, shoulders hunched, coat collar turned up, as Allan, bent to one side like a palm tree in a hurricane, struggled up the wide steps with the case. Allan hesitated at the door. With his free hand he checked surreptitiously at his waistband to ensure that his fly was zipped up before he plunged through the plate glass doors into the soft chocolate interior of the building.

The lapel badge said 'Jennifer'. She was honey blonde, and looked crisp and cool in her cream blouse and MCI cravat. He asked for Dr Telman. Jennifer gave him a gleaming professional smile, fixed him up with a security badge and phoned to announce his arrival. He stood there awkwardly with the suitcase at his feet, feeling small rivulets of perspiration running down his back, watching the girl with his peripheral vision – so confident and self-assured, so attractive, so unapproachable. The building was air-conditioned. After the breeze outside, it seemed to have the consistency and texture of warm fudge.

Rosa Telman recognised him immediately. She was quite small. He had forgotten that. At his oral exam she had seemed to fill the room with her presence. Psychologically she had towered over him. Folk said that hardly anyone ever fails a PhD oral exam but that for him seemed to make the consequences of failure even more appalling. She had given him a hard time – taken him through every twist and turn of his argument in a way that Karl Wellington, his supervisor, had never done – had never been able to do. She made him justify every assertion. At one point she had risen from her chair and rattled off some mathematics on the white board behind Karl's desk. The symbols had seemed to shoot, small, neat and ready-formed, from the end of the green felt pen. She had sprayed them on to the board. Prof. Hudson, who was there to make up the requisite number of examiners, had nodded sagaciously as if he understood. Allan had had to get up too and scribble on the board, with less confidence, bigger lettering with lots of cancellations, trying to demonstrate that his conclusions were valid. He remembered the sudden and beaming smile with which Rosa had greeted him when he turned round to face her.

And now he saw that smile again. She had a smooth oval face; her small, even teeth were very white against her olive skin. She wore no make-up and no jewellery, except for a tortoiseshell comb in her hair, which was short and black and pulled straight back. There was a crease between the dark eyebrows. It was a face more accustomed to a frown than a smile, but a frown of concentration, not of irritation. She wore a maroon blouse with an open neck and loose sleeves, and a long, loose grey skirt with huge pockets.

'Come,' she said. She moved gracefully, with a perfectly straight back and her small hands in the wide pockets of her skirt. As he moved to follow her he fell full-length over the suitcase.

They helped him to his feet – Rosa and the girl at the enquiry desk. Rosa was laughing. 'Jennifer' took charge of the case. He could guess the thoughts hidden behind her polished smile.

'You've caught us at a bad moment,' said Rosa as she led him down a long tunnel-like passageway with walls that seemed to be clad in cream leather. She walked briskly while Allan loped awkwardly at her side.

'You may have heard. There's been a tragedy. One of our people was found dead yesterday – Tommy Harkness – such a nice boy.' Her accent was slightly foreign with guttural Rs. She held open a fire door as though she was afraid Allan would try to walk through the plate glass. Her wrist was so slender he felt he could have snapped it between his fingers. 'He was one of us. One of our research unit.'

They stopped at a lift. He hadn't realised that the building had more than one storey but the indicator lights suggested that there was one floor above them and one below. The lift seemed to be stuck on the floor above them. 'It's all computerised,' she said dryly. 'That's why it works so badly.' Pause. 'Perhaps we will do a correctness check on it.' That was an in-joke. Allan's specialist subject was correctness proofs for computer programs. 'The police are here.' She made a face. 'They are going through Tommy's desk and things. It's all very distressing.' She bit her lip.

'Was it an accident?'

'They're not sure. The suggestion seems to be that he committed suicide, but the police are not telling us very much about it. They are interviewing us one by one. It is all very formal and very upsetting.' The crease between her eyebrows deepened. 'Poor Tommy. He did get a bit depressed sometimes.'

In the lift she said, 'The police are turning everything upside down.'

The research unit occupied a big open-plan office with a commanding view across the Firth of Clyde to the Arran hills. The décor was functional and predominantly grey. He noted with relief that the air was cool and breathable. Felted screens divided the office into cells which people had tried to personalise with picture postcards and coloured cartoons of an angry-looking cat with bulging eyes saying something rude – old office jokes which might just have been funny the first time around. There was a constant quiet and urgent clicking of computer keyboards and an occasional electronic bleep.

Rosa said, 'This is the only office in the building which does not have the tan and cream company colours. We're not sure why. It's what you might call a "grey area".'

Everyone had a cell, a desk and a computer work-station. Lumps of more complex computer equipment sat about on tables and in tall metal filing racks, each connected to a companion rabbit-hole in the floor by a thick twisted rope of communication cables. On a bench lay a computer board covered with black microchips laid out like a miniature housing estate. There were shelves of books perched on every filing cabinet and desk, and high on the walls were more shelves of computer operation manuals. A big coloured poster on the wall showed the labyrinth of connections of some microchip, anonymous and unseen by virtue of continuous exposure. Perhaps the best place to hide secret papers would be to pin them to the wall. Rosa took him round. They went from cell to cell. Handshakes. Names were given and most were instantly forgotten. Rosa gave a potted description of each project. Each time she was corrected by the person concerned. They were all preoccupied – and reluctant to have their work oversimplified. Allan's presence was an intrusion. There was also a hidden air of tension. Glances were exchanged.

Encryption – that was Helen Rowe, the one with the plummy Home Counties accent who made Allan think of village fêtes and jam-making. But she talked breezily of trap-door codes, transmission signals and prime numbers of prodigious length.

Handwriting recognition – Masood Qureshi. A tan stylus stuck out of a cream plastic pad on the bench. You gripped it like a pen in a bank. It did not move but the pressure of your hand was detected and the writing appeared on the screen. It also made thick and thin writing like a brush. A program could analyse your handwriting and recognise your signature. Masood was small and neat with bright eyes, a Clark Gable moustache and a broad Glasgow accent.

Software for testing processor connections – Jack Thornley. He was the only one who seemed to be completely relaxed. Dressed in tartan shirt and jeans, he sprawled in his office chair as though trying to give his spine a permanent curvature. One leg was cocked over the other so that a grubby trainer shoe waved in the air. A pair of personal stereo earphones hung round his neck and a faint buzz emanated from his head. He was a walking Heavy Metal concert. The heavy horn-rimmed spectacles seemed to be a little too big for his face. When Rosa prodded him into recognising their presence, he stabbed his spectacles back on to the bridge of his nose with a forefinger, the thick lenses making his eyes owl-like and watery. His voice had an uncertain pitch, full of squeaks and half chuckles, as though he was sitting on a private joke.

'Join the suspects,' he said, slowly unfolding his legs and shaking Allan by the hand. 'Mm . . . I see from your handshake you're not a Mason.' He shook his head with mock

sadness. 'A bad mistake, lad. The polis'll have you in a cell
before you can blink.'

Rosa was annoyed. She glanced over at a desk near the window to where a young woman and a man of about the same
age sat together at a desk. The man looked round and gave
Jack a disdainful glare.

'And this,' said Rosa, taking Allan over to the desk where
the pair sat, 'is Detective Sergeant . . .'

'McElroy,' said the man. He nodded to Allan but didn't get
up. It looked as though he and the woman beside him were
transferring the contents of the desk to a big black plastic
container which sat on the floor. The woman ignored them
and went on fanning through documents. She dropped one
into the container.

'This desk belonged to Tommy Harkness . . .' Rosa put
both hands to her face and smoothed it to recover her composure. 'Sergeant McElroy here is going through his effects.'
She turned to McElroy. 'Doctor Fraser has just joined us,
Sergeant, so I don't suppose that you will want to interview
him.'

McElroy nodded. He obviously wanted to say something
but he waited until she had finished and then said, 'Dr
Telman. I will need access to your computer – to Harkness's
directory.'

She was shocked. Her mouth opened and shut. 'I am not
sure that company policy would allow that.'

'I'm afraid I must insist. I could get a warrant.'

'A warrant to search a computer? That's a new one.' She put
a hand to her brow and thought. 'One moment. I will need to
discuss this with the director.' She went into her office, which
was a glass cubicle within the open-plan lab.

While she was away McElroy turned to Allan. 'Excuse me,
but are you the Allan Fraser who did Guillotine Route on
Carn Dubh?'

Allan was taken by surprise. 'Aye.'

'Steve McElroy.' He stuck his hand out to shake and smiled
broadly. 'I knew your face was familiar but I couldn't place

you for a moment. We met once at Lagangarbh.' Allan
couldn't recall the meeting. McElroy went on. 'I used to climb
with the Lomonds. Now I'm in the Polis club.' He smiled. He
had said 'polis' deliberately in the Glasgow style. 'I tried
Guillotine myself once and I hardly got off the ground. You
know . . .' – he pointed a finger at Allan's chest – '. . . I've got
a feeling that my Chief Inspector might want to talk to you
after all.'

Rosa returned and said that the director had agreed to give
the police access to Harkness's directory but that the process
would need to be supervised by herself or Bill Thompson,
her deputy. 'You would need help anyway, Sergeant,' she
added, 'to find your way around our operating system.'

McElroy did not look as if he believed that he did need
help but he said nothing. Bill Thompson was called over and
protested. 'I don't know Harkness's password. We'll need to
call the systems manager in.' Bill looked like everybody's idea
of an antiquarian bookseller. He even had a balding head and
a long cardigan with downwardly mobile pencil-stuffed pockets.

More phone calls were made. A policewoman in uniform
came in and spoke to McElroy and went out again. Rosa held
her brow as though she had a headache. No one spoke. They
stood looking at each other, embarrassed, like a therapy group
unsuccessfully seeking togetherness.

Another policewoman came in and said, 'Inspector
Chalmers would like to see you now, Dr Telman.'

Rosa let out a sigh. She told Bill Thompson to look after
McElroy and then she stared at Allan as if she did not know
who he was.

'Oh, Helen! Will you look after Allan while I'm away?'

Helen Rowe almost managed to disguise her impatience.
'One moment.' She put her computer terminal on to 'hold',
displaying random coloured patterns, and then took Allan
over to a cupboard and opened it to reveal a miniature kitchen
with a sink, electric kettle, and coffee machine. A row of mugs,
decorated with more office jokes, dangled on hooks from a

shelf above the sink. The inquisition started along with the extractor fan as she opened the door. She didn't look at him as she spoke. The questions just came out one after another so fast it was hard to tell the soft ones from the bumpers. No, I don't know Gairnock. Weakish with milk. I'm interested in correctness theory – same as Dr Telman. One lump. No. Not a member of the church. Fine. Just right. An atheist actually. I came down by train. Not married. Just a sister and an uncle who brought us up after Mother died. Father died a long time ago. No steady girlfriend. No, I'm not gay. The directness of the questions was breathtaking yet it was done in such a friendly, cheerful, matter-of-fact way that he found himself answering.

They went back to her cell which was also by the window and she caught his gaze drifting towards the rugged outline of the Arran hills. Yes, he liked to go hillwalking. Yes, and climbing. Yes, he would like to go to Arran with Helen and her husband some weekend. Yes, he would like to come for supper some evening. Yes, next week would be fine. No, he didn't have anywhere to stay yet. Bedsitting room, he supposed. No, he didn't have a car – he didn't even have a driving licence. His luggage was behind the receptionist's desk in the front office.

Then Helen had to go and be interviewed and Jack Thornley took over. More questions but with a different tack. Not got anywhere to stay? Would you like a shake down at my place? We can put your bags in my car. It's easy. No bother. You can use it as a base while you find somewhere of your own. Would you like a list of bedsitters? No bother. It's easy to get a list. Honest. You just hack into the computer and extract the list from the Personnel Officer's files – 'Like this – what? Yes, I suppose it is a wee bit illegal but the little prick was asking for it. I set a trap for him, and when he came snooping into my directory, I stole his shell. Look, there's the list – "just like that" as the man said.'

Allan was appalled. A 'shell' is a computer program which responds to a user as he types at the keyboard. It holds infor-

mation about his – or her – security permissions. Stealing a
shell is like stealing, or copying, a front-door key. Allan could
remember an undergraduate in his own year doing the same
thing to fellow students and getting sent down. And now,
within hours of joining the organisation he had been invei-
gled. And there was a detective sergeant in the same room. He
was going to make the *Guinness Book of Records* for career
brevity.

'It's OK, lad. All good clean fun,' said Jack, patting Allan on
the shoulder as the burning reached his ears.

After the personnel manager had rung to arrange an induction
course for Allan, no one knew quite what to do with him. He
was left in a corner with a pile of technical literature.

The systems manager bustled in. He was young, wore a
neat suit with an MCI logo on his tie, and he was in a bad
mood. His watch was on the inside of his wrist and he looked
at it often. He, McElroy and Bill Thompson sat in a huddle
round a computer work-station.

'I've cancelled the password,' the manager said in a loud
voice, 'so you should be able to log-in as Harkness without
one.' He looked at his watch again. 'But be quick, I can't leave
it like that for long.'

From his position in the corner Allan could watch this
cameo and Jack Thornley at the same time. As the manager
spoke, Jack twitched. McElroy typed slowly, watched by the
manager and Bill Thompson. Jack typed quickly. The tape-
drive on Jack's machine burst into life.

The systems manager suggested that he was not needed
anymore and went without waiting for anyone to contradict
him. Bill Thompson lifted a manual and thumbed through it.
He pulled a notebook out of his pocket and began jotting
down a few notes. McElroy was at his elbow but might as well
have been on Alpha Centaurus.

Jack got up, went over to the coffee cupboard and opened it.
He had a self-satisfied grin on his face. He selected a mug and
was spooning instant coffee powder into it when he looked up

and saw Allan watching him. His eyes flicked over to the detective and back again to Allan. He grinned broadly.

McElroy removed a computer tape from the tape-drive beside the work-station. He arranged for two constables to come and carry away the plastic bin full of Harkness's papers and then he and the policewoman left the room. There was a sudden lifting of the tension and people converged on the coffee machine. Allan was forgotten about as they chatted. Voices were raised. Jokes. Banter.

Moments later the door opened and a man came into the room with McElroy in close attendance The man was about fifty, tall, with broad shoulders, and he looked around for a moment before McElroy guided him over to where Allan was sitting.

'Can I introduce Dr Allan Fraser – Allan – Chief Detective Inspector Chalmers.'

The room had gone totally silent. The redness was coming again to Allan's face.

'Bob Chalmers,' said the man, extending his hand. He had clear blue eyes that probed like an endoscope. 'Steve here has told me about you, Allan, and I had to come through and meet you.'

Allan's mouth was wide open and Chalmers laughed. 'Sorry, I should explain. A few months ago you pulled a young man off a crag on Ben Dearg and saved his life. That was my nephew – my sister's boy. I think you probably saved my sister's life as well as his.'

'Oh that,' Allan stammered, conscious of the eyes on his back. 'I wasn't the only one.'

'I know what happened. My nephew told me and I also checked with the helicopter squad. They said he was a dead duck but for you. I think my sister sent you a note but I just wanted to say thank you myself.' He shook Allan's hand again and then they left. Allan turned. The rest of the group were standing by the coffee machine, looking at him as though he had just slithered out of a flying saucer.

★ ★ ★

The big houses which fronted on to the shore road and faced out across the water regarded Fetterburn Road as beneath their faded upper-class dignity. They turned their backs on it and coldly cut it off with high walls topped with broken glass. A few condescended to acknowledge its presence with a garage or a small gate buried in the masonry. On the other side ran a broken line of modest houses, mostly single storied and stone built.

Jack turned left off Fetterburn into Iona Gardens. It was a short cul-de-sac. At the far end were railings and beyond these was a dank, wooded hillside glinting wet in the yellowing evening sunlight. On the left was a once handsome block of terraced houses, three storeys, sandstone, badly needing to be refaced. The houses looked into a small park with mature trees. The soil between the trees was bare black earth, beaten flat. In the centre of the park was a clearing with a children's chute and what had once been a set of swings. Chains without seats hung unevenly in a row like mediaeval dungeon furniture.

Jack's Citroën 2CV stretched with relief and shook itself as they eased Allan's suitcase out of the back seat. The flat was on the top storey. There was one bedroom and a sitting room to the front, a small bathroom and a big kitchen to the rear. He offered Allan the sitting room.

It had been an elegant room, well proportioned with a high ceiling and wide bay window overlooking the park, but the cream paint on the sash windows was cracked and peeling and the wallpaper was torn and dingy. Posters on the walls. Fold-down divan. A microcomputer with printer, disc unit and cables a-dangle. Computer magazines on the table and the floor. A big potted rubber plant by the window. Several other potted plants. Hi-Fi. Tapes and CD cassettes everywhere. Only the greenery was a surprise. Somehow Allan could not see Jack as a Beechgrove Garden enthusiast.

In the kitchen the sink was piled high. Two pots stood on the stove, one crusted with brown curry, the other containing something blackened and unrecognisable. A naked light bulb dangled

over the table and the whole kitchen smelt of overheated fat.
Jack filled the electric kettle, switched it on and washed up two
cups. He eyed the sink distastefully.

'D'ye fancy a Chinese kerry-oot?'

While Jack was out, Allan attacked the sink and had most of
the stuff clean and piled up on the draining board by the time
he got back.

'Oh gee. Thanks. You didn't need to do that.' Jack grinned
and jabbed his spectacles back on to his face. 'Shall we dine?'

He cleared a space on the table by pushing aside a sauce
bottle, a toaster, a plastic carrier bag containing clothing and
a loaf. He had bought a local evening paper and studied it,
with his bottom propped on the edge of the sink, while Allan
unpacked the Chinese food and laid the silver-foil trays on the
table.

'Computer Ace Death Probe,' he read aloud. 'The death of
computer ace Tom Harkness is being treated as suspicious, a
police spokesman said today. The spokesman refused to rule
out a link with the death of another worker at the top secret
research unit at the MCI plant . . . did you know we were top
secret? It's really secret when the people working there don't
know that it is. In't it?' He went back to the paper and pretended to read. ' . . . The spokesman said that the CID
thought that the next one to die will be Dr Allan Fraser.'

Allan ignored him and opened the foil packs, laying the lids
in a neat pile. Jack laughed. He pulled two bottles of Beck's
out from under the sink and sat down at the table. He pushed
one of the bottles over to Allan and spooned some chicken
with cashew nuts on to his rice. He said, 'So what do you
think of life in Death Row?'

On the table-top he spread the newspaper. There was a
grainy picture of a thin young man – almost a boy, he looked –
with eyes close together and a nose that was bent to one side.

'Did you know Harkness well?' Allan ignored the bottle.

'Yeah. A bit. Tommy was an oddball. Not your normal,
regular, well-behaved, well-adjusted guy . . . I mean, he
wasn't a bit like me.' There was mischief in his eyes. 'It was

not easy to know him well.' He extracted a large Swiss army knife from his pocket, selected a tool and opened one of the bottles with it.

'What did he do? No – no thanks.' Allan waved a hand to stop Jack opening the second bottle. Jack shrugged, put his opener away and said, 'Do? – Oh, you mean what was he into? He wrote testing software for processor chips.' He lifted a spare rib and nibbled. Brown gravy ran down his chin.

'I didn't think you built the chips here. I thought that was done in Taiwan.'

'It is,' said Jack. He got up and pulled a piece of paper towel off a roll to wipe his chin. 'We just assemble the machines from parts. But you know the chips are over-connected. More bloody connections in them than anybody could possibly want. So down on the assembly floor we customise them by burning out some of the connections. Then they have to be tested before they get cooked to make it permanent.'

'So Harkness wrote the software that tested the connections. You do that as well, don't you?'

'Aye. Same thing – different chip. He did it for communications chips, I do it for graphics chips – we both start with the same basic processor, the MC65000. But we only do small modifications. The main bit is done by programs written in the States or down at HQ in Ocean Springs.'

'So you would know better than most what he was doing recently.'

Jack looked up and their eyes met. Pause. He grinned again, slowly this time like a small boy owning up to raiding the cookie jar. He raised a conspiratorial finger to his lips in the gesture of silence.

'Well, not really,' he said. 'I just do what I'm told, I really don't understand it much.' As he spoke, he got up from the table, moved over to the wall by the door, unclipped the telephone handset from its hook on the wall, unplugged it from the socket, moved over to the sink, opened a drawer, placed the phone in it, covered it with a kitchen towel, closed the drawer, and turned on the radio, Elton John, too loud. Allan watched him with a growing sense that he wasn't really seeing what he was seeing.

Jack said, 'OK. So you saw me. So what?' He sat down again, shrugged and forked rice into his mouth. 'It might be fun to do a little detective work on his files.'

'Why?'

'Why what?'

Allan said, 'Why did you do that? Do you think you are being bugged or something?'

'You never know. Can't be too careful.'

'But.' Allan closed his mouth. After a moment he said, 'My sister's paranoid too.'

'Paranoid?' Jack seemed unconcerned. He reviewed the residue in the foil container and helped himself to more rice.

'She thinks she is being bugged. It makes her feel important.'

Jack waved a fork at him and spoke with his mouth full. 'It's a way of life at Marble's. They bug everybody.'

'Why would they want to do that?'

'Listen. They're the ones who are paranoid. They think we're spying on them for their business rivals. Why does your sister think she's being bugged?'

'She's in the SNP.'

'And they bug everyone in the SNP?'

'No. But she thinks they do if you climb over the wire at submarine bases or you have friends who blow up electricity pylons.'

'And do they?'

'She says that if she arranges a demo with her friends by phone, the police are always there before she is. I think that she just makes it up to convince herself that she is a serious threat to the establishment.'

'I meant do they blow up pylons?'

'They might. I don't know. Sometimes I wouldn't put it past them but Jean says that the only people who do that are the Agents of Provocation, otherwise known as MI5. You're not serious about being bugged.'

Elton finished his song, high notes dying away with a slow meditative cadence on the keys. The disc jockey began asking a phone-in caller about her love life. Jack waited until the music started again – jazz trumpet.

He said, 'I like this one,' and paused. 'Everyone at MCI knows that the company goes in for bugging. It's not anything personal; it's just the way they are. They need to control everything around them. Jimmy Wilson once heard his own voice being echoed back to him on the phone. Not just an electronic effect. It was the whole last sentence of his conversation after his caller had hung up.'

'Who's Jimmy Wilson?'

'Just a guy on the assembly line.'

'If you *are* being bugged then the phone isn't the only thing you have to worry about. There could be a bug under this table. If you really believed this stuff you'd go off your rocker with suspicion and never open your mouth.'

'Naw. It's not like that. They can't afford to plant bugs everywhere. That costs real money. I'm a nobody. They have no reason to be particularly suspicious about me. But you can turn a phone into a microphone at the touch of a button from an office miles away. It's hard-wired into the exchange.'

'They have to get a warrant from the Home Office for that.'

'Correction,' said Jack. 'They are *supposed* to get a warrant. Anyway, one warrant covers one tap. One tap bugs a thousand lines. One line carries hundreds of calls.'

'The police can get a warrant. Private companies can't.'

'Private companies that make and sell telephone exchanges have a head start on everyone else. Its called line testing. Every exchange has a tap point so that they can test the lines for faults. One man's line test is another man's bug.'

'And I suppose they have an army of people listening in to your every word?'

'No. Just a computer analysing the tap for keywords and recording the chunk of conversation which follows. It's just a random trawl in the hope that something will turn up. But once you are on the hit list they'll give you the full works.'

Allan thought about that. Jack seemed to be serious and there seemed to be no chance that he would recognise the absurdity of his suspicions. Jean, Allan's sister, had suffered the same delusions. The world was a conspiracy and she was its target for dirty tricks. He tried a different approach.

'Would "hacking" be one of the key words?'

'May be, but if Tommy's death was not suicide or an accident, then the word "Harkness" will be one of the key words.'

'It doesn't stop you, does it?'

'It would be a dull life without a bit of hacking.' He took a swig from the bottle.

Allan said, 'You could get the sack.'

He thought about that, then shrugged. 'So what? That wouldn't be the end of the world.'

'You could also be convicted for hacking.'

'No. They wouldn't be able to admit that their security was so lax. Too embarrassing to charge me.'

'Where is the tape now?'

Jack's eyes were alive with glee.

'I put it in Tommy's desk after the polis had gone. Seemed the least likely place for anyone to look now that the rozers have ransacked it.'

Allan laughed in spite of himself. There was something wonderfully childlike in Jack's attitude. He sat back and put his hand over his eyes to rub the weariness out of them. 'Why did you not just bring it here?'

'Two reasons. One, I have no equipment here that can read a quarter-inch tape. Two, it's quite difficult to get a tape out of the department. Every now and then they frisk us. Did you not see the detectors at the door? It's like an airport. Most of the time they're switched off. But they switch them on randomly and make you turn out for inspection everything which makes the detectors ping. It didn't seem to be worth the risk, since I would just have to get the tape back in again to read it . . . unless . . .' He looked at Allan speculatively. '. . . unless you know someone with a quarter-inch tape-drive.'

'You still haven't said why you did it.'

'For fun. To see if it could be done.'

'That's a feeble argument.'

'No, it's not. I could be doing them a favour. Showing them that they've got a hole in their security.'

'That one's past its sell-by date. Every hacker in the business uses that excuse and it won't wash. If I leave my door unlocked would you be doing me a favour by walking in?'

'Not the same thing.'

Allan dug into his chow-mein, making a mental resolve to distance himself from this cheerfully deranged criminal.

'Will you be asked to take on his work?'

'Aye. Maybe. They might ask you.' Jack laughed and helped himself to more black bean sauce.

'Not my field,' said Allan.

'Ah, but you can't expect to go on living in your ivory tower. We all have to graft with the bread and butter stuff, you know.'

Allan changed the subject to flats. Jack made tea and they took their cups through to the sitting room. They sat on the sofa under a Picasso poster and studied the list that Jack had extracted from the personnel manager's files. Jack pointed out the places, good and bad – mostly bad.

'You won't get a wink of sleep there . . . the Hellfire Disco is just round the corner . . . that area's not bad – used to be grim but it's coming up in the world . . . these days you can see a few BMWs parked in the streets . . . some of them even have wheels on instead of bricks . . . that place is too near the docks . . . main road . . . heavy traffic . . . that'll be Alison, my girlfriend.'

There was a scuffling at the outside door and then the sitting-room door opened and a girl walked in. Mid twenties. Dark curly hair. Broad face. Small round mouth. Multi-coloured shell-suit. Chunky blue pullover. A good inch taller than Jack. Jack introduced them. She shook hands with Allan and dropped her jacket-top in a crumpled heap on to the floor. Slumping down on the divan beside them, she put her arm round Jack and her chin on his shoulder. Her advice was rather more positive than Jack's and she seemed to know

Gairnock better. The number of places Allan could highlight with fluorescent pink increased.

Alison went into the kitchen and reappeared almost immediately with a teapot in her hand. She began to use it to water some of the plants. Green-fingered mystery explained. Allan followed her back into the kitchen and tried to help as she prepared tea. Jack was tinkering with the audio equipment and a sudden blast of Runrig's 'Loch Lomond' filled the flat. Crockery in the cupboard began to emit a resonant trill. The newspaper was still on the table.

'That's really sad,' she said, looking at the picture of Tommy Harkness. 'You won't have met him, of course.' She had a high-pitched little girl voice and nice hazel eyes.

'No.'

'He was shy and very serious – not like Jack. Jack doesn't take anything seriously.'

'I'd noticed. He got that list of flats out of the personnel manager's files.'

'That's our Jack. I hope he's not leading you into any trouble.' Alison spoke in a matter-of-fact way as she spread biscuits on a plate. 'He's got a bit of a habit of doing that.' She looked at the wall by the door. 'He's done it again to the phone.' She opened the top drawer by the sink and found it. 'He's always doing that. He's out of his mind.' She shut the drawer but left the phone where it was.

'Did he lead Tom Harkness into trouble?'

'No, I don't think they had much time for each other. Tom was very quiet. I think he disapproved of Jack.'

She lifted the tray and Allan held the door open. They went into the sitting room. The walls were shuddering under the weight of sound from another Runrig track.

Jack crouched over his microcomputer. Small coloured gnomes were hopping around the screen. Occasionally one would disintegrate in a multicoloured shell-burst to the accompaniment of grievous noises. Alison put a cup of tea down beside him. It trembled. She came over to the sofa where Allan sat but conversation was impossible. He looked at the tea in his cup. The surface danced in an intricate pattern as it resonated to the sound waves. Alison turned the pages of a magazine idly as though unaware of the cacophony.

Allan felt the floor begin to sway as though in a heavy swell. The lights seemed to blur and move in time with the sound. Nauseous and claustrophobic, he made an excuse and escaped into the quietness of a cool dark evening where raindrops pattered gently on the pavement and street lights shimmered in the puddles. He took huge gulps of salt-tanged air and walked until after midnight.

His badge said 'STANLEY Quinn: Assistant Personnel Manager'. He shook Allan's hand limply.

There were three other people in the room, sitting round a sectional conference table in cream plastic and chromium steel. In front of each was a finely pointed MCI pencil, a pristine note-pad, also with the company logo, and a black wedge-shaped name-plate. A similar place setting awaited on the left. The name-plate said ALLAN. There were no windows and the atmosphere had that familiar fudge consistency. At the far end of the table was an overhead projector and beyond that, a large flip chart on a stand.

'Gentlemen, perhaps you would introduce yourselves, starting here'

Quinn pointed at a sandy-haired man in a lightweight grey suit. The man half stood up and said in a flat voice, 'I'm John,' and thereby confirmed the accuracy of the name-plate before him. The others in turn said their first names.

Allan said 'hello' and realised too late that he was supposed to say 'I'm Allan.'

'Good to meet you, Allan,' said Quinn, with heavy emphasis on the name. He walked up to the top of the table. 'We have a full programme, Allan. I have just been through the intended schedule with John, Simon and William here, but for your benefit I will repeat it.'

The sandy-haired John closed his eyes and opened them again slowly and with difficulty. Simon bent his head forwards and fiddled with his MCI pencil. William looked straight ahead, focusing on infinity. His shoulders sagged.

Quinn turned his flip chart back to the first page and ticked off in red felt pen the items listed there in green felt pen – company structure, product lines, marketing strategy, assembly technology, and others which passed through Allan's head without pausing to inhabit it. Quinn flipped to the next page. Diagram of company structure. Next page – more boxes with lines joining them. Next page – products item by item. Next page . . .

'We are one big family here, Allan . . .'

Allan was startled into full consciousness by hearing his own name. The flip chart was showing a page he had never seen before. Quinn was saying '. . . and we like to ensure that everyone is kept informed about what is going on, so that everyone can identify with the company.'

The door opened and a girl in MCI livery poked her head round. There was a rattling of cups and the end of a coffee-trolley was visible. Quinn looked at his watch testily.

'Oh. Oh yes, Angela. You are early but you can bring it in. Just put it there.' She pushed the trolley against the wall behind the door and left. Quinn turned back to his flip chart.

'The structure of the comp—'

John stood up and made for the trolley with determination. Quinn looked startled but before he could speak Simon and William also stood up and converged on the trolley. Quinn bowed to the inevitable. 'Yes. Just help yourselves, gentlemen.'

Other people came after coffee. They expanded at length on the outline given by Quinn. Each sounded positively enthusiastic about their own department. Allan had never before studied a pencil in such detail. Lunch was in the company cafeteria – up-market motorway service station – with Scandinavian pine décor. Afterwards they went on a tour of inspection.

'This is the main hall, Allan,' said Quinn. The continuous and gratuitous use of his first name chalk-squeaked on Allan's nerves. It was so persistent that he suspected it was either the result of a directive from above or was a deliberate device for committing people's names to memory. The ceiling and walls were clad in cream acoustic tiles and the floor was a mosaic of cream and brown carpet tiles. Chest-high partitioning – brown with a cream ledge along the top – divided most of the area into a honeycomb of office spaces.

'It is divided, as you can see, into an assembly area, a testing area and an administrative area.'

For Allan, the thought of working in an open-plan office of these dimensions was a recurrent nightmare. The department building at University where he had done his PhD work was a rabbit warren of small passages and unexpected nooks and crannies where an introvert like himself could hole up for weeks without human contact. You could open a window and breathe fresh air straight from the quiet cool of a churchyard, but here every breath of air, scrubbed and knocked back into shape by modern air conditioning plant, had already inhabited a thousand lungs.

The assembly area, separated from the rest of the hall by a long straight passageway, was populated mainly by robots. Each stood in its allotted place on a long, thin pedestal like a one-legged wading bird. Robot hands fed by plastic tubes dropped black beetle-like microchips and other components on to the computer boards passing beneath them. The boards were almost the only things in the building which were not cream or brown. Dark green, with a glitter of gold connections and an array of black components like a miniature model town, the boards advanced down the assembly line, through the molten solder baths and on to the testing area, serenaded as they went by the pneumatic puffs and wheezes of the robots.

The group was led along like VIPs inspecting a guard of honour, stopping here and there to see how defective parts were identified by pitiless robot eyes and how the mutants were removed by ruthless robot hands. Humans, in the inevitable cream overalls, intervened in this process only towards its final stages. The boards were stacked by robot arms beside the human operators who gave them a final visual check before testing began. One of the operators – a dark-haired girl with hazel eyes – looked up at the group. It was Alison, Jack's girlfriend. She smiled briefly but her eyes glazed over as she heard Quinn holding forth.

'I've got a lot to show you Allan, John . . .'

' . . . over here, William, I have the assembly area . . .'

' . . . now here is my testing area, Simon.'

He contrived to give the impression that he owned the plant personally.

They followed the whole process through from the customising of the chips to the assembly of complete computer systems and the testing of some of them to customer order. Allan found himself stifling a yawn and caught John's eye.

It was a relief to get back into the research department. Rosa's office was a glass box within the research unit. She had managed, probably in contravention of company directives, to wall herself off from sight with filing cabinets and bookcases and with notices stuck to the glass panels.

She sat him down on the other side of her desk and they talked shop for an hour. Later Allan wondered whether Rosa had appointed him just to have someone she could talk to about her pet subject. She had, after all, virtually invented it or at least the specialist niche within it which she and Allan inhabited. He had read everything she had published on the subject. She had made the initial breakthrough, mapped the landscape and laid down the markers which everyone else used to orientate themselves. He had followed and broken new ground. They were like two trappers in a wilderness talking about their best tricks, their favourite haunts. She had little time for active research herself. Even during their talk her phone was seldom silent, but when she talked to him the crease between her eyebrows disappeared and she seemed younger, nearer to his own age.

One of the phone calls was for him. Henry Quinn had fixed him up with digs. Mrs McCulloch, 22 Loch Ranza Road. Rosa wrote it down for him.

She was embarrassed about asking him to take on Tommy
Harkness's job. They gave him Harkness's desk and his log
book and records. The programs were very straightforward,
they said, in a computer language he knew well and to speci-
fications which were very clear.

'It's just to tide us over,' she explained. 'We will get down to
serious research when we have got everything straightened
out.'

3

MAY

Languid as a lemur, he climbed. The cliff overhung but the crack which split it like a sabre slash took a jammed fist nicely. As he moved upwards his lean frame swayed gently, rhythmically, reptilian, conserving strength. The rock was smooth and grey and flecked with the metallic glitter of mica, but it was dry. Friction and wrinkles gave purchase to the hard rubber of his climbing shoes. Above, the wall leaned outwards into a true roof overhang but he did not look up at it. It would come soon enough. He had been there before.

He moved steadily upwards. The wall began to lean out and more of his body weight dragged at his arms. Muscles stood out like rods. The wrinkles were no longer sufficient and he had to wedge his feet in the crack. He was pushed further backwards as the rock curved out over his head. The crack narrowed – too narrow now for a fist. He dipped his hand into the chalk-bag dangling at his waist and then, with thumb curled across the palm, he wedged the hand sideways into the crack, bracing his fingers to increase the friction.

The strain increased. His arms were trembling. He was now horizontal, face upwards and a few inches from the stubborn rock, clinging like a cat. Big unyielding boulders littered the

hillside at the base of the cliff, two hundred feet directly below
his back.

The crack was splayed now and useless for a hand-jam. He
dipped again for chalk and groped. A wrinkle within the crack
gave him an indifferent finger-tip hold.

This was uncharted territory. Don't stop. Move on or retreat.

He shifted his right foot to a higher position and moved outwards, taking most of his weight on the fingers. He took air in
rapid gulps, blowing like a tank engine through pursed lips.
Only seconds left. He reached beyond the edge of the overhang, urgently exploring the smooth surface – nothing. He
released his left foot and thrust with his right. Still more strain
on his right arm and hand but a few more inches for the grasp
of his left. A ledge – slim as a pencil. His urgent fingers closed
it and pulled to ease the strain on his other hand. The ledge
broke. A flake the size of a roofing slate went spinning out of
sight and his whole weight lurched backwards on to the fingers
of his exhausted right hand. He held on, willing strength into
his fingers and right arm. Time held still until there was a clatter as the flake hit the boulders below. With the left hand he
groped again round the overhang. The broken flake had left
behind another ledge, lower than the other and wider – by a
fraction. He grabbed it and pushed outwards so that his head
shot out from under the overhang and for the first time he
could look directly up the cliff above to the fluffy clouds sailing
past overhead, giving the impression that the cliff was toppling.
His foot came out of the crack and his body was swung free, a
dead weight on his arms. As he swung he brought his right
hand out from under the overhang to join the left on the narrow ledge at eye level. For a fraction of a second he paused.
Then as his full weight came on his left hand he snatched with
his right at the duralumin 'nuts' which dangled on nylon lan-
yards from his waist and tried to slam one into the slender
crack which split the rock just above the tiny ledge. The nut
was too big. He let out a despairing gasp. His fingers straightened and he fell.

He fell about ten feet before he fetched up at the end of the

rope and bounced like a puppet, swinging inwards with a powerful pendulum motion. He got a foot up in time to stop
himself being slammed into the cliff face. There was a ribald
cheer from the gallery below. Someone shouted 'hard luck!'
Clapping. There was blood coming from somewhere. 'That
looked a right cunt'i'a position!' That was Harry's voice. There
must be women about. Harry was always deliberately crude
and loud-mouthed when there were women about.

Hamish was cramped on to a ledge about sixty feet below,
threading the brightly coloured ropes through a snaplink. He
grinned hugely and paid out more rope, lowering Allan until he
could touch the ledge with an outstretched foot.

'Well done, lad! You got at least six feet further than Johnny
Wentworth.' Such praise! Johnny Wentworth was the current
TV-media climbing person.

Allan examined himself. He had a gash on his left forearm
which was dripping blood and he had split the thumb nail on
his right hand. That would have been when he tried to cram
the oversized nut into the crack.

They organised the ropes and abseiled down.

More sardonic applause came from the group lying about on
the boulders below. A middle-aged man in breeches with a
balding head, a beard and a pipe. A group of three unshaven
and pimpled youths. Their attention was split between Allan
and the pair of girls in shorts and bikini tops. The girls had
long, slim brown legs which disappeared into chunky white
socks and oversized climbing boots. Ian and Harry were there
too. Harry was lying back with his hands clasped behind his
head, looking extremely pleased with himself. Anoraks and
ropes and rucksacks and packets of sandwiches and oranges lay
all around like flotsam on a beach.

Ian offered him a swig of orange juice from a plastic bottle.
The middle-aged man came over.

'Was that Gibbet you were on, lads?'

He was looking at Allan. The girls were looking at him as
well. Allan fumbled with his harness. Hamish said, 'Aye –
Gibbet Corner.'

'Does it have a grade?'

'Pure dead bloody impossible,' said Hamish – he jerked his thumb in Allan's direction – 'but Spiderman here got higher than anyone has ever got before.'

Allan pulled a jumper over his head and took his time about getting it clear of his face which was glowing like an electric fire.

'Can it be done, do you think?'

'Sure,' said Ian. 'See next time? Dead cert. What do you say, Allan? Next weekend?'

Allan shook his head.

'Not next weekend.'

'Oh, of course,' said Harry, standing up and putting on his red jockey cap which said KING SIZED BURGERS in fluorescent green. 'The brand new job and all that. The weekend after, then. We'll all come up in your Rolls-Royce.'

Allan smiled weakly and wished that Harry would shut up. The man was still there looking at him.

'Can you do it? What was it like at the overhang?'

Allan unclipped his harness and dropped it to the ground. He looked up at the climb.

'Maybe.'

But he knew that next time he would do it. Next time he would know what to expect. Next time there would be no flakes breaking off in his hand. He would have a nut of the correct size in his teeth as he swung round the corner, so the upper part of the climb would be protected. He would get to the crux more quickly and with more energy in reserve so he could finger-jam up the slim crack until he could get a foot on the thin ledge.

For a while Ian and Hamish played around on another climb over to the right. Harry hung around the girls, telling them exaggerated stories, pointing out climbs. The sun went and grey clouds welled up from the West. Spots of rain began to fall half-heartedly, swirling in the eddies round the cliffs like thistle down, cold isolated spots landing on bare arms and foreheads. They packed up and began to make their way down.

* * *

Allan hated pubs. There was the problem of buying rounds. If only everyone would just buy their own. There was all this hassle about making sure you didn't fall behind in the round-buying stakes and the problem of explaining that he did not drink alcohol, and the noise of canned music, and the tobacco smoke, and the smell of beer, and the uncomfortable seats and drinks being knocked over by semi-drunks. Sometimes it was not so bad in the winter when they would go into a quiet country hotel and he could have a mug of soup in front of a log fire while the others boozed, but often it was not like that and he would have to drink cold ginger beer standing up on a stone floor while the melting snow trickled down the back of his legs and squelched about in his boots, while the others got congenially warm from the inside, and all he wanted to do was to get back to the hut or the tent and get out of his wet clothes.

Harry put a round of drinks on the table. 'So what's all the funny goings on at the new job, Allan? I hear they are dropping like ten green bottles.'

'Two bottles. And they're not connected. So the polis says anyway.'

Ian said, 'An' what do you say?'

'I didn't know them. They tell me the guy who was in our department, Tommy Harkness, was a quiet wee fella who minded his own business. Hardly the stuff of conspiracy and gang warfare. The polis have just announced that there are no suspicious circumstances.'

'Do you believe that?' said Hamish. 'The papers keep saying there was some kind of secret work. Are you sworn to silence?'

Allan said, 'No. There's nothing cloak and dagger about the work. The company doesn't like its competitors knowing what it is about but all these hints about secret projects are a bit over the top. I can't tell what to believe but the folk in the department were a bit surprised.'

'So what sort of thing are you doing?' Ian asked. 'Hasn't it got something to do with your thesis stuff?'

'Well, it was supposed to be about that, but with Tommy Harkness gone so suddenly they've asked me to take over his

desk in the meantime. I've been writing programs to test out
the chips. It's not my line really, but quite interesting, I suppose.'

'You don't sound very enthusiastic.'

'Well. Yes. It's a bloody bore actually.'

'Why were they surprised?' Ian offered crisps around.

'He's supposed to have hanged himself, on the back of a
door. The trouble is that the hook he hung himself on was so
low his feet could touch the floor.'

Hamish said, 'Yes, I saw that in the paper. Seems distinctly
improbable. It all sounds pretty creepy to me, Allan. You'd be
far safer up a rock face. What happened to the other guy?'

'Drove his car off a cliff, just down the coast a bit from the
MCI place. I'm told they didn't know each other but neither of
them were reckoned to be suicidal.'

'And you're doing the old job of one of them,' said Ian.
'Does that worry you?'

'No. Of course not.'

But it did.

There was the tape that Jack had copied. It sat there in the desk
at the back of the second drawer down on the right. He
couldn't forget that it was there, sitting among the other, legitimate tapes. It was not as if there was much danger in it being
discovered and anyway, the date on it predated his own access
date to the computer, but it was as though it had a kind of
radioactivity which irradiated him all day long with beams and
particles of nagging anxiety. It probably glowed in the dark.

For four days he had tried to ignore it, four days, in which he
had found his way around Gairnock, found temporary digs at
Mrs McCulloch's place and moved in, been assigned
Harkness's old desk, and been given official access to the files
on the computer which had belonged to Harkness. He had
even been able to give the files a cursory examination. It
seemed routine stuff, all fully documented in the work schedule and every update fully authorised. He was able to copy the
files to tape for safekeeping – and to do so legitimately. He

stored these tapes beside the illegal one. There was nothing to worry about. They were identical – or were they?

For four days he had thought about it. If he restored the tape by loading its contents on to the disc, the amount of space he required would double. Surely someone would notice that. Once the contents were there on disc there was no way of being absolutely certain that the data would not be monitored. Jack's suspicions about bugging were ludicrous, of course, and yet – bugging a computer user was the easiest thing on earth. The systems manager could install a special program so that everything you typed or printed on the screen was carbon-copied elsewhere and you wouldn't ever know.

To complete his own log of work he needed to recheck the contents listing of a tape. He reached into the drawer and for a moment his hand hovered over the illegal tape. Suppose he made a mistake and loaded the wrong one? That would be an explainable mistake which he could not be expected to detect until he had printed out the contents list.

He did not have the sang-froid of a natural criminal. His hand trembled as he withdrew the tape from the drawer and loaded it into the tape-drive. One command and the tape contents were displayed and transferred to the printer. Interminable seconds dragged past while the printer hummed and spewed paper before he could delete all trace of his action from the screen. His actions could have been monitored but who would think to check such an innocuous listing? He repeated the operation for a second legal tape and then placed both tape cartridges back into the drawer. Trying to look casual, he glanced round the office. Everyone seemed fully occupied. He laid both printed lists together on the desk. The illegal tape contents list was longer than the other. That meant that some of Harkness's files had been deleted. And the contents of those files were on the illegal tape.

He slipped both pieces of paper into his satchel.

How easy. How trivial. The kind of thing Jack would have done ten times a day without blinking, but for Allan, looking back on it afterwards, it was some kind of private Rubicon

which he crossed that day. It was the first occasion in which he
had ever knowingly breached regulations about computer use.
Strange that he should be so fearful of being caught in breach
of regulations, and an insignificant breach at that, which at
worst would have meant a simple reprimand. Doubly strange
when he so willingly placed his life at stake every weekend in
the mountains. For him, however, physical danger was well-
explored territory. He had no map to the pitfalls of human
relationships, just a big label, 'Here be Dragons'. But cross the
Rubicon he had done. The next step came later and came a little more easily.

The two girls who had been on the mountain came into the bar
and the bald-headed man was close behind. Harry chose the
prettier of the two girls and sat down beside her, unnecessarily
close. She recoiled.

'It's all right, hen. You're quite safe,' said Harry, patting his
breast pocket. 'There's a big fat wallet between us.'

The girls laughed. The bald-headed man came over and
asked what they would have. Allan shook his head but Hamish
said, 'A pint of export and Allan'll have an apple juice – won't
you, Allan?' The man sat down at their table and breathed
pipe fumes.

'I don't suppose you've got a sponsor?' He was talking to
Allan again.

'A'm his manager,' said Harry instantly. He had his arm
round the waist of one of the girls. 'Ye'll need to talk to me.'

'Seriously,' said the man. 'You looked pretty good on the cliff
today. If you were interested then I am sure my company would
be. We could put you in for the autumn trials. You would do
well.'

'What about it, Allan lad?' said Ian. 'You might earn a crust
and get yourself on television like Johnny Wentworth.'

'Go on, Allan,' said Harry. 'I can just see you in a pair of lurex
tights and with an advert for double glazing across your back.'

'More than a crust,' said the man, 'and it's home security
systems, actually.'

'Allan gets embarrassed if more than three people look at him at the same time,' said Hamish. 'He'd be paralysed on television.'

The man offered his business card. Harry materialised at the man's side with his hand out and received a card but Allan took one too. Somehow Harry talked the two girls into giving him a lift back to Glasgow. That left the other three to travel in more comfort in Ian's car. Allan wound himself into the back seat with a pile of rucksacks and fell asleep as they trundled down the Loch Lomond road.

He woke to find that they had come to a standstill in a queue of cars some distance North of Balloch. Out on the loch, which was now still and glassy, a water-skier was making a splash, leaping the wash of the powerboat, swaying to and fro to the limit of his tether, but with no freedom to decide, compelled to go as the powerboat dictated. Was he like that? Was he being towed into something? Hamish and Ian were discussing plans for a trip to the Alps. Normally he would have joined in but his preoccupation with events at Gairnock took over. It had been so easy to take the next step.

He had shown Jack the two lists. They were sitting in a pizza place in the centre of Gairnock. Jack had got very excited and ordered a 'knickerbocker glory' and a 'Death-by-chocolate'. He ate both when Allan declined. He kept saying, 'We're on to something, de-fin-ite-ly.'

Allan wondered if the copy of the files which the police had made had contained the two extra files. He supposed so, since the two tapes were made only minutes apart. But if it did not . . . Well. That would really point the finger.

'We've got to do it,' said Jack. 'We've got to get a print-out of those two files.'

'They may be big files. It's one thing to print out a contents list, quite another to print out two whole files without being spotted.'

'We've got to get it out of the building and run it through another computer,' said Jack.

So that was what they did. Jack stuck the tape in his briefcase and walked calmly through the detectors which were switched off. Later he dropped the tape off at Allan's digs.

'What do you think, Allan?'
    He started out of his reverie. 'Sorry! What about?'
    'About the Dolomites. D'you fancy it this year?'
    'Oh. Oh aye. Yes, I suppose so.'
    'Well, don't get carried away, will you?'
    'Sorry. I was thinking about something else.'
    'What's eating you, Allan?'
    'Nothing. Nothing really. Hamish, do you have a Unix-box with a quarter-inch tape-drive in your department?'

The University was a voracious devourer of properties. In some places the original houses had gone completely, totally digested and replaced by an excretion of concrete, but other areas had been fenced in and were being fattened up for consumption at a later date. In the meantime they led a precarious existence, their exterior stonework cleaned and windows refurbished, but internally their fabric prey to a burrowing parasite which had pierced them through with connecting corridors, communication cable ducts, fire doors and unlikely staircases which turned the block into a spongiform of academic life. Each front door in the terrace had a maroon noticeboard with the University crest and the name of some obscure department, a niche for the survival of rare and highly specialised academic species.
    The Department of Economic Forecasting and Statistics was the third in the block. It shared a doorway and a noticeboard with the Industrial Intelligence Unit – a contradiction in terms, mused Allan – and the Institute for Innovative Practice – something to do with whips and brass-studded leather, perhaps. At that late hour he had to ring the bell and wait. On the third pull he heard someone coming down a staircase four steps at a time and in a moment Hamish opened the door.
    'Sorry! I was at the other end of the building.' He closed the door and latched a pair of locks. 'We're supposed to be security

minded these days. Somebody walked in last week and lifted a wallet and a handbag from one of the offices.'

He led the way up the wide and once elegant staircase with heavy carved banisters, through a door in the mezzanine landing, up two steps, round a right-angled bend, through another door, down three steps and along a corridor. At the end of the corridor they went up a spiral staircase, along a short corridor through another door and down another staircase like the first. Hamish's room was at the top of a short curved staircase above the ladies' toilet. It was an L-shaped room with one curved wall and a window you couldn't see through for foliage. It was the kind of building Allan liked.

'So what's the mystery then? I would have thought the one thing you would not be short of at MCI would be a computer.'

Allan pulled the tape cassette out of the pocket of his wind-cheater.

'No. We're not short of computers but we are short of a computer I can use without someone else breathing down the back of my neck.'

'Hello! Skulduggery afoot! That's not like you, Allan. Somehow I hadn't cast you in the role of anarchist.'

'Times are changing, Hamish. And so am I.' He waved the tape. 'Can I stick this into a tape-drive? It's high density, quarter-inch "tar" format.'

Hamish scratched his head for a moment and then led the way out of the room and through another series of Escher-like manoeuvres to arrive at a large room with two sets of bay windows. There was a wooden bench along one wall with three computer work-stations and a shoe-box sized tape-drive. He inserted the tape and sat down at the terminal.

'So what do you want done?'

'I want a print-out of these two files.' Allan laid his own print-out on the bench. Two of the file names were highlighted in bright pink. Hamish logged in to the computer and typed the commands as Allan suggested. The tape-drive hummed – reading the files.

'Great. Now how about a print-out, or better still, do you

have a PC on the network? Could you dump the stuff to a three-and-a-half-inch floppy?'

'Sure.' Hamish remained sitting at the screen. He held out his hand like a collection plate. There was a pause, then Allan started.

'Oh! Sorry!' He dug into another pocket and produced a floppy disc.

'You didn't think I was going to give you a whole floppy for nothing, did you?' He led the way on another mystery trip. 'This is a university, mate, not a rich multi-national company. We don't buy even paper-clips here. We rent them.'

They came to another room where a large piece of computer machinery of ancient vintage was sitting under dust sheets. It was disconnected and derelict. It also looked as though some of the guts had been cannibalised. In the corner of the room was a modern PC. Hamish stuck the floppy into the drive and typed a few commands. Minutes later he pulled the floppy out and handed it to Allan. 'There you are. Was there something else?' He didn't really want to know.

'How about a quick look at it on the screen?'

Hamish's fingers rattled on the keys. 'Big files,' he said, and then the screen filled with gibberish, bleeping and squirming, with just a few decipherable words like 'ERROR 22'.

'That's enough,' said Allan. 'Kill it. It's just a bloody executable.'

'Not a secret code? How dull. I thought it would be a plan to assassinate the Prime Minister, at least. What's an executable when it's at home?'

'That wouldn't be a secret, just a bore,' said Allan. 'Everybody's got a plan to assassinate the Prime Minister. An executable is just a program which has already been compiled. So it's in machine code, ready to run on the computer. It's just ones and noughts, so it's not meant to be read as text.'

'How do you know it's an executable and not a cipher?'

'Because there are so many non-printable characters and a few strings of clear text. You don't get that in a cipher. I don't suppose you would have a dis-assembler on your machine?'

'Come again?'

'A dis-assembler. A program which will translate the code back into assembly language so that we can read what the program is trying to do.'

'We're statisticians, Allan. We *use* computers here, mate. We don't climb inside them.' After a pause he said, 'Was there something else then?'

'My tape,' said Allan.

Hamish snorted, 'At least we keep fit here,' and off they went on another tour. When the tape was back in Allan's possession Hamish said, 'D'you fancy a drink? I'll buy you an orange juice.'

'No thanks. I've got to get back to Gairnock.'

When they reached the door Hamish said, 'Are you going to tell me what the hell you're up to?'

Standing on the doorstep, Allan considered that for a moment. Then he waved the tape cassette and said, 'This is a tape of the files which belonged to Tommy Harkness, the guy who died and used to work in my department. The files you copied for me were deleted from his directory by person or persons unknown. I just want to see if there was a reason.'

Hamish made a whistle shape with his lips. 'You watch it, lad.' He wasn't joking.

'It's OK. I thought it might be a document or a letter or something that would give some clue about his death. No one at work seemed to believe the suicide verdict. But it is just an executable so I guess it's nothing to get uptight about. I'll just drop it. Forget it, Hamish.'

'This is not like you, Allan. What would you have done if it had been something to get uptight about?'

'Well . . . Do you remember the lad we pulled off the Dearg Slabs? The one who was up on the rock? Well, he was the nephew of the Chief Inspector who is in charge of the investigation. I would have handed over the stuff to him and asked him to keep me out of it.'

Hamish leaned on the door. He spoke as though explaining

to a child. 'You shouldn't have those files, right? If you think the police would "keep you out of it" then you must be daft. My advice is to throw that bloody thing away. See you in gaol.' He closed the door and locked it twice.

The train down to Gairnock was empty. Allan let his forehead rest against the window and dozed as points clattered and yellow street lights chugged past. Hamish was right, of course. The whole thing was daft and he was relieved to find that the files held nothing mysterious. That was definitely the end of the cloak-and-dagger stuff. He would tell Jack in the morning that he would have nothing further to do with his stupid schemes.

As he rounded the corner from Shore Road into Loch Ranza Road he told himself it was a temporary place. That was supposed to raise his spirits. It didn't work. The road was short, pot-holed and dingy. Polystyrene carry-out packages littered the gutters, and the gardens, such as they were, looked as though they had been pounded by pneumatic hammers to the consistency of black concrete. But at least it wasn't carpeted in broken glass as some streets were and the place had one advantage over others. It was cheap.

That was one of the surprises of his new job. He hadn't expected to be hard up. His salary from MCI was enormous when compared to his income as a student, but somehow it had disintegrated under the impact of unexpected expenditure. He had a student loan to repay. He had arranged with his sister Jean to make a monthly payment into her account to pay his whack of Uncle Roddy's upkeep and then he had had to lash out on new clothes. When he sat down to calculate the remainder he was shocked to find himself poor yet again. The advance he had got from MCI didn't look as though it would stretch to the end of the month.

Mrs McCulloch's house had a narrow frontage in the middle of the block which was two storeys high. His room was on the upper floor and his window overlooked a derelict courtyard and gave him a view of the backs of other buildings and a dirty patch of earth. Here some enterprising child had dug an earth-pit and surrounded the shrine with a number of offerings – a plastic lorry with no wheels, a headless horse which did have wheels but only three of them, and a spade. Not the kind of plastic spade you buy along with a bucket for playing on the beach but a real navvy's spade with the shaft snapped off just above the spit.

The room was damp. It had an unnatural chill and an aura of sadness about it as though the walls had absorbed the emotions of life's flotsam and jetsam which had lodged there over the years. He had a bed, a small table, two chairs and a ply-board wardrobe containing a large collection of wire coat hangers which jangled like distant cow-bells as he moved about the room.

He threw the tape cassette and floppy disc on to the bed and looked round. It was just a temporary place, he told himself yet again and now that he knew there was no mystery about the files he could put all that behind him. His aberration was over. No more tension. He would get back to doing what he wanted to do and what he was good at – working on the theory of computer correctness and mountaineering. Perhaps with a bit of care he could afford the Dolomites this summer. And of course there was the problem of not having a girlfriend. That deserved some serious thought. He fancied Jennifer on the enquiry desk and now he wondered how he could engineer an introduction. She was probably spoken for.

He lay in bed with his hands behind his head and stared at the hideous floral pattern of the wallpaper. The lack of a television set did not worry him. He enjoyed the peace to think his own thoughts. Why, he wondered idly, were those two files not on the log of work which Tommy Harkness had kept so neatly up to date, and why were they so much larger than the other files?

4

JUNE

Walking was a habit. Taking a bus meant learning the bus routes and that meant asking people for directions. He had given that up long ago. Most men seemed to triangulate their world by pubs. Faced with Allan's total lack of knowledge on that score they took off their caps, scratched their heads and were at a loss to know how to surmount such a culture barrier.

And it was no use asking a woman. A woman would always turn and enlist the help of a passer-by, and *he* would say 'Aye, ye catch a number nine at the corner by The Fiddler's Arms and get aff at MacLintock's Bar.' So Allan walked with a street-map in his pocket, keeping the dark secret of his pub-blindness to himself.

Within the span of his early childhood, Glasgow had wakened from a doss-house demeanour and begun the task of recovering its self-respect. The process had been accompanied by a great deal of self-mockery and nostalgia for the camaraderie of poverty, but the effect had been a revelation. The tenement block where he had been brought up and where his sister Jean and Uncle Roddy still lived, once soot-grimed and dingy, was now spruce with the warm pink glow of clean sandstone. Years ago Uncle Roddy had explained to him that the gardens had once been respectable, full of grass and flowers. That was before they had suffered the indignity of having their wrought-iron fencing removed during the Second World War. Allan's earliest memory was of small patches of bare earth surrounded by low sandstone walls like toothless gums, pockmarked with the stumps of old railings. Now the fences were restored and grass and flowers were recolonising.

The hallway was a collector's piece. It was half-tiled in two shades of green with buff walls above. At the first landing there was a tall stained-glass window with a Macintosh-esque design. He could hear the noise of children's feet in the stairwell above him. His boyhood persona was slipping over him.

He rang the bell with the old familiar da-di-da-da to tell them it was him and then let himself in with his own key. Jean was out and Uncle Roddy had been asleep. Roddy's bed was in the kitchen where there had once been an old box-bed. The blankets were leaden and rumpled. Allan had tried to tell him about the superior insulation properties of a downie and why it was wrong to put heavy blankets on top of it, but he had given up. The lightness of a downie made Roddy feel naked and scientific facts could not cure his psychological coldness.

'It's yersel, Allan lad!' He was struggling to sit up.

Allan put the bunch of flowers on the table and punched up Roddy's pillows. Although he had a great fondness for the old man, he found conversation with him difficult. Roddy's lively, if untutored, intelligence had gone, and in its place was a jumbled collection of memories which mixed up generations and relived favourite events of his childhood like a sports TV programme full of golden goals.

At the bottom of the bed was a pile of newspapers and magazines – the *People's Friend*, the *Sunday Post*, last week's *Oban Times*. On a chair beside the bed was a pile of *Time Life* magazines – a complete series on space which was at least twenty years out of date. Roddy liked space. He was fond of reading astounding facts out loud and as a boy Allan had found his astonishment infectious. 'D'ye ken it takes three thousand million years for the light o' that galaxy to reach us – think on it –

three thousand million years!' Roddy did not read the magazines much these days. His universe had collapsed, bounded
by the four walls around him except for what was visible
through the time-warp window of the *Sunday Post*. He showed
Allan a drawing of Dunvegan Castle on the front of the *People's
Friend*. Dunvegan was his favourite castle. He also showed
him a postcard from his sister in America. It had a picture of
some people fishing on a lake set among fine mountains. He
had shown Allan the same postcard on his three previous visits. Allan asked how he was feeling.

'A' hae wan foot in the grave, son, and that's a fact.'

Then he asked Allan about his work. Computer theory was
not the stuff of family conversation so Allan said he was fine,
and tried to explain about the company, its worldwide sales of
computers and its head office in South America. 'America!'
Roddy exclaimed. He said that Allan must be sure to look up
his cousins in Seattle. Allan tried to explain that he didn't
actually work in South America and that anyway it was a long
way from South America to North America but Roddy patted
his hand and said it didn't really matter.

Jean returned while Allan was making a cup of tea, banging
the outside door and swearing as she fumbled and dropped
something with a bump in the hallway. She was small and wiry
and exuded a kind of aggressive energy. She wore a navy raincoat and a dark red Paisley headscarf. She had a Marks and
Spencer bag in one hand and with her other arm she was
wrestling with a large package which might have been a small
surf-board. Glaring at Allan, she propped the package against
the wall, dumped the M&S bag on the table and said, 'So
you've turned up.' She did not say 'at last' but the words hovered like birds of prey.

Allan had the teapot in his hand. As he hesitated in front of
the kitchen shelves, Jean, without saying a word, reached past
him, grabbed the tea caddy and thrust it into his hand.

'Allan's going to emigrate to America,' said Roddy.

Jean was taking off her shoes. She stopped and looked at
Allan with venom in her eyes.

'Not exactly, Uncle Roddy'.

Jean lit a cigarette, picked up the M&S bag and marched out, closing the kitchen door with rather more force than was necessary. By the time she came back he was trying to clear the table to make room for the tea tray. A pile of school exercise jotters were sprawled across it. He was especially careful with the one that was open, the one with the graffiti of red marks across a semi-literate pencil scrawl. And books of course. The flat was smothered in books – *Creative English for Grade III*, *Interpretation Exercises No. 2*, and books by Fay Weldon, Germaine Greer and Dale Spender, a resentful literature which throughout his childhood had been a constant reproach to Allan, reminding him that he was an oppressor, a scoundrel and a potential rapist. It was not any single one of them. It was the cumulative effect which eroded his self-confidence. And then there were the Scottish books, books with titles like *Scotland the Wealthy Nation* and *A Vision of Scotland*, books with the same sense of grievance, the same finger of scorn, even if it was directed at another target. It did not help that he sympathised to an extent. If anything, it made it worse, because he could not then wear a mental suit of asbestos. The feminist thing hurt. It had driven him to the conclusion that only men liked sex. Intellectually he knew that that was non-sense but his gut told him otherwise and it was his gut that mattered when he was in a girl's company. Unless the girl took the initiative he was paralysed by inhibitions.

Jean returned but would not sit down. She unpacked the parcel, brushing aside his offer of help. It was a new ironing board. She busied herself in the sink for a while and then went into the sitting room and began to hoover the carpet. Later she came back and began loading the washing machine.

'Can I help?'

She paused, read the washing instruction on the label of a blouse and then looked up as though she had only just heard him.

'No. You have your annual chat with Uncle Roddy.'

She went on loading the machine and then started it up on

its cycle. Roddy told him the story of the wee lassie who thought that God lived next door because she had overheard someone shouting 'God! Are you not up yet!' Allan laughed as though he had not heard it before. Later Roddy fell asleep with his spectacles on his nose. Allan went through to the sitting room where Jean was ironing and watching a television programme on wild-life with one eye.

'Have you time to talk?'

'Not really. I'm watching and recording this programme. It's for my class tomorrow.'

'I thought there was a law against recording programmes for public performances.'

She took a puff at a cigarette smouldering away in an ashtray at her side and then stubbed it out. Her voice was husky and her face was developing the deepening creases that suggest a lifetime of submersion in nicotine.

'If I had enough textbooks to go round the class I wouldn't need to.'

He sat down and watched the programme with her. When it was over she lifted a pile of freshly ironed clothes and went out of the room. He considered folding up the table for her but guessed that he would just get it folded when she would come back with another pile of clothes to iron. There was a big bundle of handbills on the sideboard. The heading said that it was *The Maryhill Citizen* but it was obviously a piece of SNP party political stuff purporting to be a local newspaper. He was reading a copy when she came back.

'If you want to do something to help, you can deliver these for me.'

'Where to?'

'All the houses in this street and as far as Canal Road.'

There was no escape, not that he wanted to escape really, though he disliked politics. The economic management of a country, he had decided at an early age, was a task which outstripped the capabilities of mankind. The politicians might strut and proclaim their faith but the complexity of it was beyond them. Like the weather, it had a will of its own, and all they could hope to do was to modify it slightly. You might if you were lucky avoid long-term disasters like global warming but you could not hope to predict and prevent anything specific. He had listened to interminable lectures from Jean and her cronies and developed deaf ears. But his cynical apathy had not prevented him from helping her with her ploys. Often and often she had had him, a lanky schoolboy, stumping the doorsteps with election literature. It was a way of earning her approval and though he did not accept her opinions, he did value her approval. She bothered his conscience, for she had been his mother as well as his sister. When his mother died he had been a toddler. His father had been dead since before he was born and so Uncle Roddy had stepped into the breach. Then when Uncle Roddy became infirm Jean shouldered the family burden. It was no wonder really that she was bitter. Her career had been sacrificed and romance blighted while Allan had been allowed to go to University. Only in later years when he had reached his teens and been able to fend for himself to an extent, had she been able to take up teaching as a 'mature' student. How she hated that description. Her response had been to pour her energy into Scottish politics. She was a political streetfighter. Sometimes he had ridden shotgun for her when she was canvassing. It was a tough district but getting better.

It took him an hour or so. He remembered the old trick. You went to the top of each stair and delivered on the way down. He encountered only one aggressive nutter. The man opened his door and came out on to the landing waving the paper which Allan had stuffed through his letter-box. Obscenities echoed after him and the noise of ripping paper. Shreds of *Citizen* floated down the stairwell.

Jean had supper on the table when he got back. As she directed he put some bits on a plate and mascerated it into the pulp which was all that Roddy's toothless gums could manage.

'Fine, son. That's grand,' said the old man as he handed it to him and helped him sit up. Jean had softened a bit and even managed a smile. 'So what's this about America?' she said when they sat down.

And so he explained. Jean considered him to be a traitor just
for working for a multinational company, especially one that
was originally American. She did not like the real story any
more than Roddy's version but the doorbell rang before she
got into her stride about the iniquities of multinationals. It
was Andrew Coltart so they retired to the sitting room and left
Roddy watching his favourite soap on his personal TV set.

Andrew had sparse hair, a round red face and a broad grin.
His was a face well known on Scottish Television, for he was
often the SNP's spokesman on discussion programmes. He
had also had a brief moment of glory when he won a famous
by-election only to lose the seat a few months later at the
General Election. He did not have the benefit of a university
education but his command of legal matters and the way he
could produce economic facts and figures like a conjuror often
left his more sophisticated opponents punch drunk. He shook
Allan's hand the way he handled the press, with a robust bon-
homie that left you surreptitiously easing your fingers apart
and straightening your knuckles.

'So you're Allan,' he said when Jean had gone off to the
kitchen. 'I've heard a lot about you. Jean is always telling us all
that she has a young brother who is a genius . . . No, no
really . . .' he went on when Allan spluttered his objections,
'. . . no, she does . . . She thinks the world of you . . . and we
need people like you . . . when us old party hacks have won
Scotland's independence we're going to need the technical
experts like you if we're going to make Scotland into a modern
industrial state.' His fat little index finger was jabbing the air in
Allan's direction.

Jean came back in time to hear that. 'Is that you on your
soapbox again, Andrew?'

Andrew grinned but he held forth again. His current hate
objects were businessmen who claimed that Scottish
Independence would create 'instability' and be 'bad for business confidence'. In his vocabulary 'stability' was an expletive.

They began to talk about a demonstration. Allan remembered those demonstrations. He had a vivid memory of

standing forlornly on Calton Hill in Edinburgh on a wet, miserable, gale-torn Sunday afternoon surrounded by people
dressed in wet SNP tee-shirts and drooket bedraggled Scottish
Saltire flags. As Allan went out through the door with a pile of
dishes he heard Coltart say, 'Jean. Would you be able to organise a small demo for me?'

He hovered outside the door and heard Jean reply, 'I've got
a lot on at the moment, Andrew. Term started last week.'

As he returned, Andrew was saying, 'I suppose I could ask
Mike.'

'Mike!'

There was a pause and a meeting of eyes.

'I suppose I could do it if you ask Mike to help me.'

'Fine, Jean. I knew I could rely on you.'

And then Coltart was standing up and saying his goodbyes.
'Cheerio, Allan! Nice to have met you!'

When he was gone and Jean had closed the door she turned
and laughed at Allan's puzzled expression.

'Just a little subterfuge,' she said. 'You've got to be very
crafty these days.'

'What's up, Jean? Is he getting you involved in something?'

'I *am* involved, Allan. But don't worry. I'm not one of the
front-line troops.'

Allan was still puzzled so she explained. Big sister telling a
bedtime story.

'Look. The police watch our every move and our phones are
bugged.' Allan opened his mouth to protest but she waved a
hand to silence him. 'There is absolutely no doubt about that,
Allan. If we make arrangements for a demo by phone, the
police turn up in strength and film everyone there. When we
want to surprise them we make arrangements for an imaginary
demo by phone and then have our real demo somewhere else.'

'Don't they get wise to that?'

'Of course they do. So we sometimes use a double diversion.
Diversion number one is a fictitious demo. Number two is a
real demo with lots of people which is arranged without phone
calls, but there are so many people involved, the information is

bound to reach the ears of the polis, especially if the person you ask to help with the organisation is a known police informer. The real demo involves a much smaller group of people.'

'So the demo he was asking you to organise . . .'

'Is diversion number two.'

'Where is the real one?'

'I don't know and if I did know I wouldn't tell you.'

'You'll land in prison, Jean.'

'That would be very awkward for you, wouldn't it? You might have to give up your yuppie existence and do something about looking after Roddy, wouldn't you?'

'That's not fair, Jean.'

'Why the bloody hell isn't it fair?'

After supper she mellowed. 'Tell me about this Telman woman then.'

They were sitting on either side of the fire. Allan had washed up and Jean had taken off her slippers, tucked her feet up on to the armchair and was cradling a small tot of pure malt in her cupped hands.

'Rosa's brilliant. She knows the business of program correctness like no one else.'

'And that's important to you. This computer correctness. What use is it – really?'

'Jean . . .' He groped for words. 'There are computers everywhere. Not just in businesses and banks and whatever. Nowadays they fly aeroplanes and control nuclear power stations. And if one of those programs goes wrong, it's not just an embarrassment – it's a disaster. And the problem is that it's often not possible to test a program for every eventuality. It's not just that you can't foresee absolutely every possible event; it's that, because you are working with time and an infinite variety of possible coincidences, the number of different combinations is virtually infinite. If you tried to test every one of them, you would still be at it when the universe ran down.'

'So that's where you come in, is it?'

'Aye. Well, in a way. We can't do it properly yet. We are trying to prove that certain things cannot happen when a program runs – and I mean prove like in mathematics. The way we do it is to assume the opposite – assume the accident *can* happen and then try to prove that that leads to a logical contradiction – like something being in two places at the same time. We can manage it at present with certain types of program and they have got to be written in a certain way. What Rosa and I have been trying to do is to show that the same techniques can be used for a wider range of programs. Really big programs that do some funny things and are not as well-behaved as the little ones that people do it for at present. The real goal is to find a way of doing it automatically, because until we can do that it's so laborious no one in his right mind would try to do it for a program of any size.'

He paused, trying to think of an example.

'There's a story going around at the moment,' he said. 'I don't know if it's true, but it might be. It seems there was an American fighter plane which was a fly-by-wire machine. Everything was under computer control. It had been tested and had been flying successfully for a long time but there was still a bug – a fault – in the control program. When the plane flew over the equator to the Southern Hemisphere one of the readings from the gyroscopic compass became negative and the plane instantly flipped on to its back. Someone had just forgotten to correct for negative readings.'

'So you work with . . . Rosa. Is anyone else involved?'

'Well, actually we're not doing that kind of work at all at the moment. We plan to, but right now I am filling in for that guy who killed himself. It's just routine stuff, so it's a bit boring, but when they get a replacement I'll be able to get back to the correctness proofs.'

'Are you sure they're not just taking advantage of you?'

'No. Really. Rosa is as keen as I am to get back to it. She is fighting a battle with the boss. He's called Wensley Halpern – a very smooth operator. Rosa shouts at him over the phone every day. He wants to break the team up and disperse it to other plants.'

'Why?'

Allan shrugged. 'I don't know. Maybe he just doesn't like Rosa. Jack – that's a pal at work – thinks he's afraid of her – frightened she might make some kind of breakthrough and upstage him. Jack might be right for all I know.'

'So where does this Halpern guy want you to go?'

'Well, he hasn't said it exactly . . .'

'Where?'

'South America.'

'Christ!' Jean put her head back on the chair and closed her eyes.

'It's OK, I'm not going.'

'You might not have a choice.' She kept her eyes shut for a while and spoke without opening them. 'What's she like?'

'Who?'

'Rosa Telman.'

'Oh . . . She's got dark hair.'

'Very informative. I'm sure I would recognise her from that description.'

'She's about forty. She's small and olive skinned and got a wee bit of a foreign accent.'

'Is she married?'

'Oh aye. Her husband is some kind of professor – or he was. They say he's taken early retirement and now he's some kind of consultant – accountancy, I think.'

'Any children?'

'I didn't ask.'

'You're hopeless.' She snorted but she was laughing. She sat up, leaning over to the table to pour a drop more into her glass. 'Is she attractive?'

Allan hesitated. He hadn't considered Rosa from that point of view.

'Aye. I suppose she might be, in a way.'

'Is there more than one way?' She snuggled back into the chair.

'I like her but I don't want to climb into bed with her.'

'But you might if you were asked.'

He looked disgusted. 'Don't be daft. She's a lot older than I am.'

'It's been known.' Jean smiled at him over the top of her glass and then took a sip.

'She's flying out to South America next week – with Halpern. It's some kind of heads' meeting. It's an annual event but it's the first time Rosa's been invited along.'

Rosa Telman sat erect and cool in a cream linen dress as she watched the Andes sliding by the windows of the executive jet. A wide-brimmed hat lay by her side.

On the other side of the cabin Wensley Halpern had no eyes for the scenery. Throughout the flight he had worked hard at his 'portable office' – a lap-held microcomputer work-station which stored his working papers and which could put him in direct satellite data-link connection with the computer in his office back in Scotland. He had the clean-cut, squash-playing image of an after-shave advert. His chin might have been a little on the large side with a tendency to fleshiness, but his flat stomach and deep tan spoke of long hours on the exercise bicycle and under sun-ray lamps.

Halpern bristled with electronic gadgets and executive toys. Rosa had found that the business of going through the airport checks in his company was acutely embarrassing. Everything had to be unloaded and examined before he could pass through the electronic screening device and the airport staff obviously found it difficult to keep their faces straight while he produced for inspection his radio scrambler telephone, his portable microcomputer office work-station, his miniature appointment diary-alarm databank, his solar-powered lapel-button kidnap-emergency location-homer transmitter, his office-contact bleeper and his domestic-contact bleeper (the 'wife-alarm', as some colleagues called it). He even carried a fountain pen in rolled gold which was quite useless as a writing implement but which housed in its cap a miniature electronic bug detector and sweeping device. He liked to demonstrate this at the commencement of important meetings to illustrate his attention to detail and his concern for security. But such was the arsenal of electronic gadgetry which he carried on his person that inevitably and inexorably it always homed in on himself.

Rosa and Halpern shared the final leg of the journey with two others, Gunter Mach from Marble's German plant and Peter Tan from Taiwan. Gunter was a tall, heavy man with a very long thin head and gold-rimmed spectacles, who liked to crack jokes at Halpern's expense in slow, heavily accented but perfect English.

'Well, Halpern,' he had said as they climbed aboard the jet. 'I think perhaps now you are going to check the plane for bugs.'

Rosa had met Mach before only a couple times, both of them formal occasions, but she knew Peter well. They had been graduate students together at Berkeley. Peter had moved from research to management but he was still one of the few people in the Marble organisation for whom Rosa had respect and it was rumoured that the relationship between them might, at one time, have been more than just friendly.

But the Andes stole the show – a changing pattern of peaks and ridges and deep V-shaped valleys gliding past. As they flew, the predominating colour changed from grey-green and white to rust-brown with an occasional purple outcrop. Then they swung away from the mountains and the greenery of the Ocean Springs complex glided into view.

'Ocean Springs' was a misnomer. Not only was the Pacific fifty miles away, but the nearest natural source of water was a salt swamp about half an hour's drive along the dusty desert road to Chimbero. At one time the place was called 'Campo del José' which means 'José's Flats'. It was rumoured that the new name was thought up when the property development plan was still on the drawing-board and the intended location was California. That was before financial arrangements fell through and the Marble Corporation declared an interest, offering to collaborate with 'Sunrise Properties'. The location was switched to Chile where the tax laws were advantageous and the government docile, and the nature of the project changed from a purely speculative one to a well-planned complex which was to become the new headquarters of the Marble empire.

But the name stuck. Perhaps the image makers thought that it brought a touch of cool freshness to a dust-brown place of shimmering heat, trapped in the plain between the Andes, the Pacific and the Atacama Desert. Anyone driving in from Chimbero or Copiapo would see the signposts proclaiming 'A new concept in urban environment for life and work', but might well reflect on why no one had bothered to translate the message into Spanish. The 'Springs' bit of the name was not so wide of the mark. In that low-lying area the water table was not far below the surface and modern boring equipment brought it up easily. The place became an oasis of greenery in a parched landscape. Avenues were tree-lined and lawns sprinkled among the residential properties so carefully and tastefully arranged beside an artificial lake. From the centre of the lake spumed a two-hundred-foot jet of water, casting spray and rainbows.

The lake was shaped like a padlock and the hotel and conference centre were on the island formed by its hasp. On the far side of the creek was the industrial complex holding Marble's main computer manufacturing plant and research centre. Other companies were there too but if you dug deep enough into their affairs, you would probably find a connection to Marble's lurking in their foundations. The buildings there were low-rise slabs of cream concrete and the Marble colour scheme was maintained by the brown plate glass which shut out the glare of the desert sun.

The Marble Corporation was what is called a 'holding' company. But if Jason Confield of the *Financial Analyst* was to be believed, it was more of a holding, squeezing dry and devouring company. It held, owned and controlled many others and it was rumoured that it also owned several governments.

Its founder and president was J. Norman Marble Jnr. Business admirers called him 'Productivity Norm' while sycophants and employees within earshot called him 'Quality Norm'. He guided the fortunes of his empire with a quiet ruthlessness that terrified his competitors. When he decided to increase the Corporation's stake in computers, several small companies with big ideas were swallowed as a whale swallows krill and Marble Computers International (MCI) was born. Expertise was assimilated and brought to the Ocean Springs complex – 'The New Technological Camelot' as *Time* magazine called it. Businesses acquired around the world were either closed or sold off to management buy-out teams which were left with products having modest current sales but absolutely no future. New assembly plants were opened in other continents to take advantage of cheap labour and some of these were granted small research centres to make it possible for MCI to tap into whatever research expertise was available in these places. A residual presence remained in the United States, concentrating mainly on marketing, but Ocean Springs became the focal point of the empire. Whatever it lacked in amenities was brought, wholesale, vacuum-packed and shrink-wrapped from the States. Marble moved his personal office into the penthouse suite in the Conference Centre Building – the 'Shower Tower' as the locals called it, because of the way the spray from the fountain drifted against it when the wind was in the South. Telecommunications antennae and dishes on the roof of the building put him in direct touch with the outlying parts of his empire.

A small satirical magazine once portrayed Marble on its front cover as a huge, malevolent spider at the centre of a global web in which were caught up a number of flies, each of which bore a striking resemblance to a well-known political figure. Knowledgeable observers were not entirely surprised when the magazine went into liquidation shortly afterwards.

Gunter Mach wore a poncho blanket and ornate boots with golden spurs the size of saucers. A sombrero hung on his back from its lanyard. He twirled a six-shooter clumsily on his finger and then pointed it. 'Make my day,' he said, grinning.

Shivering in the chill breeze which often blew across the flats before dawn, they had boarded the rotor-jets. The distant

mountains were black silhouettes back-lit by a pink glow in the
eastern sky. They had flown up a valley between dark cliffs
while a hard edge of bright sunlight crept down the mountainside towards them. The rocks were bands of maroon and
purple and huge slopes of dark red scree threatened them from
above.

They landed on the flat valley floor in the midst of a sea of
stones, rounded and bleached. Already the sun was uncomfortably bright. The river, a mere trickle which meandered
through the middle of the stone desert, was fringed by blond
grasses high as a man's head. Nearby was a ranch where horses
were coralled behind wire fences supported by tall, spindly
poles. A girl called Randy met them. She had a Texan drawl
and a side-kick, a boy called Chico who was dressed like a
South American cowboy. Rosa had photographs of them. She
reckoned they were too Hollywood to be real. At the ranch
everyone was kitted out in new Levi's and sombreros. There
was much guffawing by the group as they caught sight of one
another dressed up like film extras.

It was the last day, the day of the excursion, the day of cor-
porate togetherness, a day for 'entering into the spirit'. But
Rosa was not entering into any kind of spirit and she had never
felt less 'togetherness'. She was extremely angry.

The 'Rainbow Room' was on the tenth floor of the 'Shower
Tower'. Sliding glass doors ran the whole length of one wall
and opened on to a veranda which was almost under the falling
spray from the water plume. The air which wafted in was deli-
ciously cool.

They were about twenty in number, not counting the wel-
coming party and the supporting cast of hostesses in the
company livery. A sleek young man with an improbable tan
stood at a lectern on a slightly raised platform and did the mas-
ter-of-ceremonies thing. Gunter was introduced to the group
as the MD who had presided over the greatest rise in productivity. Peter Tan had captured the greatest increase in market
share. Joe Delago of special contracts had landed the largest

single order to supply computers for the new computerised electoral system which was to be installed in Europe. Willard Gerstone, the South African MD, had achieved the lowest manpower cost. Wensley Halpern got his pat on the back for highest quality standards. Each was the greatest this or the best at that – except for Rosa.

At the sound of her own name she had risen, as had the others, to receive the applause, but she was described as being 'from Gairnock in Scotland'. Just that. Two claps which died on the wing, then deathly silence. She had sat down again, suddenly, spilling coffee on to her dress. A hostess had descended upon her solicitously offering sympathy and Kleenex but Rosa had had to repair to the women's room to dab out the stain and recover her composure. Moments earlier Sherman Olafsen, her arch rival and head of the Ocean Springs research unit, was introduced as 'the world authority on the theory of program correctness proofs for holistic programs'.

Afterwards, when she was telling Allan about the trip, Rosa admitted that she had been shaken. But Allan was puzzled. Given that Rosa had a poor opinion of almost everyone in the higher management, he could not understand why she would want praise from that quarter, but he supposed it was the suddenness – like being bitten by an unloved but docile family pet. Rosa was convinced that the whole thing was a set-up and that Wensley Halpern had known about it in advance. Later, when the initial meeting was over, they had been split up into small groups for detailed discussion of reports and analyses of strategy. At one of these private sessions it was explained to Rosa and Halpern that Gairnock was not to be given the prestige development and verification of the new Labyrinth operating system. Instead Rosa's team would be given some routine work on quality-testing software. Halpern had actually spoken in her defence but Rosa maintained that Halpern's weak protests were a sham, prearranged with the senior management and not intended to succeed. The real hurt was that the project she wanted would be given to Olafsen's team.

She admitted that she had behaved badly. She had been shrill; she had not put her case well and the others present, all male, had exchanged glances. She reserved her most vitriolic comments for a man – she had never discovered his name – in tinted, rimless, octagonal spectacles who had sat at the elbow of Harvey Walsh, the Vice President, and fed him bits of paper from a black briefcase. He it was who produced a copy of Rosa's terms of employment when she had talked about resig- nation. The terms stipulated that Rosa, on leaving MCI, could not work or publish in any topic on which she had worked with MCI. It was no empty threat. MCI had a history of vindictive legal suits against people who had broken their contracts.

After that she had found it almost impossible to get a private word with anyone at the conference. Every minute of each day was scheduled in a round of working parties, discussion groups and panel talks interspersed by meal-times and coffee breaks. She was excluded from most of the serious private ses- sions and she fretted away hours listening to discussions on marketing strategy. Marble himself put in an appearance at one of the buffet luncheons, to give them a platitudinous pep talk and to mingle with the troops for a few minutes with wine glass and diminutive sandwich in hand. She tried to button-hole Peter Tan at coffee but he would only talk about the weather.

Rosa stood apart from the others. She felt ridiculous in Levi's and sombrero. She watched, smouldering, while, to much applause, Chico lassoed horses in the corral with a lariat made of plaited leather. Horse flesh was slapped and there was talk of girths and withers. The horses were saddled up in South American style with huge wooden stirrups like clogs and one by one each of the visitors was eased up on to the back of a patient horse.

The power of the sun increased with the hour and Rosa dis- covered that the sombreros were not ornaments. Because of the dust on the trail, the old bandit trick with a handkerchief round nose and mouth was also a sensible protection. As they climbed a narrow trail diagonally up the flank of the valley and the higher hills came into view, the blackness of her mood dissolved.

They lunched in a high alp and here Rosa was at last able to corner Peter Tan in a secluded spot. He was sitting with his back to a large boulder some distance away from the main party. With his lean jaw and oriental eyes she reckoned the cowboy outfit suited him rather better than the rest of them. He looked somehow just right and the appearance was not deceptive. Peter was very adaptable as well as being intelligent. He was a survivor, and if somehow they had been thrown into this life for real, Rosa reckoned that Peter would have emerged as the natural leader, able to turn his hand to roping horses and handling a gun. Peter was the kind of person you would want to have on your side in a tight corner.

'What's going on, Peter?'

She sat down beside him like a little girl, for once dependent, subdued. She offered him a drink from her water bottle. Peter went on gazing at the high snow-clad hills framed by the purple slopes at the end of their valley. He sighed.

'Rosa,' he said, 'you are one of the most intelligent people I have ever known, probably –' He looked round at her and then back to the distant hills. 'Probably *the* most intelligent. But when it comes to office politics you're a babe in arms.'

'What's it all about, Peter? Tell me.'

'It's not personal, Rosa. They don't underestimate you. They know very well that you would do a better job on the operating system than Sherman's mob but they want it for themselves, Rosa. You are clever and therefore you are dangerous.'

'Dangerous?'

'The whole company is geared now to the new Labyrinth chip. It will be the central technology for the next twenty years. The operating system is a strategic bit of that technology and the proof of its correctness even more so. It would be dangerous to put that into the hands of someone who was not totally their man. That little charade in the Rainbow Room, the way they insulted you, that was just a warning shot across the bows of anyone else who might have felt disposed to come to your aid.'

'So what shall I do?'

'Do nothing. You can't get them to change their minds by protesting. The more you protest, the more they will be certain their judgement was correct. Find something else to do which will give you a focus for your talents. You're still young.' He turned round to her, met her eyes, and with a quiet smile took the water bottle out of her hand. 'It would be a waste to eat out your heart on this.'

She watched his Adam's apple jumping as he drank. He screwed the top back on the bottle and said, 'There's another reason why you can't win when it comes to office politics. You actually want the job to be done well. The people who win political battles don't care about that. They only care about being in charge of the job. So they concentrate on advocating whatever will get them promoted, no matter what that is.'

There was a long pause.

'What a beautiful place this is,' he said suddenly as he handed the bottle back. He dropped his voice. 'Just watch what you say, Rosa, and who you say it to. This place has more bugs than a hobo's underpants.'

They had got back to the ranch late in the evening. Everyone was walking about stiffly with bandy legs. They hefted saddles and saddle-bags on to the low wooden counter for Randy to collect and pack away.

'Ah, Wensley,' said Gunter in a basso profundo, 'are you not going to check me out for bugs?'

There was a glint in Halpern's eye. He produced his gold-topped pen and began to scan Gunter's person minutely – in his ears, up his trouser legs, until the others began to giggle and Gunter began to get annoyed. Then Halpern waved the pen about the room. As the pen swung across in front of Rosa the small red light on the tip of the pen lit up. He paused, puzzled, and swung it back towards Rosa. His smile was gone. At that moment Randy took Rosa's sombrero from her and carried it off, but as Rosa handed it over she saw or thought she saw that the bauble on the end of her hat string had a set of little perforations in its base.

5

JULY

Rosa's home was called 'Fairways' and it was halfway to Kilmalcolm, a low ranch-style house sitting on a small loop road off the Kilmalcolm Road, facing fields with cows and a few mature sycamores. It backed on to a golf course within easy range of a deviant tee-shot at the sixteenth. Rosa joked about that. She said that when they sat out on the lawn on a summer's afternoon, they handed round tin hats with the cucumber sandwiches. He asked her about her husband but all she would say was, 'Maurice is in business.'

Allan watched her as she drove. Yellow blouse open at the neck contrasting with her black hair. Short sleeves. Olive brown arms. Small hands on the wheel. She sat upright, concentrating uneasily on the road ahead as though she wanted to be doing something else. She joked but there was no happiness in her laughter.

There was no one in the house when they arrived. Rosa sat him down by the fireplace in a huge open-plan room – was it a room? With lots of glass and chromium, it had the flavour of executive lounge about it. If a loudspeaker had announced the departure of flight 405 it would not have seemed surprising. There was a tidy pile of logs but there were no flames in the fireplace. Beyond a bar-counter and a raised step there was the

gleam of copper kitchenwear and polished pine worktops. Rosa
put an apron on over her skirt and blouse and began straight
away to deal with the stuff she had brought in with her. Plates
rattled. The microwave hummed. She was apologetic, shouting
across to him as she worked, 'I hope you don't mind frozen . . .
It's all I could get . . . for speed you know . . . Maurice puts me
to shame.' She laughed nervously. 'He's such a gourmet.'

Maurice appeared at that moment, heavily built, balding,
red face, bushy sideburns.

'How do you do,' he said from across the room when Rosa
introduced Allan, but his attention was on the worktop where
Rosa had dumped her purchases. He held up a packet and
read what it said on the side with distaste. Then he put it down
and said 'Extraordinary!' and left the room.

He came back later when they were sitting at a pine kitchen-
style table eating defrozen savoury pancakes with pecan sauce.
It was not bad. Allan, doing the polite thing, said how nice it
was. Maurice poked it uncertainly with a fork and then said, 'I
think this needs some wine.' He went off again and returned
with a bottle of Burgundy. He was a bit huffy when Allan said
his no thank you.

Maurice gave them a lecture on the wine. He had bought it
at some 'cave' in France and went into minute detail of how he
had found it, and the way he had struck the bargain. Allan
asked him about his work and made the mistake of calling him
'Professor Telman'.

'Watson, actually,' Maurice said, without looking up. Then
he looked at Rosa and said, 'Rosa has done the feminist thing
with her name, you see.'

He had been a Professor of Accountancy and now he was on
the boards of half a dozen companies. But he was still a professor, and Allan and Rosa were his students. He gave them
another lecture, this time on business management, on the
absurdity of Trade Union leaders and on the need for
'Stability' and 'Business Confidence'. Those words again.
Allan smiled inwardly. Pious words to Maurice and his kind –
invective to Jean and her SNP friends.

The monologue was interrupted at that point. There was a roar of a car with no silencer, a pattering of gravel against the front of the house and a leitmotiv played fortissimo on the accelerator pedal.

'Bob,' said Rosa.

The door burst open and a young man and woman came in accompanied by a blare of pop music. The young man wore a bomber jacket. The girl had green hair and carried a ghetto-blaster in her hand. Rosa made hand signals to her to cut the music, which for a while the green-haired girl pretended to misunderstand, briefly turning it louder. Then for half an hour these two, Bob and Julia Watson, Maurice's children, Rosa's stepchildren, created a maelstrom. They weren't much younger than Allan but somehow he felt a generation apart.

'Is this all we've got?' Julia said, standing with the fridge door open with her hip cocked to one side. Cupboard doors were banged. The microwave hummed again.

Allan was fascinated by the way Rosa reacted. At work she was so self-assured. Everyone deferred to her judgement. Here, no one gave a damn about her and she behaved like a nervous child, hesitant, trying vainly to put in a word here and there. The crease between her eyebrows deepened. She introduced Allan. Bob said 'Hi!' and went on putting slices of ham into a roll. Julia ignored him and said to Maurice, 'We're going out.' And they did shortly afterwards with another concerto on the accelerator pedal, leaving the ghetto-blaster blaring somewhere in the house. Rosa went looking for it and switched it off.

Soon afterwards Maurice went to meet a friend at the golf clubhouse. Rosa relaxed, settling down like a leaf after the passage of a whirlwind.

'Do you never drink?' she said.

'No, never. I'm not a reformed alcoholic.'

'I'm sorry. I didn't mean . . .' She was straightening things out, tidying away dirty dishes, getting a bowl of trifle out of the fridge, putting the coffee on to perk, just the two of them again on opposite sides of the table.

'Let's go into the garden,' she said. 'It's getting dark, so there will be a cease-fire with the golfers until morning. I just hope no one ever invents luminous golf-balls.'

It was dusk and the coffee was good. A blackbird was still warbling.

Rosa asked him about his home and he told her about Uncle Roddy and Jean. She said, 'It's not been very exciting for you since you came. I'm sorry. I didn't mean to involve you in the testing software. I really intended to let you carry on with your work on correctness theory. How do you feel about it so far?'

Allan protested politely and truthfully – he understood completely – and dishonestly – he was perfectly happy.

'I wondered.' She leaned back in her chair. Even in the growing darkness he could see she was smiling. 'I wondered if you would like to help me with a small project.'

'What kind of project?'

'More or less the work we both want to do.' She put her cup down and folded her hands in her lap. 'You see, now that MCI have taken it away from us, there is no chance that we can get into that work officially, but there is nothing to stop us doing a little bit of work on our own.'

'Would they know at MCI?'

'Not if we didn't tell them.'

She was full of surprises. But sister Jean's influence was strong. He tested the idea for hidden trapdoors. The blackbird had stopped. Some other bird was singing more quietly in the stillness.

'What would it involve exactly?'

'Well . . .' She was thinking as she spoke. 'I thought that we might work together on the idea in our spare time. I could make sure that you were not given too much at work so that you would have some spare time. We could work in the evenings and exchange notes during the day.'

'But what would the project be?'

She offered him more coffee from the pot but he declined. She poured more for herself then sat back again, holding the cup in her lap.

'More or less what we originally intended. We could prove

the correctness of the new Labyrinth operating system – no deadlocks, no unfairness, no starvation.'

These were the technical terms for a well-behaved operating system that gave all users a proper share of resources. But he was puzzled.

'But I thought that that problem was being given to the Olafsen team. Are we going to be given the source code?'

Proofs were done on source code. Without that you were high and dry.

'Ah. Well. You see, that is the difficult bit. But there is a way round it.' A gleam of light from the darkening sky was reflected in her eye. She leaned forwards and put her hands together as though praying, thumbs just under her chin. 'You see . . . I think we can do it on the machine code.'

No one did that. The machine code was a hideous jumble of instructions. Some of the code was even ambiguous. But he didn't protest. He knew that she knew that. There had to be a catch. He took a deep breath.

She said, 'I'm not mad, Allan. It can be done. You see, the order code for the Labyrinth is structured and it's orthogonal. It doesn't have the same problems as other order codes.'

He stretched and clasped his hands behind his head, frowning, doubting, but all ears.

He said, 'Supposing we could do this. How could we tell anyone, let alone publish?'

'We'd find a way. Through some of your university friends perhaps.'

He couldn't quite see that but wondered if it mattered. They wouldn't succeed anyway. Of that he was sure. But trying might be good fun. Better than the stuff he was doing, and it would keep him active in the field while he looked around for something else.

Rosa spoke again. 'There's something else, Allan. If we managed to find an automatic proof method for the operating system, there's no reason why we couldn't do the same for any program running on the Labyrinth.'

He spluttered. 'Oh come on!'

'I'm serious, Allan. The programs are in the same machine code.'

'But you've got no specification for what the programs are trying to do!'

You needed a spec. There was no other way the proof system could know what the program was supposed to do and therefore no way to prove that it was doing it.

'For most programs, perhaps. But for some we could write the spec. ourselves. The important thing is to prove that it is possible.'

'A spec. in machine code!'

'No. In logic notation. We would have to find a way to resolve the variables.'

She was mad – or was she? He finished his coffee, which was cold, keeping the cup up to his lips between sips while he thought.

She said, 'More?'

He shook his head and put the cup down. The fun thing was to try. Success was relatively unimportant to him. Getting back into it, into the literature, running back through the logic expressions again . . . Something would come out of it even if it wasn't the impossible objective Rosa was setting for them.

'OK,' he said. 'I'll give it a try.'

It was really dark now but somehow he knew she was beaming at him.

6

AUGUST

'So what are you going to do, bugger-lugs? Up sticks and off like Bill?'

Joe Willaby had had too much to drink but to judge by the colour of his nose that was not an unusual occurrence. He leant forwards towards Allan, red in face, eyes a shade unfocused, and pointed a finger of the hand which was holding his glass. He placed the other hand on Jenny's knee. Jenny – the delectable Jennifer of the enquiry desk – was sitting beside Joe and looking uncomfortable.

'I wouldn't blame him if he did,' said Jack. 'If he stays here he'll be stuck doing hack programming when what he really wants to be doing is his high-powered theory stuff. That's right, isn't it, Allan?'

Jack had had a few too but he was in better shape. Bill Thompson put another round of drinks on the table. Allan made room by lifting the plate with his bit of quiche. The noise of the canned music was making conversation difficult. He felt that a smile would suffice for an answer.

'What do you say, Bill?' said Joe.

'About what?' Bill sorted the glasses and pushed an apple juice in Allan's direction.

'About leaving now that your team is being shut down.'

'It's not being shut down, Joe.'

'Good as,' said Joe. 'From what I hear, Rosa's going to plant an axe in Halpern's head. Rosa the rebel, eh?' He wiped froth off his lip with the back of his hand.

A waitress pushed in and collected glasses. Alison, Jack's girlfriend, ordered lasagne for herself and Jenny. Gorgeous Jenny. She had a white roll-necked jumper.

'And some crisps, darlin',' said Joe to the waitress.

'When do you move?' Jack asked Bill.

'I'm going down next week but the wife and kids will stay here till I get a house down South.'

'Sold the house?'

Bill nodded. 'But entry is not for a couple of months.'

Joe stood up and stumbled. He leant heavily on the shoulder of a red-headed man sitting at the next table beyond Jack.

'Sorry. Sorry,' said Joe and made his way uncertainly towards the gents.

The man did not seem to mind but his companion did, a thin woman in a print dress.

'Going away party?' said the man.

Jack said, 'Yes. Bill here is departing to parts South – Surrey University – lucky bastard.'

'You all with MCI then?'

'Aye,' said Jack. 'For our sins.'

'The new gurus,' said the man. His female companion was not happy. She looked at her watch.

'Underpaid gurus,' said Jack.

Jenny spoke to Masood, who was sitting beside Allan. 'Do you mind if we change places?' Allan knew it wasn't his magnetic attraction. It had more to do with the repulsive force of Joe Willaby, but he wasn't complaining. Jenny settled beside him and pulled her skirt down over her knees.

'I'll hold that for you,' she said, seeing that Allan was stuck with a glass in one hand and a plate with a slice of quiche in the other.

'I don't believe that,' said the man to Jack. 'You guys will get a good salary and these days you're lucky to have one at all.

Anyway, you can always make a bit on the side, I'll bet.'

Bill hooted scornfully and turned his attention to Alison.

Jack said, 'We don't work with CDs and microwaves, you know. The stuff we handle has no resale value.'

'I don't mean like that,' said the man. 'You guys can hack into computers, can't you?'

Jack warmed to one of his pet subjects. 'You've been watching too many thrillers on TV,' he said. 'In fiction an expert in computers is supposed to be able to walk up to a machine he has never seen in his life before and hack straight into it. It's not like that, you know.'

'But you lot make the computers,' said the man. 'In the old days the men who made safes were the best at cracking them. They just kept a spare set of keys. I bet you could do the same.'

Jack put his glass down and for once had nothing to say. He took his spectacles off and cleaned them on a paper napkin. Joe Willaby pushed his way back into the group. He seemed annoyed. Perhaps it was because Jenny was out of reach.

'Have you never drunk alcohol?' Jenny asked Allan.

'No.'

'Why not?'

'I don't know. My uncle who brought me up never did either. I just picked up the habit – or rather, didn't pick up the habit.'

The woman beside the red-haired man stood up and straightened her dress. The man downed his glass and nodded goodbye to Jack. Jack watched them as they shuffled sideways towards the door.

Alison said, 'Jack! You're thinking. I can tell.'

'He's right, you know.'

'Stop it, Jack! Just get the idea out of your head right now.'

Bill said, 'He's not right It would need a massive conspiracy to do it. You'd need to fiddle the operating system and then be able to follow the machine right through sales to its destination and then you would need physical access to the hardware which might be on the other side of the world. You would never keep a conspiracy that size under wraps.'

'Why the operating system?' said Jack. 'Why not the chips themselves?'

'It's time we were getting back,' said Helen. She was driving and had stayed on lemonade.

'Who's going to drive Joe's car?' said Alison when they reached the car park.

'No one,' said Jack. He lifted his hand and showed them a small black plastic gadget.

'Is that what I think it is?' said Bill.

Jack nodded.

'What is it?' said Jenny.

'Rotor arm from Joe's car,' said Jack.

They piled into Helen's Space Cruiser.

Jack said, 'You know, that guy was right. Usually it would be the operating system but in the 65000 the encryption function is on the chip. If you did spike a chip, the only problem would be beating the testing procedures on the assembly line.'

'I told you to stop that,' said Alison.

7

SEPTEMBER

'Once and for all, Jack Thornley, I am not playing a part in your stupid games.'

Alison spoke softly through clenched teeth. There was a pause between each word.

'OK. OK.' Jack held up his hands as though submitting to a bank robbery. 'I give in. Say no more about it.'

'You're damned right we'll say no more about it.' She lifted a soapy hand out of the sink and pointed with her whole arm at the kitchen door. 'One more word about tapes or chips or secret passages and I am walking out of that door.'

'Cross my heart,' said Jack. She had turned back to the sink. He came up behind her and put his arms round her waist. She flounced her hair and caught him a crack on the nose with the back of her head.

'Ouch!'

'Serves you right, you smarmy weasel.'

She tipped the teapot into the vegetable strainer and banged it down on the draining board.

Jack rubbed his nose and lifted the local evening paper.

'So what's it to be tonight then – pictures?'

'I'm going to wash my hair.'

He dropped the newspaper on to a chair and brought a pile

of dirty crockery over from the table to where Alison was washing up.

'You're still angry then.' He lifted some food scraps from the
top plate of the pile and dropped them into the pedal-bin. 'It
wasn't a big deal, you know. Just a switch of tapes for a few
minutes.'

Alison, with both hands in the sink, shut her eyes and
dropped her head as though waiting in submission for an axe to
fall on her neck.

Jack went on, 'I would have given you all the right codes to
recognise the boards and you would only have needed to do the
switch and press a button and then repeat the operation a few
seconds later. And it was only a test. One way or another we
would have known whether it was really possible to put a secret
passage into a chip.'

Alison opened her eyes again and sighed deeply. Then she
took her hands out of the water and dried them. Without a
word, she went over to the kitchen door and removed her jacket
from the hook, put it on, opened the door and went out. A second later he heard the outside door slam.

Allan steadied the tray on the glide-rail with one hand and
tried to tuck his shirt-tail into his waistband with the other. He
caught sight of his own reflection in a glass display case. Hair
awry. He patted it ineffectually with the spare hand.

'Sorry.'

The man behind him was trying to get past. Allan gripped
his tray in both hands and made his way hesitantly towards the
table.

It was now or never.

'Can I join you?'

Jenny was at the table. Alison was with her. They sat facing
each other, deep in conversation. Alison pulled a chair back for
him. Jenny smiled. It was a nice smile but not a very interested
smile. He sat down and arranged his plate.

'Would you pass the salt, please?'

Alison handed him the salt cellar without looking at him. She said to Jenny, 'You know, I don't think he should have done that. It was rude of him to butt in.'

Allan's knife and fork paused in mid-air, then slowly and with ears burning, he detached a piece of meat.

Jenny said, 'He's like that. It's just his way. He doesn't realise he's being rude.'

Allan cut more meat.

Alison said, 'No girl would put up with a man who behaved like that.'

Jenny said, 'She would if she loved him.'

His hand shook. He went on cutting.

'More fool her.'

He drew his knife through the lettuce several times.

'So what do you think will happen next?' said Jenny.

Alison said, 'Well, we'll see what happens in tonight's episode.'

Jenny turned to him. 'Do you watch *Neighbours*, Allan?'

Alison looked at Allan's plate. 'Do you always cut your food up like that? It looks like mince. Would you like help with your spoon and pusher?'

Jenny said suddenly, 'Why don't you ask Allan to speak to Jack?' Alison looked dubious but she didn't say anything.

Jenny turned to Allan. 'Alison's having trouble with Jack. He keeps asking her to help him with some silly hacking thing he wants to do and he won't take "No" for an answer. Do you think you could tell him to stop it?'

'I think it would need someone with a crowbar to get sense into his head,' said Alison.

Jenny said, 'He might listen to you, Allan.'

'I'll try.'

Later that evening, in his digs, he lay in bed looking at the key-stoned blocks of light projected by the window panes on to the dark ceiling and thought about Jenny. A lost cause. The conversation had gone all wrong.

Holidays. She flew on package tours to Benidorm. He hitch-hiked to Chamonix. She said where was that? What was the night life like? His most exciting night at Chamonix had been spent in a bivouac-bag suspended from a steel peg on the West Face of the Dru, thousands of feet above the surface of the Mer de Glace.

Music. She liked James Last and Richard Clayderman!

Films. She liked – thingamy and whatsit – names he had never heard of. She went to the pictures by car and he couldn't even drive.

But she was nice. She was bloody lovely. What malicious Cupid had arrowed him with desire for a woman so nice but so . . . so . . . disappointingly normal?

The promise to speak to Jack had been a mistake too. He tried it when they were having a pizza together at Alfonso's. He had known as he started to speak that it was a bad move. Jack shovelled in another forkful of pasta, stabbed his spectacles back on to the bridge of his nose with a forefinger and grinned horribly, showing lots of teeth, his eyes enlarged to wet moons by the lenses. Allan had made his day.

What was it with people like Jack? Their sense of right and wrong switched itself off when it came to 'systems'. Hooked on being bloody smart Alecs. To them computer files were not personal property; they were a challenge – coconuts in a fair-ground stall sitting there just waiting to be knocked off.

Anyway. What the hell? Climbing and computing defined the axis of his life and currently he was not getting enough of either, not real climbing and not real computing. Withdrawal symptoms. Time to pull his finger out. A woman would appear from somewhere, though just at that moment he couldn't see from where exactly.

He bought a bike. There was a sports centre on the outskirts of the town, an uncompromisingly ugly building of pebble-dashed concrete halfway up a narrow country road which was used by council garbage lorries on their way to a landfill site. The sports centre had a climbing wall and that solved the problem of keeping in shape for the weekends. Perhaps, he thought, he would also find a suitable female there.

What he did find was a troop of boy scouts. They were all over the surface of the climbing wall, weaving a network of multicoloured climbing ropes. It looked like a garish tartan on the loom. The scout master strode up and down, shouting encouragement and checking rope-handling technique. Afterwards he gave Allan a ticking off for climbing without protection and showing his boys a bad example. 'We come here every Thursday,' he added. 'Would you like to give me a hand?'

'Aye. Maybe. If a'm here.'

They were in Rosa's office. She said, 'I got this out of stores for you.' She reached behind her desk and brought up a cream and brown metal-bound suitcase. She laid it on the desk-top, flicked the catches and lifted the lid. It was a portable micro-computer. 'Every research worker is entitled to one of these on a more or less permanent loan,' she said. 'I thought you might find it useful.' Her eyes opened wide and her eyebrows lifted high and twitched. He whistled and ran his hand over it. An MCI machine, of course, but with more raw power than the machine which had been shared by everyone at his old university department.

'And you can probably make use of this.' She waved a floppy disc. She switched the machine on. 'It runs on batteries as well as mains power. Look.' When the operating system had booted she slipped the disc in and showed him how it worked. 'I've got the same machine at home,' she said.

The software did logical transformations. Type an expression and the name of the operation you wanted and hey presto, the transformed expression was displayed. No more writing out expressions by hand. No more transcription mistakes, no dropped indices or primes overlooked. Just point it in the right direction and press the trigger. *Zap!* A Kalashnikov instead of a bow-and-arrow.

Rosa said, 'You have to bring it back every six months for a service but otherwise there is no restriction on use. I thought you might like to dabble with that idea we discussed. In your own time, of course. Here are some of my ideas.' She handed him a brown envelope with more floppy discs.

That was how it started. In the evenings they both worked away at their respective keyboards and in the morning they exchanged the brown envelopes furtively, like pornographers, bundling the contraband with legitimate correspondence. During the working day Allan had the greatest difficulty in wrenching his thoughts away from the project and focusing his attention on to the work he was supposed to do, and Rosa seemed to be affected the same way. She left the day-to-day running of the department to others. She came in later in the mornings and looked sleepy all day but supremely happy. The others commented on it. What's happened to her? I think she's got a lover. Rosa? Never! Well, how do you explain the faraway smile? She doesn't care about this place anymore.

She sat at her desk, writing in her small, neat script, and when anyone came in to her office the page was always quickly buried under others.

I tell you, she's writing to her lover. I don't blame her. Maurice is a pain in the arse.

Allan tried to organise his time the way he had done when exams were looming. In the early evening he went to the sports centre. Once per week he had supper with Jack at Alfonso's Pizza Parlour in the High Street, talked shop and argued about the ethics of hacking.

After supper at his digs he would settle down to the micro. Often he sat up half the night trying to meet the schedule dictated by Rosa's fertile imagination. Her brain fizzed like soda water. At one point he did three nights in a row and felt he was beginning to hallucinate. His weekends in the mountains more or less stopped. Ian phoned occasionally and told him what he was missing.

The assembly line. Silence except for the hum of machinery and the puffing and wheezing of the robots.

Alison Crawford was thinking colours. She had decided on black. Bright colours did not suit her skin. A one-piece swimsuit rather than a bikini. It would make her look slimmer. She had seen the very thing on a display model in the window of the big department store which she passed every evening. It had a little bit of red trimming along the top edge and a daring plunge of the neckline which made her tingle with a mixture of apprehension and excitement.

She lifted the next board from the batch in her 'in-bin' trolley and did the required eyeball check. She could do the work on autopilot while much of her mind was free to roam on more interesting topics. The board with its array of black components and gold connections slotted smoothly into the rack like a book between book-ends. She pressed it home with a firm click. The other boards followed until she had exhausted the batch. Next she keyed in the serial number of the batch on to her console, called up the display of test procedures and selected one on a small touch pad. While the computer program read the stored number of each board and probed the innards with a pattern of instructions, her mind wandered back to the holiday she had planned along with Jenny. Jenny, of course, would wear her white bikini. She had such a good figure, with no worries about slimness, and white went so well with her honey-blonde hair. Together on the beach at Ibiza they would swivel more than a few heads. Eat your heart out, Jack Thornley.

The printer began to chatter as it spewed test results. She tore off the print-outs and scanned them. All clear. She removed the boards one by one from the rack, placed them on her out-bin trolley, initialled the control chart and clipped the test results to it.

Next batch.

'Psst!'

She wondered whether she could afford the towelling beach-coat which went with the one-piece suit in the window.

'Psst!'

She looked up. Jack was leaning over the partition of her work-place cell. For a moment she just looked at him blankly, unable to believe he would have the gall. Then she returned to her work, trying to concentrate on staring at the next board,

slotting it into the rack. Next board. A voice inside her was
shouting 'go away' over and over again. She was looking at the
codes, punching in numbers. She looked up again.

'I need your help.'

She looked at him but not at him. The printer began to
chatter. Ignore him! Pull the boards out of the rack. Put them
in the out-bin. Sign the control chart.

Next batch. Look at the board. Ignore him! Look at it!

'I'm in trouble, Alison. I need your help.'

Slot it into the rack. And the next. Select the codes. What
code? What code? She looked at him. He had a small piece of
paper in his hand which he dropped over the partition on to her
bench.

'That's the number of a board. Fail it. You must or I'm for
the high jump.'

'Start jumping,' she growled.

Next board. She remembered with a shock that she had
signed the control chart of the previous batch without checking
the test results.

'Put this one in its place. When it fails put the original one
back in its right place.'

He had a board in his hand now. Where had that come from?
He lowered his arm over the partition and put it on the bench
in front of her, then turned and walked away. It lay there like an
accusation.

Next batch – no! Finish off the previous one. Pull the boards.
Check the results. Load the out-bin. Then she reached up to
the level above and checked belatedly the results of the previous batch but one. OK! Thank goodness! But the board was
still there and the slip of paper with the board number.

Jack was no longer in sight but she could see Peter Humble
coming down the assembly line, pushing a miniature train of
in/out-bins before him, having a word with each operative as he
passed. She lifted the scrap of paper. The batch and board
numbers were both there. It was in the next batch. She lifted
the first one out of the in-bin. Not that one. Check it. Check it!
She had almost placed it in the rack without scanning it for

obvious physical defects, especially on the pin connections. Slot it in. Next board. Not that one either. Peter Humble was one cell closer. Jack, you bastard! Great holiday, Jenny! My ex-boyfriend? He got the sack because of me. Now he can't get a job anywhere. Next board. Not that one either. Slot it in. Next board. That was the one!

Alison took the board in her right hand and Jack's board in her left. She looked up the line. Peter Humble was still three cells away and chatting to Jill Watt. He was collecting her out-bin, still chatting as he moved away to the next cell. Alison closed her eyes for a moment and then slotted Jack's board into the rack. The original board she placed on a shelf under her bench by her knees. Punch in the batch number. Select the codes. Press to start. Wait while the electronics did their job. Wait with hands clasped in her lap while Peter Humble came to the cell next to hers. Wait while he chatted to Petra Lambert about some TV programme.

The board would fail the batch, of course, but how could she swap the original one back into the batch with Peter standing next to her? The printer was chattering.

'See you, Petra.'

Peter was alongside her cell. Delivering a fresh in-bin, holding out the control chart for her to sign. She initialled it.

'Did you see *That's Life* last night?'

Alison shook her head.

'My niece was on it. She was interviewed by Esther Rantzen.'

Alison smiled at him, wondering if she could chat to him and get him to wheel away the out-bin before she unloaded the faulty batch. Then she could do the swap when he was gone.

Peter said, 'That batch finished? I'll just take it too.'

Alison tore off the print-out and scanned it for the error messages and then realised with a shock that there were none. With Peter watching she removed each board, placed them in the out-bin and initialled the control chart. He wheeled the bin with its shelved layers of batches away. And Jack's substitute board was still in the batch. The real one was beside her right knee on a shelf beside her handbag. And there had been no errors in the print-out. The board had passed unrecognised. Alison sat back in her chair and wiped her hands over her face, pressing her fingertips into her eye sockets. You wait, Jack Thornley. You bastard. I'll get even yet.

Jack opened the door with a smoking saucepan in one hand. It was black, acrid smoke and when he took the lid off it belched. He led the way back into the kitchen where he placed the smoking pot in the sink. On a shelf close by were two other blackened objects which had once been saucepans. Allan poked the contents of one with a finger.

'Hmm. That looks interesting – black meringue. So what was it you wanted to talk about?'

'Plan B,' said Jack. 'There's a fish and chipper round the corner.'

They took their carry-outs into the park where the swing chains dangled. Some enterprising child had tied an old tyre on to the end of one of them with a piece of plastic-coated clothes rope, so Jack insisted on having a swing before joining Allan on the bench nearby and tucking in to his chicken supper.

'So what's the matter?'

'Nothing,' said Jack and put another chip in his mouth.

'You seemed anxious enough in the car park this evening. Is it about Tommy Harkness's files? Here they are.' He pulled the floppy disc out of his pocket. 'It's just a program – no secret messages or diaries or political jookery-pokery. Just a program like the others.'

'Is it really like the others?'

'I won't know that until I've decoded it, will I?'

'So what's stopping you?'

'It's not very important to me, Jack. Is that all it's about then? Do you want to take the file yourself?'

He offered it but Jack shook his head. Allan looked at him with a level gaze, drew in a deep breath and then let it out again. He turned his attention back to his chicken supper.

'It's nothing – really,' said Jack again. 'Well. It's just something funny that happened the other day.'

'Funny peculiar?'

'Aye.'

Allan was determined not to make it easy for him. Not to rise to the bait. Not to break the silence. They sat munching. The street was wet and the sodium lights were repeated upside down the length of the street. The trees dripped. Jack popped the last chip into his mouth, screwed up the packaging and dropped it into the litter bin beside him.

'You remember that idea I had? The one about putting a security bypass into a chip.' He took a sip of Coke from his can. 'Well. Well, it sort of worked.'

Allan tried not to react, but the last sentence was uttered as he was drinking from a can of orange juice. It went down the wrong way and he spluttered. Jack slapped him on the back.

'Sorry,' said Jack. 'I didn't mean to startle you.'

'I don't want to hear this, Jack.'

'Yes you do. It's fascinating.' He said the word slowly, drawing out and separating the syllables. 'You're all burned up about proving programs correct and here am I telling you that no matter how good your programs are, it is possible to slide round any security protection you care to devise.'

Allan said nothing but Jack was determined to get an answer. 'Don't you think that's fascinating?'

'In principle, yes.'

'OK. Let's talk in principle. In principle the idea sort of works.'

'And how, in principle, do you know that?'

'Because, in principle, I did it.'

'You spiked a chip.'

'Yes.'

'How?'

'What do you mean, how?'

'How did you, in principle, do the trick?'

'I modified one of the programs which customises a communications chip so that when you type my name instead of a password it does not check the password at all.'

'Your name! You used your own name!'

'Yes. "jackthornley" all one word, all in lower case. It goes straight through the security protection like a dose of castor oil – in principle.'

'Jesus! You used your own name! And where is this wonder chip?'

'Ah now. That is the really funny part.'

'Do tell – in principle.'

'I don't know. That's the laugh. It's out there.'

'Where is out there?'

'Out in the world. On a board made by MCI, in a computer somewhere. It may not even be an MCI computer. It could be any machine made by anyone who uses MCI boards.'

'You mean really?'

'Yes really – in principle, of course.'

'How did you get it there?'

'I didn't, actually. Alison did.'

'What!'

'Alison did. She didn't know what she was doing exactly. You see I made up the chip. Then I nicked a board and swapped my chip for the one that was already there. Then I told Alison that one of the boards in her in-bin had been modified by me and please would she stop it going on down the assembly line. I gave her my board and told her to swap it. But you see the one she took out was OK. It was the one I gave her that was spiked and so she really put the spiked board into the assembly line.'

'You're a bastard, Jack!'

'I know. But listen. The really, really funny bit is this. I thought that the testing program would find the bad chip and throw it out. The idea was to see what error messages it would print. Just to see, you understand. I was testing their security.'

'Doing them a good turn, I suppose – in principle.'

'Yes – in principle. But, you see, it didn't.'

'Didn't what?'

'It didn't detect the spiked chip. And the board went on down the assembly line and now it's God knows where.'

Allan was speechless. He gasped and then lowered his forehead on to his hands with elbows propped on his knees.

'Have you got no conscience at all, Jack? Doesn't it worry you at all? You're telling me that somewhere there is a computer that thinks "jackthornley" is its best friend and that if you type your name into it it will let you through its protection mechanisms? It could be in a bank or a government security database and you've built a secret passage straight through into its innermost secrets. You could write yourself a cheque for a million pounds or get yourself promoted to be the head of MI5.'

'Yes. Well. Yes, it does worry me a bit.'

'Only a bit? Which bit?'

'The bit that says I don't know where the bloody computer is.'

'Oh for God's sake!'

Allan screwed up the packaging of his fish supper and made as though to hit Jack with it. Then he tamely shied it at the litter bin, and missed.

'Now look what you've done,' said Jack. He giggled and wagged a finger in mock censure. 'Destroying the environment.' He picked up the bundle and placed it in the bin with exaggerated care. They sat side by side staring at the dangling chains.

'That's where you'll end up, Jack,' said Alan, pointing. 'Hanging in chains.'

'You don't see it, do you? You don't see the really funny thing about it.'

'I'm not laughing – much,' said Allan.

'The thing is,' said Jack. '*Why* didn't it find the fault in the bloody chip?'

They stared some more at the seatless swing. Allan shivered. A fine drizzle was falling again, but still they sat. Down Fetterburn Road at a distant corner a neon sign had gone wrong and was flashing the message 'King-sized . . . gers'.

'Your local Celtic supporters won't like that,' Jack said, pointing.

Jack was right. That was the really funny peculiar thing. The implications were . . . He couldn't express it properly.

'important' was too tame a word. If Jack's chip had not been trapped there was nothing to say that all of the chips were not spiked.

'How could it be checked?' said Jack.

'In principle –,' he checked himself. 'I mean, you could check the testing program itself. It may just be a bug. The proper check may never have been programmed into it. But it could be that the checks have been overridden by a modification. It should be possible to check that.'

'That's the cock-up versus conspiracy theory again,' said Jack. 'How exactly could it be checked?'

'It could be put through a dis-assembler to get it into a form which is readable. Then it would just be a case of going though it carefully line by line and working out what it was supposed to be doing.'

'I thought that's what you would say. That's what you said could be done with those files we found in Tommy Harkness's directory, isn't it?'

Allan nodded but didn't take his eyes off the neon sign.

'Here.'

He looked round. Jack was offering him a small package wrapped in brown paper. It was the size and shape of a paperback book.

'What's that?' The hair on the back of his neck began to tingle. He knew what it was but he didn't want to believe it.

'Here,' said Jack again, and dropped the package on to Allan's lap. 'It's a quarter-inch tape cartridge. It's the testing program. I stole it and I can't think of a better person to check it out.'

8

OCTOBER

Two weeks later he got back to his digs from the sports centre and there was a new white Rover sitting outside the front door in the pool of light cast by a streetlamp – an alien visitor from another planet. He remembered Jack's comment about the neighbourhood and looked for the piles of bricks, but there were none. Perhaps they were an optional extra peculiar to BMW.

Mrs McCulloch objected to his bicycle sitting in the hallway so he carried it upstairs. She objected to his doing that too. Usually she came up the stairs after him, examining the wallpaper for damage and making small but clearly audible clicks with her tongue. But that evening she just opened the kitchen door by a chink and looked at him through it as though she had recognised him from a photofit shown on *Crimewatch*.

He was surprised to find the light on when he opened the door and even more surprised to find Rosa sitting in his armchair.

'I don't think your landlady approves of me,' she said in a whisper, 'but I waved my micro at her and told her it was strictly work.' She got up and closed the door quietly. She was laughing. A brown and cream micro lay on the table.

He leaned the bicycle against the wardrobe. There was not

much room left. Rosa ran her hand along the mantelpiece and
flicked the dust off her fingers.

'I've seen more salubrious dens,' she said, 'but at least you
don't have pop music blasting your eardrums and Maurice's
boring business colleagues droning on and on.'

'Coffee?' he held up the pot. Rosa nodded and settled down
at the table. She opened the case of the micro and looked for
an electric socket.

'There's only one, I'm afraid, and I've got the kettle plugged
into it.'

'No matter. I'll switch to battery. How do you manage normally?' She was being very business-like and enthusiastic,
setting out the cables, like a child packing for a picnic.

'Sometimes I swap with the kettle, but often I use the batteries and . . .' He froze in mid-sentence. There was a pile of
books on the window-sill beyond Rosa. Buried in the middle of
the pile were the two tape cartridges he had got from Jack.
Rosa was sitting beside them but did not appear to have
noticed. She looked up from the micro.

'. . . and . . . and I recharge them overnight,' he stammered.

He tried not to look in that direction, busying himself with
the teapot and the cups. He put the cup down beside her.

'Here, I'll make more room,' he said and lifted the pile of
books. The top of the wardrobe seemed to be the best place.

'I thought we might connect the machines back-to-back,'
she said. 'It would save a lot of toing and froing with discs.'

They sat facing one another with the computers between
them. They connected the cables so that the screens displayed
the data from both. It was as though each was looking over the
shoulder of the other. They began slowly, pausing to comment
as they typed but the conversation died as the pace quickened.
Ideas poured out and fingers flew on the keyboards. The coffee grew a skin.

There was a tap at the door – Mrs McCulloch with an invented
story about someone behaving suspiciously with Rosa's car.

'Is that the time!'

It was 1 a.m. Rosa wouldn't wait for fresh coffee, but made off hurriedly. Allan carried the micro for her downstairs. She put her hand on his shoulder and squeezed it as she took the machine from him at the door of the car.

Next morning he phoned in to explain that he would be delayed. Later, on the way to work, when the post office opened, he sent both the tapes in a padded envelope to himself at Jean's address.

Rosa came round to his digs quite often after that. Sometimes she brought food and cooked it for them in the microwave which she persuaded him to buy. The single electric socket made it difficult but he used some old camping tricks, wrapping a dish in pullovers to keep it warm while she cooked up a second one. Sometimes she brought a bottle of wine and apple juice for him in a wicker basket with French bread and cheese. She usually had only one glass and after a few visits she took to leaving the re-corked bottle with Allan for the next time. If he was not her secret lover then he was fulfilling some part of that role.

Once she had been for him a figure of immense stature, but although his respect for her did not diminish, she was now a real person with foibles and needs. She obviously enjoyed his company for its own sake and not just for the intellectual excitement of their project, although that was a good part of it. Sometimes, after they had eaten, she did not want to rush straight into work but would sit in his armchair, talking about old times at Berkeley and about Peter Tan and the trips they had taken into Yossemite. Sometimes she wanted to talk about Allan and drew out of him all about Jean and Uncle Roddy and his climbing.

'I must come and watch you at this sports centre,' she said. 'I don't think I could get up a mountain nowadays.'

One evening Rosa had two glasses of wine. She seemed particularly relaxed and cheerful, joking a lot about Maurice and her stepchildren. Then she wanted to know what hills he had climbed recently.

'None at all. There hasn't been time.'

'That's no good,' she said. 'I'm taking up all your time.' She laughed. 'If you couldn't get to the sports centre you would go rusty. Where else could you go?'

'It's amazing what you can find if you're desperate.'

'Where would you go?'

'At home when I was a boy I used to climb around the flat. I could go from the front door across the hall, through the sitting room, into the broom cupboard and up through the trapdoor into the loft space without touching the floor.'

'You're joking!'

'No. Really. You wouldn't notice but there are all kind of holds and things around a house. I mean, there's a ledge above every doorway and toe-holds on the skirting boards. It's possible to get on to the top of a doorway and stay there.'

'I don't believe it!' She was enjoying herself and poured a third glass of Chianti.

'Honest.'

'Prove it! There's a doorway.'

So the gauntlet was cast and he had to do it. That meant stripping down to shorts and his hard narrow climbing shoes. The door was close by a corner of the room. He started by stepping up on to the edge of the skirting board at the point where it was wider by the door. He gripped the ledge above the door and pulled, walking up the face of the door as he did so, and then moving straight into a push-up with elbows akimbo. For balance he placed one foot on the wall with which the door made a right angle. Then, taking his weight on one bent arm, he snatched the other hand away and slapped it palm upwards on to the ceiling. The friction that provided stopped him falling over backwards as in the same flowing movement he brought up one foot and placed it on the ledge beside his left hand where his right had been. The ceiling was high so that there was just room for him to pull up the other leg and sit hunkered on the ledge with both hands on the ceiling and bottom sticking out like a back-to-front gargoyle, and twice as ugly.

It was at that moment that Mrs McCulloch, attracted by

the scuffling noises, tapped on the door and walked in. For a second she did not see Allan crouching above her, half naked, in simian pose, his bottom inches above her head, then she screamed and shot backwards out of the room.

The following day Mrs McCulloch told him that she would need the room.

Jean came to see him. She drove down from Glasgow that Saturday, leaving a neighbour to look after Roddy. It was her first and last visit to Gairnock. She stood at the door of his bed-sitter with her hands on her hips, ran her eyes round the room and said 'I should bloody well think so' when he said he was looking for somewhere else.

The business of looking for a new place solved the problem of what they would do for the day. They drove round and looked at a few places. After supper they took a look at some outlying villages.

'This is daft,' said Jean. 'How'll you get in and out?'

'Bike.'

'When are you going to realise that you're not a student any-more?'

On the way back she pulled in to a lay-by. The autumn colours glowed in gentle watery sunlight. The hedgerow was spangled brightly with red berries. Jean gathered up the sand-wich packages and the apple cores and Allan dumped them in a roadside bin. That was when he saw the cottage.

On the other side of the road from the lay-by a farm track ran off between bushes. It was tyre-rutted and muddy but the gable end of a small building was visible through the rust-brown and yellow foliage. Jean was reluctant to get her shoes muddy but she came with him, stepping warily on the stones which projected through the mud.

It was a traditional butt and ben with two small cracked and cobwebbed windows, a low paint-blistered door and a roof that sagged between the chimney stacks like a hammock. A rusted corrugated-iron shed was stuck on the further gable. The front end of a blue Fordson Major tractor stuck out.

'You can't be serious,' Jean said, doing her John McEnroe impersonation.

She stayed by the door while Allan threaded his way round the back. The ground rose sharply behind and trees and bushes grew close so that he had to push his way through. There was one small square window in the centre of the back wall. Jean was startled when he opened the door from the inside.

Allan was captivated. It was like the bothies he had slept in all over the Highlands, but in better condition. The floor was stone. The front door opened into a narrow passageway. The kitchen was on the right and the other room on the left. A doorway from the kitchen led to the tiny pantry. The pantry had two windows, one to the back wall and the other into the passageway directly opposite the front door. There was an old iron range in the kitchen and genuine fire-dogs like instruments of torture. There was a deal table with a drawer, two upright chairs and one armchair which looked and smelled as though it had mice nesting. In the bedroom the remains of blue floral wallpaper was damp and sagging. There was a big damp patch in the centre of the ceiling. The kitchen had a sink in the window. The tap was dry. Running water came from a tap on the front wall by the door. Tiny round two-pin sockets showed that there had once been electricity. The toilet was a lean-to outside on the back wall.

He said, 'Let's go down to that farm beyond the lay-by and ask who owns it.'

Jean said, 'You *are* serious, aren't you? Jesus, what a midden!'

Andrew Jamieson had not really considered renting the cottage, but he was delighted to find that there was someone who did not mind climbing on to the roof to fix a slate or two, who had no need for a telephone, or electricity or an inside toilet, let alone central heating or a jacuzzi. The fact that the building had been condemned as unfit did not worry him if it did not worry Allan and so long as no one else knew. His only requirement was that he should be able to have access to his tractor shed. The deal was struck.

Jean had her say. It's filthy! There are mice in that chair.

There's no electricity. How are you going to wash clothes? How can anyone get in touch with you when there's no telephone? There isn't even running water, for Heaven's sake. Can you imagine using that outside toilet in winter? What happens when you get a dose of flu?

After that she drove them back to Gairnock in silence. He imagined evenings with a roaring log fire in the old range, a modern chemical toilet, bottled gas, a tin bath in the kitchen. Jean had no experience of such things. When she saw how cosy he could make it she would be . . . amazed.

When she drew up at the door of his digs he got out and came round to the driving window which was open. With a hand on the roof of the car he bent to ask if she would like a final cup of tea or whatever, but she beat him to the punch. She said, 'You're stark raving mad,' and drove off, leaving him leaning on nothing.

For two weeks all other spare-time activities were dropped while he breathed life into Burnside Cottage. Two weeks of hard work and uncomplicated pleasure. Jack and Rosa, at different times, gave him a lift out with his things. The auction rooms in Gairnock were prepared to deliver, so he made a bonfire of the old armchair and the mouldering bedstead and installed furniture of a reasonable vintage. He transported a chemical toilet on the back of his bike, imagining the headline 'Man knocked down by lorry, three die of asphyxia'. Mrs Jamieson, the farmer's wife, gave him an old bookcase and a chest of drawers. He found loose slates and nailed them back into position and added a few more from a disused quarry. The pipe to the kitchen sink was disconnected but he managed to re-establish the connection using plastic press-fit connections.

Masood Qureshi helped him sweep out the pantry and give the old pine cladding a coat of white emulsion. Jack helped him hang new wallpaper in the bedroom. He hacked away some of the bushes which had overgrown the ditch on the far side of the cart track so that he could see the burn which ran there. In a junk shop he found a huge copper urn and installed that on the range as a source of hot water when the fire was lit. He bought a lorry-load of logs. Mrs Jamieson brought him a huge home-made apple pie. She stood in the kitchen, looked round wonderingly and said 'My!' Rosa came with more bottles and they had a celebration. She gave him a painting of the white sands of Arisaig and a distant view of Eigg and they hung it over the fireplace.

That night he lay cosily in his second-hand bed (with a new, mouse-free mattress), watching the flickering embers in the grate and listening to the wind soughing in the chimney and the slates rattling. He thought about Jenny and of what might have been.

9

LATE OCTOBER

He settled into a routine, cycling to work each morning and bringing back each evening a set of charged batteries for his micro. Rosa seemed to like the cottage. She came often in the late evening and they would work together until after midnight. Increasingly she left the detailed work to him, preferring to sit in his old armchair by the fire drinking soup, discussing possibilities.

But the business of Jack and the tapes was still lurking in his mind. Not many computer installations would have the software for what he wanted to do, but doing it at MCI was out of the question. What he needed was a co-operative university department – a real computer science department – not a statistics outfit like Hamish's. His old department would do nicely but he did not want Karl Wellington, his former supervisor, to have any suspicion that he was operating – as Jack would have put it – 'outside normal parameters'.

The solution came by post. As a research student he had been the target for computer junk mail. Conference announcements, advertisements for new technical books, cut-price software and the like poured though his letterbox, and the stuff still kept coming, redirected to him 'Care of A. Jamieson – Easter Howe Farm'.

One day a buff envelope came with an invitation to an academic seminar on software testing. It was to be held in his old department and as he read it Allan recognised an excuse to drop in on Karl and the lads. He smiled a wicked smile. They always liked to show off their latest toys. Once the discussion got going it would not be hard to introduce his own problem: trouble with the slowness of his version of the dis-assembler (he would name a rather old version). Bit of a bore really. Did they have a more up-to-date version (they would have)? Would they mind if he did a comparison of processing speed? A little flattery would help. That's a nice machine. It's faster than ours (it wouldn't be). Just these couple of tapes – it won't take long. Then maybe a print-out – for comparison. Not important really. Just if they could spare a little computer time – for comparison, you understand.

A seminar on software testing. Yes. Rosa would wear that. A day off for 'staff development' would look good on the departmental progress report. So he asked her.

Deception was becoming surprisingly easy and he was looking forward to seeing the results at last. Then maybe he could put behind him all this nonsense that Jack had wished upon him and concentrate on important things.

'Are you all right, Allan?'

'It's a bit airless in here. Open a window, Sam.'

'When did you eat last – want a cup of tea? You'll remember it. It's still the glorious stuff we used to have when you were here. Takes the lining off your stomach . . . Sorry!'

'I'll get some water.'

'No. No need, Karl. I'm OK. I'm OK. Honest. I think I may have a virus or something. I should be hitting the trail.'

'Sure you're OK?' said Karl. 'I'll give you a run to the station if you like.'

'No. I'll be all right. The air will do me good. Sure, I'm fine. I'd better not forget my tapes, though. I'll read the print-out on the train.'

'Do you want them both? They look identical to me.'

He stuffed the tapes into one pocket of his anorak and the thick roll of print-out in the other. It stuck out quite a long way.

'I'm OK. Honest.'

On the way to the station he bought a *Scotsman* and wrapped the print-out inside it.

The train was deserted but he chose a corner seat nevertheless. He felt safer with a partition behind him. Carefully, he unwrapped the print-outs. He didn't need to check them line by line. The two were identical.

The implication had hit him the instant the second print-out had started chattering off on the serial printer. Tommy and Jack had stolen the same thing. And Tommy had been killed. He rolled the stuff up again. If Jack was right, that was the program which was cheerfully putting a stamp of approval on all of MCI's chips – chips with a secret passage built into them. So there would be no need to trace each chip to its destination. Every computer would have the same type of chip and every chip would have the same modification – the same password – everywhere.

Want a pay increase? Just say the word. I'll modify your payroll record. Need a small boost to the finances? Name your figure. I'll write you a cheque with the compliments of any bank you care to mention. Promotion? Hang on a tick. I'll stick a few stars on your personnel records. See that guided missile. Let's misguide it. Want revenge? Give me his name. I'll change his records so that he becomes an alcoholic, child-molesting, murdering rapist with a low credit rating.

Know the password and you had the key to Aladdin's cave and the evidence that such a password existed was here in his hand, wrapped up in a newspaper. Men had been killed for less.

Telegraph poles glided in procession; wires dipped and rose in endless curtseys, fields with placid cows rotated and allotments with cold-frames and cloches slid by in ordered sequence.

The wings of the seat caught him awkwardly in the shoulder blades so he squiggled down on to the tail of his spine with his

body half under the black-topped table and his feet under the
seat opposite. He shut his eyes. A face floated before his. A thin
face from a tabloid front page. It had narrow eyes and a squint
nose and a calm knowing smile.

The method of Tommy Harkness's death was a reproach, so
gratuitously brutal, so . . . so . . . disdainful of that thing which
had been a person with feelings, done, not in a fit of powerful
emotions, but dispassionately, a task to be fulfilled, a quota to
be completed. Tie a rope round his neck. Hold him. How many
men involved? Two? Three perhaps? Pin his arms. While his
legs kicked and he struggled for air, hitch the rope to a hook on
the back of the door. Then pull downwards, adding the weight
of several men. Watch his eyes bulge while the life was squeezed
out of him. Then walk away and call it suicide. Official!

Official! What was his name? – Detective Inspector
Chalmers had thanked him for saving the life of his nephew.
And he had walked away from Tommy's death and called it sui-
cide.

A door slammed and a man with a briefcase brushed past.
Allan watched through half-shut eyes as the man hesitated and
then sat down on the seat across the passage and diagonally
opposite. The carriage was empty. Annoying. There was no
need for the man to sit there. He took a book from his case and
settled down to read.

Allan shut his eyes again and thought furiously. No one but
he and Jack knew he had the tapes. Was that true? Bugging,
according to Jack, was a way of life at MCI. He had to get rid
of the stuff. Knowing what he did, he could not now dump it
on Jean.

'Tickets please!'

He put the roll on the table and struggled upright. As he
searched his wallet the bundle unrolled. The ticket collector
ignored it but the man across the passageway looked straight at
it. As Allan gathered it up their eyes met before the man
returned to his book. At Queen's Street Allan pretended to be
asleep to give time for the other man to get clear, but the man
touched him on the shoulder.

'We're in Glasgow!'

'Oh! Oh, thanks!'

The man alighted and walked past the window. Allan followed, keeping thirty yards behind, noting each passenger and porter. The man turned right and made for the newsagents. Allan went straight ahead for George Square, feeling ashamed of his panic reactions. He couldn't go through life being suspicious of every stranger. No one else knew about the tapes. He could not have been followed.

The main post office was on the other side of the square. It had a display of stationery so he bought a padded envelope, stuffed the tapes and print-out inside and had it weighed and priced. For a moment he considered removing one copy of the print-out. He had not yet read it all the way through, analysed the content for proof of deliberate malpractice. But he sealed it as it was, addressed it to himself, Poste Restante at – he hesitated again – the main post office in Edinburgh and dropped it into the parcel mail chute. Then he walked to Central Station to catch the Gairnock train.

On the train down to Gairnock he began thinking more clearly, going over recent events and assessing the extent to which he might have drawn attention to himself. Computer records? He was sure he had left no pointers except for that simple file contents list which would not be noticed unless someone was looking for it specifically at the time. Bugging? Suppose Jack was right and bugging was a way of life at MCI. All their conversations about the tapes had been in Alfonso's Pizza Parlour or in the park across the road from Jack's flat. Jack himself? His friendship with Jack was common knowledge. What traces had Jack left behind him with his stupid ploys? Jack had to be persuaded to cut out the hacking completely. Not easy. Jack was the weak link.

Did he want to get involved at all? Should he not just sink out of sight and forget the whole affair? Somewhere – yes – he dug deep into an inside pocket – he had a card. He pulled it out.

Havelock Home Securities – A. G. Simpson – Sales Director.

What was it Harry had said – loud-mouthed Harry – that day in the pub when the bald-headed man had offered him his card? A pair of lurex tights and an advertisement for double glazing and earn some of the crinkly stuff. There was the escape tunnel if he wanted it. What would he lose?

The project with Rosa. Nothing else. No emotional ties. Not yet. Damn it!

There was a dark blue Ford Escort parked in the lay-by opposite the track to Burnside Cottage. Allan dismounted and stood quietly in the dark, listening and looking, but it was his nose which registered. Pungent wood smoke. He pushed the cycle silently up the track. There was a loom of light from the windows. He leant the bike against a tree and tiptoed to the window. A cheery wood-fire was burning in his grate. The room looked unusually tidy and the tilly-lamp was alight and standing on the mantelpiece. Someone was sitting in his chair. He could see an elbow and the top of the head – dark hair. It had to be Rosa, for only she knew that he kept a key in an old milk can in the tractor shed.

She was slumped comfortably in the chair with her legs crossed, a book in her lap and a glass of wine in her hand. As he pushed open the kitchen door she raised the glass in toast and said, 'Hello! How were things in Edinburgh?' She was wearing jeans and a heather mixture pullover with a deep, wide collar that enveloped her in loose folds. The sleeves were pushed up to expose her slender forearms and a lock of her hair, normally so tightly controlled, had fallen over her forehead. She pushed it back with her wrist. Allan knew his mouth was open.

Rosa said, 'I took the afternoon off. Wensley was having one of his bloody meetings so I threw a headache. I think there should be a law against working on Friday afternoons.'

He hung his jacket on the back of the door. 'I didn't recognise your car. I nearly burst in with the wood chopper in my hand. I thought you had a Rover.'

'The Rover is Maurice's car. The Escort is mine.'

He sat down on the upright chair by the table.

'Something smells delicious.'

She raised her eyebrows and a finger like a stage magician and eased herself out of the armchair. With a cloth she pulled open the oven which was built into the old iron kitchen range and lifted out a chipped black casserole dish. She put it on the table before him. An aroma of chicken, thyme, marjoram and onions wafted up as she lifted the lid. Dark mushrooms bobbed in the bubbling gravy.

'There,' she said. 'Now you see that I am not just a pretty face,' and she laughed. 'After making you buy that microwave, I felt I owed you a meal. I've never used one of these old ranges before. It was quite a challenge.'

There was wine for her and apple juice for him. She had also brought a pavlova and fresh ground coffee which she made in an enamel saucepan on the open fire. At her suggestion he lit candles and turned off the harsh white light of the tilly-lamp. She asked him about the seminar and he managed a plausible account of the talks, though he found it a strain to remember what they had actually been about. He said nothing about the tapes. Then when it was quite late she said, 'Well, shall we do some work?'

Warm, well fed and relaxed, he had been on the point of falling asleep but he washed up while she set up the two micros.

'I thought we might explore an alternative approach,' she said. 'I had an idea last night.'

So they explored her idea and for an hour they went round in logical circles. Then she said, 'It's no good. My brain is pickled tonight. But you go on.'

'I don't want to chase you but it's after midnight. Won't Maurice be worried?'

'Maurice flew to Brussels this afternoon. He won't be back until Monday. Julia has gone to stay with friends in London and Bob is driving that buzz-bomb of his in some rally or race or something down in the Borders all weekend.'

She settled down again into the armchair.

'Which is just as well,' she went on, 'because I've had too much to drink and you can't drive me home, can you?'

His hands froze on the keyboard and he looked at her.

'It's all right, Allan. I won't assault you. I'll just curl up in this chair for a few hours. Could you put a few more logs on the fire?'

He took the log basket outside and filled it. As he bent over the pile of logs in the dark he felt his face flush red and then to his alarm he started to have an erection. There was a loom of orange light in the sky in the direction of Gairnock. In the other direction a few stars blinked clear. He stood for a while in the darkness, in his shirt sleeves, calming himself before he returned with the basket.

'Do you mind me staying, Allan?'

As he passed the chair she ran a hand over his forearm, raising a tingle in the hairs. 'Gosh, you're cold,' she said and gripped his arm more tightly. The log basket was still in his arms. He put it down and turned to face her. She stood up and put her arms round his neck.

They built up the fire, spread the mattress and quilt before it and dowsed the candles. His strongest memories were of the way the flickering firelight drew a golden line round her naked silhouette as she knelt, sitting upright on her heels, head back, one erect nipple caught in the light, and of drawing his open mouth and tongue along the line between the black and golden halves of her body from her thigh, over abdomen and breast to her open lips.

In the morning while it was still dark he rose, slipped on his trousers, pullover and shoes and went out into the chill of the pre-dawn to return with more logs. There was still a glow among the embers and shortly, after he had slipped, naked once more, into the warmth of the down-filled covers, the logs crackled and burst into flame. Later, as the early light of dawn filtered through the window, they made love again.

Later still he woke to the aroma of coffee and the yeasty smell of fresh baked rolls. She had been down to the village a couple of miles away in her car and was now sitting in the armchair with her book open in her lap. She looked up as he stretched.

'So! The sleeper awakes.'

After he had dressed she said, 'We've got two days to ourselves, Allan. What would you like to do? Go for a walk? Visit a historic castle? Swim naked in a river?'

They walked. He had such energy. She had to restrain him from bounding up the heather. They lay among ancient stones and kissed and dined on apples, cheese and cold burn water.

They made love again that night. She went at midday on Sunday. He walked her to the lay-by and stood there waving until the car was gone and aware that he was also waving goodbye to his escape tunnel.

The cottage was now a lonely as well as a happy place to be. For the moment work on 'the project' was impossible. He mooned about, taking pleasure in simple routine chores, trying to tidy things but in reality simply shifting the untidiness to new places. All this business with the tapes and Tommy Harkness was now just a bad dream. The tapes and the incriminating print-outs were safely stashed. There was nothing further to worry about on that score.

The microcomputer was sitting in a corner with a box of floppy discs. He picked up the box to put it with the others and then he remembered. He had made a copy of one of the tapes on to a floppy disc, or rather, Hamish had made the copy for him, and he had forgotten all about it. He had not put the floppy in a safe place as he had done with the tapes. It had been there all weekend and with Rosa in the cottage by herself for a part of that time. He opened the box. It wasn't there. He looked again, refusing to believe it. Definitely not there. He pulled out the other boxes and searched. Not there either. Again he looked – still not there. He sat down thinking furiously. It had been unlabelled. It was impossible that Rosa would bother to read through the contents of his files and recognise an unlabelled disc with unprintable jibberish as something sinister. And yet it wasn't there. He had last seen it the night he went to see Jack and was given the second tape. He had put it in his pocket.

And he had never taken it out! His anorak was on the back of the bedroom door. He ran through to the bedroom and searched it, quickly feeling the exterior of the garment for the hard square shape. And of course it was there after all.

So he put the disc in an envelope and addressed it to himself – Poste Restante, Motherwell. Then he cycled down to the village and slipped it into a pillar-box.

10

NOVEMBER

Thursday. The Scouts were there. The Scout Master was called Kenneth. He talked Allan into it – demonstrating moves, showing how to hold the rope, climbing up alongside a boy in trouble, encouraging, showing him how to use pressure holds, explaining the importance of balance and agility rather than strength. The boys gathered round.

'Sir! Can you go up that without your feet, Sir?'

'Can you do it, Sir?'

'Go on, Sir!'

'Stop calling me "Sir". I'll only do it if you stop calling me "Sir". OK?'

'Yes, Sir,' they said in unison.

Later the boys were on the wall and Allan was helping, checking that each boy who was holding a rope had gripped it correctly.

'Hello.'

He looked round. A young man was standing beside him. He was dressed in a tee-shirt, black tracksuit trousers and PAs. His face was familiar.

'Hello . . .' Allan turned back to the wall. 'That's good!' he shouted to the boy above them. 'Now try to move left on to the holds at the level of your knees. You'll find hand-holds under

the ledge above. Remember to lean back slightly.' And then
'. . . Sorry. Have we met?'

The young man stuck out his hand. 'Steve McElroy.
Remember the policeman at your work a few weeks ago?'

'Oh yes.' Allan took his hand.

'I was watching you just now. Very impressive. Can you do it
without hands too?'

'I don't usually do that kind of thing. The boys . . .' His voice
trailed away.

'Doing your bit for youth. That's impressive too.' Steve was
mocking him. 'When will you knock off?'

'I'm just going, as a matter of fact.'

'I'll buy you a coffee,' said Steve. 'The stuff at the cafeteria
here is just about drinkable.'

'No. No thanks. I must be going.'

'There's no one waiting for you back at your cottage, is
there?'

Allan froze, but Steve just laughed. 'Come on, I might even
buy you a bun as well.'

Steve took two sugars. He stirred the cup for a long time and
then looked up at Allan.

Allan said, 'You've been checking up on me.'

'Aye, we have.'

'Why?'

'We're interested in you.'

'This wasn't an accident, bumping into me tonight then.'

'No, it wasn't.'

'So?'

'So I'd, I mean, we'd like a little help from you. It's quite all
right, we don't suspect you of anything. Not anything criminal,
that is.'

He dunked a doughnut in his coffee and watched the brown
stain creeping upwards through it. Allan's mind was darting
about in search of an explanation. Nothing.

'One of the reasons why we are interested in you is because
we don't suspect you of anything. You arrived at Gairnock

after Tommy Harkness was killed, so we know you had nothing to do with it. And Bob Chalmers, my boss, thinks you're OK because of that stunt you pulled off when you saved his nephew. . . What's the matter? Do you have something against Bob Chalmers?'

'No.'

'Come on. What is it?'

'Nothing.'

'He thinks a lot of you,' said Steve. 'That's why he asked me to keep an eye on you.'

'Thanks for nothing.'

'We need your help, Allan.'

'Why?'

'There are a lot of loose ends in the Harkness case. You could help us to tie up.'

'I thought you decided it was . . . suicide.'

Allan said the last word with scorn.

'And you don't think it was suicide?'

'Do you?'

'No.'

Allan was surprised. 'Then why have you said it was?' His coffee was getting cold. He took a sip.

'We didn't. It was the Procurator Fiscal who said that.'

'So why don't you think it was suicide?'

'I can't tell you that. But Bob Chalmers might. I'd like you to come and see him.'

There was a long pause.

'When?'

'Soon.'

'What do you want from me?'

'Just some information. You see this whole thing revolves around the work which Tommy was doing. We got a copy of his files from your computer but we can't make head or tail of the stuff. I'm supposed to be our local police expert on computing. I've got a degree in computing – I have – don't look so surprised. But I don't have your kind of expertise.'

'Do the police not have their own experts?'

'Yes we do. But . . .' – he fiddled with his spoon – '. . . we don't want to bother them at the moment.' He met Allan's eyes directly. 'Let's just leave it at that for the moment, shall we?'

'What if I say no?'

'It's a free country,' said Steve. 'We can't force you.'

They sat. Steve took another sip of coffee. 'I was wrong. It's not drinkable.'

'Is that all then? I have to go.'

'Tommy Harkness was murdered and it was a particularly brutal murder. The people who did it are still walking around. Doesn't that worry you?'

'The *people* who did it!'

'It takes more than one person to string up a conscious and fully fit man like Tommy.'

There was another long pause during which Allan studied the surface of the coffee in his cup. A group of the scouts burst through the glass swing-doors. The cafeteria echoed to shouts and yells. Two of the boys were scuffling. Another had a half nelson on his companion. Kenneth was trying to call them to order.

Allan turned back to Steve. His voice was sarcastic.

'So what do you want me to do? Accompany you to the station?'

'Actually, we would like to keep the whole thing quiet. Do you know a pub called The Gantocks in Cable Street?'

The Gantocks lay in unfamiliar territory, but he reckoned that he could find it as a moth finds a mate, by travelling up the scent-gradient of the alcohol fumes. That strategy was frustrated, however, by the presence of a bar on every street corner. Some had lost large chunks of their names and on others the lettering was hidden among an even larger freehand script in rainbow coloured spray-paint which declared the allegiance or denounced the hate objects of the local street gangs.

Chalmers and Steve McElroy were sitting together at a table in the inner recesses. He didn't see them at first and, not having the self-confidence to walk up to the bar and order a drink, he stood dithering until Steve raised an arm and waved him over.

The Gantocks was a rough place devoid of the civilising influence of women. Stained wooden tables, dark green Victorian glasswork and discoloured gold-edged mirrors with adverts for extinct species of tobacco, formed the basis of what might be called 'the décor'. A stone floor and hard wooden benches suggested that no luxury was allowed here to deflect a man from the purpose of serious drinking. The odour of beer and tobacco was so strong that Allan suspected it would cling to his clothes for a month.

'Glad you could come, Allan,' said Chalmers, half rising to shake his hand. 'What'll it be?'

'Eh, an apple juice please.'

There was a distinct pause as Chalmers gathered up his smile and put it back on his face. He slid a banknote across the table. 'Steve, would you do the honours?' Then he turned again to Allan. 'So you found the place then.'

'Oh aye.'

Another pause. Chalmers looked round over his shoulder to see what was keeping Steve. He drummed his fingers on the table. He had thick, short fingers and muscular hands which curled easily into fists. Steve put the change down beside Chalmers who gathered the coins carefully, frowning as though he believed there should have been more.

'Steve explained what we are about.'

Steve said, 'I didn't explain very much. You said . . .'

'Aye. Aye, we want your help, Allan. We need the help of a computer expert like yourself to tidy up a few loose ends. Nowadays everything seems to have something to do with computing and old cops like me are finding it harder and harder to keep abreast.'

'What can I do?'

'We need someone to go over some computer stuff for us and tell us what it means. Steve here knows a thing or two about computers but even he is a bit flummoxed. We got a lot of stuff from MCI which used to belong to Tommy Harkness, and we want to close the file on Harkness, you see, and so we need to know what it's all about.'

'You want me to go through the computer files and translate them into . . . into what exactly?'

Chalmers screwed up his eyes. Then he wiped his face with the flat of his hand and ended up, elbow on the table, with his chin on his fist.

'I don't know what. I'm groping, Allan, and that's a fact. There is something badly wrong . . .' – he thumped a fist gently on the table – '. . . and I want to know what it is and I don't know where to start. I need you to look at the stuff and tell me what it means. What was Harkness doing? What was his job?'

'I can tell you that without looking at the files because I'm doing the same job myself at the moment.'

'Now you're talking. Go on, tell me.' He took a swig of beer and wiped the froth off his lips with the back of his hand. Then with both elbows on the table he looked straight into Allan's eyes. His eyes were pale blue and they had a very disturbing directness about them. Allan took a deep breath.

He described the way the chips were made in Taiwan and then shipped to Gairnock. He told how the basic chip design was over-connected and how the chips were then modified for special purposes and then further modified to customer order. He told them how the bulk of the processing was carried out by programs sent over from headquarters and how at Gairnock they only made minor modifications to take account of customer requirements. He told them about the testing programs and about the burn-out process which fixed the modifications and made further testing impossible.

As he talked, Chalmers seemed to wait on every word and Steve nodded in agreement. But Allan was becoming increasingly irritated. He knew his description was superficial twaddle – the sort of thing Henry Quinn spouted on his induction courses or which anyone could read every week in the *Computer Guardian*. Steve with his degree in computing could have given Chalmers the same chat and probably better. They hadn't brought him all this way for this?

Chalmers said, 'Would Harkness have been able to change any programs without telling anyone?'

The question stopped Allan's mind dead in its tracks.

'That's difficult to say.'

'Try.'

'I suppose he could have reprogrammed one of the programs. His difficulty would have been to swap that for the real program on the assembly line. Has . . . has this got anything to do with his death?'

'It might have,' Chalmers said slowly. His expression did not change and his blue eyes were unblinking. 'How difficult would it be to make a swap?'

'I don't know. I haven't tried.'

Chalmers sat upright and rocked on his chair as though rearranging his buttocks. He folded his arms and leaned forwards again.

'How about finding out for us?'

Steve looked uncomfortable. He was stroking his chin, watching the bartender clean glasses, checking his shoes for dog-shit.

Allan said, 'No.'

'Another drink?' Chalmers pointed at his glass.

'No thanks.'

Chalmers laid the palm of one hand flat on the table and drummed with the other. He looked at the ceiling. He considered Allan's face for a while and then said quietly, 'Allan. I need your help. It's important.'

'To tidy up loose ends? To close the file?'

'Keep your voice down, please. No, not to tidy up loose ends. To solve a murder. A particularly cruel and vicious murder of a young man who was . . .' – pause – '. . . a decent sort of guy.'

'You knew him?'

'I just want to find out why he was murdered.'

'Why are you so sure he was murdered? The official verdict was suicide, remember?'

Chalmers unfolded his arms and sat up straight. The palms of both hands were flat down on the table as if he was going to do press-ups.

'No one commits suicide by hanging himself from a hook with his feet still on the ground.' He rocked forwards, emphasising each sentence with his forehead. 'No one commits suicide immediately after phoning his mother and arranging to see her that weekend. No one commits suicide when . . .' His voice had been rising but suddenly it was quiet and his anger deflated. '. . . There are other reasons as well.' He sat back and closed his eyes for a second. The fingers began to drum again.

'Will you do it, please, Allan? We need a computer expert on the inside, so to speak. Someone we can trust.'

'On the inside? Do you mean inside MCI?'

Steve took a long breath, rolled his eyes and looked away from Chalmers.

'What if I said yes? What would you expect me to do exactly?'

'You tell him, Steve.'

Steve leaned forwards and it was Chalmers' turn to study his shoes.

'First of all we would like you to decipher the computer files we got from Harkness's directory.'

'But that could take weeks working full-time.'

'And we would like you to find out certain things for us about how possible it would be for people within MCI to do certain things. For example, would it be possible for a worker in MCI to trace a chip on the assembly line all the way to its final location in a computer?'

'You want me to be a spy inside MCI?'

'. . . Yes. In a way.'

Chalmers broke in. 'We want certain questions answered which can only be answered by someone who actually works for the company. We are not a rival company trying to steal company secrets for commercial advantage; we are policemen trying to solve a murder.'

'I still don't see why you don't get the information the legitimate way by asking MCI. The police have powers, don't they?'

Chalmers spoke slowly and deliberately, looking him straight in the eye. 'Not if they are officially off the case.'

The light dawned.

'This is unofficial. You want me to be an unofficial police spy. And you want me to translate the files for you because you can't ask police experts to do it for you . . . because it's unofficial. And if I went snooping around in MCI and they rumbled me, you would never have heard of me . . . would you? . . . because it's unofficial.'

Steve said, 'You'll have to tell him.'

Chalmers looked at Steve for a long time. The fingers drummed. Then he faced Allan again. His voice was low and calm and almost sad.

'You're quite right. It is unofficial. We have been told to drop the case by the Procurator Fiscal. Officially we can still tidy up loose ends but we are supposed to be closing the file.'

He stopped and stared into his beer and kept his eyes there as he went on. 'But unofficially the file is not closed and it is not going to be closed.' He was looking at his glass but he wasn't seeing it. 'Tommy, you see, was our man. Not a policeman but a friend who agreed to help us.' He lifted his glass and drained it.

'How do I know all this is kosher?' said Allan.

Chalmers thought for a while. He reached into his inside pocket and pulled out his wallet, a notebook and a pen. He extracted a business card from his wallet, found a page in the notebook and wrote something on the card. He offered it to Allan. It was Chalmers' own card. He had written another address on the back.

'That's Tommy's mother. Why don't you contact her and have a chat and let her tell you how inconsiderate it was of her son to commit suicide?'

Allan read the address. 'I take it that's Perth, Scotland?' He put the card in his pocket. 'OK,' he hesitated. 'I'll think about it.'

'I need another drink,' Chalmers said. He put a handful of change and a couple of crumpled notes on the table. 'Set them up, Steve.'

When Steve had gone to the bar Chalmers said to Allan, 'Whether you agree to help us or not, I hope you'll be very careful. If you ever want to contact us don't use my number on the card. Here. Give me that card again.'

He wrote another number on the back.

'You can contact Steve at that number. Just phone there and leave a message and he'll meet you at the sports centre.'

'Is that really necessary?'

'I don't want you on my conscience as well.'

He watched Steve talking to the barman, then let out a sigh and turned to Allan again.

'Only Steve and myself and Jocylin McCarrie, that's Detective Sergeant McCarrie, who's in my team, know what we are about. And now you, of course. I'm taking a risk by telling you as much as I have. It is important that the information goes no further. I may explain a bit more to you if you decide to do what we ask. But in the meantime, for your own safety as well as that of others, don't breathe a word of this meeting. To anyone. Do you understand?'

He offered cigarettes.

'No vices at all? Well, not that kind anyway. Eh?' He lit up and put the packet away, smiling to himself. 'I'm worried about you living in that country cottage of yours. It's too isolated. And with you cycling about, you're a sitting duck for a hit-and-run driver. It is not as though I could spare men to keep an eye on you.'

Steve returned with the glasses.

'Why do you drink that gnat's piss?' Chalmers said, pointing at Allan's glass.

'Can't kick the habit.'

'I was saying, Steve, that his cottage is too isolated for his own safety.'

'It has some advantages,' said Steve.

They both laughed. Allan looked from one to the other and they both laughed again.

'Are you going to explain the joke?'

'That's quite a love nest you've got there, Dr Fraser,' said

Chalmers as Allan blushed angrily. 'It's OK, lad. We're men of
the world, aren't we, Steve?'

The following Saturday, early, Allan cycled to the station,
caught the first train to Glasgow and from there travelled
through to Edinburgh. The package was waiting there for him.
Then he caught a train to Perth.

At the tourist office in Perth he got a map of the city and
information on bed and breakfast places. He chose a terraced
granite building overlooking the Tay. The landlady didn't mind
him sitting in the room for most of the afternoon. Alone at last
in the quiet of that room, he unrolled the bundle of print-out
and began to read.

By mid-afternoon on the following day he was satisfied. The
'Jack-tape' and the first file on the 'Tommy-tape' were identical. The second 'Tommy-tape' file was similar. It was a
program to check another type of chip. He wasn't sure which
type, but buried in the middle of both types of program was a
short sequence of code. It forced the program to skip one of
the checks. If the program hadn't skipped it would have found
Jack's secret passage. So the checks did exist. They hadn't been
missed out by mistake. Conspiracy, not cock-up.

He had come prepared with another envelope. The 'Jack-
tape' went into this and, as he made his way back into Perth, he
stopped off at a small sub-post office and posted the package to
himself – Poste Restante – Fort William. He wrapped the
'Tommy-tape' with its print-out in a plastic bag and stuffed it
into his haversack. He checked the telephone directory and
then walked to the north side of town. In a housing estate off
the Inverness road he found a semi-detached bungalow with a
red tile roof and a small well-kept garden. As he hesitated by
the gate, the door of the house opened and a small woman
appeared. She wore an apron and gardening gloves and she
carried a wicker gardening basket. She had grey hair and a sad
expression. Mrs Harkness had good cause to be sad. He
walked on to the end of the road, stopped for a while and then
set off towards the station.

Back in Gairnock, late that Sunday evening, Allan phoned the number Chalmers had given him. The person who answered sounded like Steve's father.

'Is that all? Just "See you at the sports centre tomorrow"? Shall I ask him to phone you back? No? OK, I'll tell him when he comes in.'

Before making his way back to Burnside Cottage, he cycled round to Jack's place. Jack, he had decided, had to be told before the clown did something they would all regret.

The ledge, wide as a pavement and covered in sharp ribs and bumps, sloped outwards to an edge. Nothing was visible beyond the edge except billowing mist. The ledge was also covered in running water which was being delivered from above. Whether it was simply rain or surface water dripping down from the cliff above was not clear, but it was cold enough not to be liquid.

He was soaked through, his fingers were numb, his boots were full of water and yet Allan was happy. He was securely belayed to a spike on the wall behind him and with one foot propped on another spike in front of him he drew in the rope carefully, feeling for the moving resistance which marked the progress of the climber below. And as he did so he sang Dougie McLean's nostalgic ballad 'Caledonia', or as many of the words as he could remember.

'. . . that you will see the changes that have come over me.'

A hand suddenly appeared over the edge and closed on a rocky rugosity. A torrent of water was instantly diverted over the hand and down the sleeve of the arm attached to it.

'Eeeyyyaaarrrch!' said a voice.

Ian's head appeared over the edge and then another hand. He let go with the first hand and held his arm out while a mugful of water poured out of his sleeve. He looked up at Allan.

'See today. Today's a hell of a good day for being bloody miserable. . .' – he stepped up and took a higher hold – '. . . and so . . .' – he climbed on to the ledge – '. . . I don't see what the hell you have to be so bloody cheerful about.'

They rearranged the rope, retied the belay and Allan set off up the cliff. The climb was getting steadily easier and soon degenerated into an upward walk. Ian and Hamish joined him shortly and they untied the rope.

'. . . Caledonia here I come . . .'

'Have you ever seen this guy so bloody cheerful?' said Ian.

'No,' said Hamish. 'It's positively obscene.'

'You mark my words,' said Ian. 'There's a wumin at the bottom of this.'

'I take it things are going well, then,' said Hamish. 'Did you get that business of the tapes solved?'

'Yup,' said Allan. 'See things. Things is goin' well.'

And they were. The 'Tommy-tape' and the print-out had been handed over in a plastic shopping bag to Steve McElroy at the sports centre. He had told Jack. He had told him that the matter was in the hands of the authorities now and that he was to cut it out. Definitely out. O.U.T. Out!

'You told us before that you had been given some job you found boring.'

'Ah, that's finished,' said Allan. 'They brought a guy over from the States to do that. He's OK. But they've put me on another job helping with voice recognition systems. It's still not my scene but it doesn't have daily deadlines so I can spend some of my time thinking about other things.'

'Thinking about women, I'll bet,' said Ian.

He was right, of course. Allan did spend quite a bit of time thinking about Rosa. But their project had taken centre stage again. There was a subtle change in his relationship with Rosa. Even when he had been at Mrs McCulloch's place in Loch Ranza Road it had seemed to him, and much to his surprise, that he had the edge over Rosa as far as sharpness of mind was concerned. Perhaps it was because she was preoccupied with office politics, perhaps it was, as she said, because she was 'over the hill'. But the advantage he had over her had increased in recent weeks. Rosa continued to call in the evenings, but they tried to avoid rekindling the passion of that amazing

weekend. Rosa made it quite clear that she did not intend that
the affair should continue, but now and again, in little ways,
there were sparks which showed that the fires were still alight.
Once when they were standing together at the table looking at
some document, both leaning forwards, supporting their
weight on their hands, she suddenly drew her little finger across
the back of his hand, raising goose pimples. And once as they
were going in through the front door of the cottage, she in the
lead and a step higher, she turned round to find their eyes on
the same level, and they had to embrace. But they stuck to their
task, with Allan taking more and more of the initiative.

He persuaded her that they had been tackling the problem in
the wrong way. They had been trying a frontal assault. His
approach was more subtle. It required a flanking move, putting
in place additional and seemingly peripheral aspects of the theory, nibbling away at the problem.

And something else. He found evidence of a side of Rosa he
had never suspected. Some of his dirty clothes disappeared
and reappeared a few days later washed and ironed. New
things, like washing-up cloths and scouring pads, appeared
mysteriously in the cupboard under the sink. Old things, like
tea-caddies and pots of marmalade, moved to new, tidy but
unexpected positions in his kitchen. It was as though he had
acquired an invisible guardian angel. He tried telling himself
that this was really helpful, but he found it mildly irritating nevertheless. Control over his own domestic arrangements, too
recently wrested from Jean, was in danger of slipping from him
again.

He was happy when he was alone tackling the hard clean
rock of theory rather than the shifting scree of personal relationships.

Ian and Hamish were for going down by the quickest route but
Allan talked them into coming with him to the summit. At
first they grumbled, but the rain stopped and the mist became
luminous and spirits lifted as they emerged from the clouds
into a hard, brilliant light to stand on the sunlit ridge. Their

shadows were projected on to the white billows below them. Each saw his own shadow surrounded by a halo. The shadow arms were huge, extending outwards from the centred head like the hands of a massive clock, sweeping the rainbow circumference. An archipelago of glinting peaks, in a white ragged cloud-sea, stretched to the horizon.

11

NOVEMBER

Halpern's parties were something of a legend at 'The Tunnocks'. For one thing the setting was a bit out of the ordinary. Garloch House was grander than one would have expected as a home for even a senior executive in MCI and managing director of the whole Gairnock plant. It was rumoured that his wife had money. It was also rumoured that her old man couldn't stand his son-in-law.

The house sat in private grounds amid lawns, rhododendron bushes and mature chestnut trees. There was a small lochan – the original 'Gar Lochan' – behind, and round about were the rolling Ayrshire hills. The house was built in sandstone, big rough-hewn blocks which projected at the corners to give it a notched appearance. This was enhanced by the rafters which supported the steeply pitched roof. They extended downwards at the eaves to hang above the walls like pointed teeth.

Another thing which people talked about was the food. Folk who had been to previous parties told the others in hushed tones of the huge haunches of venison, the array of salads, the mouthwatering sweets and the copious supply of booze. But the thing which was the most talked about, and joked about, was the way Halpern used his parties as weapons of office warfare and instruments of control. His technique, it was said, was to corner some unwilling subordinate, whose resistance had been suitably weakened by alcohol, and then to blackmail them with subtle hints of embarrassment in front of the other guests if they did not agree to some change in working practices or reassignment of duties which increased the control that he had over the working parties and committees of the plant.

'You'll be OK, Allan,' they said. 'He won't be able to get you pissed. But watch out for the sherry trifle – it's 100 per cent proof.'

Helen Rowe and her husband Roger gave Allan a lift from their house where he had showered and changed out of sweaty cycling clothes into his good suit.

'He does this about three times a year,' said Helen. She was in the front passenger seat while her husband Roger drove but she had swivelled half round to talk to Allan. 'Each time he invites a different group of staff, carefully selected to give him maximum leverage.'

'You keep saying what a clown he is,' said Roger to his wife, 'but everything you say about him suggests that he is a pretty shrewd operator.'

'He's both,' said Helen. 'He is completely transparent. Everyone knows what he is about and despises him for it, but he still gets his own way every time.'

'Sounds like he should be in politics,' said Roger. Roger was built like a front-row prop forward, which was not all that surprising, because he was a front-row prop forward. He had played for West of Scotland. Helen was in awe of Roger's physical presence. 'Even his muscles have got muscles,' she told Allan with a giggle and a hint of pride.

'So what's his scheme this time?' Roger asked. 'Who's to be the target?'

'I think it's Rosa,' said Helen, lowering her voice and warming to the gossip. 'He's invited the whole gang of us and he's been calling her at short notice into one meeting after another. Her face gets longer each time.'

Roger said, 'He's the boss. Why does he need to go through

this fandango just to manipulate her? He can just tell her what he wants.'

'Oh, that would be too easy. He gets his kicks by manipulating people. It's the cat and mouse game he enjoys.'

'Well, at least that means it's not you that he's got his knife into,' said Roger without enthusiasm.

'Well no, actually,' said Helen. 'If he *is* after Rosa then we're all involved. He may try to use us to embarrass her. He softens people up that way. So watch out. Especially you, Allan. It's a good thing you don't drink. One of his favourite tricks to get one up on a manager is to get the members of that manager's team really drunk and making fools of themselves . . . This is it, Roger! Turn in here!'

A half-moon of tarmac set in from the road, all but the central area covered with copper beech leaves. Sandstone walls with grey-green lichen and ivy. Two massive pillars and heavy gates which looked as though a century had passed since they were last closed. A long drive, single track with depressed tyre tracks and grass bursting up through the middle. Then the house. Roger whistled.

'Have you not been here before?' said Helen. 'No. I remember, I came the last time with Bill Thompson.'

'Now that's a nifty bit of real estate,' said Roger. It was a professional opinion. He was an estate agent.

The tarmac gave way to a wide expanse of gravel before the house where a fair-haired, lanky youth in a leather zipper-jacket and jeans waved them down. He was wearing earphones and the faint buzz of heavy rock could be heard as Roger wound down the window.

'Would you park round the back please, to the right.'

'That's Stephen Halpern,' said Helen as they crunched over the gravel. 'He's a computer freak.'

There were outbuildings to the rear and a splendid view over the loch and a lot of cars. They walked back round the house where there were a couple of steps and a pair of stone lions. The front door stood open. Roger paused with a foot on the first step and a hand on the head of one of the lions. 'Damn,' he said. 'I forgot the garlic and the crucifixes.'

Watch out for the peppers. They're so hot they suspend them in a toroidal magnetic field.

Some Nuits-Saint-Georges?
   No thanks, I'd prefer wine.

I wish I could wear a sari. It's so cool and elegant. Roger, do you think I could wear a sari?

Have you seen Dianne yet? Dianne Halpern. She's here some-where. She's the one with the pure white hair.
   You mean the one with the legs?
   Yes, and the black and white flounces. She looks like a chess-board.

Twin cams. Supercharged. Straight through outlet manifold. Racing tyres. Goes like a sewing machine.
   So that's why he's a prick.

Get a load of that! They're going to pop out any minute. How do they stay up?
   She must have counter weights hanging down her back.

Watch out for Dianne, Allan. If she gets her gimlets on you she'll eat you alive.

Who's the crow?
   That's Jack's latest. She is like a crow, isn't she? It's not just the black outfit, it's the beaky nose.

Do you think it would kill her to crack a smile?
   Sullen disdain is in this year.

Hello Jack! Is that attractive girl in black with you?

Dianne! How lovely to see you again. That's a lovely dress. Super party. You are clever to get it all together. I hear you handled the catering arrangements.

Who's the gorgeous hunk?
  Hands off, Dianne. That's my husband Roger.

Rosa! Is that Maurice I see over there trying to seduce Eleanor Halpern?

Being of a non-circulating species, Allan hovered in the vicinity of Helen and Roger. Roger set about the food with some determination and reported back frequently to headquarters with his survey results while Helen concentrated on social topics. Between them they provided adequate coverage of the event from every angle and Allan benefited from the spin-off.
  No one had met Masood's girlfriend before. Very graceful in her sari, she added a touch of oriental elegance to the company and it was quite startling to hear her talking, like Masood, with a Glasgow accent even down to the 'see this, see that' vernacular. Allan had always defended this trait from its detractors by pointing out that Glaswegians were actually ahead of the world in incorporating the formal standards of computer languages into everyday speech. When you wrote a program in most computer languages you had to provide preliminary information to the compiler by identifying or 'declaring' every variable:

```
integer x;
integer y;
```

Then and only then could you indicate how they were related or what was to be done with them:

```
{read(x,y);}
```

A true Glaswegian would do likewise:

```
See fish;
See ma maw;
{Ma maw hates fish;}
```

If everyone did likewise, Allan argued, it would be much easier to process 'ordinary' or 'natural' language by computer.

It was Dianne, Halpern's daughter, however, who turned the heads. Tall and leggy, she wore a slim black dress which exposed acres of leg and bust, huge gold earrings and several cables' length of necklace hung in multiple loops. The whole ensemble was topped by a tall mass of chalk-white hair. She could not have been more than nineteen but had the self-assurance of a woman twice her age. She seemed to be in charge of the catering arrangements and had frequent exchanges with the chef in the white hat who presided over the carvery and with the two young women in demure white blouses and black skirts who hovered behind the drinks table.

Halpern cruised among his guests but it was noticeable that he manoeuvred people away from groups and cornered them individually the way a sheepdog does with sheep. His favourite pose was standing sideways on to his target, with a drink in one hand and his other hand on his target's shoulder, while his gaze settled on a part of the floor two feet in front of them both. Usually the victim was pinned in a corner. The hand on the shoulder riveted him to the spot and the sideways-on stance made it easier for Halpern to keep others at bay while he nodded his head and concentrated on what the petrified victim was saying. Allan's turn came quite late in the evening, sometime after Halpern had had a long discussion with Rosa.

'Ah, Allan Fraser, isn't it? I hope you're keeping your glass filled. Enjoying yourself? Splendid. Splendid. You're in Rosa's team, aren't you? Yes. Splendid. How long have you been with us? Yes. And how are you finding the work? Let me see, you came to us from . . . Edinburgh, wasn't it? And you're in the same line of country as Rosa. Splendid. We're all very proud of Rosa's reputation, you know. Yes. Tell me, what are your plans? How do you see your career at MCI developing? There are lots of opportunities, you know, for a young fellow with no family ties. How would you like to spend some time at our headquarters in South America? Work with the people there and get to know them. It could be an invaluable experience. My daughter tells me you're something of a celebrity. What? Yes, I mean a celebrity. One of the young ladies over there . . .' – he waved the hand with the drink in it in the vague direction of the buffet but did not shift the other, which remained firmly on Allan's shoulder – '. . . is a friend of Dianne's and she says she saw you doing remarkable things on a cliff somewhere. Seems you have had offers to climb professionally. That true? Goodness. What it is to be young and talented! Eh? Wish I was a few years younger myself. Used to be a bit of a sportsman myself, you know. Not mountains. No. My interest was in rowing and in horses. Used to ride quite a bit. And gymnastics. Used to be able to do handstands and walk round the room. That was my party trick. Have you got a party trick? No, I'm sure you have, I'm sure you have. Now that I think about it, that is a splendid idea.'

His hand was still on Allan's shoulder but he was addressing the room. There was sudden silence.

'Listen, people. We're going to witness a remarkable feat. Allan here is a famous mountaineer and he's going to give us a demonstration.'

Some clapping and a startled gasp from Helen. Allan felt the room swaying, a burning sensation creeping up his face and a buzzing in his ears.

'Outside everybody. Dianne! switch on the outside lights!'

'I can't . . . I . . . I . . . I've got no shoes . . .'

'Stephen! You're about his size. Can you help him out with a pair of trainers or something?'

People were filtering out of the French windows on to the lawn. Helen was at his side.

'You've got to do it, Allan. You've got to call his bluff. For Rosa's sake. For all our sakes. Do it, Allan! Just do it!'

The drinks ladies were taking trays out on to the lawn. Powerful spotlights suddenly illuminated the dark house, throwing shadows upwards. More clapping. Stephen Halpern handed him a pair of filthy trainers. People were giggling on the lawn, standing about. Some of the women were holding their arms and shoulders and the more gallant of the men offered them their jackets. Halpern shepherded him out with a hand on his back to be greeted by more clapping.

'Ladies and Gentlemen! Allan Fraser will now ascend the vertical wall of the house!'

Allan was wretched and nauseous. He looked at the house. The sandstone blocks were rough-hewn. He went over to the wall and ran his hand over the surface. The clapping started again and then died as he did not leave the ground. A grip here, a toe-hold there. He looked up at the eaves. The rafters projected down towards him, big handy rafters, just the right size for a full-palmed grasp. He placed a foot experimentally on the wall and tested the friction. Quite good. He tried various angles to get the maximum angle at which a foot would slip if placed flat on the wall. Then he walked back out on to the lawn. The crowd behind him disappeared from his mind. This was an interesting problem. The blocks projected at the corner of the house a few yards away. He walked over to that point and tried another experimental foot. The edge of the first notch made a very good foothold. He reached upwards and found the block two notches above gave a sideways handhold and because the two walls were at right angles they could be used alternately and in opposition to one another.

He took his jacket off and dropped it on the grass. He wiped the sole of his right shoe clean on the leg of his trousers. To hell with good suits! He had never felt comfortable in the thing anyway.

Reaching up, he took handholds and stepped up on his right foot. Then he wiped the sole of his left shoe on the other trouser leg. He looked up the corner to the eaves. Thirty feet – ten metres. Over to the right was an open window set as a half-dormer into the roof space.

Now!

Gently, like a candle flame, he swayed up the corner, alternating hands and feet, his balance to one side countering the handgrip on the other side as he moved a hand to the next block. His shadow, caught in the powerful cross-beams of the spotlights, exaggerated his swaying motion, leaping from one wall to the other. There was a gasp from below.

'Splendid!' That was Halpern's voice. 'Come down now.'

Twenty feet. He kept going. Twenty-five. Thirty. Halpern led the clapping.

'OK Allan, come down!'

His head was under the eaves. The spiky rafters were right by his head. He leaned back and for a moment was out of balance as he transferred his grip to the first rafter. He stepped higher on to the next block. He was leaning backwards now almost at forty-five degrees, feet flat on the wall, hands underneath the rafters, his weight hanging on his hands and pressing his feet against the wall in a classic lay-back. He moved right and transferred his grip to the next rafter.

'Come down, Allan!'

And the next. And the next. And the next. He was walking sideways across the wall from rafter to rafter. The window. He stepped on to the window ledge, ducked and stepped through into a room lined with bookshelves.

There was applause from below and a lot of laughter. He went over and tried the door. It was locked. A door banged in the house below him. He was in a study. He was in Halpern's private study. Feet were pounding up the staircase within the house. There was a chair. He sat down by the desk. Marble pen and ink stand. Clock. Telephone. Fax machine. Microcomputer. Papers. Lots of papers and a pile of tape recordings for a normal tape recorder all neatly labelled. A photograph of Halpern, his wife and two children – like a corn-flakes advert.

A key was rattling in the lock. He stood up and went over to it as Halpern, very red in the face, threw it open. Halpern did not look happy.

'That was just marvellous!' said Helen, who was driving. 'I've never seen him so deflated!'

'He was apoplectic,' said Roger, who was pissed. 'It was jusht shuper. Talk about putting his gas at a peep!'

Helen said, 'You'll need to be careful though, Allan. You won't be his favourite person.'

Allan did not say much as they drove back to Gairnock. He was concerned about what Halpern might do but he was more concerned about something else. What the hell was Halpern doing with a tape-recording of a conversation between Rosa Telman and himself?

12

NOVEMBER/ DECEMBER

They were sitting in the sports centre cafeteria again. They had gone to the far corner, well away from the other customers. There weren't many other customers anyway. Steve said, 'What we want to know is – is this a bit of local enterprise or is it a worldwide conspiracy?' He lifted the top off his beefburger and shook the ketchup over it. 'You see, Allan, it's possible that someone at the plant has found a way of spiking these chips, but it's also possible that the secret passage is built into them at source. That would mean – do you see what it means?'

Allan bit into his egg roll and took a mouthful of tea. 'You've got enough to reopen the case. Why don't you have a word with your Fiscal? Then we could drop all this secrecy. A've got enough to think about.'

'That's the problem,' said Steve. 'It was the Fiscal who stopped the enquiry an' we don't know why. Maybe he was leaned on by someone above him; maybe he was told by Special Branch that they had the matter in hand or maybe he is part of the conspiracy himself. We just don't know and we'd like to know before we take your stuff to him. The crucial thing is – is it local or is it global?'

'An' you want me to find out. If it was Special Branch, aren't you in danger of getting in the way of an official investigation?'

'It can't be an official Special Branch enquiry or we would have been told. We just want some information. Could the secret passage be built into the chips right at the start?'

Allan shook his head. 'No. At least, I don't think so. That would mean that the circuitry would be changed physically. You can take a chip and grind the surface off it and look at it under a microscope and actually photograph the circuitry. If you did that layer after layer you could redraw the circuit. That's what the Soviets used to do to Japanese and American chips to copy them. It's laborious, but when there's a lot of money at stake it's worth it. Anyway, if someone did that, they'd find the circuitry of the secret passage, so I don't think anyone would take the risk. It's much more likely that the modification is inserted when the chip is customised. Then the modification is in the state of the junctions which can't be observed in the same way. It would be undetectable. The only way to find it would be at the testing stage before burn-out. After that the customisation is fixed and not even the testing programs could get at it. Incidentally . . .' He took another sip of tea. 'That's why MCI have been able to put the encryption function on to the processor itself. For a long time the US Government wouldn't let any American computer company sell a machine outside the USA with an encryption chip in it. Then MCI came up with this way of making chips secure. So now it can be built right into the chip. That's the laugh. It's supposed to be good for security but it makes the whole secret passage thing possible. The operating system just presents two strings to the processor, one in clear and one scrambled and the processor says "Bingo!" if the scrambled string is the encrypted version of the clear one. It's a one-way system. You can't use it to get back to the clear string if you know only the scrambled one.'

'And I suppose,' said Steve, 'if you put in the special pass-word in the clear register it will say "Bingo" no matter what the other string may be.'

'You've got it.'

'And if the testing program was modified as we now know it was?'

'Then you've got an undetectable secret passage.'

Steve thought about that for a while, looking round the cafeteria as though fascinated by the mural of sporting heroes. Then he said, 'Where do the testing programs come from?'

'From America – no, sorry, from South America. The company headquarters are in Ocean Springs in Chile. Except for the little extra bit we do in Gairnock.'

'How do they come? On tape? In the post?'

'No.' Allan shook his head. 'MCI has a global computer network. All company software and notices and things are shipped around on the network.'

'Do you have access to the network?'

'Yes, but you can just forget that idea. I'm not going to hack into the network for you.'

'I didn't mean that. What I am getting at is this. If you have access to the network, then so had Tommy Harkness. Could that be where he got those tapes you gave us?'

Allan shrugged and took another mouthful of tea. He hadn't told Steve about Jack. He had just let them think he had found the stuff in Harkness's directory.

'Tell me more about the network.'

'We have a network within the plant. The filing system is a network system. If you ask for a file you don't need to know which computer it is actually stored on. You can if you want, but it does a lot of work for you and just delivers up the stuff on to your screen without telling you where it got it. But it's different if you want to access stuff on a computer outside the plant, in America or Europe or wherever. Then you have to open a channel and use a password and make a connection to the computer you want. There are directories to help you find the machine you need but you have to name it yourself. Then, once you have made the connection, you just start typing in the normal way and your stuff goes from the local machine to a network node, to a microwave relay station, to a satellite, to a receiver, to another node and into the machine at the other end. It's all very straightforward. I imagine your police network is very similar.'

Steve nodded. 'And what kind of data can you access?'

'Noticeboards mostly. Files where people dump information of general interest like bugs which have been found in operating system commands and how to avoid them. And people can send messages to one another, so long as it's company business. Of course, some people have a funny idea about what *is* company business and so you get friends chatting away halfway round the globe at company expense.'

'So the official testing software would come to Gairnock via the network.'

'I guess so. Most new bits of software come that way. Of course, once it's here it's stored on the local machine, but that kind of access needs special passwords.'

'Who has those passwords?'

'Not me.'

'But who?'

'The assembly line manager, I imagine.'

'Who is that?'

'A guy called John Seaton.'

'Would the managing director have the right kind of access?'

'Halpern? . . . Suppose so. But he wouldn't be doing that kind of thing for himself. He'd get a flunky to do it for him.'

'Is Seaton a flunky?'

'We're all flunkies.'

'Can I get you something else?' Steve pointed at the counter of the cafeteria where a disconsolate waitress was laying out a trayful of cups.

'No thanks.'

'Aye, it is pretty awful, isn't it?' He sat back with his hands in his pockets, feet flat on the ground and wide apart. 'What it boils down to is this. To do this thing you would need to modify two kinds of program – the program that customises the chip by putting the secret passage into it, and the program that tests the chip for mistakes, which would find the secret passage if you didn't nobble it. Is that right?'

Allan nodded.

'Right. Both programs come to Gairnock via the company network and both could have been modified at source. Right?'

'Aye.'

'But both could have been modified *after* they reached Gairnock. Right?'

'Yup.'

'So either there's a very large conspiracy going on and it's completely out of our league, or there are some smart alecs at Gairnock building themselves a little nest egg on the side. Right?'

'Aye.'

A lad in a red track suit and a girl in a green leotard were bringing trays in their direction.

'And there are no other alternatives. Right?'

'Wrong.'

'Why so?'

'It could be both.'

Steve's eyes narrowed suspiciously. 'How come?'

'There could be a global conspiracy going on and some locals could have found out about it and used the set-up for themselves.'

The couple sat down at the next table. The girl was angry. She banged her tray down and spilled some milk. The lad looked anxious. He scurried back to the counter for tissues.

'Shall we go then?' said Steve.

In the car park he said, 'That's an interesting idea. Perhaps we should bring Bob Chalmers in on that.'

'It's just an idea. It's a possibility. Ah didn't say it was likely.'

'There is one thing we badly need to know,' said Steve. 'Did the tape you gave us come from Gairnock or from the network? I mean, did Tommy Harkness lift it locally or from source? We need to know if the program on that tape is being used locally at Gairnock.'

Allan froze. He hefted the keys of his bike padlock in his hand. Then he said, 'It is in use at Gairnock.'

Steve looked at him accusingly. After some thought he said, 'You haven't levelled with us. Not completely. Have you?'

'No.'

'Why not?'

'Ah don't want to involve other people. Just believe me, the modified program is in use at Gairnock.'

'That's not good enough, Allan.'

'It's all you're going to get.'

'You're in this too deeply to pull out now. Who is it? Rosa Telman?'

'No.' He was walking towards the cycle-rack but Steve was in pursuit. He grabbed Allan's arm and swung him round.

'It is. Rosa's in this with you. Isn't she?'

'No. It's not Rosa Telman.'

'I have to know, Allan.'

They stared at each other for a long time and then Allan said, 'It's Jack Thornley. The tape I gave you came from Harkness's directory but Jack nicked another from the assembly line and it's the same program.'

'Jesus, Allan! You should have told us.'

'Maybe Ah should've. But Jack got his girlfriend Alison to help him. She didn't mean to. He tricked her into it. Ah reckoned she didn't deserve to get dragged in.'

'Jack's in danger – does he know?'

'Aye. Although sometimes Ah think Jack's stone-deaf to good advice.'

'Maybe we should let Bob Chalmers persuade him.'

Of all the people who visited Burnside Cottage it was Bob Chalmers who found himself most at ease with his surroundings.

'My Granny had a range just like that,' he said. He moved round the kitchen, picking things up, running his hand over them and smiling as though he had found a long-lost friend. 'I used an iron like this once.' He held it flat side uppermost and slapped his free hand on to it as if he was swearing an oath. 'I went to stay with my Granny when I was twelve and she let me help her about the house. But I never thought I would handle a thing like this again.'

'I found it in the back room when I moved in,' said Allan.

'Look after it well,' said Chalmers. He had settled into the armchair by the fire.

Jocylin McCarrie was there too, the remaining third of the Chalmers team. She was very business-like, with hair pulled back severely, sitting on the edge of her chair with notebook at the ready. Jack arrived later. His 2CV bounced up the track like a mobile trampoline.

Jack told them the whole story, beginning with the copying of Harkness's files from under the noses of the computer manager and Steve McElroy. He sat cross-legged on a stool with his back against the table. Steve was perched on the window-sill. Chalmers sat in the armchair and gave Jack the penetrating stare treatment.

Chalmers shook his head ruefully. 'You're lucky to be still alive,' he said. 'OK lad, what you did was foolish, but it has helped us a lot. Just promise me you won't go doing anything more like that without consulting us. Steve. Will you sum up the technical stuff as we see it?'

When he had heard Steve out, Jack was keen to hack straight into the network.

'Have I been talking to myself?' said Chalmers. 'We don't want you hacking in anywhere. This has got to be a well-planned operation with no chance of either of you two being identified.'

'We don't have the right kind of access,' said Allan.

'So who has?'

There was some scratching of heads. Allan and Jack looked at one another.

'John Seaton,' said Allan. 'He's the assembly line manager. He's the only one I can think of at the moment but there must be others.'

'Yeah, Seaton's the guy,' said Jack. 'We only need one. We could try a Trojan Horse.'

Chalmers looked mystified. 'Steve?'

'A Trojan Horse,' said Steve, 'is a program which carries another inside it or tacked on to it. The idea is just like the Trojan Horse the Greeks used. The victim sees a harmless program and loads it into his own directory and runs it himself without realising that he is also running the extra bit of program that's tucked inside it. That way you get the victim to run the program himself so you don't need to know his password.'

Jack said, 'If Seaton is a special user he doesn't even need to use a password to get into the network. He would have special privileges.'

Jocylin was taking shorthand. She flipped a page.

Allan said, 'So if we wrote a program which copies the files you want from the network on to a tape-drive on a machine in our department, we would only have to insert that program into another and get him to run it for us. Problem is, where do we get the Trojan Horse? What kind of program would he load and run himself? The usual way is to give someone a present of a new computer game but Seaton doesn't strike me as the type of guy who enjoys zapping space invaders.'

'I don't want any risks taken,' said Chalmers.

'We'll think of something,' said Jack, stroking his chin. 'What kind of program would he not be able to resist loading and running?'

'It doesn't need to be a program,' said Allan. 'It could be mostly data with a small program for retrieving the data. There must be some data somewhere he'd like to get a look at . . . most people would like to see their own personnel records.'

He and Jack looked at one another and the lightning struck simultaneously.

'Henry Quinn!' they said in unison and laughed. Jack clapped his hands.

'Want to share it?' said Chalmers.

Allan explained. 'Henry Quinn is the personnel manager who has files on everyone. It's all supposed to be open under the Data Protection Act so that every employee can get access to his own records, but everyone suspects that that's eyewash. There will be other records we don't see. So if a tape of personnel records marked "Personnel Records – Senior Management – Highly Confidential" should happen to fall Seaton's way, well . . . He's the same as everyone else at MCI. He's paranoid. He'll just have to see what's on it.'

'I can get a suitable tape off Henry's directory any time,' said Jack. 'A've got his shell.'

Chalmers was looking backwards and forwards like a puzzled spectator in the centre court.

'The difficulty will be making the drop in a plausible way,' said Allan.

'This is all way out of line,' said Chalmers. 'Even if it was an official enquiry, this would be illegal.'

There was a long silence. Steve and Jocylin looked at each other. Allan and Jack looked at Chalmers.

Chalmers said, 'I want you both to be very careful.'

Getting the data file was easy. Jack lifted the data from Henry Quinn's directory by copying it to a tape-drive on his own console. Later he walked out of the building with the tape in his pocket. Allan covered for him by going ahead through the metal detectors with a load of scrap iron, keys, pen-knife, etc., in his pockets. If he had set off the alarms, Jack would have suddenly remembered something he had forgotten about in the office.

Writing the program was harder. Allan did that, but he had to involve Hamish, his climbing pal at the Department of Economic Forecasting and Statistics. Jack said, 'What a mouthful.' Hamish was not too happy about it, because they had had to sit all night in the department building while Allan bashed out the code.

'This is criminal,' he said. 'I don't think I want to be involved.'

'It's your civic duty,' Allan told him. 'You're helping to solve a murder mystery.' And that was how Hamish got sucked into the 'Circle of Friends', as they called themselves.

The program was designed to access the network with all the rights of a privileged user. It would copy the basic customising program and the basic testing program and dump the stuff on to the tape-drive on Jack's console. All that was needed was the unwitting co-operation of John Seaton. There was a danger,

however. Once the program was planted, they could not be
sure that it would not fall into the wrong hands. They had discussed the problem over several pizzas at Alfonso's. Allan
found the conspiratorial atmosphere was becoming infectious.
They had hit on a strategy that seemed foolproof. The program
would check the identity of its user and would not work at all
if the user was not John Seaton. So if Seaton was an honest
man, which they doubted, and just handed the tape back to
Quinn, Quinn would not be able to run the program properly.
It would instead just delete itself.

They were worried, however, that in these circumstances
the evidence would still remain on the tape. There was a
thumb-turn knob on each tape cartridge which, if turned into
the right position, would prevent the contents of the tape being
deleted or overwritten. So Jack modified the thumb-turn so
that no matter which way you turned it the tape could never be
protected and then Allan made sure that the last thing the program would do was to delete the tape.

'He'll just think it's rewinding,' Jack said. 'He'll never twig
that it's wiping itself blank. But here, I've an idea! Just to make
sure he doesn't give it back to Henry afterwards, let's put a
tape-deleted message into it.'

So Allan put that into the program too. After the tape was
deleted the program would print the message: 'This is a read-
once-only tape – tape now deleted'.

'That'll gee'im the shakes,' Jack said. 'He'll know then that he
can't give the tape back to Henry and pretend he hasn't read it.
So he'll just have to get rid of it and not let on. It's beaut! All the
best stings make use of the victim's own dirty tricks against him.'

The drop, it turned out, was the easy bit. Jack simply slipped
the tape into a box of tapes destined for John Seaton's office.
Allan distracted the messenger's attention by spilling a pile of
print-out at his feet and while Allan and the messenger were
gathering up the fan-folds Jack did the deed.

'What a performance!' Jack said. 'You're about ready for the
Royal Shakespeare Company.' And Allan was quite pleased

with himself too. He had controlled his blushing. A little bit of embarrassment fitted the part, but not too much.

The hardest bit was waiting for the output. It was possible that Seaton would ignore the box for several days, or forever. But if it did happen, they had to be on hand to pull the tape out of the drive and remove the tell-tale message on the screen. There had to be a message. They could not afford to get the tapes muddled up with some other person's data.

The other problem was that there would be a lot of data. Uncertain of which files needed to be copied, they had set the program to cast its net wide. The stuff could take a long time to be copied and for all of that time the tape-drive would be running and running and other people in the office might start to ask questions.

'Let's put a time control on it,' Allan had suggested. 'Bung the program into background so that it zaps the files in the network during the night when everyone else has gone home.'

'What happens if Seaton works late? It could do its thing while he's there.'

'He won't work that late. He's got a family. What family man works late this close to Christmas?'

'One that's fed up hanging balloons.'

'Or fancies his secretary.'

'We'll need to chance that.'

They put a blank tape in the tape-drive and worked out a shift rota. Allan made an excuse about getting some work ready for the morning and stayed on late. The idea was that he should be the last person out and that Jack should be the first person in the next morning. Even that would be dodgy because the incriminating tape and its message on the screen would be waiting there all night.

Masood decided to work late too. Allan sat at his own console with one eye on Jack's machine, listening for the whine of the tape-drive. Masood's desk was on the other side of the office so there was a good chance that he would not hear the tape even if it did start to operate.

Allan wrote a program, typing slowly and carefully, still watching the tape-drive on Jack's machine. The program did not do anything in particular. He compiled and ran it, corrected the errors and ran it again, and again, and again. Jack's machine was still quiescent.

He heard a noise and looked up. Masood was walking over in his direction, in the direction of Jack's machine. He had a tape in his hand. Allan watched, appalled, as Masood bent and tried to push his tape into the drive. Then he saw that it was occupied and went off to find another.

Allan deleted his useless program and started over once more, using a different style. He laid it out very neatly, taking great care with the indentations.

Still the tape did not come.

He made coffee.

Masood switched on a radio. 'Feed the world! Do they know it's Christmas time at all!' That would help to drown out the noise of Jack's tape-drive but Masood switched it off again. He came over to join Allan at the coffee cupboard. Someone had hung paper streamers around the coffee machine and paper puff-balls from the ceiling.

'Working late?'

'Yes, just something I need for the morning.'

'Rush job? What's on then?'

Allan's mind went blank. But Masood didn't wait for an answer.

'Want to see my latest?'

Masood gave him a demonstration of his new handwriting detector. He was trying to recognise handwriting style, even without signatures, from the characteristic way letters were formed.

'But I change my writing style all the time,' Allan protested.

'No you don't,' said Masood. 'The letters may look different but you still have a set of characteristic letters and the pressures and slopes are still the same. What's the matter?'

He followed Allan's gaze over to Jack's machine.

'Nothing. I thought I heard the night guard coming round.'

'He won't be for another hour.'

Masood went home soon after that. Allan read a chapter in a book on phoneme recognition. His eyes closed. He started awake as the door banged.

'Are you going to be much longer?' said the guard. He was tall with greying hair and over his tan uniform he wore a leather shoulder bag. He seemed untouched by Christmas cheer.

'I'm just waiting for a program to finish.'

'You didn't sign the late-book.' The guard was offended. He opened the shoulder-bag and clicked a button on the gadget inside to record his location and time.

'I'll go down in a minute and sign it. This shouldn't be much longer.'

'I want you to sign it now, Sir.'

Argument was useless. Allan followed him down through the dimly lit building to the control desk and signed the late-book. He scanned the names. Seaton's name was there. He had signed out only two hours before. And they had used a four-hour time delay.

The guard insisted on coming with him all the way back again.

'Twenty minutes more,' he said. 'And then I have to lock up. That's the rule.'

'OK. OK.'

He closed the door of the office behind him and walked back towards his own desk. He stopped. Jack's machine did not look the same as it had before. The screen was different. Then he became aware of the noise. He leaned closer and there was the single word on the screen.

'BINGO!'

The tape whined on, and on. He had no way of knowing how long it would take. The guard might return while it was still running.

He forced himself to sit at his desk and read the next chapter in the book. His eyes skimmed over the words without absorbing anything. Ten minutes. The tape-drive was still running, jerking from file to file. Fifteen minutes.

And then it broke into a continuous high-pitched whine –
rewinding!

Sixteen minutes. Seventeen.

The guard was officious. He would probably be back before
time.

The tape stopped. He snatched it out of the tape-drive,
slipped it into his pocket and typed the 'clear' message to wipe
the screen. Rucksack in hand, he made for the door but with
his hand on the door handle he stopped, went back to his desk,
took the tape from his pocket and put it into a drawer.

As he passed through the security point he shouted a cheery
'Good night!' to the guard, who was glowering at him from the
security desk, and as he did so the bunch of keys in his pocket
triggered the alarm bells.

The following evening he walked out of the building with the
tape. This time Jack acted as the alarm detector. Allan was
pleased that he was able to do it, to find that his emotions
were under control. All it needed was a little time to think
about it and a little more experience of subterfuge. He was
becoming an expert.

Jocylin McCarrie drove him to Edinburgh the following
Saturday. She used her own car and she was a good driver.
Allan reckoned she was a cut above Steve, who was too fast and
took too many chances, but Jocylin went pretty fast for all that.
They stopped for a snack at the Harthill service station. Over
the noise of canned Christmas music he tried chatting her up.
It was obvious that she regarded him as just another job.

'Where exactly is it we're going?' she said.

'My old department at Edinburgh University.'

'Why?'

'Because they have the kind of computer and software I need
to dis-assemble the stuff we got on the tape Jack and I hacked.'

'Is that safe?'

'Karl's OK,' said Allan. 'He'll keep quiet if we explain it to
him. He was my supervisor.'

'And he knows we're coming?'

'Aye.'

Karl Wellington was waiting for them. He came out of his house in a pullover and slacks as soon as they drew up at his gate, and flopped into the back seat.

'This is not like you, Allan,' he said. 'You're the last person I would have expected to get caught up in something like this.'

'I've been surprising myself recently.' He made the introductions. 'Karl Wellington, my old supervisor . . . Detective Sergeant McCarrie.' After a pause he added, 'Jocylin's riding shotgun today.'

Allan gave the directions as they drove round to the department. 'Great place to work,' he had told Jocylin earlier. 'I really enjoyed being a student there.'

'Now. What exactly is it that you want?' said Karl when they were in his office and sitting in a threesome round a terminal. Karl was in the middle with his hands on the keyboard.

'Just a dis-assembly of the stuff on the tape.' Allan leaned forwards and pushed the tape into the drive.

'Is this what you were on about that day you were through here before?'

'Aye.'

'You sly bugger!' said Karl.

'It's still hush-hush,' said Allan. 'Please keep it under your hat, Karl.'

'That's important,' said Jocylin.

Wellington promised and did what they asked, but it worried Allan that yet again the circle of friends had been expanded. There seemed to be no way to contain this thing. The print-out was enormous.

'That's a hell of a lot of paper,' Karl said. 'Are we going to get paid for this?'

Jocylin said, 'I'll talk to my boss.'

They got back to Burnside as darkness fell. He made tea while they discussed what to do with the bundle of paper, which was about a foot thick. Allan wrapped it in a polythene bin-liner sack and stashed it in a dustbin in the tractor shed.

Sunday. The three of them, Bob Chalmers, Steve McElroy and Jocylin, were at his door at eight a.m. It was scarcely light.

Chalmers said, 'Did you have any trouble?'

'No. Everything went OK, but Karl Wellington wants to be paid for the computer time and for the paper we used.'

'Mmmm,' said Chalmers.

Jack arrived an hour later.

Jocylin made it clear she was not there as tea-lady. She organised the space, clearing the table, setting out the chairs and retrieving the print-out from the tractor shed. Then she went for a walk. It was Chalmers who kept the tea and coffee flowing. Steve did his best to help but he had little knowledge of the assembly language, so the burden of the analysis fell on Jack and Allan. They split the bundle between them and began.

'Don't write on the print-out,' said Allan, seeing Jack wielding a ball-point. 'Don't leave anything on the page which will identify you.'

Chalmers was going to say something about that but changed his mind. Steve wandered out and shortly afterwards Jocylin came back and settled down by the fire with a paperback.

An hour later they knew. The program from the MCI network had been nobbled in the same way as the local Gairnock program. The conspiracy was 'global' and as Chalmers had put it 'was out of their league'. The detective thrust his hands deep into his pockets and walked out of the door. They listened to his steps receding.

'What will he do?'

'He has contacts in Special Branch,' said Jocylin. 'He'll probably use them and try to take it to the top.'

'Is he quite sure that it's not at the top already?' said Allan.

There was a scuffle at the door and Steve walked in.

Allan said, 'Are you three keeping watch or something?'

Steve said, 'Just a precaution,' and stared back at Jocylin.

Jocylin said, 'You know, it would be hard to plant a bug in this house. Most eavesdropping gadgets these days are made to look like electric sockets or light fittings, but they would look a bit out of place here.'

'There are other ways,' said Steve.

Lunch was corned beef sandwiches and tea and then they started again. They had no easy guide as to the content and significance of the other files. Each line had to be read and identified. On separate sheets of paper they scribbled notes, trying to decipher the logic, the purpose of each program. Jocylin stood behind Allan for a while and watched him. Most of his notes consisted of little boxes with labels to represent blocks of code. Spidery lines drawn between them represented the flow of control and there were sketches of what looked like irregular chessboards representing arrays and data of other kinds. He tore up some paper into strips so that he could rearrange the order of the blocks.

'What are these?' Jocylin said, pointing.

Allan explained without pausing. He was scribbling hard. She went back to her book.

The light faded early. Allan lit the tilly-lamps and placed one on the mantelpiece. The other was hung from a large rusty hook which dangled from the ceiling.

'Handy for if you're contemplating suicide,' said Jack and then added '. . . sorry' when no one laughed.

Supper was a repeat of lunch. Chalmers' cooking skills were limited. Steve went outside for a while and Chalmers slept in the armchair. Jack and Allan read on. A log crackled occasionally and settled in the grate. The tilly-lamps hissed quietly. The only other sound was the repetitive turning of the pages.

Two hours later Jack said 'Bingo'. He looked at Allan. 'This is it.' Jocylin got up and came round behind them to see. Chalmers was still asleep.

There was a two-way radio lying on the table. It bleeped and Steve's voice said, 'Hold it.'

Jocylin snatched up the radio. 'What's up?'

'Car. Dark blue Escort. It's stopping.'

Jocylin still had the set in her hand. She went over and touched Chalmers on the shoulder.

'Someone's coming,' she said quietly as his eyes opened.

Steve's voice sounded again. 'He's getting out the car . . . sorry . . . she. Hold it. It's Dr Telman.'

'Damn,' said Allan and blushed.

'She's looking at our cars . . . she's coming up the track . . . she's seen Jack's car . . . she's stopped . . . it's OK, she's going back . . . all clear.'

Faintly in the distance they heard a car door bang and the sound of the engine.

Jack looked at Allan and winked.

'You'd better relieve Steve, he'll be frozen,' said Chalmers to Jocylin.

She said, 'They've found the program. The one that does the customisation.'

'You mean the one that inserts the secret passage?' Chalmers was alert.

'If our guesses are right,' said Jack. 'Now all we have to do is to find the password itself.'

They split the pages of fan-fold between them and carried on.

Half an hour later Allan knew for certain that he was looking at it – a long string of characters which the program loaded into the chip. He copied it down carefully among his notes and slipped the sheet under the bundle. Pretending to doodle, he wrote it a second time on the wooden table top itself among the cracks, grooves and coffee stains. A few minutes later he said, 'Here Jack. What do you think?' He spun the bundle of print-out round for Jack to read. Steve was out getting more logs. Chalmers was dozing again. With brow furrowed, Jack scanned the page. He looked up for a moment at Allan with bright eyes and then dropped them again on to the page.

'Hmmm. Let's see.' He wrote on his notes, boxing off a paragraph with a wavy line and then linking it to another. More writing. He lifted a page and slipped it under his other notes.

Steve came back in, struggled with the door, and dropped a log on the stone floor.

Jack said, 'I guess so. I think it must be.' He spoke flatly, denying the excitement which was flitting behind his eyes as he turned the page back to Allan.

Allan looked at Chalmers.

'We've got it,' he said loudly. 'That's it.' He pointed with a finger at the line of code. 'That's the password.'

Chalmers and Steve banged heads as they bent to look.

'Hang on,' said Jack, 'I'll just note this down,' and he began copying the characters on to his notes.

Chalmers reached for the page. 'I'll take charge of this from now on,' he said. 'And I think I'd better have these notes as well.' He lifted both sets of notes from the table. Jack and Allan exchanged glances.

They sat round the fire and drank the harsh black tea which Chalmers had made.

'There are a few things we still have to clear up,' said Chalmers, 'before I take this higher. I think we have enough to reopen the case but the implications are so serious I'd like to be sure of a few points before I move.'

'You worried about the local enterprise theory?' said Steve.

'Aye.' Chalmers looked into the mug of tea which he held between his ample fists as though trying to crush it. 'You see . . . .' He looked at Steve as he spoke, checking Steve's reaction to his words. '. . . There are a couple of people we've had our eye on for some time. I want to check them out . . .' He hesitated and then seemed to make up his mind. 'But I don't want to involve you two in that aspect. I'd just like you to keep your eyes and ears open at MCI. Especially if you hear of anyone making a quiet pile for themselves. Someone spending money freely, more than you'd expect them to be able to afford.'

'I'm freezing,' said Jocylin's voice.

Steve laughed and stood up. 'Hang on, princess, your prince is coming,' he said into the radio. 'Just let your hair down a wee bit.'

When he had gone Chalmers said, 'I'm worried about you two. I suppose there's no way anyone could find out that you were responsible for this little lot?' He waved a hand at the pile of paper.

Jack laughed. 'If they identify anyone it will be John Seaton.' But Chalmers was not amused.

'This is deadly serious,' he said. 'Two deaths already. John Ford driving over a cliff and then Tommy hanged. I don't want more. From now on I want you both to keep a very low profile.'

'Yes Sir,' Jack saluted American GI style.

Jocylin came in and went to the fire. She held out her hands to the flames.

'Are we going soon?'

Jack sat in the armchair with his eyes shut while Allan cleared away and washed up.

'I'd better be going too. Pity he nabbed the password,' he said. He was looking at Allan for confirmation '. . . In'tit?'

When Allan did not answer he said, 'You've got it, you bugger. Where did you put it?'

'I want a promise, Jack.'

'Promise.' He held up his hand to take the oath.

'I'm serious, Jack. How can I trust you? You're a hack-o-holic.'

'I'm reformed. I've signed the pledge.'

'No, Jack. I'm scared. It's got to remain secret.'

'Well bugger you! I'm the one who cracked this thing in the first place.'

It was a fair point. Allan knew Jack should not be told and yet his sense of justice rebelled. In the end, after more argument and many promises, he showed Jack the tiny characters scribbled into a crack on the table's surface.

'You crafty bugger! I thought I'd fool him by writing it down fairly obviously, but he guessed I'd already written it in my notes, the swine.'

Jack got out his diary and was about to copy the password down but Allan stopped him.

'That's a dead give-away Jack,' he said. 'Let me show you a way to encode it.'

So, with Jack at his elbow, Allan set to work with pen and paper. First he counted the characters in the password. There were thirty. Then he wrote down the sentence 'Weesleekitcowrintimrousbeastie' as a single word without spaces. Next he wrote down the numeric computer code for each character in the sentence and did the same for the characters in the password. He paired them off with the poem sentence and added them to produce a new set of thirty numbers. Every character in the numeric character set was a number between 32 and 127. By adding and subtracting from the new numbers where necessary, he mapped the new set of numbers to the range of numeric characters. These he translated back into character form.

'Copy that down,' he said, 'and for God's sake, never leave the real password lying about.'

'OK, Gov,' said Jack cheerfully, and Allan's heart sank.

When he heard the sound of Jack's car moving off he began again with a new sentence. This time it was the names of his three favourite mountains, in Ordinance Survey Gaelic, strung together as before without spaces. With the blade of his pen-knife he detached the backing page from inside the cover of his diary and wrote the converted password on the inside of that page. He wrote it with spaces between the characters and in the spaces he placed other arbitrary characters to give a new password sixty characters long. Then he put an X on the front for good luck. Finally he glued the page back into place and scrubbed the table-top until all trace of the password had gone.

Afterwards he tried to put it out of his mind. He told himself that he had played his part in exposing the conspiracy. The matter was now in responsible hands and he could look forward to getting on with the project with Rosa.

The logs burned brightly. With the glare of the tilly-lamps turned off, he sat staring into the flames. Rosa had come that evening. She had seen the cars in the lay-by and Jack's Citroën parked by the cottage and she had gone away again. What had she thought? He did not like to think of her being hurt.

Jack would surely come to his senses. As before, he and Allan would have a weekly pizza at Alfonso's and they would talk about nothing more significant than . . . than . . . well maybe not wine, but definitely women and song.

13

DECEMBER

'It's for you, Spiderman.'

Helen Rowe shrugged her shoulders and made a mystified face as she handed the phone to him. The whole office, indeed the whole plant, had got hold of his nickname. The catering assistant at the party must have been one of the girls who had watched him trying Gibbet. He had thought her face was familiar. Now he was notorious. The story had gone round the plant within twenty-four hours and had grown somewhat in the telling. The height of the wall had increased from thirty to sixty feet, the rough sandstone blocks had become as smooth as glass and he had not lay-backed along the rafter projections, he had dangled from them, swinging from hand to hand like Tarzan.

When he wasn't 'Spiderman', he was 'The Milk Tray Man'. One of the girls on the assembly line, urged on by a backing group of giggling colleagues, had button-holed him in the corridor and told him that she 'just loved Milk Tray' and would he please deliver a box to her that night. As the group disappeared into a lift one of her pals shouted 'And don't forget the diamonds!'

He took the phone. It was a woman's voice. English? Scottish? He wasn't quite sure. A nasal, upper-crust voice with just a hint of Scottish vowels.

'Hello? Is that Allan Fraser? This is Dianne. Dianne
Halpern – we met at my father's party. Yes. I was wondering.
We're having a little get-together tomorrow night and I wondered if you were free. Just a few friends. You are? Oh good.
Shall we say eight o'clock? You'll find us easily enough, won't
you? Just drive down the – What's that? You don't have a
car? . . . and you can't drive . . . Christ!'

The sophistication had slipped for a moment and then was
recovered.

'. . . How quaint!'

She seemed to have her hand over the mouthpiece but he
could still hear some talking – or was it shouting? – going on at
the other end. Then she was speaking again.

'That's all right. I've made arrangements. Daddy'll give you
a lift.'

As he put the phone down Helen said, 'Was that Dianne
Halpern?'

He nodded. 'My God!' said Helen. 'The lad is about to
enter the lioness's den.'

He wondered if he could have refused but both Helen and
Rosa told him not to be ridiculous. Of course he had to go. The
whole office expressed an opinion. Jack made as though he
was eating a cockroach sandwich. Masood beamed, rolled his
eyes and made motions with his hands as though stroking a
bosom.

The following day Allan brought his good suit to work in a
suitcase tied to the back of his bike. He had spent the previous
evening with a nail-brush getting rid of the mud stains from the
trouser legs and pressing it as best he could with the ancient
iron heated in the open fire. Throughout the day he had a
series of phone calls from Halpern's secretary to arrange,
rearrange and re-rearrange the time at which he was supposed
to present himself at Halpern's office. But the appointed hour
duly arrived.

Halpern emerged from his inner office with two brief-cases,
stopping with the door open, giving final directions to someone
inside. 'I want the Sellbourne meeting set up for Thursday . . .

Cancel everything else that day . . . Who? . . . No, put him off . . . I must have a clear twelve hours . . . Get the letter to Johnston away tonight and . . . yes . . . Yes, include that . . . No . . . Tell George I must have it Wednesday noon at the latest . . . Oh, you're here . . .'

He had looked round and seen Allan. 'I've been told I'm to give you a lift or something.' Then he was talking back into the room again. 'OK, Angela . . . That OK? . . . Good . . . Good night.'

He turned back to Allan. 'Here. Make yourself useful.' And he held out one of the brief-cases which was stuffed until it was almost spherical. He still had another, thinner case in his hand and then, as Allan took the fat one from him, he bent down inside the door and picked up his portable microcomputer.

'This wasn't my idea,' Halpern said. His eyes were intent on the road ahead. He seemed to have an aversion to dipping his headlights. 'I'm just the foot soldier who does what the General commands. Are you dining with us?' and then with resignation he added, 'I don't suppose I will ever understand my women-folk.'

Later he said, 'Have you thought about the idea of transferring to headquarters?'

Allan knew it was politic to be enthusiastic. 'I am very interested, but I'm also interested in the work I'm doing with Dr Telman.' There was a pause and then Allan added, 'But, of course, my real interest is in the work I was doing at university. I would like to go on with that.'

'What exactly are you doing with Dr Telman these days?'

'I'm helping with a project on speech processing.'

'And what you were doing at university?'

'Proof of program correctness. I'd like to try my ideas on the operating system for the new Labyrinth.'

Dangerous ground, but Halpern knew where his interests lay – it would have been suspicious if he hadn't plugged his own interests. And there was that tape recording. Halpern might already know about the project. From the date on the cassette he had worked out that it had been recorded on the day he had had supper with Rosa and Maurice. It could, of course, have been an office conversation, or it could have been made as Rosa put the idea of the project to him.

Halpern said, 'So you're interested in the Labyrinth . . . bloody fool! . . . sorry, not you . . . that car in front . . . that's good, but if you want to do well in this company, Allan, you will have to learn to adapt. Every newly graduated PhD wants to carry on with their thesis work. They would be no bloody good if they didn't . . . What the hell do they think they're doing? . . .'

He changed down, swung out and accelerated the Merc past the object of his wrath.

'. . . But the ones who are most useful to us soon realise that the universe doesn't revolve around them and their ideas. There are a million things to be done before the launch of the Labyrinth. Not just the operating system to be written and tested. When MCI puts a new chip on the market it gives the user a complete package. We don't dump it on the users and leave them to develop their own software . . .'

Braking. Turning left off the main road. The car behind braked too. The horn blast dopplered down an octave as it swept past. Narrow road now. Trees on both sides.

'. . . The Labyrinth is going to be *the* strategic technology for the next two decades. We have advance orders for it from a hundred companies who are developing products based upon it. And that doesn't take into account the products we are basing on it . . .'

They came over the crest of a hill fast. Allan's stomach levitated.

'. . . We even have advance orders for the Galaxy range of computers that will use it. It's going to be everywhere, Allan. It will be big in the defence industry. We may be phasing out the old range of nuclear weapons – blunt instruments of mass destruction – but the emphasis is now switching to super-smart weapons, weapons that can select their targets. We'll almost have them flying through key-holes soon. The great emphasis will be on intelligent recognition of visual and sound patterns . . .'

Maybe Halpern was practising a sales pitch or an after-dinner speech.

'. . . The Galaxy-Superwarp will have multiple Labyrinths. It will be the number cruncher and it's going into twenty or thirty countries all over the world. It will handle economic models. Think on it. At long last the world will have the economies of the world harmonised. No more unexpected slumps or booms triggered by one country doing something unexpected. Business confidence needs stability, Allan, and we will give it to them. We will even handle their electoral procedures. Democracy is spreading like wildfire hand in hand with market economics . . .'

Allan had read stuff like this in leader columns, or was it in *Spitting Image*? They had slowed down, turning again on to a quiet road with overgrown verges.

'. . . There will be a piece of the action for you too, Allan, if you want it and are up to it. But you must adapt and be ready to throw your weight behind the projects the company has identified as important and at the time the company needs them. It's team work that counts now, Allan. There really is no place for the brilliant individualist any more. Think on it, Allan. A move to South America would be a good career move for you.'

The old MCI 'first-name' habit. Or was it a disease? Silence for a while and then Halpern said suddenly. 'That was quite a stunt you pulled at the party the other night.'

'I'm sorry, Sir,' said Allan. 'I had no idea what room I was climbing into.'

'Mmm,' said Halpern ruefully. 'I suppose I asked for it. My wife and daughter were highly amused. In fact everyone seems to think you were the star of the show. My secretary asked me yesterday if I was thinking of installing a better burglar alarm system. She was smirking all over her face.'

'I'm sorry,' said Allan. 'I didn't mean to embarrass you.'

They were pulling in between the gate pillars. Gravel

crunched. The stone lions again. A small corner of an Ayrshire
field that is forever Trafalgar Square.

Carrying the heavy brief-case, he followed Halpern and
stepped into an American soap opera – the kind with lots of oil
money sloshing about, where people got shot and came alive
again thirty-two episodes later. Big hallway, wide staircase –
just waiting for Scarlett O'Hara to be carried up it.

'Dianne will be somewhere,' Halpern said. He took his case
and disappeared upstairs. Allan waited, hands in pockets, then
with hands out of pockets. Loud pop music upstairs. He sat on
a carved wooden chair. A door banged and female laughter
came from a passageway beyond the staircase. Dianne
appeared. She had changed her hair. She was a blonde now.
Pink dungarees. The trouser legs were rolled up to just below
her knees. Nice calves. Bare feet. Tanned. He stood up. When
she saw him she stopped as though surprised. Her hand went
to her mouth and she bit the back of her wrist for a moment.
Then she gave a start. 'Allan! How nice of you to come.' She
advanced with her arms out. Did he shake her hand, embrace
her or kiss her? She presented a cheek for him to peck. Then
she stood back and looked at him. 'Oh my Gawd!' she said. 'I
don't believe it. That's the same suit you were wearing the
other night.' She yelled over her shoulder, 'Stephen!', then
went on more quietly but still forcefully to Allan, 'We're not
going to Hell on Wheels with you looking like that.' She turned
and yelled again, 'Stephen!'

The lanky youth Allan had seen at the party appeared round
the banisters at the top of the staircase. Red on white, his tee-
shirt said 'Whales are Sexy'. Dianne was studying Allan. She
said over her shoulder, 'Stephen, I need access to your
wardrobe.'

'No, Dianne. Nothing doing!' His voice wobbled uncertainly
between soprano and baritone.

'Come on,' said Dianne to Allan. She hooked a finger for
him to follow and marched upstairs.

Stephen's room was in the roof space of the house. It ran
from the front to the back of the house and had dormer win-

dows at either end where the ceiling sloped down to waist height. Half the room was filled with computing equipment. There was even a 'virtual reality' nacelle and 'adventure' gear – broadswords, mailed fists and a helmet with electronic umbilical cord. Dianne strode to the cupboards which lined the far wall. She slid open the doors and began rummaging, occasionally pulling out a shirt on its hanger and trying it against Allan's chest for effect. At last Allan was stung into a response.

'I'm not sure that I want to . . .'

'Shut up,' she said. 'What do you think, Stephen? No. The turquoise does not go with your eyes.' Allan could see down her cleavage. He was glad he had had the foresight to wear tight underpants.

'Not my best shirts, Dianne,' said Stephen plaintively.

Allan said, 'Maybe I'm not your idea of fashionably dressed . . .'

She was holding a white shirt against his chest. It had wide sleeves caught in at the wrist and a silver thread woven into it. The collar was high and flared. She was looking at the shirt, frowning.

He said, 'I'm not taking this lying down, you know!'

Her eye flicked up to his face and back again to the shirt. Her tongue ran round the inside of her lips, trying to suppress a smile.

'Well, we'll just have to see if some other position suits you. Yes, I think the Spanish flamenco style will do.'

From the wardrobe she pulled out a hanger with a pair of black high waisted trousers with flares and flappy bits at the ankles.

'Stevie? Are these trousers too loose for you?'

'No, they're a perfect fit and . . .'

'Good.' She hit Allan in the chest with the hanger and trousers. 'Try them on. Stevie's slimmer than you are,' she said, 'so you should bulge nicely,' and stalked from the room.

'Have you played The Ivory Fangs of Dungeon Doom?'

Stephen was holding a red helmet with a spaceman visor and
Norseman horns.

'No, I don't believe I have,' said Allan. 'What is it? A xylo-
phone?'

'Here,' Stephen was offering him the helmet. It had a tail of
twisted cables. 'Sorry about the wires,' he said. 'I tried to get a
remote sensor helmet but my father said it was too expensive.'

At a rough guess Allan reckoned the equipment Stephen
had would have bought an average family saloon. The centre-
piece of the set up was an MCI computer. It was the same as
Allan's but a couple of points up the range. Allan had his
trousers off by that time but he took the helmet and tried it on.

'Just stand here.'

He guided Allan into a structure like a round pulpit and helped
him on with the gauntlets. The broadsword was only three inches
long in the blade but the handle and hilt were full size.

'OK. Just wait a minute and I'll start the game.'

There was a clicking of keys and then Allan found he was
standing in a square room like a wire frame. He raised his
sword hand; a wire-frame sword rose before his eyes.

'Point your left hand and click with your thumb to move.'

Allan raised his left hand and pointed ahead through a wire-
frame doorway structure. He brought his thumb down on a
small button and found himself sweeping forwards through
the doorway. The harder he pressed the faster he went. In the
passageway ahead of him a green man-sized spider dropped
down from above. He struck it with the sword and it vanished
with a satisfying explosive noise.

'Yes. Very impressive.'

'That's just version two,' said Stephen. 'Version three has
solid panels. The wire-frame figures are all I can run on this
machine.'

'It's still very powerful, Stephen. You've got about twice the
power I have in my machine.'

'You should see the one Dad's got. It's the X3 model.'

He rattled off the technical facts like a computer magazine –
its RAM size, its disc size and transfer speeds, the games it

could run. Allan was still wandering around the simulated
environment of the game – it was some kind of castle structure – and despatching sundry horrors with a thrust of his
trusty excalibur.

'I thought so!

Dianne's voice pierced the battlements.

'Have you any idea how ridiculous you look, standing there
in underpants and shirt-tails with that stupid helmet on, wag-
gling your hand about in space?'

They ate in the kitchen at an oval table of plain oiled pine.
Allan sat down with care to avoid splitting the trousers and
admired the row of brightly polished copper pots and pans on
the wall. His crotch was uncomfortably tight. The trousers felt
like the compression suits worn by old-time diver-bomber
pilots. Dianne was dealing plates on to the table-top like a
croupier. There were bowls of salad and Mrs Halpern brought
a steaming bowl of baked potatoes. It looked as though Dianne
and her mother ran the household. A female oligarchy. Stephen
and his father were waited upon and ordered about cheerfully
as though they were mentally handicapped. There was no sign
of the 'few friends' Dianne had mentioned on the phone.
Halpern stood at the table and applied an electric carving knife
to a large boiled ham.

'So where are you two young people off to?' he said.

'Hell,' said Dianne.

'Dianne, darling,' said Eleanor Halpern. 'I don't like you to
go to that place.'

'It's fine. Hell's OK, Mummy. You shouldn't believe those
stories. Anyway, Allan will look after me. He'll see me to Hell
and back. Won't you, Allan? Oh, and Mummy, my Fiat's acting up. Can I take your Volvo?'

'You said something about other people,' said Allan.

'Oh, George and Cynthia will be there.'

'Hell on Wheels' was a roller-skating disco in Ayr with a reputation for being a place where you could get a fix. Dianne said

the management had invented the story to boost their popularity. She drove the Volvo estate with panache but not much skill. He shifted his position uneasily.

'Are you OK in those trousers?'

'Yes,' he said doubtfully, 'but I think I will get an attack of the bends when I take them off.'

Dianne parked in a dark alley behind the club and threw her imitation fur coat on to the back seat.

'Shouldn't you put it out of sight? Someone might . . .'

'Daddy's insured,' she said, slamming the door. She was wearing tiger-skin tights and a matching top with about six inches of bare midriff. Her hair was combed back into a straw-coloured mane.

Hell was appropriately Stygian. Flickering crimson flames were projected upwards on the walls behind the tables where scantily dressed demons with long red tails served coloured water for twice the price of champagne. In the central space, black silhouetted figures gyrated on roller-skates over an underlit, fluorescent orange floor. A whirlpool of humanity. The roar of the wheels almost drowned the blare of the disco music. 'Hell on Wheels' was close to Allan's idea of Hell on Earth.

George and Cynthia were there already with another couple. In the gloom Allan never managed to work out who was who. He wasn't even sure of the gender of their companions. A waitress brought them skates and drinks. Allan asked for water. The waitress gave him a filthy look and marched off. She didn't come back.

'Have you skated before?' Dianne asked.

'Not really. I've ice-skated.'

'Well, you're halfway there. Just hold on to me. Tightly.'

She took his arm, wrapped it round her bare waist and snuggled up close. They plunged into the maelstrom. People were packed so closely that it was almost impossible to fall down but he managed it, bringing Dianne and quite a few others crashing down beside him. After that the noise, flashing lights and congestion gave him another attack of claustrophobia so that he had to go outside for a while. He spent the rest of the evening sitting in the cafeteria near the door while Dianne danced and skated with the half-naked and ambiguous George/Cynthia person. He, she or it was tattooed or painted and wore multiple loops of gun-metal chain. Allan bought drinks for them all and got concerned about the steady disappearance of his carefully husbanded supply of bank-notes.

'So you don't like the bright lights.'

She took his arm as they left the club, and wobbled slightly as they went down the steps.

'That was the bright lights, was it? They seemed pretty dark to me. Shall we walk somewhere and get a cup of coffee?'

'No, I'll make you coffee when we get back,' she said, slurring the words a little.

'Is that wise?'

'I'm never wise,' she said, waving an arm to the world. 'Being wise is a bore, an absolute bore. Come on.'

She unlocked the car and climbed in.

'Dianne, I don't think you should drive.'

She wound the window down and looked up at him. 'If you want to stay here that's OK by me.' She turned the ignition key. He climbed in beside her, fixed his seat belt and sat rigidly with staring eyes and feet pressed hard against the floor in front of him as the car lurched out into the street.

When they got beyond the town limit and the streetlights disappeared she was late switching on the headlamps so that for some distance they travelled in near total darkness. Several times they veered off across the central line and he made a grab for the wheel. But she batted his hand away and straightened up. And then she said suddenly, 'OK, let's stop here,' and pulled sharply leftwards into a long loop of lay-by which ran away from the road and down behind some trees. She parked beside a notice which said 'No Overnight Parking'. When she switched off the headlights it was totally black. She giggled. He reached out a hand towards her and met her hand halfway.

★ ★ ★

'You're a very surprising woman, Dianne.'

'You're a bit unusual yourself. You know what attracted me? The way you deflated my father. I've watched him do that so often to people. He gets them to do party tricks and humiliates them. He's a bastard really.'

'Why does he do that?'

'Oh, I guess it gives him a feeling of power. They say that powerful people, or people who like power, are basically insecure. They have to get control over other people to make them feel secure in themselves. He does it to Mummy as well.' She wrapped her arms round his neck. He had one arm round her and the other hand was up inside her tiger-skin top. The fur coat almost covered them both. 'But he's afraid of you,' she said.

'I don't believe that.'

'It's true. I heard him say to one of his people that – what was it? – Rosa Telman was a spent force but that you were dangerous.'

'Dangerous! How could I be dangerous?'

'I don't know, but that's what he said.'

'Who did he say it to?'

'John . . . Beaton or Seaton or something.'

'A big guy with white hair?'

'Yes.'

'That's John Seaton. He's in charge of the assembly line. Nothing to do with me. Not now they've moved me from the testing software section.'

'Maybe that's why they moved you. Anyway, he does think you're dangerous. So what have you been doing to him apart from climbing in through his windows and dating his daughter?'

She undid the buttons on his shirt and clamped her mouth on his nipple, exploring it gently with her tongue.

'You may like to know that I consider the dating of his daughter to be the highest achievement of my entire career. Apart from that, I haven't been doing anything.'

She bit his nipple.

'Ouch! Do I get bitten every time I pay you a compliment?'

'No. You get bitten every time you tell a lie. What have you been doing with Rosa Telman?'

'Nothing – ouch!'

'Yes, you have. I heard my father saying that you and Rosa were as thick as thieves.'

'I've not done anything with Rosa Telman – ouch!'

'What's she like in bed?'

'That is not a proper question for a lady to ask a gentleman.' She transferred her tongue to his other nipple.

'I'm not a lady and you are not a gentleman. Answer the question, pretty boy, or lose your nipple.'

'Give over. That's my favourite nipple. I'm very attached to it.'

'Talk!'

'Rosa's nice. I like her. She and I have common interests, but it's theoretical. Sometimes we talk about it.'

As he was talking he ran a hand down her back to her waist and over the curve of her rump. She pushed closer to him. He was short of leg room, and a twinge of cramp made him gasp. He arched his back and straightened his leg, suddenly pushing hard.

'What's this then – rough sex?'

Later he could see her face. Dawn was not far away. She slept peacefully in his arms under the big travelling rug.

He rubbed his arm, trying to restore the circulation. 'Am I going to see you again?'

'If you want to.'

'I do. But next time we'll do my kind of thing.'

'Oh. Isn't this your kind of thing then? Are you kinky?'

'No, I mean the disco and that. It's not my scene really. Do you ever go walking, Dianne?'

'Walking! My Gawd, what have I got here – a bloody PT instructor?'

'Well, I'll think of something. But I'll be in charge. Right?'

'Oh!' she mocked in a little-girl voice. 'How masterful you are!'

'I'll phone you.'

'I can't wait.'

Pink strands of cloud were visible in the eastern sky as they
pulled up at the house. He showered and changed into his suit
and was asleep with his head amongst the coffee cups when
Halpern came into the kitchen with a waft of aftershave.

14

DECEMBER

In the darkness he could just make out the two heads. Chalmers' voice said, 'We've got a problem.'

Steve was at the wheel, Chalmers in the passenger seat.

'I thought we had it all neat and tidy,' Chalmers said, 'but they're acting like I handed them a bag of snakes. Where'd I get the stuff? How did I know it was kosher? What did it mean anyway? This bothering you?' The red spark of his cigarette drew circles in the blackness.

Steve said 'Yes' and coughed. Steve had his window down. A fitful draft of cool air let them breathe intermittently. Spots of rain too.

Chalmers said, 'You trying to catch your death?'

Steve said, 'Pneumonia is curable, lung cancer isn't.'

'I didn't want to call you,' said Chalmers, 'but we had to have another chat. Thing is, we're dependent on you for technical know-how. Special Branch have taken all your stuff, they say for analysis, but they're already making like they think I'm trying to pull an April Fool stunt.'

Allan was uncomfortable. It wasn't just the smoke. His knees were pressed against the back of Chalmers' seat. Chalmers took a drag. The red glow showed him the two heads and two headrests in silhouette and a cloud of cigarette smoke like a picture of a nebula in one of Uncle Roddy's space books.

He said, 'I don't see how there could be any doubt. It was plain enough on the print-out.'

'Plain enough to you. Not everyone has your expertise.'

Steve said, 'There's a car coming.'

They watched in silence as the loom of light got stronger, the tops of the trees suddenly white and gleaming, spangled with water. Telephone lines drew white lines in the sky. Chalmers was slewed half round to face Steve, his profile outlined in white. Steve had his hands on the wheel. The windscreen sparkled with points of light and then the car swept past, unseen behind the trees. They heard the tyres sizzling on the road. Then total darkness again and the dying sound of the car.

'It's a good spot, this,' said Chalmers. 'The bend at the railway bridge holds a driver's attention. No one ever notices this lay-by, and the trees screen it completely.'

'Good spot for a murder,' said Steve.

'It's a bit far,' said Allan. 'For a night like this.'

'Thought you were bursting with energy,' said Chalmers. 'All that biking.'

'Head wind,' said Steve. 'You must be soaked. Time you got yourself a car, Allan.'

'How're the driving lessons coming along?' said Chalmers.

'Not bad. I go for my test in two weeks.'

'Did you go to BSM?'

'No. ACME.'

Chalmers laughed. 'Not Cyril McAllister. I thought he'd folded. We ought to pull him in for having no visible means of support. Does he have an MOT certificate for that old banger?'

'Is that the guy with the wee shed at the top of Ivanhoe Road?' said Steve. 'That shed should be exhibited in the Demarco Galleries. The graffiti work on it is a classic example of Naive Scottish Street Art. It's got more obscenities to the square inch than an American crime novel.' After a moment he said, 'Why is it that there are more Rangers supporters than Celtic supporters?' Without waiting, he supplied the answer. 'Because if you're working with a spray can it's quicker and easier to write something rude about the Pope than it is to write it about . . .'

Chalmers chimed in, in unison, '. . . The Moderator of the General Assembly of the Church of Scotland . . .'

'. . . Aye, we know,' said Chalmers. 'What school did you go to, Allan?'

Allan said, 'I'm an atheist.'

Steve said in his Rab C. Nesbit voice, 'But ur y'a Protestant atheist or a Catholic atheist?' and they both laughed.

Allan said, 'Do the police have an MCI computer?' and the laughter stopped dead.

Steve said, 'You mean, why don't we just log into a police computer with the password?'

'Yes. Special Branch couldn't argue with that.'

'Well,' said Chalmers and took another drag on his cigarette, 'we did think of that, but that's where we have a problem.'

'We don't have the password,' said Steve. 'They took away all our paperwork, even our notebooks.'

'And you haven't got a copy anywhere?'

'Nope.' Steve said it quickly as though speed would disguise embarrassment.

'Not at all? Not even in your private diary?'

'Nope.'

Chalmers lit up the car with his cigarette again and then said, 'We thought maybe you wrote it down somewhere?'

'You took all my notes. Remember?'

'I thought you might have memorised it and written it down later,' said Chalmers.

'A jumbled string of thirty characters. Are you joking?'

There was a rushing noise. On the embankment above them the railway lines twitched in anticipation. Then, obscured by thick foliage, a procession of lighted windows hurtled past with the beat of a heavy diesel engine and a sound like falling water. Chalmers waited until the noise died away.

'Might Jack have written it down?'

'You took everything.'

'Then we're stymied,' said Chalmers.

There was a long pause. Chalmers puffed away. Allan opened another window and put his face to the wind.

'Is that it then?'

Steve coughed. Chalmers said, 'How would you and Jack like to do it again?'

Allan laughed but he was not amused. 'No way.'

'I understand,' said Chalmers. 'We wouldn't ask you if it wasn't necessary. But we do need to prove the thing, once and for all. Maybe Jack would do it himself.'

'Do they know about me and Jack?'

'Special Branch? No. We made sure of that.'

Steve laughed. 'Jocylin was livid. The boss here made her photocopy all the print-out and all your notes so that your fingerprints wouldn't be on it. We destroyed all of the originals. She was standing by that photocopier for hours. Fanfold is not the easiest stuff to photocopy. Kept muttering about women's lib and women having to do the skivvy jobs.'

Chalmers said, 'And that's why we're meeting here in this God-forsaken spot. This isn't even our car. It belongs to Steve's father. We borrowed it so that there would be no danger of bugs or of being tailed. We drove round for a long time before we came here.'

'I noticed,' said Allan. 'I stood in the rain for half an hour.'

'Will you do it?'

'I'll think about it. I might have a word with Jack.'

'Could you do it without taking risks?'

'No.'

'Thing is,' said Chalmers slowly, 'I'm not sure whether they really believe me or not.'

'I don't get it. You said . . .'

'Thing is,' said Chalmers, 'they might just be pretending to disbelieve. It might be a ruse to get us to reveal our sources.'

It had stopped raining but big drops were falling from the

trees and landing noisily on the roof of the car. There was still a lot of wind. It sounded like waves on a pebble beach. After a while Allan said, 'What do they know?'

'Damn all. I let on we got everything from Tommy Harkness. But he's been dead eight months now. Why'd it take you so long? they said. I'm a slow worker, I said, and they looked at each other. Four of them. My pal Larry wasn't there, just his superior and a guy he kept calling Commander and two other spooks who didn't open their mouths. The Commander did most of the talking. He wouldn't let it go. He kept on asking me about my sources. For the first time in my life I have some sympathy for the villains of this world. Interrogation isn't funny.'

'You think they may be part of the thing themselves?'

Chalmers stubbed out his cigarette. 'That's one explanation. It's not one I like much.'

'Is there another?' said Steve.

'Only if I don't believe you experts that the evidence is crystal clear. It's very frustrating for old fogies like me. I'm out of my depth on the technical side. I just have to make up my mind which set of whizz kids are telling me the truth.'

There was a long pause and then Allan said, 'And have you?'

'Aye, I have,' said Chalmers. 'But I don't like what that leaves me looking at. It means this thing is much bigger than we suspected.'

'You've always said it might go beyond MCI,' said Steve.

'I thought that it might reach out and touch a few local officials, but Special Branch is something else. It means, Steve, that we may be looking at something you and I can't resolve. It would mean the thing has some kind of official sanction and the ordinary rules don't apply. There may not be a villain to catch.'

'The boss of MCI is a guy called Norman Marble,' said Allan. 'I wondered if he was behind it.'

'I've heard of him,' said Chalmers, 'and I dare say he is involved, but if Special Branch and the Procurator Fiscal and other officials here are involved too, that puts it higher still. An octopus with tentacles everywhere. Chop one off and it will grow three more.'

'You're not serious,' said Steve. 'Official sanction! Why the hell would governments be involved? What would they have to gain?'

Allan said, 'MCI chips are everywhere. They're in government computers and equipment all over the world.'

Steve said, 'It still sounds far-fetched to me.'

'But if it's right,' said Allan, 'then you two and Jocylin are in the hot seat. If I got you the password that could just make things worse.'

'Aye,' said Chalmers. He lit another cigarette, his hands cupped round the match, his face bathed in yellow light before he waved his hand and extinguished the light. In darkness again he said, 'That's why I told Jocylin this morning to apply for a transfer . . .' Allan felt the car lurch on its springs as Steve reacted. Chalmers went on, '. . . and why I'm about to suggest to this man beside me that he does the same.'

'Bloody hell,' said Steve.

Allan said, 'And what about you?'

'Well. I just have to know. One way or the other. I have to know.'

'So do you still want the password?'

'If I'm not there who's going to use the password?' said Steve.

'I will,' said Chalmers. 'Will you get it?'

'I'll get in touch,' said Allan.

'When?' said Chalmers. 'Where are you going to be during the Christmas break?'

'Christmas at my sister's place in Maryhill and Hogmanay . . . somewhere else.'

'So when will you do it an' how'll you get in touch?' said Steve.

'I didn't say a was going to do it. I'll think about it. Is there somewhere I can send a letter?'

Again they listened for a while to the wind and to big raindrops plopping on to the roof. Then Chalmers said, 'My sister's address. You got somewhere to write it down?'

That evening under the hissing tilly-lamp he decoded the password from his diary. The following morning he posted the letter on his way to work.

15

DECEMBER/JANUARY

The Giuoco Piano

This venerable opening, which was played as long ago as the fifteenth century, derives its Italian name (meaning slow or mild game) from the contrast it offers to the various gambit openings; but as a matter of fact, it can be as violent as the most perturbed of all these openings.

Allan read the words again. Harry Golombek – *The Game of Chess*. The book was one of his most treasured possessions. He had found it when he was thirteen while rummaging in the loft at the Maryhill flat – now Jean's flat. It had been their family home. The flat was on the top floor and so they had a loft, unlike the others in the building. The loft was his den. A small section of the floor space had been laid with planks but most of it was just rafters and dust-laden plasterboard, and water tanks and water pipes lagged with brown carpet felt. It was a glory-hole with cardboard boxes full of papers, rolls of lino, a wicker-basket full of old pots and pans, a chip-pan, a wok, a box of tools.

The book was in a tin box of his father's things – a dog-eared, musty-smelling paperback covered in dust and cobwebs,

but it had small neat handwriting in the margins which could
only be his father's hand. Suddenly he had been filled by a
need to read and understand the book so that he could read
and understand those margin notes. Through them the father
he had never known spoke to him.

He had found a small travelling chess-set in the same box,
and spent many an afternoon there in the loft under the dim
glimmer of the skylight, reading, playing games with himself,
trying out the variations – especially his father's variations –
until the light faded and the rafters had compressed a groove in
his bottom.

And now he read the words again, sitting in his own kitchen
at Burnside Cottage by the fading light of the evening and to
him the Giuoco Piano seemed exactly right. For in the same
way he and Rosa had opened gently, mapping out the problems, preparing the ground, preparing the weapons, circling
the heart of the problem, preparing themselves to strike.

The light faded early for it was coming to the end of the year.
With his departure to South America planned he had taken
some days of his holiday allowance to give himself a real break
at Christmas and New Year. Dianne had gone to Austria to ski
with a group of her swinging friends. Rosa had gone with
Maurice and her loathsome stepchildren to Dunbar to stay
with her in-laws. Ian had flu and Hamish had gone to a conference in Geneva. A deep depression had swung into the
North Sea and was drawing gales and sleet down from the
Arctic. Floods were reported at Fort Augustus and Inverness.
He had been to see Jean and Uncle Roddy the previous weekend. He had laid in a stock of logs, and food and batteries for
his computer. So now he could stretch himself into the old
armchair, snuggle down before his log fire and look forward to
days of solitary work on the 'problem'.

He had now done the preliminary work, and he was ready
for the head-on attack. The logs stirred. He threw another on
the fire, settled back and fell asleep thinking of the Giuoco
Piano . . . which was just right . . . as violent as the most perturbed of all these openings.

He worked and slept and ate and worked and slept and ate without regard to the chronology of the days and nights. He slept on hard problems – short sleeps measured in minutes, drank tea when his brain grew fuddled and refused to think of anything else for fear of disturbing the geometry of his thoughts.

The speed of his mind increased. He paced the room when excitement drove him and woke from his catnaps with new thoughts and new urgency.

His mind was loaded now with the problem. As in a chess game, all the alternatives were simultaneously present – right there, bouncing and rubbing against one another.

The periods of sleeping and waking merged into one so that it was difficult to remember when he had eaten or slept last. He tried each possibility in turn, exhausting every angle and nuance of it before discarding it and trying the next. Each was tested with his new theoretical tools and each was found wanting until – on the eighth day – or was it the seventh night? – or the morning of the ninth? – he was not sure which, but he knew for certain that he had the answer. He had the method by which the correctness of a certain kind of program could be checked automatically. He had the litmus test. He had Rosa's Holy Grail and he was as pleased for her as he was for himself. She had seen the possibility. She had equipped him for the task and had handed him the torch. And with that thought he slept.

He woke with a start to find the fire out and the cottage as cold as death. It was black dark. Something had roused him. He heard again the knock at the door. It was the farmer Andrew Jamieson and his wife, come to bid him a happy New Year. Mrs Jamieson was shocked to see the state of the cottage and was set to light a fire and cook Allan a meal, but her husband took her away with a reminder that they had others to visit. They toasted the New Year – the Jamiesons with whiskey and Allan with water straight from the tap, in a tin mug.

After they had gone Allan kindled a fire, washed himself, cooked himself beans which he ate from the pot and then fell asleep again.

It was light when he woke again. A light snow had fallen and the ploughed fields were ribbed in white and brown and the dark grey clouds were pierced by a bright metallic glitter. The fire was out again but there was still a glow in the embers which caught the fresh supply of logs. He set about tidying the cottage with more determination and got the place looking reasonable by the time he heard another knock at the door.

This time it was Rosa.

Rosa poked the logs with a stick.

'That's it, Allan. You've done it.'

There was sadness and tiredness in her voice, like the sadness after love. They were sitting on either side of the fire, Rosa deep in the old armchair, a lock of her hair straggling free from the tortoise-shell clasp. Allan was on an upright chair. He sat leaning forwards, with elbows on his knees.

He corrected her. 'We've done it.'

After a long look into his face she said, 'No. You've done it.' She tended the fire again. 'I've waited a long time for this.'

All afternoon until the light faded she had checked through his working while he found chores to do. Sometimes she brought him over to her side from the sink to clarify a point, sometimes she stopped him as he hung clothes to dry on a string across the fireplace and pointed to a line on the computer print-out, and sometimes she just looked up, caught his eye and smiled.

'I said it could be done and it *has* been done and I'm not at all worried that it was you rather than me who finally did it.'

Did she mean it? He wasn't sure.

'We did it. The concepts were yours. I put them together.'

The last of the light was fading over the fields. Moving to the window, she stood, arms folded, leaning against the wall, watching the vanishing of edge between hill and cloud.

'I'm sad you're going to go to South America, but I'm also glad. It's right for you now. I'm more or less at the end of my creative life, at least as far as computing is concerned. I'm all washed up at MCI. I'll have to find somewhere else and some other field to work on.'

'Nonsense!'

'No. It's true, Allan, and I don't care now.' He knew that wasn't true. She went on. 'I've reached the end point – the objective I set myself. So it's right for you to go now. I'd really like to get back into academic life. A fellowship, perhaps.'

He did not know what to say so he said nothing. And then Rosa said, 'Can I stay the night here? I mean, I won't be getting in the way, will I?'

The flames in the old range held their attention as they talked. Rosa suggested that Allan should publish.

'You haven't done any work on this field for them. You still need their approval before you launch into print, but there is no reason why they should withhold.'

'I can't publish without you. Don't be silly. Anyway, they would never give their approval.'

'You wouldn't need their approval if you resigned – after you've been to Ocean Springs. It's worth getting them to pay for the trip. It'd be a good experience for you. But afterwards they would have no hold over you the way they have over me.'

The thought made him uncomfortable – taking the credit for what was really a joint effort, but he let it lie – better not to stir the idea.

Later, when he was making ready to pull the mattress through to the kitchen she laid a hand on his arm and said, 'No, Allan. Leave it. I'd rather just sleep here in the chair tonight.'

So he built up the fire again and left her there with blankets. Before she left in the early morning she said, 'I came here one night a few weeks ago and you had company. I saw some cars in the lay-by, so I went away.'

'Oh, that would be some of my climbing friends.'

He had prepared the lie, justifying it to himself with the thought that Steve was a climbing companion of a sort and that it was best for Rosa not to know. Knowledge was dangerous.

The logs had burned out and cold gripped the cottage. He lifted the log basket and opened the door.

'Be careful, Allan. I don't want anything to happen to you.'

'Why should anything happen to me? I climb very carefully, you know.'

'It's not the climbing that worries me,' she said. 'I keep thinking about Tommy Harkness and wondering why he died. I don't believe it was suicide.'

He didn't speak. She went on, 'You didn't hear the news last night, did you? There was an item about a man who gassed himself in his car with the exhaust pipe. He was found in a lay-by on the A1 somewhere in Yorkshire. This morning I heard that it was John Seaton, our assembly line manager.'

16

JANUARY

Steve's mouth was moving but the words were torn away by the wind. Allan put a gloved hand behind his ear to show that he hadn't heard and Steve leaned nearer.

'Have you any idea what the Andes are like?'

'Where I'll be?'

'Aye.'

'Not like this! Dry. Near the Attacama Desert.'

The ridge was shredding the mist like a comb. A strong wind was blowing from left to right and the mist was being formed by the ridge itself, flowing out to the right in long, ragged streamers, pouring through the snow-filled gaps between the red finger-points of crag and then swirling under to fill the corrie with grey billows, obscuring everything. The left side of the ridge was in bright sunlight; with its snow cover it was almost too bright to look at.

The draw-cord on Allan's anorak hood was broken, so he kept it in place, denying the wind its pleasure, by wearing his balaclava outside his hood.

Steve raised a mittened hand, measuring a height.

'How high?'

'Higher than the Alps.'

They had tried with the rope but the wind pulled it out to

the right in a horizontal catenary between them, adding to the wind-drag. The going was not so hard that they really needed it. Steve touched him on the arm.

'You passed your driving test then. Where d'ye get the bus?'

They were creeping sideways along the crest from pinnacle to pinnacle, keeping three-point contact. On a windless day they would have scrambled over the spikes but with gusts threatening to lift them off their feet they avoided most of the 'gendarme' on the sunny side.

'D'ye not recognise it? It belongs to Cyril McAllister.' When Steve wrinkled his nose he added, 'ACME School of Motoring.'

'You didn't buy it!'

Allan shook his head. 'Naw. Hired it!'

Steve beamed. 'Did he give you a receipt?' and his smile broadened further when Allan shook his head.

Beyond the pinnacles the ridge rose to a minor summit. The snow slope was brittle, bubbly stuff that gave way easily. The scree below was encased in clear ice.

'Not nice!'

Allan nodded. At the summit they found a sheltered nook behind rocks. The wind shrieked overhead.

Steve said, 'It had nothing to do with you.' He was digging into his rucksack. He offered chocolate and Allan took some. 'We had our eye on Seaton for a long time. He was living beyond his means. We knew he had a racket.'

'What has that got to do with it?' Allan mumbled through the chocolate. 'We set him up. We thought we were being bloody smart and we just set him up.'

'You didn't. He set himself up.'

'How do you make that out?'

Cloud was boiling in the corrie at their feet, lifting and blowing clear to reveal a huge white bowl ringed by broken reddish crags. Beyond, the next hill, a great whaleback of white, was dazzling.

'Remember your theory of global conspiracy plus local enterprise? Well, Seaton was the local enterprise.'

'Is there anyone else I should know about? I mean, is some-one else at MCI likely to strangle himself or stab himself in the back?'

Steve wiped his nose with the back of his mitt and looked at Allan. His eyebrows were encrusted in hoar. He reached across and took the sandwich which Allan offered. He took a bite and then said, 'Halpern'.

'You mean . . .'

Steve waved a hand in a dismissive gesture.

'I mean Halpern and Seaton were thick as thieves and, as we now know, probably *were* thieves. It really was a beautiful set-up. Insider trading is the way to make millions with very little risk. The money you get is paid over legitimately. It could be a lucky fluke like a bet on a horse. It's only when you do it repeatedly that people begin to suspect. The weak link is the connection, the information source which can be traced. But in this case there's none. All they had to do was to tap into the computer of a large merchant bank which handles takeovers. They're all using networks and have remote network connec-tions. They don't use desktop machines, at least not in isolation. All their memos and reports will be on their net-work. They could even get their information from several sources and so we would be put off the scent completely.'

'So Halpern might be for the chop?'

'Not necessarily. Not if he's been careful. But yes, if I was him I'd be having a look over my shoulder.'

'Shouldn't he be warned?'

'That's Chalmers' strategy,' said Steve. 'He's planning to contact the guys in charge of the Seaton investigation and sug-gest that they interview Halpern. And then he hopes to interview Halpern himself and lean on him a bit in the hope that he blows the conspiracy.'

'You think Halpern knows about the conspiracy?'

'He has to. Doesn't he?'

'I take it Chalmers hasn't used the password yet.'

'With the Seaton thing he thought he didn't need to. How did you get the password the second time, by the way?'

'That's my secret.'

'Was it risky?'

'I got it for you. Just leave it at that. When does your transfer come through?'

'Next week. Shall we get on? It'll be dark in a couple of hours.'

'So I won't see you again? Doesn't it worry you that you won't see this thing through to the end?'

'It does a bit. But lots of cases go unresolved. You get used to it. If you get too involved you can't think straight.'

'Chalmers is involved, isn't he?'

Steve looked thoughtful. 'I'm not sure about this, but there is a rumour that he and Tommy Harkness's mother were pretty close.'

'That explains a lot,' said Allan. 'But you didn't say if I would see you again.'

'Probably not. But Bob Chalmers wants to have a way of getting in touch with you. He's a bit put out by you not having a phone but he says he'll send you a postcard. It'll be from "Uncle Bob" and it will have a date or a day mentioned on it somewhere. That's the signal to meet him on that day.'

'That's a bit vague.'

They were standing, fixing the straps of their rucksacks.

'Not really. The date on the postcard will indicate the time to meet and the place to meet will be that lay-by where we met before.'

'OK for him. I've got to get there by bike. Look at that!'

He pointed west. A wall of green-black cloud was bearing down upon them.

'Let's get to hell out of here,' said Steve and made off along the ridge.

'What exactly do you do with Rosa?'

'Are you jealous?'

Dianne lay naked beside him, pinning his right arm down with her stomach. He was on his back and she was trying to arrange a lock of his hair in a romantic curl across his brow.

'No, I'm not. I'm curious to know why my father is so worried about you.'

'Is he worried? I don't know why he should be. Did you know he wants me to go to South America?'

'Yes. They say Ocean Springs is a beautiful place. Will you go?'

'Yes. I'm not sure. I'm thinking about it.'

She treated Burnside Cottage as a kind of quaint beach hut. She had only been a couple of times. The first time she tried sitting outside with a book in the sunlight but the sunlight was an illusion. A chill wind drove her indoors again.

She talked a lot about 'Charles', who had a yacht and a lot of other yuppie toys. Allan was not too concerned. Her affections, he knew, rotated like a lighthouse. When it was his turn to be caught in the beam he was transfixed like a rabbit but at other times he could be sanguine. The trip to the opera, however, was a score. It had just the right ingredients. Dianne turned up in a peach-coloured off-the-shoulder gown which she set off with jet black hair. The opera was pretty good too. Afterwards they went to a fashionable café and dallied over a vegetarian dish. A driving licence had released his love life from a logistical strait-jacket. They took Dianne's Fiat and he drove back. She had stayed that night with him at the cottage.

'He makes tape recordings of people. Did you know that?'

'Who does?'

'My father. He has recorders all over the place and he's got a whole collection of conversations between people. When he's not playing with his microcomputer he listens to the tapes and makes notes. He's paranoid.' She gave up on the lock of hair and ran a finger down his nose to his mouth where it stopped and began tracing out the shape of his lips. Her finger-nails were long and pointed.

'He's even got a recording of you.'

'How do you know that?' The finger at his lips made him mumble.

'I heard your voice one day when I was outside his room. I knocked and went in and he was alone, and he switched the tape recorder off in a hurry.'

'Well . . .actually I did know.'

Suddenly alert, she raised herself on her elbows, exposing a tantalising vista of dangling breast and then shot a hand under the bedclothes and seized his testicles.

'How do you know?'

He gasped and folded up, but her grip tightened.

'Come on. How do you know?'

'Ouch! The day I climbed into his study . . . Ahhhaaa! . . . there was a tape recording of Rosa and myself lying on his desk.'

Dianne let go and rolled over on her back and let out a peal of laughter.

'That's why he nearly swallowed his tie that night! Caught with his pants down. What a hoot! Did you take it?'

'Of course not!'

She had pulled most of the bedclothes off him. He struggled to get them back.

'I would have,' said Dianne. 'Here! Maybe I could get it for you.' She turned to him, leaned over and kissed him on the tip of his nose. One nipple brushed over his. 'If you're nice to me, that is.'

'What does he do with his microcomputer?'

'He sits up in his room with it for hours every evening. Sometimes I think he's having sex with it.'

'Now that's what I would call "virtual reality".'

He grabbed her round the waist and pulled her close.

'I wonder if I could program you into Stephen's adventure game. Of course, I would need to gather a lot of data first, by first-hand experience, you understand.'

His hand was exploring, gathering information. She wriggled against him.

'I don't want to be in Stephen's game, thank you. I'm not having little brother seeing me in the altogether. Did you know Daddy has a radio transceiver built into his computer and he talks to people all over the world? He's got a broker in Tokyo who buys and sells a lot of shares for him. He's a bit of a wizard at it, actually. He bought Mummy a cottage in France last year on the proceeds.'

'I thought your mother was the one with money.'

'She used to have. But all her money is tied up in Garloch. No, he's the one with the purse strings so I have to stay in with him, even if I do think he's a bastard. Are you going to go to South America?'

'Yes, I think I will. But not just yet. I've said I'll go in the spring. I've got some unfinished business here.'

She stiffened again but he warded off another attack on his private parts.

'What kind of unfinished business?' she demanded. 'Are you talking about me, or are you talking about Rosa Telman?'

'You've got Rosa Telman on the brain.'

'I'm afraid you may have her on something else. I might come out and see you in South America. Just to keep an eye on you.'

'That would be nice.'

Jack poked a finger into the eye of the CD machine. Like a stone idol on some Polynesian Island, the eye glowed yellow and the tongue extended slowly and deliberately in a rude gesture. He fed it, laying the disc like a sacrificial offering on the surface of the tongue, and poked the eye again. The tongue retracted. There was a click and a second later the sound of a rock band shook the room. The stone idol was venting its anger.

He sat down at his computer and stared at the exaggerated technicolour landscape on the screen which was rushing towards at him at an impossible speed. The control lever was by his hand but he made no effort to grasp it. He watched, passively, as a large pointed mountain rotated into centre screen and exploded in his face. The noise of the impact was horrendous but barely audible over the industrial clamour of the CD player. He went on staring at the screen while the message displayed told him he was not only dead but had been demoted to novice-level 2.

Life had lost some of its zest. Flying rocket machines through simulated landscapes or defeating animated slime patches from the planet Zontor no longer held his interest. Depression, someone had told him, was a symptom of suppressed anger or desire. Jack had several suppressed desires. One was a simple sexual desire for Alison. Another was a desire for a well-cooked meal of the traditional non-carry-out variety. But the third and most pressing desire was the burning urge to break his promise to Allan not to use the password to the secret passage. Someone, he argued to himself, had to prove that it could be done. Unless it was proved, everything was hypothesis.

Jack found it hard to admit to himself that the motivation was actually a need to demonstrate his prowess – to score where others failed or feared, to show that he had knowledge which others lacked, that he could find his way around the 'system', that incredibly complex maze. He wanted to demonstrate that he could walk through it in ways that others did not know existed, to pop up like a wraith where he was least expected, and then to disappear again, leaving others stunned and disbelieving.

When he made the promise he had done so with sincerity, but he was secretly surprised that Allan had trusted him. He would not have trusted another with the knowledge Allan had given him. He would have pretended to have done so, and given the unsuspecting 'other' a false password which would have left him thinking he had the key to the universe, and then made him promise not to use it. That would be beaut. What a con! Dead ultimate!

And then an uncomfortable thought struck him. Perhaps that was exactly what Allan had done to him. The thought began to eat into his soul as his rocketship crashed yet again on the planet Zor-2. Dead for the second time and demoted to novice-level 1.

17

FEBRUARY

Hamish and Ian decided that Allan's departure required some fitting escapade and so they chose Bheinn na Cailleach. The mountain was tucked away at the end of a winding single-track road in the North-Western part of Scotland but it was also shapely, with fine crags and gullies, and Allan loved it perhaps more than any other. The great hollow bowl of the northern corrie held some of the finest cliff scenery in Scotland and the jagged spurs which descended into it from the summit ridge were famous for their length and difficulty.

For efficient climbing in the limited winter daylight they needed two pairs and so they invited Dougie Barr, who was a forestry graduate and lived and worked not far from the mountain. It was agreed that Dougie, being local, would make his own way, with a key to open up the mountain bothy which gave shelter to the climbing fraternity within the northern corrie itself.

Cold clear weather with hard snow was what they wanted but what they got, on the long drive north, was wind gusting to eighty, throwing bucketfuls of sleet at the windscreen. With some difficulty they ignored the attractions of the hostelries along the route and pressed on, for was it not a special trip? and besides, Dougie would be waiting for them, up there on the mountainside, in a cosy bothy, soup at the ready.

By midnight, when they climbed out of the car at the foot of the mountain, the wind had dropped and the sleet was holding off.

'Whose idea was this anyway?'

'Some infidel. It's against my religion to drive past a pub during opening hours.'

The packs were heavy, so they took the slopes with a slow, steady swing of the hips, rucksack straps creaking in rhythm with their pace, each cocooned with his own thoughts. A quick shower soaked them and then passed, leaving a dark, ragged sky and a few stars. They walked by torchlight. The path was good for the first three miles and then the ground steepened and the path degenerated. In places they were ascending the boulder-strewn bed of a small burn. Two hours later, high on the shoulder of the hill, they lost the path for a while and Hamish stuck his leg into a bog up to the knee. As he withdrew it, covered in black slime and with a great sucking noise, Ian put his finger in his mouth and added the plop of a cork.

Higher still, they crossed over a crest and dropped down into the lower end of the northern corrie, where the wind vanished and the hollow resonance of their footsteps suggested big cliffs on the right. More stars pierced the blackness above, hanging like lanterns. They reached the snow line. It was getting very cold and sweat-laden clothes were beginning to freeze.

'I don't see any light from the hut.'

'You can't see it from here. There's a bump between us. But don't worry, lads. Dougie'll be there. He'll have picked up the key this afternoon and he'll have the soup ready. You'll see.'

Another half hour's toil on slippery snow took them over the bump. Dougie was not there.

The hut was black and the door was locked and the place was built of massive masonry as though to withstand an assault by bulldozers. The door was iron-bound, with a keyhole big enough to admit a child's hand. The windows were deep set into the walls and had iron bars padlocked across them. The roof was of corrugated iron, tightly nailed.

They found out afterwards that Dougie, having forgotten

about the arrangement, had gone to see his girlfriend in Dundee, but Ian insisted that Dougie was merely held up and would be along shortly. A circuit of the hut revealed an evil-smelling dry lavatory and a big box with a sloping top held shut with a metal hasp. They prized the hasp with an ice-axe and found a rescue stretcher with sledge runners lying on a pile of coal.

'Toss,' said Ian and won.

'I bags the stretcher,' he said. 'You two in there.' He pointed at the lavatory. 'Dougie'll be here soon, so there's not much point in getting your sleeping bags out. Besides,' he added gleefully, 'ye'd get them all mankie. That cludgie's mingen.'

The lavatory shed was roughly the size and shape of a telephone box, with solid stone walls and a flimsy wooden door. Even with the toilet bucket removed, the stench was abominable. In total darkness and the temperature of a deep-freeze cabinet, Hamish and Allan stood back to back and then front to front and then front to back and then front to side.

'Do you think we could sit down?'

'What on?'

'On our hunkers.'

They slid down slowly, backs against the freezing stone walls. It was very tight.

'Aaargh!' said Hamish. He reached up desperately for the lock and as the door burst open he rolled out into the snow. 'Bloody hell!' he said, rubbing his leg and holding it out straight. 'I don't think that was a very good idea.'

So they stood again in the blackness, back to back then front to front, then back to front.

'We could sit on our rucksacks.'

They tried it. That was better, but it was difficult not to touch the walls, which would have frozen a candle flame.

'Do you think Dougie's really coming?'

'If he isni', he's going to die a slow and horrible death.'

Hours later, cramped and exhausted, they gave up and opened the door.

'Have you slept at all?'

'Are you joking?'

'Listen!'

They were silent.

'The bugger's snoring!'

Hamish lifted the lid of the box and shone a torch in Ian's face. He was stretched out peacefully on the stretcher and he was in his sleeping bag.

'What's the matter with you two? Can y' no let a fella sleep?'

'Time's up,' said Hamish. 'Next shift.'

'What's the point? Dougie'll be here soon.'

They dragged him out and tossed again. Allan won. It wasn't exactly comfortable but it was bliss after the toilet shed, and as he drifted into sleep he heard Hamish and Ian arguing. Minutes later . . . was it really two hours? . . . the lid was lifted and he was dragged out and Hamish sank gratefully on to the stretcher.

It was a fiercely cold night, now full of stars and deathly still. You could see the shapes of the hills against the not quite black sky. Ian was swinging his arms.

'That's a hell of a cold doss,' he said, nodding at the toilet shed. 'What do you say we get the stove going?'

They lit a stove. Ian pumped it hard and placed it on the ground at their feet. They stood over it with legs apart.

'Jesus, that's hot!' said Ian.

They left the door open so that they could beat a quick retreat into the snow and for the rest of the night, as the light in the East grew and the hills took solid grey form, they alternated between frigidity and searing heat.

Ian was for waking Hamish.

'He hasn't had long enough,' said Allan.

'Would y'look at that mountain!' said Ian.

The massive cliffs of Bheinn na Cailleach were iced like a wedding cake. The gullies were ribbons of green ice, and festoons of snow smothered the rocks, which rose in gigantic steps into a clear pink dawn. You got a crick in your neck just looking at it.

'It's going to waste!' Ian said. 'We've got to get that lazy

bugger out of his pit.' His breath hung round him like ecto-
plasm.

'Let's cook breakfast first.'

So they did that. In the stillness the stove burned easily in the
open. Allan fried up bacon, eggs, haggis and beans in a single
pan into a glorious hash. Ian lit another stove and placed a
dixie full of snow on it. He stood over it, adding more lumps of
snow as it melted and the volume reduced. When it boiled he
kicked the coal box.

'Wake up, princess!'

If the night had been Hell, the day was Paradise.

'Hadn't we better go down for the key?' said Allan.

Ian was adamant. 'Dougie'll be here tonight – for certain! It's
too good a day to waste.'

A wickedly sharp blade of rock split the corrie into two
smaller bowl-shaped hollows. Looking up it from the hut, they
saw it rise in huge, irregular steps. The last and highest one,
just below the summit itself, soared into the tower which gave
the blade its name – 'An Casteil'. Its tip was aflame as the sun
caught the crusted snow.

The right flank of the blade formed a tremendous precipice
and running up the cliff was a shallow, twisting groove. This was
Yggdrasil. From the sunless boulder-strewn floor of the corrie it
ascended vertically, splitting as it did so into smaller cracks like
the branches of a tree. In late spring, when the sun had shifted
most of the snow from the crags, a thin seam of snow would
often linger within the groove so that it resembled a bleached,
skeletal hand reaching up from the gloomy depths of the corrie
towards the sunlight which touched the summit ridge.

'Why's it called Yggdrasil?' said Ian.

They were moving up hard, steep snow in the corrie below
the climb. They paused and leaned backwards to look at the
precipice above them.

'Because it's shaped like a tree,' said Allan. 'The Yggdrasil
was a kind of tree.'

The cliff above them was foreshortened by the angle but they could see the way the groove branched and branched again as the narrow band of green ice, trapped between the white crusted rocks, soared upwards.

'Never seen one. Where does it grow?'

'It's a mythical tree. It's in the old Norse Sagas. Its branches, trunk and roots are supposed to hold together Heaven, Earth and Hell. But it got all burned up on the Day of Ragnarok – that was a sort of Twilight of the Gods.'

The axes gave purchase. They had two each. The downwardly curved blades bit solidly. Hamish in the lead kept up a steady rhythm. The snow accepted the bite of their crampons with a squeal like harvest mice.

Hamish said, 'That must be a hell of a tree. Which is which?'

'Which is what?'

'Are the branches Hell or are the roots Hell or what?'

'The branches are Heaven and the trunk is Earth or ordinary life and the roots are in Hell. They dip into a spring which is the "Spring of all Knowledge".'

Ian paused and considered that, leaning forward on his axe. His breath hung white in the still air. Their mouths tasted the coldness of it. 'Useful for examination purposes,' he said.

'Aye,' said Allan. He paused below Ian and buried the shaft of his axe deep. 'But there's a price to pay if you drink there.'

'Knew there'd be a catch. What's the price?'

'Odin had to sacrifice an eye.'

The climb was perfect – solid green ice the whole way at a terrifying angle. Whiles they used ice-pegs and dangled to ease the strain on arms and feet, whiles they moved upwards on 'lobster claw' crampon points and the hooked 'pterodactyl' ice-axes.

From the narrow neck behind the tower and onwards they were in gentle evening sunlight. At the summit they lingered, watching the purple shadows pushing the pink off the surrounding peaks one by one. The outer isles were visible, floating, so it seemed, above the silver of the western sea.

'That bastard Dougie had better be there,' said Hamish.

★ ★ ★

The events of the next two days represented a triumph of exuberant optimism over common sense. For two more nights they suffered as they took turns at standing in the upright toilet shed and sleeping on the stretcher.

They aged ten years.

Each morning the weather was so perfect that the thought of returning to sea level for the key was unbearable and they went climbing – and the climbing was the stuff of paradise – solid vertical ice and rock covered in snow with the solidity and texture of timber.

On the last night, as Hamish and Allan shivered in the vertical ice-bound tomb of the toilet shed, Hamish said, 'What was all that business with the tapes and the programs you wrote on my machine?' Perhaps it was that Allan's brain had become chilled and drained of the ability to dissemble by sheer exhaustion, or perhaps it was the effect of a camaraderie born of shared adversity, but it seemed the natural thing to do. He told him the whole story.

Hamish whistled. 'You've opened a can of worms, my son. What do you suppose they're after?'

'Money?'

'Naw. More like power. Some people are switched on by power the way you and I are by a hard climb.'

'You're right, but I think it's partly fear. The more power they've got, the more afraid they become about losing it. They want things tightly controlled so that nothing can shake their control unexpectedly. Keeping control needs still more control. That's why they keep prattling on about "stability". Stability's a good thing mostly, but if you make it a religion then nothing can ever change for the better.'

Hamish said, 'And you're going to South America. That's a bit like putting your head in the lion's mouth, isn't it? Hold on, I'm getting cramp.' They were sitting on the rucksacks. Hamish shifted his position.

'I think I'll be OK so long as they don't begin to suspect. We've been careful so far and not drawn attention to ourselves.'

'Can you trust that guy Jack? He sounds a bit of a tearaway.'

Silence. After a while Allan said, 'Hamish. Would you be willing to act as a post-box?'

'What do you mean?'

'Well, I can communicate on MCI's computer network to the folk at Gairnock, but that will be monitored and I'm afraid a letter would be intercepted. But a letter to you would not ring any alarm bells. I could send a postcard to Rosa. If it is a picture with mountains on, it will be a code to tell her that there's a letter lying at your department.'

His thoughts were often with Rosa. She wasn't part of the circle, but he wanted to keep their closeness to themselves.

'Sure. But do you really think it's necessary? Seems a bit . . . excessive.'

'I don't know if it's necessary. How can I know? All I know is that there is some kind of conspiracy which is worldwide and seems to have enough clout to control the Procurator Fiscal in Gairnock. Chalmers is obviously worried about who he can tell within the police force. It seems to go to the top in MCI but it may also go to the top elsewhere as well.'

'You mean governments?'

'Who knows? I'm freezing. Shall we try a primus stove for a while?'

In the morning their will broke and they made their way to the valley. The weather broke too. A front swept in from the West and soaked them to the skin as they descended. They changed into dry things by the car, standing naked in the roadway in a lonely glen watched by a herd of inquisitive cows.

As they climbed into the car Allan said, 'Thanks, lads. That was something special.'

Ian squeezed the water out of his trousers and said, 'Y'know, I think that was the best three days of my life!'

Jean's idea of a farewell do was to press-gang Allan into making up the numbers of an SNP demo. He protested, but his protests were half-hearted and he went along. His feelings of guilt, of deserting Jean, were enhanced by the deterioration in

Roddy's health, but the old man still seemed to be inordinately proud of him.

'So they're sending you to South America,' he said. 'They must think an awful lot of you, son. Be sure to visit your cousin in Seattle.'

They marched to the site at Bannockburn and listened to speeches, including one from Andrew Coltart. Colourful invective was his refrain. It was amusing for the faithful and made good headline items but Allan kept wanting to tell him that the insulted seldom became the converted. His main target was the Labour Party and his thesis was that Labour was the unwitting tool of the 'Westminster Establishment', a harmless repository for the votes of the Scottish electorate, a dumping ground which could never threaten the unassailable control which the Establishment had over Westminster. It was good tub-thumping stuff and got a lot of cheers. He also gave them a warning about opinion polls, which he claimed were manipulated by the Establishment.

'Scotland will not be free,' he roared, 'of the Westminster yoke, until the Scottish electorate ends its love affair with the Labour Party or the Labour Party in Scotland ceases to be the harlot of Westminster.'

The crowd cheered him hysterically. A pop group sang Scottish songs to steel guitars at a volume which imploded Allan's ears, and then the rain came down and soaked them.

Afterwards they all went to a pub in Stirling. Allan found himself wedged between a sober man in a navy-blue suit and a woman whom everyone called 'Hettie' and who had had too much to drink. Hettie wanted to get her arm round him. The sober man drank orange juice and looked as though he was suffering as Allan was with the din, the congestion and the tobacco smoke. He turned to Allan.

'What did you think of Andra's speech?'

'I think I agree with a lot of what he says, but the way he says it tends to put some people off.'

'Aye. He is a bit of a street fighter.'

'I don't believe his theory about the opinion polls though,' said Allan.

'Why don't you believe it?' said the man, suddenly alert.

'How could they do it?'

'Opinion polls,' said the man, warming to the subject, 'are based on samples. Each opinion poll company has its own way of constructing the sample, based on representative groups of the population, a kind of cross-section. Each canvasser is told to interview ten or twenty or fifty people made up of people in the same proportion as the cross-section. It would not be hard to weight that cross-section to give a bias to the results. You only need to modify ten returns in a sample of a thousand to give a two percent swing to the result. There are no official checks on the results. No watch dogs.'

'What good would it do them?'

'If they made out that an election was a close-run thing, the middle parties would be squeezed and folk who might be inclined to vote for the SNP might opt instead for Labour. Of course, they can't risk being too wrong when the actual results are announced so they have to have "a late swing".'

'Are you serious?'

'Deadly,' said the man.

Allan shook his head. He wondered if the man really was sober. There was no smell on his breath but he had in his eye the intoxication of fanaticism.

'Do you think they are too nice?' said the man. 'Do you think they don't have the resources to do it? Do ye think people who would murder Jack Kennedy or Willie McRae would think twice about fiddling a few polls? Ah tell you, it's gaun t'get worse. We're heading for the big bang. We've got the British elections soon, this year anyway, the Euro-elections, the American presidential elections and now we've also got the Eastern European countries in the act. The motivation for fiddling or influencing the results couldnae be greater. With the technology we have today there is no need for them to send out the Imperial Guard to cut down the revolting peasants. They just manipulate the supply of information and the peasants vote the way they're tell't.'

At closing time they debouched on to the pavement. A group

was already there and began singing 'Flower of Scotland'. Jean was drunk. She was in a group close behind. Allan could hear her saying, 'That's my wee brother. He's . . . he's a genius . . . no . . . A'm serious . . . An' he's going to South America to work for some bloody multinational. A don't think he should go. Do you think he should go? . . . no . . . but do you think he should go?'

She gave Allan the keys and he drove them back to Maryhill. Uncle Roddy was asleep and so was Jean, when he let himself out of the flat.

Allan chopped his spaghetti small so that he could fork it easily. Other times he had tried with the spoon and the twirling fork trick. It wasn't so hard, but the stuff tasted the same whichever way you did it, so what was the point? He waited, glancing at her several times. At last he said, 'So did you get it?'

Dianne was doing the full Italian thing but the effect was spoiled a bit by the way the strands of spaghetti flailed her lips. She sucked an errant one into her pouting mouth, dabbed away the bolognaise sauce with a paper napkin and said, 'No.' She took a sip of wine and then twirled again. 'This is a nice place,' she said. 'How did you find it?'

'Jack and I come here for a pizza when we want to talk. You couldn't find it then?'

'No. Well, not really. I didn't look exactly. I walked into his study and said, "Can I have the tape you made of Allan and Rosa Telman talking?" ' She said it in a flat voice, very casual.

'You didn't!'

'I did!' She took some more wine and made a face. 'The food's good but I'm afraid this is plonk.'

'Sorry.'

'Not your fault – I ordered it.'

'What did he say?'

'He pretended for a minute not to understand. "What tape?" he said, and I said, "The tape Allan found the night he climbed in your window." '

'Dianne!' Allan put his fork down. Elbows on the table, he

covered his eyes, not knowing whether he should laugh or cry.
'You don't mess about, do you?'

'What's the point? I wasn't going to rake around in his den
when he wasn't there. Not my style. He said, "Why are you
asking?" all huffy, and I said, "I want to give it to Allan as a
going-away present." '

'And what did he say to that?'

'He hummed and hawed for a bit. He said something about
"company policy" but that was just bluster. Then he said, "Tell
that young man of yours" . . . Did you know you were my
young man?' She laughed and took more wine. 'Anyway, he
said, "Tell that young man of yours that he had better be careful, especially when he gets to Ocean Springs." '

'Was he mad?'

'He wasn't angry, if that's what you mean, not really, more
worried. He's been behaving in a funny way ever since that
friend of his, Seaton, committed suicide.'

'In what way funny?'

Dianne finished her spaghetti and dabbed her mouth. She
said, 'He's been drinking a lot, and he's started forgetting
things. He looks worried out of his mind. He had a big row
with Mummy.'

'Is she worried about him?'

'She's leaving him. Shall we ask for the menu again?'

They settled on profiteroles and fruit salad.

'That must be upsetting for you,' Allan said when the waiter
had vanished.

'What is?'

'Your parents splitting up.'

Dianne was either totally unconcerned or acting cool. 'Don't
be silly. Mummy will be a lot better off without him. She's
going back to Sussex where her family lives. Her brother has
the ancestral pile.'

'What will you do?'

'Oh, Charles is being transferred to London. He's got a flat
there. He's asked me to marry him. The profiteroles are for
me,' she said, seeing the waiter hovering.

Allan was learning. He took a spoonful and ate slowly. He said, 'This is nice. How are your profiteroles?' and then caught her grinning at him. She said, 'You haven't asked.'

'Asked what?' Dead innocent.

'Asked whether I'm going to marry him or not, you bastard! Don't you care?'

'Oh that!' He put down his spoon. 'I hope you'll be very happy.'

She said 'Bastard!' again, but she was laughing.

Two more spoonfuls. A suitable pause and then he said, 'Well, will you? I can't see you in domestic bliss somehow.'

'Neither can I . . . I'll give it a whirl maybe . . . Not marry. But I'll probably move in and see whether I like the guy.'

'Don't you know?'

'Not really. A yacht and a Porsche tend to obscure a girl's real feelings.'

Allan was shaking his head. Laughing. 'You're going to make somebody a horrible wife.'

'But a bloody good mistress,' said Dianne. 'But getting back to Daddy, I'm worried about him.'

'I thought you didn't like him. Coffee?'

'Yes, please. I don't like him, but I didn't say I didn't love him. He is my dad. Anyway – after he showed me the tapes . . .'

'Tapes! Did you say "tapes" – plural?'

'Yes. Didn't I tell you? He has a box of them. What I don't understand is how he's got the time to listen to them. Anyway, he came down to breakfast the next morning and that was unusual. Usually he's away before I'm awake. But he came down all grumpy. He'd been drinking. He sat down, took some black coffee and said, "Tell Allan Fraser I'd like to have a word with him – in private." '

Meeting places. Everybody had them and their choice said something about them. Halpern chose a country inn, with a carvery and wines at fancy prices and waiters who could spot a substantial tipper at a thousand paces. A suspected non-tipper, like, for example, someone turning up on a bike, someone like

Allan, was waiter-invisible. It was Saturday afternoon, so the place was busy. At a rough estimate the car park had a quarter of a million's worth of automobile soaking up the weak wintry sunlight. Rooks wheeled with ratchet calls in the tall trees behind the car park.

Allan thought about their meeting place. Halpern could have called Allan into his office and told his secretary not to disturb them. He didn't do that. He could have called Allan on the internal phone or sent a memo in a buff envelope. He didn't do that either. He used Dianne to convey the message and he chose this toffee-nosed joint for their chat. That said a lot about MCI. And if anyone knew about MCI, Halpern knew.

'Of course you don't, do you?' said Halpern, veering the bottle away from Allan's glass. 'Pity. This is rather a good wine.'

Allan's open-faced sandwich looked better than it tasted. The beef was stringy. Halpern had a stuffed cabbage leaf. It smelled spicy. He put the bottle back in its ice-bucket and said, 'So you're off to South America. When exactly?'

It was a good act. If Dianne had not forewarned him he might have been taken in – for a while. The old assurance seemed to be there, but Halpern's eyes were constantly on the move, like a fighter pilot checking for enemy planes coming out of the sun.

'On the tenth . . .' He stopped himself saying 'Sir'.

'Looking forward to it?'

'Very much.' Allan spoke quietly, keeping his eyes on Halpern, wary, watching, waiting to spot the ace appearing from the sleeve.

'I wanted a word,' said Halpern, attacking his plate, 'because I thought I could give you some advice.'

'That's very kind of you.' Still the quiet voice, expressionless.

'Several bits of advice in fact. . .' – Halpern switched on the charming smile – '. . . and the first one is – don't go climbing in any windows, will you?'

'I'll try to avoid any necessity for that,' said Allan.

Halpern said, 'Oh, very good. Very diplomatic. That's me put in my place. Hasn't it? But about that, Allan, I believe, from

something Dianne said the other night, that when you climbed
into my study you saw something you shouldn't have seen.'

'I believe I saw something which should not have been there,
yes.'

Halpern studied his face for a moment and then held up a
finger. A waiter materialised instantly. 'I think my young friend
would like some horseradish for his sandwich.' He pointed,
avoiding Allan's eye. Allan said nothing but pointedly ignored
the sauceboat when it arrived.

'What you have to understand,' said Halpern, taking some
wine, 'is that in a company like MCI there are many projects
being carried on and some of these are very hush-hush. It's not
just the defence contracts, you know. To keep our competitive
edge we need to keep the opposition guessing.' More wine.
A look at Allan to check his reaction. 'From time to time
an enthusiastic employee might stumble upon one of these
projects.'

Allan put his knife and fork down. He folded his hands in his
lap, looking straight at Halpern, cool, in control of himself, but
angry. Halpern was looking at his own plate and he was still
talking.

'It is also necessary for a company such as ours to keep an
eye on its employees, to ensure that their enthusiasm does not
get out of bounds. It's been known, for example, for some
employees to start up a little project of their own, quite unofficially and for that project to encroach on some official
project and cause difficulties.' Now at last he looked up and
met Allan eye to eye. 'We don't like that,' he said. 'It's very ill
advised.'

Allan just went on looking. Halpern blinked first. He glanced
round the room then went back to his plate.

'I am giving you this advice, Allan, in a friendly way,' he
said, talking to the plate. 'At the moment this is completely
unofficial. I have kept what I know to myself and if the problem
stops here it will go no further. However, if the problem were
to continue when you are in South America, I would not be
able to protect you, Allan.'

When Allan said nothing Halpern added, 'Do you under-stand that, Allan?'

Allan said, 'I'm not sure that I do understand you, but I'll think about it.'

'Do that,' said Halpern. He turned his attention to his stuffed cabbage. For a moment the old confidence was back in his voice.

Allan finished his sandwich. He sat back. 'Tell me,' he said. 'What exactly have you been protecting me from?'

The last fork-load of cabbage stopped in mid-air and then returned to the plate.

'Look, Fraser.' The façade of cool detachment was slipping. The eyes were darting about again, especially at the glass doors, where a couple in ski-pants and matching Pringle jumpers had just come in. Talking in very loud voices. Putting on a performance for the other diners. Halpern lowered his voice. 'Don't push your luck. Stop poking and prying into things which do not concern you. And drop this silly thing with Rosa Telman. You could have a future in the company. She has none. I could help you, Allan. All I ask is a little co-operation.'

Bingo! That was it. Everything else was bullshit. Allan waited to let the dust settle on that one and then said very quietly, 'To do what?'

Halpern took a drink, rather a large one. There was a trem-ble in his hand as he put the glass down. He met Allan's eye for a moment and then looked away.

'It's a pleasant afternoon,' he said. 'Would you care for a stroll? There's a forest path in the woods behind the inn.'

He had a stick in the car and walked at a military pace. He pointed out a magpie. He seemed to know about birds. Deep in the trees he said, 'It's like this, Allan. I could use an intelli-gent pair of eyes and ears in Ocean Springs.'

Allan played innocent. 'What exactly? . . . can you explain? . . . how could I do that? . . . how would I communicate? . . . what kind of data? . . .' and Halpern spilled. He wanted to know more about the inner workings of the Labyrinth operating system. He was particularly keen to know about anti-hacking devices. When could a user be identified and so on. Communication would be easy and secure. Halpern would be at the Ocean Springs heads' conference. 'In July,' said Halpern. 'It's been put back a month. I'm told the Labyrinth operating system development has hit snags. I think the delay has something to do with that.'

Allan let him believe they had an agreement. In return for information, Halpern would keep quiet about Allan and Rosa's project, would make it easy for Rosa to get a Senior Fellowship at the university of her choice, funded by MCI, and would do his best to promote Allan's career. The career thing did not worry Allan. But he calculated that Halpern would not understand and would be suspicious of a person who did not put his own career above all else. So he tried to look keen. The Rosa thing did matter. It was what she wanted.

Thinking back to their meal together, Allan wondered if he should have been using a longer spoon.

18

MARCH

Rosa spent the last weekend with him at Burnside Cottage, busying herself with domestic things. Allan tried to help her do things he didn't think needed doing but eventually gave up and left her to it. She had brought food and made supper but the sexual thing between them did not arise. She seemed just to want to chat. Allan did not know and did not ask what story she had told her husband, but as they sat with cocoa mugs by the fire she told him that she was intending to leave Maurice.

'I'm going to leave Gairnock altogether,' she said. 'My mind's made up. There's nothing left there now.'

'Where will you go?'

'Wensley has suggested that I get a fellowship at a university. There's an MCI fellowship grant and he says he'll put my name forwards. I think I'll take him up on it.'

'You've often said that that was what you wanted most, but you won't be able to work in the field.'

They both knew which field he meant.

'That doesn't matter to me anymore. It's run its course. I'm tired of fighting political battles. I just want a quiet life with something to keep my mind occupied. Will you keep in touch, Allan?'

So he told her his plan about using Hamish as a post-box address. She looked very puzzled.

'Why? I mean, why go to all that trouble? You don't seriously think anyone would get their noses into my correspondence?'

'I think they might.'

She was mystified and a little annoyed. 'This is paranoia, Allan.'

And so he told her – not every last detail, just enough – about Tommy Harkness being a police informer and about Chalmers and about the possibility that there was a conspiracy within MCI. She was angry.

'Why didn't you tell me, Allan?'

'I didn't think it would be safe for you.'

'I'm not a child. I'm your boss, for heaven's sake!'

'You're more than my boss, Rosa.' She blushed at that. 'And I'm only telling you now because you're getting out of MCI and I want you to take sensible precautions.'

'You've changed, Allan.' She seemed deflated. 'When you came you were just about the shyest thing I'd ever seen. But now you seem to be bursting with self-confidence and ready to run the whole show.'

'It's all your fault, Rosa.'

She came over and sat on his lap.

'What have I done?' she said, running her fingers through his hair. 'I've created a monster.' She leaned back, looking into his eyes. Her hands slid down the sides of his face to his shoulders.

He said, 'Are you by any chance measuring me for a neck-bolt?'

He had packed everything. As he looked round the old place he was surprised by his own sadness at the thought of not seeing it again. Two boxes, mostly of books and climbing gear, and his big suitcase had already been despatched. Only his rucksack and an airline hold-all remained with enough stuff for the last night. And the microcomputer, of course.

Rosa had offered to run him to the airport in the morning. He ran his hand over the smooth wooden back of the kitchen chair, browned with age and polished with use like a saddle. The wall above the mantelpiece looked naked without the picture of the Arisaig sands – the picture Rosa had given him. Only a picture postcard remained. A montage of 'Bonny Loch Lomond' and the scribbled note from 'Uncle Bob'. Tonight. Chalmers wanted to meet him at the lay-by tonight. Probably to say cheerio.

On the kitchen table the patch where he had removed the password was scrubbed clean.

The microcomputer sat incongruously in the centre. It had a cream and brown plastic case, and it jarred. Not a single other item of plastic was visible, only seasoned wood, stone worn with age, black iron and chipped china. The computer was squat and modern and ugly and . . . and threatening. It had not occurred to him before how alien it was in these surroundings. He remembered the words Jocylin had used . . . most eavesdropping gadgets these days are made to look like electric sockets . . . they would look out of place here.

The micro looked very out of place and as he looked at it the conviction grew that it was a malevolent presence.

The screws turned easily under the blade of a kitchen knife and the top of the case lifted easily too, exposing the expected array of chips and printed circuit boards and cables of multi-coloured wire. Without a schematic it was impossible to read the circuit, but he could identify the main components – transformer, battery voltage-multipliers, processor chip, memory chips and the like. No sign of anything like a microphone, but there was a square black chip, roughly the size of a pack of playing cards. No identifying label and very few connector tags. He could think of no function which would need a chunk of silicon that size. A monitoring device? It was an interloper. The interior of the case was custom-built to hold the layout, but a section of stiffening panel had been cut away crudely to accommodate the big black chip and the board it was mounted on had been pig-a-backed on another. The layout had been modified after the machine left the factory.

Was it possible that the device held some record of the work he had done on the machine? He had done no hacking with the micro, just his theory stuff. Legal, but private. And the machine had to be handed back 'for maintenance'. Pulverising it would be too drastic and hard to explain. Something more subtle. Something which could be put down to simple chip-failure.

He opened the drawer of the kitchen table – a blue paper-clad battery oozing pus and caked in verdigris, one yellow rubber kitchen glove for the left hand and with the index finger missing, a length of string with two knots in it, a length of baling wire folded into a hank, three coloured marbles of various sizes, a rusty tin-opener, a dried-up bottle of blue-black ink, assorted cutlery all of different patterns, mostly bent and with broken handles – Yuri Geller cast-offs perhaps – and two panic-stricken spiders.

He picked up the baling wire and bent it several times until he snapped off a section about six inches long. The rubber glove was too small to admit his hand but he could get his fingers into it. Holding the wire between thumb and second finger he leaned over the machine, switched it on and identified the power-pack. He found the high tension point which served the screen display and touched one end of the wire on to that point. Then he touched the other end on to each of the connection tags of the mysterious chip. A thin wisp of smoke ascended from the chip and there was a slight smell of burning.

When the smoke had dissipated there were no external signs of damage. He screwed the top of the case back on and closed the machine. It was ready for return. Rosa had a machine like his. He would explain to her on the way to the airport how he had dealt with the problem. She would be amused. He looked at his watch. Plenty of time for a nap before he set off for the lay-by to meet Chalmers.

He woke with a start. It was black dark. Match. Damn! He should have been at the lay-by already. Anorak. Bike out of the shed. Switch on headlamp. Nothing. He hit it with the side of his hand and the light came on but it flickered as he bounced down the track. A mist had formed.

A bridge. He had passed the lay-by. He stopped and walked back. The lay-by was twenty yards back, an old loop of road which had been by-passed like an ox-bow lake when they had straightened out the corner approaching the bridge. It dived away from the road behind bushes and trees.

There was a car. A Ford Sierra. Dark green. He leaned the bike against a tree. The courtesy light came on as he opened the door of the car. There was a brief-case in the back seat, its contents spilled across the seat and on the floor. Papers, a pair of leather gloves, a pocket calculator. Gold initials 'R.C.' tooled into the leather. There was a rubber torch in the door pocket

He took the torch and flashed it about. Bushes dripping with moisture. Soft drinks cans and fast-food packages littering the verge. Dark trees, tops lost in thick mist. A barbed wire fence with a stile. A narrow path leading from the stile up an embankment towards the railway line. Footprints in the mud. Lots of them. Sheep wool and shreds of grey cloth hanging on the uppermost wire at the stile.

Allan gave a low whistle and waited. The sound of water dripping. Far away the noise of a car horn. He stepped over the stile and followed the footprints. The path became black and gritty, covered in cinders. It climbed a steep bank between gorse bushes. Another fence at the top. No stile. He flashed the torch beyond. Lank foliage. Brambles. Black sleepers. Railway lines glinting silver in the torch beam. A bundle of material lying on the line. Clothing. He stepped over the fence and took a closer look. A body.

Fawn windproof jacket. Grey trousers. Shoes, brown, brightly polished. Allan looked down at his own shoes. Covered in mud with a dusting of black ash. He looked again at the body. No head.

He retched. A white object a few yards down the line to the right. A head. Neck and jaw smashed and bloody. Hair wet and plastered down on to the skull sequinned with fine water droplets. Eyes open. Staring. Bob Chalmers.

He retched again, an acidic taste in his mouth. He stepped quickly back over the fence.

Beside the Sierra he stood for a while, trying to think. He heard water dripping from the trees. What had he touched? The door handle on the outside. The door pocket. The torch. There was a box of Kleenex on the passenger seat. He opened the door again, took a tissue and wiped the things he had touched. He kept the torch.

He set off but stopped half a mile down the road and threw up.

19

MARCH

According to ancient Highland legend, the Cailleach Beur, or 'Old Witch of the Peaks', or 'Winter Hag', does battle with the Sun-God for supremacy, and the waxing and waning of her powers dictates the cycle of the seasons. Each spring, in late March or early April, when she realises that she is losing the fight, the Hag takes a fit of temper. She steals three days of storm from the depths of January and hurls them into the battle to gain a temporary advantage.

As Allan boarded the plane at Glasgow airport for the first hop to Heathrow the old Hag was at it again. The first green leaves might have been appearing on the trees, but the hills of Cowal were blanketed in white and sleet was driving in sheets across the airport tarmac.

'Buenos dias.'

The air hostess doing her thing with the cool professional smile. He stepped out of the plane on to the wobbly step-way and the sun hit him like a hammer directly on the top of his head. And this was supposed to be autumn! He shielded his eyes. No trees. A flat dust-brown desert.

That last leg of the trip flying along the Andes from Santiago to Copiapo had been spectacular. It made up for the others.

The long flight down the Atlantic had been boring. The hop from Montevideo to Santiago over the mountains had, disappointingly, been done at night and in the company of fat businessmen.

He had scanned the newspapers on board and at every stop, but the *New York Times*, *Le Monde* and the London *Times* were not interested in a body on a railway line in Scotland. He had had to wait for the connection for ten hours in Santiago. The airport had a plastic and concrete concourse like every other and he was left exhausted, tight-faced and with a feeling in his mouth as though he had been sucking aluminium. His only gain was a wallet full of pesos which he got with his MCI credit card – a tangible consequence of his salary increase.

The terminal building at Copiapo airport was a large wooden hut. He was lost amid luggage collection points and empty space and a few people talking rapidly in Spanish. He dug out his Spanish phrase book and looked around. In the far corner there was a row of enquiry desks, one of which had an illuminated sign with the MCI logo. There was no one at the desk but he hit the bell on the counter and waited. At the third press a door opened behind the next kiosk and a man with a white shirt and epaulettes looked round the corner and said something in Spanish.

Allan shook his head. '*Ingles por favor?*'

'Ocean Springs?'

Allan nodded.

'Wait there.' He pointed. 'Someone come in after.' He held up three fingers. '*Tres hora.* Maybe. Maybe tomorrow.'

'Can I get into the town?'

'You wanna go Copiapo?'

'Yes. *Si.*'

'Taxi.' The man pointed. 'Autobus.' He pointed in another direction.

Taxi sounded safer. Perhaps he would be fleeced but at least he would reach his destination. A bunch of taxi drivers were chatting over cigarettes, lean men with brown, deeply creased faces and check shirts.

'Copiapo? Hop in,' said one, opening a door after the initial abortive exchange in Spanish.

'What place?' said the man when they were hurtling down a straight, dusty, white concrete road.

'Hotel?'

'What name hotel?'

'Any hotel. *No mucho pesos.*'

The driver looked disappointed. The streets of Copiapo were crowded. Banners and flags festooned the shop fronts and the sound of angry, urgent voices emerged from every lamp post and every tree. The noise was dreadful. The taxi driver took Allan to the door of a low building with pink stucco walls and no windows. He also took too much money, reaching out to pick the notes from Allan's grasp as he thumbed through them, trying to determine the denominations.

The only opening in the outer walls of the Hotel San Miguel was a wide, dark entrance. Inside he found himself in a pleasant, cool courtyard with lots of greenery and a pool and a fountain in the centre. Rooms, dark, cool-looking rooms, opened off the courtyard through tall louvred doors which stood wide. The din of the street had gone. In one of the rooms was an enquiry desk with a small ornate brass bell. When he rang it, a woman with a broad face and broad hips appeared through a bead curtain.

'*Tiene una habitacion libre?*'

The phrase book told him the words but he had no idea how to pronounce them. The woman stared at him uncomprehendingly. He tried again.

'*Habla usted Ingles?*'

She wiped her hands on her apron and then let out a sudden piercing yell.

'Maria!'

A young girl of perhaps fourteen or fifteen appeared through the bead curtain. Although her youth was evident, she was already a very well-formed young woman. The older woman spoke rapidly and Maria disappeared. Allan stood with his rucksack and hold-all, not knowing if he had been told to go away or had been admitted. Shortly, Maria returned, bringing with her another, older girl in a blue dress and a clasp in her long black hair.

The girl in the blue dress spoke. 'Good afternoon. I speak English a little. Can I help?'

He wanted a bedroom for one night and some help in contacting MCI to arrange for transport. The girl in the blue dress was helping out of kindness. She worked in the bank next door. She smiled shyly and shook her head at his offer of payment. She fixed him up with a room and arranged to phone MCI in the morning. He'd get a message at the desk. He thought of asking her to have dinner but she was blushing. She'd get the wrong idea. So he began his South American adventure by lying out on his bed throughout the long afternoon, brushing off flies, sleeping off the exhaustion of travel.

And dreaming about Chalmers. The eyes watched him.

In the evening the hotel offered a plate of soup with a large island of beef in the middle, a reef of potatoes round it. Spoon, knife and a fork, together. He ate the soup with the spoon. Wispy white streamers floated in the soup. A raw egg. When nothing else had appeared, it dawned on him that he was supposed to make a second course of the meat and potatoes with the knife and fork. Once he had recovered from the culture shock, he found it was good – very good.

Morning. The Banco Americana had a marble entrance but the rest of the building was pink stucco like the hotel. No sign of the girl in the blue dress.

The town was not yet completely into shrink-wrap. Traditional leather and woven stuff. European-style clothes shops. Posh glassware. Food shops with smells of ham, coffee and tobacco like a wee general store in a Scottish village used to have. A man on horseback, wearing a poncho blanket and a wide-brimmed hat, mingled easily with cars and pedestrians in the crowded streets.

Allan bought a pastry, handing over a dirty bank-note. They were puzzled by his accent and amused by his dismal Spanish.

They turned him into a roadshow involving everyone in the shop, customers as well as staff. They gave him smiles but no change. Nor did they ask for any. All transactions were to the nearest note. He found out afterwards that this was the practical 'people's solution' to a national shortage of coins. In the street, lots of noise – music, words, lots and lots of words. The citizens were still being harangued by angry, excited voices from loudspeakers hung on every conceivable vantage point. Later, at the hotel, a message. He should make his own way to the Ocean Springs and ask for 'Geraldine' at the reception centre.

Decision time.

At the bank the girl in the blue dress was there. He explained what he wanted and she gave him directions and then when it was obvious that he was still mystified she went off and returned with a brochure for the bank that had a small map of the town. She marked the places he should try.

He found Bernardo's on the outskirts of town. The office was a dingy hut which reminded him of the ACME School of Motoring without the graffiti. There was also a corrugated iron shed and a number of cars and pick-up trucks in various stages of repair and disrepair lying about. Wheels and tyres and oil drums rusting in the sun. There was no one in the office but he heard a metallic knocking in the shed and eventually discovered Bernardo in an inspection pit under a rusty bus.

'*Buenos dias señor. Automovile?*'

Single nouns. Grammar was beyond him. Bernardo was fat with greasy overalls, a droopy moustache and a tendency to talk at the speed of a football commentator. Allan got him to slow down and do the single noun codeword thing. And hand signals. He settled on a yellow Dodge pick-up truck, four years old and rusty, but it went. Allan was no expert. Bernardo soon spotted that and tried to get him to look at another which had better paintwork but Allan stuck to his choice of the Dodge.

Allan waved his credit card and pointed. 'Banco Americana.'

So the deal was done. Allan returned to the bank and drew the cash. Two hours later he was the proud owner of his first

car and an hour after that he had acquired tools, spare petrol
can, two spare tyres, spare battery, water can, road maps, jeans,
check shirt like the taxi drivers and a gaucho hat. If MCI were
trying to set him an initiative test he had decided to pass it in
style.

OK, Chalmers. How am I doing so far?

'How did you get here, Dr Fraser?'

Geraldine was a large lady, 'a good armful' as Jack would
have said. She wore loose-fitting cotton trousers with a floral
print, which were caught in at the ankles and waist with elastic,
and a matching top which didn't quite cover her midriff. The
hair was streaky blonde/brunette, the spectacles large and
tinted. She had a Southern drawl.

'I drove.'

An understatement. Teeth clenched, gears grinding, controls cack-handed, roads mirror-reversed, road-signs
unintelligible, angry horns exploding around him, taxi-drivers
firing salvos of invective. More like his own personal D-Day
landing.

Geraldine said, 'We weren't expecting you till tomorrow,
Doctor.' She consulted notes on her desk. 'I'll just fix your
badge.' She searched through a filing drawer and extracted a
plastic badge which showed his picture. It slotted into a lapel
badge.

'Now I'd better take you to Dr Olafsen and I'll show you
where we've put you later. We've assigned you an apartment in
the Gracewell Tower. I'll come with you, but I'll just let Dr
Olafsen's secretary know we're coming.'

She punched buttons on the telephone and spoke to someone.

'. . . Dr Fraser? Dr . . .' – she looked at her notes – '. . . Allan
Fraser . . . from Scotland in England.'

Allan contemplated the strangulation of Geraldine but
decided to let it pass.

'. . . today . . .' She looked at him over the top of her tinted
glasses. '. . . He drove . . . He's here . . . no, right now, he's

standing in front of me . . . I'll bring him over . . . no, I'm bringing him now.'

She put the phone down with more force than was necessary and reorganised her face into a fixed smile.

'Right,' she said. 'I'll come with you. Where did you leave your car?'

She walked with exaggerated hip movement like a ship in a heavy sea, but hoved-to when she saw the dust-caked Dodge.

'I guess I'd better take my buggy,' she said, '. . . to get back later. I'll lead you.'

She got into a thing which looked like a golfing caddie-car complete with awning. There were lots of them about. Seemed to be the favourite mode of transport within the complex. He ground the gears and followed jerkily in the Dodge through a network of avenues. There were two basic types of building – cream concrete and tan brick. They passed a shopping arcade and a golf-driving range. Middle-aged men with shuddering thighs and bellies were jogging the pathways with sweat bands round their hair.

The Halvorne Research Institute was one of the brick buildings, single-storied, with red tiled roof projecting well beyond the walls to throw the windows into deep shadow. Short, irregularly placed buttress walls projected out between the windows to form recesses and break up the uniformity of the exterior. To the rear it was connected by a rectangular piazza with arcades to a concrete tower block. As elsewhere, lawns filled the spaces between the buildings and the pathways. Besides the golf-buggies, there were a few highly polished saloons in the car park. The Dodge definitely lowered the tone.

Geraldine walked over to the entrance and stood there waiting for him, clip-board in hand. There was a card-reader on the doorway and to gain entrance they had to swipe their identifier badges through it.

'This is Dr Olafsen's department.'

The lobby was empty and she seemed doubtful about which way to turn until Allan pushed open the glass doors on the left.

There was only a single desk in the large office but it had the
proportions of a pocket aircraft carrier and was twice as complicated. Bits of it could be lowered into hidden recesses to
keep the working surface clear of the clutter of keyboards and
telephones and monitor screens. It had a control console of its
own, with lots of buttons which winked, and the woman with
red fingernails and the white off-the-shoulder dress who sat
behind it was playing a concerto on the buttons as they came
through the door. The white dress went nicely with her dark
olive skin and her black hair which was held in place with a red
band. Her spectacles were red too and they had wings. She did
not look up as they came in, but a hand with red talons waved
them towards a nest of chairs surrounding a coffee table and
another monitor screen. The screen was split into two windows. On one Tom and Jerry were doing grievous things to one
another. On the other window were the words: 'Dr Olafsen will
be free in (32) minutes.'

Geraldine was irritated. She hesitated and then said, 'When
you're through with Dr Olafsen just give me a ring and I'll take
you to your apartment.'

She handed him a card with her contact number and then
swaggered out of the room, pointedly ignoring the woman with
the winged spectacles, who returned the compliment.

Twenty minutes later the monitor on the table beside him
bleeped and the display which had counted its way down from
'(32) minutes' to '(12) minutes' changed to '(37) minutes'.
Tom and Jerry had been replaced by Popeye.

Ten minutes later the screen bleeped again. An extra message appeared. It said 'Thank you for your patience. Coffee is
available in the vestibule vending machine.'

He could see the door to Olafsen's room and a couple of
times a man who might have been the elusive Olafsen popped
out and back in again. On the second occasion he stopped and
leaned over to examine a diary on the secretary's desk. He discussed something briefly with the secretary, turning pages
rapidly, and shot a quick glance at Allan, but then rushed back
into the room without a word and shortly afterwards the screen

display clocked up another 20 minutes' delay. Tom and Jerry replaced Popeye.

Half an hour, two cups of coffee, a magazine and forty-three dirty tricks (on Tom by Jerry) later Allan went to the desk and asked to use the phone. He punched Geraldine's number.

'I'm ready to see my apartment now.'

'Oh good. You've seen Dr Olafsen?'

'Yes. I've seen him – I think.'

He put the phone down before she could respond and went outside to wait for her. As he did so, he noticed, with some satisfaction, that the lady with the winged spectacles had her mouth open.

Geraldine's buggy again led him through the mesh of avenues to the Gracewell building. It was one of the concrete sub-species and it was a tower block. The apartment was on the tenth floor with a view that looked West and took in the conference centre and the two-hundred-foot fountain. The décor and fittings were soulless motor-lodge but comfortable and clean. Toilet and shower were en suite. Tall louvred doors opened on to a small verandah with curved mock-Spanish railings. The doors stood open to admit a welcome breeze.

He asked about the boxes which had been sent on and was told how to collect them. She gave him a 'Welcome Pack' which included a map of the complex and a Bible. There were also papers to sign – bank accounts, lease of the apartment and so on.

When she had gone he lay on the bed and looked at the too-low ceiling and wondered if he could thole the place. He reminded himself that this was not America. It wasn't even Chile. It was 'Modernia', that non-nation state with a foothold in every airport and along every motorway where the currency is plastic and the language is in pictograms. In 'Modernian' you can say what is permissible and what is forbidden but you can't write poetry. Anyone can get to be a Modernian. All you have to give up is your roots.

When he woke the room was crimson. He leapt up and went to the window. The western sky was a furnace of flaming

clouds. From the verandah he could see that the clouds went
all the way from the horizon to directly overhead and beyond,
creating the effect of standing in a huge, inverted bowl. A
thought struck him. He hurried out and took the stairs three at
a time until he burst out on to the roof through the service
door. A distant wall of blood-red mountains stretched along
the eastern edge of the desert as far as could be seen in either
direction, abrupt, clear and jagged.

Sherman Olafsen wore his blue button-down denim shirt outside his pants and as he spoke he flicked his shoulder-length
hair away from his face with a toss of his head. Mid-thirties
with a slow Boston accent, he had a disdainful air, and he was
not pleased. He was not used to people walking out on him. He
was certainly not used to a newcomer walking into the department and introducing himself to a member of his team.

Jake Learner had taken Allan round the department and
introduced him to half the staff and then taken him along to
the coffee room at half-past ten where they bumped into
Olafsen. Jake was surprised, not to say appalled, when he discovered that Allan's introduction was a piece of DIY. Olafsen
shrivelled Jake with a look and took Allan along to his office.

'I expect to meet newcomers myself, Fraser,' he said, 'and to
introduce them to the members of my team at an appropriate
time. I do not expect them to walk in calmly and get involved
without my even knowing.'

'I know you're a very busy man, Dr Olafsen. I didn't think
my arrival was important enough to disturb you.'

Later Jake took him to the canteen in the basement of the
tower block to which the Institute building was adjoined. It was
almost identical to the canteen in the Gairnock plant.

'You're a marked man, Fraser,' he said as they stood in line
for service. 'I don't think anyone's ever done that to Sherman
before and certainly not anyone from England. He's not keen
on Englishmen.'

'Ah well,' said Allan. 'I'm not too smitten by them myself.'

He could see Jake's brow wrinkle as he tried and failed to

work that one out. Anticipating more fun, Allan let the misunderstanding run on. They took their trays to a table where others in the group were sitting and Jake introduced him. He had met some of them already.

They were a casual bunch. No sign here of the Marble livery. Long hair and pony-tails were common; jeans and sneakers were universal. Some wore bands round their foreheads like tennis players. Jake had a bracelet on his wrist and earrings. They were all young, mostly American, but there was a sprinkling of other nationalities. Allan heard a French accent. There was a round-faced Scandinavian, and quite a few oriental faces. They were mostly men, but there was an Afro-American girl called Iris, and a woman called Marylin McIndoe, who wore an Indian feather and a leather shirt with dangly bits. She spoke like Damen Runyan.

'What's your speciality?' said a tall, skinny guy called Joe. He had a wobbly Adam's apple and eczema.

'I was interested in program correctness proofs but Dr Olafsen has put me in "Software Support," ' said Allan.

'Another egghead,' said Gordon, who was black and seemed to be the oldest in the group. 'Sherman never lets strangers into his own team. It's a kind of priesthood. Any idea what section of software support?'

Allan shook his head. 'I'm supposed to see a guy called. . . ' – he pulled a piece of paper out of his pocket – '. . . called Tomasco this afternoon.'

'Willie's OK,' Marylin said. 'Willie'll give you an easy time. Thinks "*Mañana*" too much hassle.'

Willie Tomasco was small and fat and he sweated a lot. His office was on the fifth floor of the Elvira Tower, which was the concrete block behind the Institute. If you came to it in the normal direction it was at the front and the Institute was tucked out of sight.

Unlike Olafsen, Willie saw him straight away. The office was MCI vernacular – wrap-around tinted plate-glass windows protected by verandahs from the noonday sun, mahogany-effect desk, cream and tan leather-effect chairs – a tidy, functional room with just a few pictures of Tomasco's family to make it personal, and yet somehow Willie had contrived to make it chaotic. It wasn't the desktop. That was a model of business efficiency. And it wasn't the piles of computer paper which stood like chess pieces on the conference table which filled half of the room. It was Willie himself. He was coming apart, mostly at the waist, but his hair also appeared to be disintegrating and his manner was vague and disorganised. But Allan was to learn later that this was a superficial impression, for Willie knew what he was about.

'Fraser? Oh yeah. Sherman left a message.' He shuffled a few bits of paper on his desk and picked up a manilla folder with a note clipped to it.

'Said could I use you? What's your field, Fraser?'

He opened the folder and flipped through it as he spoke.

'Program correctness proofs.'

'That's Sherman's own field. Why doesn't he use you himself?' He waved Allan into a seat and sat down himself behind the desk. He leaned back and linked his fingers across his stomach in a thumb-twiddling pose.

Allan said, 'I get the impression that I'm surplus to requirements.'

Willie smiled and shook his head sadly.

'Yeah. I get the picture. How are things in England these days?'

'I don't know. I haven't been there recently.'

Willie's eyes narrowed. He said nothing. Allan thought, 'Why am I doing this? I'm becoming as belligerent as Jean.' He explained. 'I'm not English, Mr Tomasco. It's a sore point with Scots that everyone keeps thinking our country is just a region of England.'

Tomasco studied him for a moment and then his face wrinkled slowly into a quiet smile.

'OK, son. I'll remember. How about we take a walk round and talk to the guys? Then I could pop you round, a few weeks here and a few weeks there. I know you're a clever guy, Allan.

I've got your CV here.' He waved the manilla folder. 'But I need to see how you fit in. After a month or so we'll have another chat and come to some understanding about where you'd like to work and where you'll be useful to me. How about that?'

'Sounds OK to me, Mr Tomasco.'

'Willie.'

'Sounds OK, Willie.'

Afterwards in his own room.

'Don't look at me like that, Chalmers. Couldn't afford to get stuck in Olafsen's team doing the same theory stuff all over again. Need access to the network and to the operating systems. OK? It'll be low profile stuff from now on. Promise.'

Maintenance is the halitosis of computer programming. Everyone knows it's there but no one wants to be seen in its company. It means going through other people's programs and modifying them. It means no scope for ego trips.

Maintenance was a sub-department of Software Support. It occupied three floors in the Elvira Building and it was also Willie's empire. He was responsible for several teams and he seemed to be on good back-slapping terms with everyone. He wandered, with Allan in tow, from unit to unit much the way Rosa had taken him around her team. Again Allan found it impossible to remember names.

Some teams looked after particular bits of software like an operating system or an accounting package. Every day, from around the world, complaints and reports on difficulties poured into the network. Every complaint was numbered and every one had to be followed up. Customers were given short-term help by staff local to their area but in the longer term the teams under Willie Tomasco were responsible for eliminating the source of these difficulties. They were the heavy brigade. They were the cavalry. The buck stopped with them.

The operating system of a computer is the program which breathes life into the machine. It controls all other programs. It

decides where files will be stored and who should get access to
them and when, so that two users cannot interfere with each
other's work. It prevents one user hogging the machine at the
expense of others. It tidies up after a user has left the system. It
is the computer's harbour master. Without an operating system
a computer is a useless heap of silicon and copper.

The operating system of a large multi-access computer has
been described as the most complicated artifact of mankind,
and Allan saw no reason to disagree with that. Bugs, or errors,
could live in an operating system throughout its operating life,
without ever being resolved. Since the program was written by
several people, usually four or five but sometimes a lot more,
no one person ever knew the entire system with total intimacy.
Small defects could hide there in the shadowy gaps between the
brightly lit areas of knowledge and the effort required to
squeeze the last few bugs out of a system was often out of all
proportion to their importance.

The maintenance team for each piece of software issued bul-
letins and bits of program called 'software fixes'. These were
sent through the network to the troops at the front line. They
were designed to correct or bypass the errors and difficulties
the customers found. Later, the fixes were incorporated into a
new, numbered, sub-version 'release' and the numbering went,
say, from version 5.3.1 to 5.3.2. Upgrade tapes would be sent
to all customers who paid their annual maintenance contract
fees and all the recommended modifications would be made
automatically.

The step, say, from 5.3.2 to 5.4 was more significant and
would involve a reissue of the whole operating system on a single tape. The upgrade by a whole number, say, from 5.4 to 6.0,
meant a rewrite of the whole system, incorporating new ideas
and introducing a whole new set of bugs and errors which
would be gradually squeezed out over a period of years as the
system crawled its way up from 6.0 to 6.0.1 and onwards.

Of course, every version had to remain fully documented,
because some customers continued to use old versions of the
system and went on finding rare errors which had escaped

detection. Removal of support from a version of the operating system was a significant step which could alienate customers and lose business. So there was a huge job for the assistants who maintained the documentation. All of the documentation was stored on the computer network and was fully accessible from every outpost of the MCI empire.

'They're short-handed in the OS65 team,' Willie said. 'I'd like you to start there so that we can see how you shape up. Remember, getting on and co-operating with the other guys is as important as being a brilliant programmer. No one can do it all by himself.'

'OK, Willie.'

Rosa's letter was friendly but subdued. She enclosed news-paper cuttings about Bob Chalmers' death. The official verdict was suicide.

20

MARCH/APRIL

'Welcome to "The Undertakers".' Silvester patted Allan on the back. He had a pony-tail and moccasins.

'Why "Undertakers"?'

' 'Cos we're putting OS65 to rest. Company trying to phase it out, see. Unglamorous, eh? You mind that?'

'Not a bit.'

'Good. Most of our boys been taken over to OS-LAB, the Great White Hope. They say it's way behind schedule and full of bugs. Anyway, '65's still got a few beauties of its own and we still gotta fix 'em. Here's the file of registered bugs. You take this one. See the date reported is here. You got print-outs, problem reports. See here? See what you can do. Fill in the fix report here. Bring it back to me an' I'll show you what we do next.'

The library was good. Not just on computers. Maps of the mountains. He took photocopies. Guidebooks. Not many. The guidebooks said the maps were bad – drawn straight from aerial photographs without ground triangulation. All warped. But better than nothing.

'Have you been to the mountains?' he asked them.

'Been to El Paso,' they said.

'What's it like?'

'Dude ranch. It belongs to the company. They show you how to saddle a horse or throw a lariat.'

'How often do you go?' he asked.

'Been there last year sometime,' said one.

'Me too. Year before. It's OK. Might go again,' said another.

'Ever been anywhere else in the mountains?'

Headshakes, shoulder shrugs.

'Do you know of anyone in Springs goes to the mountains?'

More headshakes.

Friday night. Alone. He camped near a village and watched a blood-red sunset.

Saturday morning. A crowd of inquisitive urchins watched his every move. They peeked into his tent as he slept. They watched him open-mouthed as he cooked. They giggled uncontrollably as he ate and, most embarrassing of all, made it almost impossible for him to pee or shit. Take note – keep away from villages.

The mountains were like no others he knew. No vegetation. Dust dry and appallingly hot. Take note – plan routes for maximum shade.

The height he could reach was governed by how much water he could carry from the small river in the bottom of the valley. Note – get more water bottles.

Sunday evening back to 'Springs'.

'Alone in the mountains! You not lonely?'

'No. Never.'

Never when he was alone. Only when he was surrounded by people with whom he had little in common.

'Why don't you drop round to the Flamingo bar this evening? They make the best Manhattans outside Big Apple.'

'Tried the Aconcagua Club? – play the wheels or shoot crap.'

'What's your handicap? We're looking for someone to make up a foursome.'

'Have you tried the games room? It's in Elvira. First floor.'

Curious, he wandered round to the games room that
evening. Jake was there with full helmet, gauntlets and boots,
clawing away at empty space before him. Jake offered him a
turn with the equipment and to his amazement Allan found
that when he put the helmet on he was confronted by a rock
face. With the gloves on he could move two virtual hands on to
virtual holds on the virtual rock and, with his bottom supported by a stool, he could place his virtual booted feet on to
virtual footholds and climb the virtual cliff. The real magnifi-
cent thing was just twenty miles away.

That night he hung the picture of the Arisaig sands on his
bedroom wall.

His driving was improving. He lacked experience with city traffic but he could handle the truck well on the open road and
that was just as well, because the open road was hairy at times,
especially in the mountains. On the narrow, unmetalled single-
track roads an encounter with another vehicle was an event of
some consequence which often involved both drivers getting
out, passing the time of day, offering cigarettes and negotiating
terms to allow one another to pass.

According to the map, the village of Casserone was at the
end of the road, but he had found that a passable track continued up the valley and he had formed a plan. Some of the
outlying ranches were served by a bus-service or more correctly a truck-service. He calculated that if he left his Dodge at
the farthest ranch he would be able to cross the mountains to
the North into the next valley and then by truck-service return
to get his wheels back. Even if that was not possible, the farthest ranch was near high, steep mountains and would be a
good base for a bit of exploration.

There was one snag.

He had forgotten his Spanish-English dictionary, so as he
drove, leaving a comet trail of dust and stour, the wheel leaping and jerking in his hands, he ran his tongue over the
questions he would ask. What was the word for bus/truck

again – *camino* – that was it. *Esta camino passa aqui?* – Does a truck pass here? It was later, when he got back to Ocean Springs and to the life-support system of the dictionary, that he learned the difference between *camion* (a lorry) and *camino* (a roadway). That explained a lot.

Theresa made her way towards the orange grove, picking up sticks as she went. The bundle in her arms was already quite heavy. The orange grove was surrounded by a fringe of bushes and these were a good source for sticks. She stopped to pick up another and then realised that with its shape and thickness she could, with a piece of rag, make a good doll with it. Carefully she placed it on a stone, to be retrieved later. Her mother, practical as ever, would simply see it as good kindling. As she straightened, her eye caught an unusual flash of bright yellow in the bushes ahead. A yellow dress? It was too large for a dress and as she approached she saw that it was a vehicle. It was parked beside her father's orange grove. She saw a movement in the bushes and stopped. Theresa was a brave girl. At ten years old she could do a full day's work at weekends and in the evenings after school was a genuine help to her mother with the baking and sweeping and, as now, gathering kindling. Her father worked desperately hard for the orange grove and she would defend it to the death. She crept forwards on her bare brown feet.

A tall, lean man was bending beside the yellow truck, fumbling with a bundle of orange fabric. He was pale coloured – a Gringo. Her father said that all Gringos were mad. Theresa put down her bundle of sticks so that she could run away more easily. She crouched down behind a bush and watched. The man stretched the orange-coloured fabric out on the brown earth and pushed some long bendy rods into it. He opened a small satchel of the same type of fabric and poured its contents on to the ground. Pieces of metal, sharp spikes which glittered like silver fish, poured on to the ground. He picked some of these up and went round the perimeter of the big bundle, pushing the spikes into the soil and sometimes driving them deep with the soles of his big boots. Then, grasping the bundle in the cen-

tre, he lifted and the whole thing rose up and became like a big
beehive with a hole in the side. Again the man went round the
perimeter, poking the ends of the rods into the soil, and then
he bent down and crawled into the beehive. Theresa was
amazed and in her amazement she came round the side of the
bush to see better. At that moment the man put his head out of
the beehive and saw her standing there with her bare feet, print
dress and little apron, with her mouth open.

'Er – hello,' said the man. He spoke in a funny way, mispro-
nouncing the vowels and slurring words.

Theresa said nothing. She just stared, and then she turned
and ran back round behind the bush.

The man crawled out of the beehive and stood up. He went
over to the yellow truck and reached inside and then he was
walking towards her. His hand was offering her a bar of chocolate. She recognised the colour of the wrapping from the big
posters at the side of the road she had seen down at Casserone.
She had never tasted chocolate but one of her friends at school
had. Her hand went to her mouth. The man was close. She
stretched out her hand and took the chocolate.

'Good night,' said the man. 'Er . . . good day. Hello. Thank
you.'

Theresa still said nothing.

The man stretched out his hand, took the bar of chocolate
from her, broke it into pieces and offered her back the bundle
of broken pieces. He made signs for her to put a piece in her
mouth. She tried a piece. It was smooth and sweet. Now she
could tell Maria a thing or two.

'Please,' said the man and pointed over towards the dusty
jeep-track. He walked towards it and beckoned her. They stood
facing one another on the road. Theresa's mouth was jammed
with chocolate.

The man pointed at the roadway at their feet.

'A roadway pass here?'

His voice and his eyebrows lifted, indicating a question.
Theresa's brows knitted. She struggled to understand and then
nodded slowly.

'*Claro*,' she said, showing a mouthful of masticated chocolate.
The man pointed at the road again.
'And the roadway pass here tomorrow *to* Casserone?'
Theresa's eyes opened like saucers.
'*Claro.*'
'And the roadway pass here tomorrow *from* Casserone?'
Her father was right. The Gringo was mad. She took a step
back, nodding her head to placate him.
'And the roadway pass here next week?'
She turned and ran.

Later she returned with her father. She had a little bundle of
oranges wrapped up in her apron and the strange man took a
photograph of her sitting beside her gift.

Theresa's father, Jeronimo Arostica, was small with a dark
Indian face which wrinkled easily into a smile to show a row of
broken, discoloured teeth. His hands were hard and calloused
with labour but his heart was soft and generous. He invited
Allan to have a meal. Theresa and her mother served at table
while the men ate. Allan was self-conscious about that, but
knew it would have made them uncomfortable to break the tradition. Theresa was allowed to stand at her father's side and he
put an arm round her as he talked with Allan. Talk was not
quite the right word. They conversed but body language played
a major part in the conversation. Allan built a little relief map
of the area in the dust outside the door of the ranch and
explained his intentions. He drew roadways on the map and
made the noise of a truck as he traced the route. Jeronimo
nodded in agreement but was horrified and showed with his
hands how steep the mountains were. Allan pulled some photographs out of his document bag and showed Jeronimo
pictures of himself climbing crags and also on the West Face of
the Dru in the Alps. After supper they all came to watch him as
he demonstrated on a small crag near the house. Jeronimo
shook his head and patted Allan on the back. He had seen
everything now.

★ ★ ★

'You got plans for Togetherness Day?' Mrs Tomasco leaned over and put another waffle on his plate.

Allan said, 'Togetherness Day?'

'Willie not tell you?' She looked across the table at Willie in mock-exasperation. Willie swallowed a mouthful and dabbed his lips with the napkin he had tucked under his chin.

'We got lots of specials here,' he said. 'The guys in personnel think it's good for morale. We borrow all the Chilean National Days and invent a few more. This Monday coming is "Togetherness Day". Whole day off. Parades. Speeches. You know the kinda thing.'

Sarah, Willie's six-year-old, said, 'I'm in the parade.'

Willie said, 'I think Allan's a bit of a loner. Parades are not quite your thing, are they?'

Allan nodded, smiling.

'How are they treating you?' Mrs Tomasco asked Allan. 'Has Willie given you something interesting to do?'

'Oh yes. I'm fine,' said Allan.

'I was thinking,' said Willie. 'Has anyone said anything to you about Vesuvius?'

'No. Vesuvius the mountain?'

'Nup. Vesuvius the bug. It's got a proper number but everyone calls it Vesuvius. It doesn't erupt often but when it does you know you've been zapped.'

'No. No one said.'

'It's been around a long time and no one has been able to track it down. It would be nice to nail it down before we nail down the coffin lid on OS65. Maybe a fresh mind would see something. You could take a look.'

'Sure. I'd be glad to. Oh! One thing I wanted to ask you. Will you sign for me to get a micro out of stores so I can work evenings in my own room?'

'Sure.'

'Ain't you got something better to do evenings?' said Willie's wife. 'Young fella like you.'

The weekend of Togetherness Day Allan went off on his own

again. He drove down to Copiapo and stayed at the Hotel San Miguel. They remembered him. Saturday he drove North-East and tried the mountains there and planned an over-the-mountains trip from there to Jeronimo's place.

The sports centre at 'Springs' had every conceivable exercise machine but no climbing wall and the desert was depressingly horizontal. But the Shower Tower wasn't. Each window had its verandah which protected the window below it from the noonday sun, giving the vertical columns of windows the appearance of a stack of shelves. Between the columns there was a recess, a foot deep and five feet wide, running the full height. The whole building was fluted.

Allan stepped off the path and went over to the nearest recess. He could bridge the recess easily with a hand and foot on either wall. A perfect way to cat-burgle the Shower Tower. Fifteen feet up, spread-eagled, he heard someone coming along the path and quickly dropped to the ground. He tried to look nonchalant as one of the glossy Marble hostesses clipped past in her stilettos.

He had more opportunity to study the Gracewell Building for climbable features. The only way up would have been to climb from verandah to verandah. That would have been easy with a grappling hook and an 'etrier' or short rope ladder. Not *real* mountaineering, though. More interesting would have been the descent. He reckoned he could have 'dreeped' from one verandah to another, provided he set up a pendulum motion to take him inwards as he dropped from his hands at full stretch. The idea did not get any further than an idea, however. He did not think the explanation – 'Because It's There' – would go down very well if he had been caught at it.

It was officially called 'Fault No. 25019' and it was triggered by a curious combination of circumstances which were hard to reproduce. Several customers had complained about it. There was print-out evidence. Output data would suddenly appear in the wrong window and the whole screen would lock solid.

Nothing would happen, no matter what keys you hammered. You had to bring the system down and re-boot, that is, start up again, to clear the fault. It was disastrous for the customers and embarrassing for MCI. Fortunately most customers were completely unaware of Vesuvius.

So rare and elusive was it that the Undertakers had more or less given up trying to pin it down, but they had ideas. Something interrupted a critical section, one of the bits of the program which should never be interrupted, at exactly the wrong moment.

'OK if I work late tonight, Willie?'

'Sure. What's the problem?'

'I've got an idea about Vesuvius. I'd like to try it out.'

'Want to explain?'

'No.'

Willie thought about that. 'This is a team effort, Allan. We communicate.'

'Indulge me, Willie, this once. I'll need to dump the system on to a clean machine.'

Another pause. A shrug of his fat little shoulders.

'OK.'

In the lab they had several computers which were used for testing. He chose one which was not connected to the network and installed a fresh copy of the operating system on it as though he was a customer starting up for the very first time. It took a couple of hours to load all the tapes and by that time the lab was quiet. While he was at it he loaded the source code as well. The source code was the original language of the system before it was converted to machine language. The next task was to couple a microcomputer to the machine as if it was a terminal. He connected three micros.

'Setting up your own network?'

Gordon was standing at his shoulder.

'Sort of. I'm chasing Vesuvius. I'm going to generate a pattern of interrupts.'

'We've been through that already.'

'So? I'm only wasting my own time.'

Gordon patted him on the shoulder, as one might with a senile ancient. He wandered off to the coffee-machine and got himself a cup of green pea soup with milk and extra sugar. He kicked the machine. 'Shit! How about applying your talents to this bloody thing?'

Allan waited until Gordon had wandered back to his own desk and then slipped his floppy disc into the drive. It took about twenty minutes to load and set up the software he had prepared on his own micro – all the stuff he had developed with Rosa. This was the test of the theory. He let it rip.

'Getting anywhere?'

Allan was contemplating the buttons on the coffee-machine. Gordon was back at his elbow.

Allan said, 'I'm trying to work out how to avoid getting tomato ketchup with my hot chocolate.'

'I mean with Vesuvius.'

'Oh. Maybe. I expect not.'

'Can I see?'

'There's nothing to see. It's just running through patterns.' He yawned and stretched. 'I was just hoping to eliminate some things but it will take a while. If anything turns up I'll call you.'

Some time between three and four in the morning he woke. He was lying on the floor with a seat cushion under his head. Gordon had gone. The message was on the screen. Two parts of the op-system were shouting at each other and neither was listening. A deadly embrace. Nailed!

Instantly awake, he studied the source code print-out. It was obvious when you saw it. How could it ever have worked? He drew a pink highlight pen through the lines of code.

The next step was to cover his traces. He programmed a pattern of interrupts which would throw the system repeatedly into the error condition to reproduce the fault over and over again. The screen locked solid every time. More programming created a number of alternative patterns which did not reproduce the fault, but he knew Willie would demand to know how he had found the error and he needed an alibi. His story would be that it was a happy fluke. He had run the fault to earth by trying alternative patterns. By eight a.m. he had constructed the alibi program and was asleep once more on the floor when Willie found him.

The following week Willie called him into his office. When one of the office juniors had left two cups of coffee on the table, Willie reached under his desk and pulled out a bottle of Glenfiddich. He waved the neck of the bottle over Allan's cup and raised his eyebrows and seemed disappointed when Allan declined. He splashed some into his own cup and sat back.

'You're wondering what it's about? . . . Well I wanted a word with you about security.'

Allan stiffened but tried to disguise it.

'I'd like you to help the guys in security.'

Hot with relief, Allan took a sip of coffee. It was unusual to find 'security' being handled by software maintenance but some years earlier, Willie had fought a political battle and won security for himself. He had argued that it was illogical to maintain a piece of software without at the same time maintaining its level of security. Now it was his pet topic. Maintenance is patient, routine and systematic, or it should be. Security, especially the business of identifying and countering hackers, viruses and sundry other threats to the privacy and security of a uses data, requires a bit of flair, a bit of lateral thinking.

'Anything in particular, Willie?'

'Yeah. You see, I reckon the guys here do a good job. They're a lively bunch and they have so far managed to stay one jump ahead. When someone comes up with a new wheeze it doesn't usually take them long to track it down.' He paused and leaned back in his seat. 'But I would like to get ten jumps ahead.'

He was in expansive mood and beaming. He waved a finger in the air. 'Suppose, just suppose we could take a look into the future and work out what the bad guys were going to throw at us next year, and we got ready for them.'

Allan just nodded in what he hoped was a wise and encouraging way. Willie continued.

'I've been studying your CV again, Allan, and I reckon we're not making full use of your talents . . .' – he looked at Allan hard – '. . . and I'm not convinced that the way you found that Vesuvius bug was entirely a fluke.' He waited for a while, holding Allan's eye, and then, when Allan made no response he smiled and looked down at his cup and spoke to it. 'So I think we should use you in a long-range role.' His eyes came up. 'I'd like you to take a look at the mathematics of virus attacks.'

Allan made a puzzled face. 'Can you explain?'

'Yeah. The reason we call them viruses is because they spread like real viruses or something like them. I read an article in *Scientific American* last year which described the mathematics of the spread of epidemics. Real virus epidemics, I mean, like flu and AIDS. I reckon that it might be a good idea to analyse our problem the same way. I would like to know how bad this virus thing could really get. What is the very worst they could throw at us. The AIDS thing caught a lot of people by surprise and it spread a long way before the danger was recognised. I wouldn't like the same thing to happen to us. The guys in security have built up a whole lot of data on viruses which you might be able to use.'

'Why me, Willie?'

Willie swung round in his swivel chair until he was sideways on. It was the kind of question he liked to answer.

'I like to think I'm a good manager and a good manager plays to the strengths of his people. You're a loner, Fraser. That sticks out a mile. Usually I like to integrate people into the team. They're more useful that way. But now and again you get what I call a useful loner. The Vesuvius bug business showed me that you're a useful loner. So, if you happen to have a job that's best tackled by a loner, then it's sensible to put them together. In this case there is no deadline and not much harm done if you stepped under a locomotive, so a back-up team is unnecessary.'

'OK, Willie, I'll have a go.'

Tomasco came round his desk to guide Allan out of the office. He tried to put an arm round Allan's shoulders but that would have meant that his feet would dangle clear of the ground so he just grabbed Allan's upper arm.

'I hear you slope off into the mountains at weekends. Don't go and break your neck, will you?'

And before he closed the door he said, 'Do you have a gun? There are bandits in the hills here – and I mean real ones.'

The official notice on the door said 'Software Security Section' in small, neat lettering, and underneath 'Team leader: John Passold'. The unofficial notice was much larger and written in Mickey Mouse lettering. It said 'Fort Apache – the fastest guns in the West'.

That was the first indication Allan had that he was entering a world of fantasy fanatics and ego-trip eccentrics. They called themselves 'The Cavalry' while the 'Bad Guys' or just 'The Enemy' came in three flavours.

The 'Bandits' did what they did for some understandable reason like fraud and they tried to keep their activities secret. Rarely was their expertise in matters computing up to their ambition.

The 'Indians' did it just for the hell of it and could not resist announcing their presence. Sometimes they deliberately destroyed the system or deleted data, sometimes the destruction was accidental and nearly always they left behind messages like 'You have just been Zapped by The Great Mafisto'. Indians were usually very expert indeed and the Cavalry had a kind of respect for the very best. In fact the more he saw of the Cavalry, the more Allan became convinced that they were Indian-poachers turned Cavalry-gamekeepers.

The 'Aliens' were more elusive. The purpose or motivation was unclear and indeed it was not always certain that there was anyone responsible. The presence of an alien was suspected when the size of a file changed without any record of such a change in the accounting files, or when a check total or hash total was inconsistent. Sometimes after a lot of investigation a

suspected alien turned out to be just a bug in the system and
the evidence was turned over to the maintenance people. Other
times it turned out to be a bandit who really knew what he was
about and had covered his traces well. Bandits came in all sorts
but Indians were almost always male, young and hooked on
computers.

The Cavalry were distributed world-wide. Every MCI plant
had its software support group to service the needs of the local
customers and at least one member of each group was a desig-
nated expert on security. Fort Apache was the headquarters
but because they were all in constant communication through
the MCI network they functioned very much as a distributed
team and there was a great deal of camaraderie. In many ways
members of the Cavalry were closer to each other, even if they
were thousands of miles apart, than they were to the people
next door in their own local office.

Everyone was on first-name terms. They had their photographs stored as bit-maps on the network and you could call
up an image of another cavalry soldier in Melbourne or Tokyo
at the touch of a button.

When someone tracked down a hacker and worked out how
the trickster had done his dirty work, the story would be stuck
into the noticeboard file on the network and everyone got to
know about it. Hints on how to identify and trap were also
posted but this was often considered too insecure for the most
secret methods and these were distributed by Fort Apache,
using good old post.

The greatest accolade was to have a hacking or an anti-hacking technique named after you, so if you wanted to catch a
hacker you might set a 'Passold tripwire' or install a 'Keto
Tracer'. You could also say that a particular hacker was using
a 'Morris Worm' or a 'Blackford Boomerang'.

The ethos of the Wild West was everywhere. The guys in the
lab, which Allan now joined, treated the whole thing as an
adventure game, and outwitting an elusive Indian was their
greatest triumph. When the evidence was eventually put
together identifying some miscreant, it was handed over to the

legal division of MCI for action. They had a name for the people in the legal department too. They called them 'The Hitmen'.

The Cavalry did this part of the job with great glee. It was one of the rules of the game. The enemy was zapped and would conveniently disintegrate and disappear from the network. Seldom did they actually get a person's real name. Usually the closest they got to people and the probable fate of the enemy was the directory user-name. It was a sanitised affair with no messy consequences.

Before they were fully identified, some Indians were given names like 'Cochine' and 'Hiawatha' and their exploits lived on in the mythology which seemed to be the main topic of conversation at coffee. Everyone had his own favourite and the others listened to the stories over and over again.

'Sitting Bull found that the ethernet cable passed through his room. So he built himself an ethernet monitor and read the passwords on the cable before they reached the machine and got encrypted. Then he thought he would do everyone a favour by checking that the passwords were correct. The other users didn't twig anything was wrong until he started warning them that they should change their passwords more often.' Everyone fell about and then someone would top it with another story.

Assembling the evidence could be fun too, since it often required considerable computer expertise just to understand what had happened, and the Cavalry got a good deal of sardonic amusement at the pathetically ignorant queries they often got from the legal division asking for clarification. For example – 'You state in your submission that the person identified by the code no. 1 stole the shell of the person identified as no. 2. You do not state what no. 2 did when deprived of that shell.'

Bandits were usually boring, but sometimes one came along that gave them a sporting run. These they honoured with names like 'Jesse James' and 'Billy the Kid'. The evidence was also usually boring, consisting of little more exciting than lists of data showing illegal account withdrawals.

Aliens were given names like 'Android' and 'Green Slime'. Aliens were doubly nasty because you did not know that it was not going to turn out to be an uninteresting bug and that you had been wasting your time on a maintenance job. The Cavalry regarded the maintenance teams as the drones of the organisation and themselves as the élite. Olafsen's theoretical studies team were termed 'weirdos' and 'eggheads'.

They had a fully equipped electronics lab, because some of the techniques they used involved the use of specialist equipment. John Passold showed Allan round. One of the favourites was called an 'Automatic Sampling Unit'. It was a large black chip about three inches square which could be wired into a terminal or a microcomputer and which would record into its solid state memory a sample of everything that passed through the machine. Storage limitations meant that it could not store everything, but it could be programmed to identify particular strings of characters, and if these were typed by a user, the thing would take what was the equivalent of a photocopy of everything that followed for a fixed length of time. If you suspected that a user was using a forbidden password, a local engineer could wire an ASU – pronounced 'ass-U' – into the suspect's terminal and it could be programmed for the forbidden password. If he typed it then you got a copy of what he was using the password for. John Passold was very proud of the ass-U. Allan recognised it immediately. He had cooked one to a crisp inside his own micro at Burnside Cottage.

To read the contents of an ass-U you needed an Automatic Sampler Reader – ASR or 'asser'. You connected two micros together. One had an ass-U and the other had an asser plugged into it. That way you could read the contents in the ass-U within the other micro. An asser could also be used to wipe the contents of an ass-U or to insert new, innocuous data into it. Before he left the lab that evening, Allan had slipped an asser into his pocket.

Often and often he had had arguments with Jean on the subject of 'Conspiracy versus Cock-up' theories. Jean, being paranoid, had always favoured conspiracy and Allan, being, in his own opinion, well balanced, had thought that, in general, cock-up was the more likely. Now, however, he was beginning to favour a new hybrid theory. The Cocked-up Conspiracy Theory seemed to him to have a plausibility the other two lacked, and here was an example. They bugged his micro with one hand and provided him with the wherewithal to circumvent it with the other.

It was too dangerous, he decided, to keep the asser in his own apartment or in the pick-up truck. He drove that very evening to Jeronimo's farm and walked some distance up the valley beyond. It took only minutes to climb a crag beside the trail and wedge the asser, in a plastic food container, into a crack.

Another technique of which John Passold was proud was the Keystroke Interval Signature System or 'kiss'. The idea was that when someone types on a keyboard, their fingers beat a unique rhythm on the keys. There is, for example, a characteristic time interval between the 't' and the 'h' and the 'e' of the word 'the' which is a dead giveaway. They had the 'kiss' of every MCI employee stored in a database and could tell straight away who was typing if they got more than a few dozen characters. Customers could have their employees characterised in this way too, so that hackers could be tracked immediately, even if they were using a stolen password.

The name 'kiss' gave rise to innumerable corny jokes.

'Cochine was on the network again last night.'

'Gee! Did he give you a kiss?'

Allan sent a letter to Tom describing the kiss technique and a postcard to Rosa, with a picture of Mount Aconcagua and a message to 'give my regards to Jack'.

But it was the virus data that Allan had come to study.

Within a computer there are unused spaces – suspected bad sectors on disc packs, unused space on message packets, housekeeping space used only for special purposes, and so on. Viruses live in these spaces. They travel about on the network, tacked on to the end of legitimate software and data, or they stow-away in the free space at the tail end of a package. Viruses lie dormant, waiting for a certain date or for someone to run a particular program and then they can spring into life. The most effective viruses, like the AIDS virus, spread themselves about before they let anyone know they are there. And if they *never* let anyone know? Then why should they not go on spreading for ever? What would happen to a biological virus which spread rapidly and did not do its host any harm? Why should a benign organism like that not conquer the world?

Allan collected the data on known viruses, the method of transfer from one computer to another, the method of detection, ways of avoiding detection. He was not too concerned about what the viruses did when they finally awoke from their slumber. That could be nice or nasty, depending upon the taste of its perpetrator. But he was interested in the technology of detection. The Cavalry had developed a number of anti-viral programs which delved and probed into the hidden interstices of a computer. These programs were the 'immune response' of the computer world.

He knew that one of the reasons the AIDS virus or HIV was so dangerous was because it attacked the immune response itself and he wondered if there was a computer equivalent. Was it possible, for example, for a virus to examine the software running in a computer and detect when a program was about to examine the very locations where it was itself located? If it could do that, then it could either move itself elsewhere or modify the detection program to ignore its own location.

And he was interested in more than viruses. A 'worm' is a program which bores its way into a computer by its own efforts. It does not pig-a-back on legitimate data and software. A worm can penetrate computer security protections by means of a few simple stratagems. People are careless with passwords. A good password is arbitrary and contains some numbers, but because they have difficulty remembering arbitrary strings of characters, people use their own names, and the names of their wives or husbands, and their own names backwards, and the name of their dog, cat or house, or they use a normal word in the English language or American or whatever. Word processing programs have huge lists of words and it is not hard to get hold of a list of people's names. Microcomputers can zip through these lists, trying each one in turn in a few hours, and before long they are almost certain to hit on the password of some user who has been careless.

Once the worm is inside a computer it can look at its list of users. On a network most people have access to more than one computer so the chances are that your careless user has a directory on some other computer within the network and the chances are he or she has used the same password on both. So the worm tries the same username and password on every other computer in the network. It will probably succeed. And so the worm spreads and spreads. Worms and viruses, they get about.

Because Allan's task was one of those 'it would be nice if we had the time' kind of jobs, he could wander about without pressure of time. He spent many hours in the main library, and browsing through the virus history files on the network. No one minded if he didn't work normal hours in the lab and he actually spent a lot of time in his own apartment with his personal micro, running mathematical models of virus and worm epidemics. Much depended, he found, on the 'latency' of a virus, the length of time between infection and the point at which the virus made its presence known.

It also occurred to him that a worm equipped with the 'open sesame' password for the secret passage chip would spread like a domino cascade on the MCI network. He ran a model and found that it would have infected every computer within minutes of introduction. The speed was astounding.

He lay on his bed with his eyes on the Arisaig sands and thought about that.

21

APRIL

Calle San José was on the northern side of Santiago, a narrow street off the Avenida Alambra. It ran between dark buildings with blank barred windows. Two hundred yards along on the right, a wide arch with gates and a small hut for the porter or '*portero*' gave on to a small courtyard. There was no *portero* there as he passed through the gate. Arches surrounded the courtyard to form a piazza. Under the arches lighted windows in the dusk suggested occupation.

Allan walked towards the nearest window on soft feet, for there was a stillness about the place which compelled quietness. The murmur of voices from the direction of the windows seemed to enhance the effect. He looked in and saw a classroom with steeply banked benches and a table and a blackboard on an easel. Naked light bulbs hung from the ceiling. He could see the elbow of someone writing at a table against the window wall. The elbow of a man.

He walked on to the next window. Another classroom like the other, but this had a group of people crowded round the lecturer's table as he demonstrated something.

'*Que desea?*' (Can I help you?)

Allan swung round. The man had a uniform. Probably the

portero returning to his post. He stammered out his prepared query.

'*Excusa. Señorita McKechnie por favor?*'

The porter beckoned, led him to the far corner of the court-yard and pointed through a door.

'*Muchas gracias.*'

The hallway had a flagstone floor and a musty smell. It led to another, smaller courtyard and on the far side was another lighted window. Inside a slim young woman was writing on the blackboard with her back towards him. There were about six other people in the room, taking notes as the young woman spoke, and as she turned, Allan discovered that he could read what she had written. He was watching a lesson on elementary English. She was slim with sandy hair and a sad smile.

He retreated to the hallway and sat on a wooden bench, hands deep in his pockets, wondering what kind of reception he would get from Liz McKechnie. She would probably tell him to get lost.

An hour later the door was opened and people were coming out. Happy, high-pitched voices, talking rapidly in Spanish, and laughter. He heard '*Buenos noches*' several times as he moved towards the door. She had her back to him, leaning over the table, standing, writing something in a ledger, gathering up her books.

'Señorita McKechnie.'

She swung round quickly, startled and apprehensive.

'My name's Allan Fraser. I'd be very grateful if you would spare me a few minutes to talk.'

'What about?' She had a husky voice and an accent that came from down-under. There were freckles across her brow and the bridge of her nose.

'I would like to talk to you about Peter Elkon.'

'No.' She held up a hand as if she was a policeman holding up traffic. It was a sudden defensive gesture, warding off a painful blow. Then she turned to her books. Her head tilted down, concentrating on the books as though she was willing him to disappear before she looked up again.

'I know that it's a painful subject for you, but it is important and I'd like to explain why.'

She had the books in her arms, clutched defensively up against the front of her tweed jacket. She looked at him with hurt in her eyes, blinking. Tears were not far away. He kept talking.

'Perhaps I can buy you a coffee somewhere nearby so that I can explain why I am raking up these things again.'

She didn't say anything. She put her books into a bag with long handles, walked past him to the door and then . . . she turned and waited. A slight incline of her head invited him to lead the way.

The 'Eldorado' was on the next street. It had two rows of tables with red table-cloths and bent wood chairs on either side of a central passageway. They chose the seat furthest from the door and sat down. Allan had his back to the doorway.

Liz McKechnie looked at the menu with eyes that did not see, and let out a long sigh. She put the menu down.

'I don't know. Whatever you're having.'

So he ordered two ham omelettes with green salad because it was almost the only thing he knew how to order in Spanish. She didn't want wine so he ordered two glasses of Canada Dry.

'Well?' She was looking at him defiantly.

He said, 'I work for MCI at Ocean Springs . . .' He saw her eyes shut slowly in resignation and then open again. She pulled off her Paisley scarf and stowed it in the bag with her books. '. . . I was transferred here from Scotland a few months ago. I worked for MCI in Scotland too. When I got to Ocean Springs the guys there told me about Peter. They said he had committed suicide . . .'

The girl shrank visibly and a tear formed in each eye but Allan pressed on.

'. . . They also told me about you. They said that you didn't believe it was suicide. They said you'd created quite a fuss . . .'

He watched as a tear brimmed over and ran down her cheek.

'. . . I wanted you to know that I don't believe it was suicide either . . .'

She was digging in her bag, urgently, as though it was the most important thing in the world.

'. . . No one at MCI knows I am here and I would very much like it to stay that way . . . They told me that you were Peter's girlfriend.'

She found a bit of Kleenex and dabbed her cheek. Then she looked up at him and blinked. Her throat was working hard and her eyes were brimming again. She closed them and sighed.

They sat like that for a while, not saying anything, until the waiter arrived with the omelettes. She made an effort towards normality and the waiter mixed the dressing for them as she directed – so much vinegar – so much oil – so much seasoning. When he had gone she blew her nose on another Kleenex and blinked at Allan.

'What difference can it make now?'

He ate thoughtfully, and then put the fork down.

'There's something going on at MCI which is not kosher.'

'Are you CIA or MI5 or something?'

'No, nothing like that. I'm just a person.'

'Then why are you involved? Shouldn't you leave it to the authorities?'

'The authorities aren't kosher either.'

'But why you?'

'If not me, then who?'

They ate then. It was a good omelette and the salad was crisp.

'Another Canada?'

She shook her head.

'Coffee?'

She nodded.

When the coffee came she poured cream thickly on to the surface.

'That's what Peter said.'

'What?'

'Just what you said. "If not me, then who?" '

'Why did he say that?'

'Because I wanted him to stop. I said it was dangerous. I said someone else should do it.'

'Do what?'

'What he was doing. He didn't tell me the whole thing. But he kept saying that they were doing something terrible at MCI and he had to stop it.'

'He didn't say what?'

She shook her head. 'I said he should leave the company but he just kept saying that he had to wait. He said he had to wait until "the Labyrinth came" – does that make any sense to you?'

'It does a bit. Did he say anything else?'

'He said that the "something thousand" was just a dress rehearsal. He said that the Labyrinth was the real thing. That's all I know. He never explained it to me.'

'Could that have been the "sixty-five thousand"?'

'Yes. Yes, I think it was.'

Allan sat back in his chair and took a long breath.

'He didn't ever say what the "real thing" was?'

She shook her head slowly. 'I hope this is some help to you. I don't know why I'm telling you. I suppose it's because you said the same thing as he said.'

Her elbows were on the table on either side of her coffee cup. She lowered her head into the palms of her hands. Tears dripped into her coffee.

He wanted to say something which would comfort. 'A friend of mine in Scotland was killed and that was called suicide too. I just want to do something about it.'

She looked up. 'How did he die?'

Allan hesitated, but she wanted to know. She was looking at him very directly.

He is supposed to have laid his head on a railway line.'

Liz said, 'Peter is supposed to have jumped . . . from the

tenth floor of the Gracewell Building. That's in Ocean Springs. Do you know it?'

Santiago is a city patterned like a grid. They walked together, he with her carrier bag, turning left then right repeatedly as they threaded diagonally through the lattice of narrow streets. Her flat was near the river – the Rio Mapocho – which ran as a torrent through the city between stone walls. She told him about Peter Elkon, his parents in Minnesota, his boyish enthusiasm, his love of Chile. They had both loved it, until Peter's death.

She said it was so varied, running as it did from arid desert in the North to the Polar glaciers in the South, and never more than a few miles wide between the mountains and the ocean. But now she wanted to move on. She taught English for the British Council and she thought that they could fix her up in another country if she played it right by them. She was from Auckland and had come to Chile as part of her grand round-the-world trip. That had been three years before. But she had met Peter Elkon and somehow the world-trip dream had been replaced by Peter and his world. She hated MCI.

'Did he leave any papers, a diary or anything?'

'His parents flew down from the States. They took his things back with them. I've only got his letters and a few other things. No papers.'

They turned into Calle Rossanne. On the left were narrow terraced houses with old Spanish-style frontages and on the right curved railings were overhung by big dark trees. From somewhere beyond the railings and the trees came the noise of rushing water, deep in a culvert perhaps.

'What a nice place. You're very close to the city centre but it's very quiet and secluded.'

'I used to like it. But not now.' Her voice was tired. 'Not since I got burgled. They didn't take anything. They just broke things and threw my clothes about. I had to get new underwear. I felt unclean.'

'When was that?'

'Two days after Peter died. I was in shock and that was the last straw.'

Allan stopped.

'I don't think I should come to the door of your flat. I'll stand here and watch you till you get in safely.'

'What's the matter? Do you think the burglary had something to do with Peter's death?'

'It's a possibility. I don't think it would be wise for me to be seen at the door of your flat.'

She was alarmed and he was sorry about that but he saw no way of avoiding it.

'Look, Liz,' he said, 'if you want to get in touch with me . . . You might remember something we haven't talked about tonight or . . . or anything. If you want to get in touch, ring this number . . .' – he scribbled in his diary and tore out the page – '. . . and leave a message. It's a hotel in Copiapo where I go sometimes. The Hotel San Miguel. They'll keep a message for me. Don't try to contact me at Ocean Springs and don't . . . ' he turned to face her and tried to put an imperative into his eyes – '. . . don't use your own phone when you ring.'

Her mouth was open and her face white.

'This is not funny,' she said. 'Did you come here just to scare me?'

'No. Honest, Liz. If I had realised the situation, I wouldn't have come at all. I'm grateful for the information but I shouldn't have come. I realise that now. I didn't realise that you were already known to them.'

'Who's them?'

'I don't know, but they kill people, and it's best not to give them an inkling that you know anything about them. I probably won't see you again, Liz. I wish you all the best and I hope you get to Mexico or wherever as you planned. I suggest you make it soon too. But if you do need help, send me a message to that number and I'll come.'

'Are you going back to Ocean Springs now?'

'No. I'm staying at the Hotel Madrid tonight. Then I might

go up into the mountains for a couple of days' walking. I fly
back on Tuesday.'

He stood in the shadows and watched as she walked down
the street to the house where she lived. She stopped at the
door and looked up at the house and then back at him before
she went in. He heard the door bang shut.

He stretched out a hand and was shocked when it banged
against a hard, smooth surface, not far from his face. He
groped across its surface seeking an edge, a way out. There
was a bell ringing loudly close to his head. He was climbing
with difficulty out of a deep black well towards consciousness. And then he remembered where he was. The hotel
bedroom was the other way round. He rolled over away from
the wall, reached for the bedside light and then for the telephone.

'You bastard!' said a husky female voice. 'If you were trying
to scare me, you did a bloody good job of it.'

His watch was on the table by the phone. It was 2.05 a.m.

'I'm sorry I . . .' It was a moment before he recognised the
voice. 'Oh! Is that Liz McKechnie?'

'It bloody well is. And I'm scared.'

'Where are you, Liz? Where are you calling from?'

'I'm calling from the reception desk of your bloody hotel!'

He sat upright. '. . . But . . .'

She was shouting and close to tears. 'I got a taxi here
because you got me into this and you can bloody well get me
out of it!'

He pulled on trousers and pullover over his pyjamas and
slipped bare feet into his shoes. She was standing by the
enquiry desk in a raincoat and with the Paisley scarf over her
hair. Her head was bowed and she had her hands behind her,
holding on to the edge of the desk. Long sandy-coloured
ringlets poked out from under the scarf and dangled down her
back.

'Liz!' He took her arm and led her over to the darkened
lounge but the glass doors were locked. The porter at the desk

said something in Spanish and waved his arms about. The gesture said 'you can't do that!' So he led her towards the lift. Again the porter was sending urgent tick-tack signals. Allan dug into a pocket and found some notes. He threw them on to the desk and the porter picked them up, smiling, and waved them towards the lift.

'Was that money you gave the porter?'

'Yes.'

They were in Allan's room and she was sitting on the bed.

'Why? What did he think . . . you mean he thought . . .?'

'Yes, I guess that is what he thought.'

She shut her eyes and said in a flat voice, 'I've blotted your escutcheon.' She seemed to be amused – or was it just the last straw?

'My escutcheon can look after itself. What's the matter, Liz? What's happened?'

'I've been burgled again.'

'What! When?'

'Tonight. I woke up and decided to make myself a cup of hot chocolate and my sitting-room window was wide open and my books and things were scattered all over the floor.'

'What did you do?'

'I panicked. I called a taxi and headed here.'

'Was anything missing? What did they disturb?'

'I'm not sure. I don't think anything was taken. I didn't look. I just ran.'

'Did you close the window?'

'Yes. No. I don't know.'

He was thinking rapidly. Funny how his mind speeded up when the adrenalin was flowing.

'Listen, Liz. This is very important. We're going back to your flat together . . .'

She was alarmed, shaking her head, but he pressed on.

'. . . to make sure everything is closed up again and to check on what has been taken. But you must remember when we get there not to talk about Peter. We must have some other reason why I sought you out and we should talk about that.'

Puzzlement mixed with the fear in her face.

'You said you came from Auckland, Liz. Well, I have rela-
tives in Auckland. My uncle emigrated to New Zealand sixty
years ago. He's dead now but he had sons and one of them
sends a calendar every year to my uncle in Glasgow. I've got
his address somewhere.'

He began to ransack his hold-all and eventually found a
small green address book. She shook her head, not so much in
a denial as to shake away these events and make them not happen.

'Here it is. 125, Wattanna Avenue, Auckland. Can you
remember that? Do you know where Wattanna Avenue is?
Good. Think yourself into the story. You have met my cousin,
maybe you dated him for a while.' He was squatting before
her, holding on to her elbows, trying to make her pay attention. 'Listen, Liz. He's got red hair, or reddish, a bit like yours.
I've never met him but I've seen photographs. A big guy. His
name is Lachlan MacQuarrie. Got that? Lachlan McQuarrie.'

She said, 'Lachlan McQuarrie,' and nodded without lifting
her head.

He dressed properly and they got another taxi round to her
flat. It was small but attractive with lots of dark carved wood
and tiny rooms, but the sitting room was a shambles. The
window catch had been forced and Liz, in her panic, had left
it wide open. Allan searched around and found a coal hammer
and some rusty nails and drove the nails in to fix it shut.

'That's it. If you get a proper catch tomorrow I'll fix it for
you, but that'll do it for tonight.'

'I can't stay here now!' Her voice carried portents of hyste-
ria.

'You must have friends in Santiago.'

She shook her head. He paced about, hands deep in his
pockets while she made hot chocolate for them both.

'It'll be light in an hour.'

'I can't stay here!' She stamped her foot and spilled the
milk as she poured it. He did the pouring for her. They sat on
the sofa together and drank the chocolate. He got hungry and

made bacon and egg for himself. She had toast. He began
talking about Lachlan McQuarrie. The need to pretend
seemed to calm her and she went along with the subterfuge,
acting the part of Lachlan's ex-girlfriend quite well. The
shapes of the trees across the road were becoming visible. The
sky was signalling a pink dawn. There was some noise of traffic. A church bell rang.

'You must look to see what, if anything, has been stolen.'

She shook her head again. 'I feel unclean and nothing is
safe.'

In the end he got her to look and they established that some
money had been taken from a drawer, as well as a radio and a
small silver bell. She had no jewellery. The thieves had just
gone for small, easily carried valuables. The bookcase and
private papers were untouched.

Allan examined the phone carefully. Judging from the rest of
the room, Liz had not dusted the place for a day or two but
the telephone was spotless and the table top where it sat had
no dust either.

'Well, not much damage really. I'd say you had got off fairly
lightly.'

'I still can't stay here!'

'I could take you back to my hotel and we could book you a
room. But that can only be for the weekend. I'll be away on
Tuesday and then what?'

'That's better than nothing,' she said. 'It'll give us a chance
to think of something.'

So that was what they did. She came back with him to his
hotel and they slept fitfully, she on the bed and he in an armchair until well into the morning. After coffee she signed in
and he paid for an extra room. They had lunch at a terrace
café overlooking the river. Then she gave him a conducted
tour of the city.

The most imposing street, a wide tree-lined avenue leading
to the presidential palace, was called the 'Avenida de Bernardo
O'Higgins' which he thought was hilarious. She explained
that O'Higgins had been a national hero but the juxtaposition

of ornate and exotic Spanish with the prosaic and homely Irish name still seemed incongruous.

He stopped at a shop window with gourds and bombilla and she told him what they were. He bought a couple of the yerba matte tea-sets for Rosa and Jean. He would have liked to buy sombreros for his other friends but he couldn't think how to parcel them for the post, so he settled for postcards, mountains for Hamish and Ian and a fat cowboy on a mule for Jack.

Liz was returning to normal. She made things easy for him and not just because she spoke Spanish fluently. She walked easily at his side and enjoyed the same things.

'What is all this racket?' he asked. He took her arm and guided her to a table outside a café. 'The same thing is going on at Copiapo. Loud-speakers in every tree.'

'That's the election. You're listening to party politicals.' She put her bag on the seat beside her and shook her hair free.

'Oh! When does it happen?'

'In about six months.'

'You mean they have to put up with this for six months?'

She nodded, smiling. 'It's been going for six months already. They take their politics seriously here. But I don't know why they bother. Everyone knows that if they don't like the result the army would step in.'

'Oh? I thought Chile had gone all democratic again.'

She shrugged her shoulders and pouted. With her right hand she made a gesture like a wobbling plate, palm down.

'Maybe. They're getting all modernised. That's a joke really. The people need housing and the children need schools and the old folk need better pensions, but the government is lashing out and buying American computers to run the elections.'

And that was when it hit him. It seemed so obvious he wondered why he hadn't seen it before. Halpern had told him that the company were installing computers to run elections in many countries. Hamish was right. It wasn't money they were after. It was power.

'What's the matter, Allan?'

'Oh nothing. I just remembered something. Something back home.'

Liz ordered lemon tea and chocolate cakes for them. 'Have you been abroad before, Allan?'

'Sure! I once went to Carlisle for the afternoon.'

She didn't know where Carlisle was, so the joke fell flat. She had a nice smile with small, even teeth. He bought a map of the mountains nearby. Ski-tows were marked in red, which was appropriate. These were the places to be avoided. By six o'clock Liz was back on a level keel.

'I'm sorry. I just panicked.'

'It's understandable. I could kick myself for frightening you the way I did.'

'I've ruined your trip. You were going to go walking in the mountains, you said.'

'I can do that any time. In any case, there's still time. I got a guide book and it says there's a military railway which goes up behind the city into the high valleys.'

'Yes. They say it's lovely. I've never been.'

'Would you like to come with me?'

She pressed her lips together, making a big chin, trying to suppress a smile. Allan thought it was a pity to suppress it. She shook her head, blushing slightly.

'I'm not making a pass at you. It's a straightforward suggestion. No ulterior motive. Honest,' he said and then after a pause, 'Sorry. I don't believe me either.'

After a moment he said, 'But now that we have established some kind of alibi for meeting – hey, I'll bet cousin Lachlan never suspected he would be used like that – well anyway – it would seem strange if we didn't meet up from time to time now that we . . . know each other . . . a bit. We could even call one another directly on the phone if we don't talk about Peter.'

She was putting her handbag into her carry-all, putting on her scarf.

'I'd better be going,' she said. 'Thanks for your help about the window.'

'Liz. Can I see you again?'

She straightened up and looked at him.

'Yes. OK. But I'm going to leave the country soon. This has put the lid on it for me.'

He watched her walk gracefully down the steps of the terraced café where they had eaten and raise an arm to catch a taxi. She looked back before she climbed into the cab, gave a brief wave and then she was gone.

22

APRIL/MAY

A dialogue is a conversation between a p-individual and an m-individual in which communicational messages or p-m-grams are exchanged in alternating contrapuntal sequence to explanate a plan or i-schemata held by one of the individuals with the aim of achieving a symbiosis of action termed here a p-m-account.

The abstract was pinned on a noticeboard by the coffee-machine and Allan read it with a growing sense of disbelief.

'Having trouble sleeping nights?' Silvester was at his elbow, getting himself a cup of coffee.

'Is this a joke?'

'No, Sir, that's genuine Olafsen shit,' Silvester said. 'Guaranteed to cure your insomnia.'

'You won't be going then.'

Silvester laughed. 'I can think of better ways to spend a couple of hours. But if you want a laugh I recommend a visit. It's something else. Sherman likes to think he's an academic. He has seminars every other week. Some poor junior gets slaughtered regularly. You'll probably be asked to give one some time. It counts towards departmental management points.'

'Who goes?'

'Sherman – he's always there – and other people who can't think of an excuse quickly enough.'

Allan loved the word 'explanate'. He photocopied the abstract to send to Rosa. He thought he might go to see what was going on.

It was all in the best tradition of academic ostentation. Members of staff draped themselves over chromium and leather chairs in an overheated room and looked bored. The speaker managed to say the word 'paradigm' three times and referred five times to 'McCarthy's Circumscription'. Only once did he stumble and call it 'circumcision' by mistake. He showed overhead transparencies covered in squiggly symbols written in an illegible scribble. Several times he spotted errors in the overheads and ad-libbed corrections which were also wrong, but he scribbled them over the other writing so that no one could see what he had written before or after. Olafsen sat through this miasma nodding his head in approval. When one brave member of the audience dared to ask a question, Olafsen interrupted, saying, 'I don't think that's relevant.' But Allan had actually followed most of it and one thing was crystal clear. Olafsen's team were getting nowhere. Their approach was one that he and Rosa had abandoned at a very early stage. Some of the problems that the speaker identified and attempted to solve were not actually problems at all but side-effects generated by the horrible notation. The temptation to stand up and put them all right was very strong indeed but he folded his arms across his chest and said nothing.

At night, staring at the ceiling, he thought about Liz McKechnie. He fantasised about taking her to the mountains and making love in a tent and tried to think of excuses to call her but could think of none. Anyway, he knew that it had to be her choice. If she wanted to meet again she would call and he could not force himself upon her. But she didn't call. Perhaps, he thought, she was safer without him and that thought was some comfort.

23

MAY

'He's got a terrible kiss.'

The woman ahead of Allan was talking to her female companion. He had seen her before in the cafeteria queue. She had brown hair cropped close to her skull and small silver earrings. He slid his tray on to the glide-rails behind hers and contemplated a salad.

'How come?'

Her friend's face was familiar too – an Afro girl with dreadlocks. The choice of salads was almost identical to what was usually on offer at Gairnock. Such standardisation had the advantage of eliminating nasty shocks, but it did make for boring lunch breaks, unless you were lucky enough to eavesdrop on an interesting conversation.

'It's all over the place.'

They were moving to a table. Jasper was there. He followed them and sat at the end of the table with a nod to Jasper.

'Where does he penetrate?' said the other girl. She motioned to Allan to pass the salt.

'He comes in everywhere. Sometimes it's Geneva, sometimes Stockholm, sometimes Amsterdam. He must be flitting about on the telephone network before he actually penetrates.'

Allan was becoming wallpaper to the Cavalry – a harmless

eccentric. If he hadn't known that a 'kiss' was a keystroke signature, the conversations he heard might have been
embarrassing. He ate slowly because otherwise, not taking part
in the conversation, he would be finished ahead of the others.

'What's the matter with his kiss?'

'I think he's doing it slowly and deliberately with one finger
and probably with his left hand.'

'And how does he get in?'

'God knows. But he does it very quickly. He seems to have a
password for every machine but it leaves no accounting trace of
the user name.'

'Is that possible?'

'I would have said "no" until Crazy Horse got going.'

'Would you pass the pepper, Allan? How long's he been
around?'

'Difficult to say. We spotted him for the first time about two
months ago. Is there any water left?'

'Have a beer. He doesn't leave a visiting card then.'

'Thanks. Not usually. He creeps about in moccasins. Usually
no visiting card and almost no footprints either.'

'So how do you know he's an Indian?'

'It's the places he gets into. There's no reason except that it's
difficult. And he does leave a visiting card sometimes. We left
some messages for him and he responded as we hoped. We said
"Welcome to our anti-hacking database" and he said, "Thanks,
I'll come again".'

'Bastard!'

'We'll get him. He'll keep it up until we do. They never can
resist the temptation to go one step too far.'

Another day

'This ragout is terrible. Have you seen anything of evil-eye
recently?'

'Is that cream caramel? I didn't see that at the counter. I
thought evil-eye had been traced to a device-driver bug.'

'No, seems he's around again, or maybe it's another one.'

'Ain't you thinking of the bog-monster?'

'Maybe. What're the footprints like?'
'Files altered. No change to the cyclic word check. Always financial files.'
'Suspicious.'
'Yeah. Must be a bandit.'

And another day.
'We set a trip-wire for Crazy Horse last week and the S.O.B. un-set it for us. He knows his way around, that guy.'
'What's your next move?'
'Going to get a trace through the telephone network. Find out the source.'

A week later.
'Got him! Got the bastard!'
'Who?'
'Crazy Horse. We've got his location.'
'So it shouldn't take long to nail him now.'
'Just a matter of time till he tries it again. We'll be waiting and the local lads will set a snare on the telephone lines. He's as good as in the bag.'
'Where is he?'
'In England. Some place called Gairnock. Hey, Allan. You came from there. Do you know any crazy guys in Gairnock who could be horsing about on the network with some kind of high-level password?'

In his room. Lying out on the bed. Mind racing. He went through the options and they were all risky. International telephone calls and telegrams would be monitored. He considered phoning Hamish and talking in some improvised code about the 'man who built the house' as a cipher for 'Jack' but it was too obvious and would put Hamish in danger too. He could write a letter to Hamish, using the code they had devised as they stood back to back in the ice tomb of the toilet shed on Bheinn na Cailleach. It would be slow, but it was the only safe option.

He wrote down the words, 'Please tell Jack they are on to him', and then padded the message with other words, using the pattern they had agreed. Each word occupied its ordinal numbered slot in successive sentences.

please

– tell

– – jack

– – – they

– – – – are

– – – – – on

– – – – – –to

– – – – – – – him

And the letter became:

Dear Hamish,

Please forgive me for not contacting you sooner. To tell the truth, I have not really been so busy, just preoccupied with my new car and fitting it out with gear. Tyres, tools, jack and spare water-can, etc. are all vital necessities here. It's a pity they haven't got an AA man round every corner as in Britain, but that's life, I suppose. I should ask, how are you? I was thinking about you on Saturday last when I went for a walk in the high Andes. I think you would be amused to see my gear which makes me look like the lone ranger. My command of Spanish, however, would give him a shock. I'm still struggling to say hello. Anyway . . .

The rest of the letter was junk. The keyword 'anyway' was the 'end-of-message' marker. He knew the cipher would not fool a real cryptanalyst for very long but with luck they might not realise that it was a coded message at all. He sent Rosa a postcard of Mount Aconcagua.

But there was one other thing he could do. It would be fast and direct but risky. He could use the magic password to get a message directly to Jack. The danger was that if Jack was not already blown, the message could finger him. Pacing the room didn't help.

The ass-U sampler units were probably set up as trip wires to ring bells if the magic password was used and there was only one way round that. He would have to use the password a second time to delete the contents of the ass-U. Would that work? He experimented with his own micro, knowing that he could use his stolen 'asser' to delete it if the experiment failed. First he had to decipher the password in his diary. The experiment seemed to work on the micro, so now he had to try it for real on some terminal connected to the network. He wrote the password on a tiny slip of paper and hid it inside the cap of his pen. The deed, he decided, had to be done during a working day. If it was done at night he would still need access to the building and the badge reader at the door would indicate that he was in the building at the time of the attack. The thing might slip through unnoticed, but perhaps not. There was safety in numbers. Better do it while everyone was there and he would be just one of a number of suspects. And better to use some terminal which was not on his own desk.

In the end he settled for the games room. The machines there were connected to the network and everyone had a go from time to time. The games room was on his way back to lab from the canteen.

There was no one in the games room.

Speed!

The slip of paper was stuck inside the cap of his pen. He looked about for something long and thin and found a paperclip, which he bent straight and used as a fish-hook to angle for the paper. He left it crumpled up on the desk and sat down.

'Didn't know you were a games fanatic, Allan.'

He hadn't heard Jake come into the room.

'Oh. I'm not really. Just passing the time.'

He hoped his voice sounded calm. His heart was pounding in his ears.

'Have you tried Death Row?'

'No. I haven't tried anything really.'

'It's very good. You have to think up legal loopholes to escape the electric chair.'

'Sounds like a bundle of fun.'

'It is really. Some of the wheezes are really clever.'

'OK. I'll have a look.'

Jake wandered off to the far end of the room and donned a virtual world helmet.

It had to be now. The machine went through its logging on sequence asking first for his directory name.

Password:

He unfolded the crumpled scrap of paper and typed the magic sequence, left-handed with one finger, typing fast, fumbling the characters and having to retype.

He was in – through the protection checks and with total control over the machine. He connected to the central node, one of the hubs of the network, and drew his breath in as that machine accepted him without even asking for a password. And again to the European hub. Signals travelling the Atlantic as fast as thought. The door behind him opened and Jasper came in with Marylin. Marylin waved, but they didn't come over.

His hand was shaking. He scanned the list of possible connections displayed on the screen. European node to Gairnock. List the users! Scan them. Find Jack's entry. Connect to Jack's directory. Clear the screen of tell-tale indications.

Now. Edit his log-in file.

'Have you tried Indian Reserve?' Marylin was at his elbow.

'No . . .' Indians! Did she mean hackers? No, must be a game! Innocent voice. 'No. Is it good?'

'I like it. You have to get through a sacred burial ground without getting spooked and then escape from the tribe who come after you. It's got five levels of multi-tasking combat and the most powerful spell-casting system you've ever seen.'

'Mmm. I'll have a look.'

'Shall I show you?'

'Her hands hovered over the keyboard, her elbow near his face.

'Another time maybe, Marylin. I have to get back soon.'

She wandered off. Sweat broke out on his brow as he realised that the scrap of paper with the password was lying there still on the desk. He crumpled it up and stuffed it back into the cap of his pen.

Everyone has a log-in file which is invoked as connection is first made. It sets up a user's favourite facilities and it can display a message to remind you of things to be done. He modified Jack's log-in message:

YOU HAVE JUST BEEN ZAPPED – THE PHANTOM

Then he inserted a command to freeze the screen, making it impossible for Jack to get past the message and use the computer. By the time Jack had unscrambled that, perhaps his message to Rosa via Hamish would reach the idiot.

Now! Break the connection, and the next and the next. He was reversing the connections he had made, retreating back across the network, back to his own machine.

He still had to delete the contents of the ass-U. He typed very fast the sequence of commands he had practised on the micro. No time to check that they had worked. He could see Jake heading in his direction again. Log-out! He was off the machine – evidence deleted.

'Sorry Jake. I have to go.'

There was no more talk in the canteen about 'Crazy Horse'.

It was a pleasant evening for driving, dry and bright. The sea

across to Arran was aglitter. There was hardly anyone else on
the road, but he was not enjoying himself. He felt terrible and
struggled to extract a damp handkerchief from his trouser
pocket to wipe a dripping nose. Jack glanced in the mirror.
There was a black Ford Sierra on his tail but it was some way
back.

Why tonight of all nights? All he had wanted to do was to hit
the sack with a noggin of whiskey and a hot-water bottle. The
message had been mysterious.

Must see you. Jock's Well, 9 p.m. tonight.

He had been half expecting Alison to get in touch. Although
he missed her, he expected that she had missed him even more
and he had been confident she would come back to him. But
the brief note through his letter-box was not what he had
expected. And tonight of all nights. Perhaps she had knocked
and he, buried under blankets with the CD player going loudly,
had not heard. Perhaps she had tried to contact him at work,
but he had been off for four days.

Jock's Well was a well-known lover's spot on the coast road
but he was not too sure he would recognise it. He slowed down
and glanced again in the mirror. The black Sierra was keeping
its distance.

The clump of trees was familiar. He recognised it easily after
all and slowed as he approached it. The Sierra came up behind
him and passed as he swung into the lay-by under the trees.
There was no sign of Alison's car but there was a white Metro
already parked there. A burn passed under the road at that
point in a small ravine, and a pathway ran from the lay-by
along the steep bank of the ravine. He eased himself out of the
car, coughed heavily, blew his nose again and then, shivering,
followed the path. Jock's Well was on an old drover's track
which ran parallel to the new road. Alison was not the outdoor
type so this meeting place was out of character. He was
annoyed and his cold did not improve his temper. And of
course there was no sign of Alison, or of anyone else when he
got there.

At the side of the track was an old stone drinking trough and a trickle of water dripped into it from the fern-covered banking above. The trickle was not enough to keep the water clear and green scum had grown over the surface. Below in the ravine a waterfall cascaded into a shallow pool.

He heard footsteps behind him and turned. No Alison. Two men – probably from the Metro. He nodded in greeting.

'Nice evening.'

The men did not reply. They grabbed him by the arms and threw him over the edge. Then they came down the steep banking and held his unconscious head under the water.

There was a letter in the mail-box. For a second his heart leapt, thinking it was from Liz McKechnie, but it was from Hamish. Allan examined it carefully for signs of its having been opened but to his unskilled eyes there were none. The letter began:

> *Dear Allan,*
>
> *Too many things to do, apologies for taking so long. It's late so I'll just dash this off and hope to get a longer letter to you soon. Anyway, I never was much good at letter writing . . .*

The message was simple:

TOO LATE

Allan burned the letter in the ash-tray supplied so thoughtfully by the management and rolled into his bed to lie there staring at the sands of Arisaig as the light in the room dimmed, turned pink and faded to darkness. Then he rose, switched on his micro and began to write a program. His program would need a name. He called it 'Vidar' – the one who avenged – the one who survived the Day of Ragnarok.

One week later there was another letter in his mail-box. It was from Rosa, with press cuttings about Jack's death. No suspicious circumstances – official. Tommy Harkness, Chalmers and now Jack.

I'm not going to let it go, Chalmers. I've got a plan. OK?

Trouble was, he had two plans, neither of them fully worked out. One plan was about the conspiracy. The other plan was about Liz McKechnie – not so much a plan – more a bit of wishful thinking. Since the weekend in Santiago she had been the focus of all his happiest thoughts. In the end it was his need to escape from disturbing dreams about Jack and Chalmers, rather than any expectation of success, that prompted him to write her a letter. He could at least daydream.

24

MAY/JUNE

'Hello? Hello? *Perdon. Excusa. Buenos dias, Señora. Señorita McKechnie, por favor?*'

'Hello? *Excusa. Señorita McKechnie, por* . . . Liz! Thank God! How are you? Got your message.'

'Hey! That's great. Yes, we do have a couple of days. Friday and Monday. Terrific. I'll be there. No. Nothing here I would be interested in. Barbecues, mostly, and people marching around in Chilean National dress.'

'I've nothing against Chilean national dress. But it doesn't go with Bermuda shorts, does it? Or with cheer-leaders waving pom-poms.'

He caught the plane to Santiago on the Thursday evening and took a taxi to Liz's place from the airport. He was pleased to see that she checked him out through the spy-hole before she opened the door. She was wearing a grey pullover and fawn slacks and just a hint of perfume. Her hair was caught behind her head into a pony-tail. She let him give her a peck on the cheek.

Over supper he dug out the maps and she told him what she knew about the ski resorts. He found a dot on the map marked 'refuge' and Liz said it was a German ski chalet and that the

Army railway went up to it. It was all very circumspect. They even remembered to say something about Cousin Lachlan. He slept on the sofa.

It was called the 'Army' railway, but apart from the fact that the guards all wore khaki you wouldn't have known. The rolling stock was ancient. At each station the engine stopped to gather breath. Men walked up and down and tapped things with hammers, not too hard. There were long pauses at nowhere in particular. Santiago was a long way South of Ocean Springs and the mountains here were more like the Alps. The rock was grey-black. Conifers clad the slopes and there was much more snow.

Liz was elated. Her previous trips out of Santiago had been to other towns like Valparaiso or Vina del Mar. This was a revelation. They leaned out of the window together at one stop and the narrowness of the window pressed them together. She put her arm round his waist and he held her shoulders. Clouds jostled round the peaks and gave tantalising glimpses of brilliant light and patterned shadows and patches of high-up glistening whiteness that might have been glaciers.

The train disgorged them at a tiny station full of disused wagons and rusty railway lines with grass growing between. The other passengers disappeared down a roadway to some houses that stood in a terrace below the station, but Liz and Allan went in the other direction, up the valley towards the higher hills. He had brought his big rucksack and his smaller day-sack, which Liz was using. Sleeping arrangements had been a problem, for he had only one sleeping bag, but Liz solved that one by packing up her down-filled bed cover in a plastic bag and Allan rammed it into his pack.

The roadway was good and properly metalled and they soon discovered why. As they emerged from trees they found the floor of the valley covered in a mineral white stuff that was being mined by huge machines. It was alabaster. Beyond the mine the valley opened to a wide expanse surrounded by mountains. The lower slopes were littered with the unsightly industrial junk of a ski resort in the off-season, pylons, wire ropes, ash-covered car parks and derelict snow-cats.

They stopped to look at the map and then took the smaller, higher road which branched off to the right, and after climbing some distance over a ridge, the refuge came into sight. It was large, half-timbered like a Bavarian chalet, with a distinctive herringbone pattern painted maroon on white. Green shutters on the windows. No signs of life. Allan told her the story of his three nights in the toilet at the Bheinn na Cailleach hut and she didn't believe a word of it. 'No one could be that stupid,' she said, pushing him sideways.

The windows were small in comparison to the size of the rooms and the hut was distinctly gloomy, but there was someone in residence. The hut guardian was a thin man with a bald head and a beaky nose. He explained the darkness as they signed the visitors' book.

'*No gasolina*,' he said, rubbing his hands together, '*pero muy romantico*.'

He leered at Liz and handed Allan two candles.

He gave them a small room under the eaves with a view of the valley. The clouds had thickened and light rain fell that evening. Allan went outside, stretched out his arms and turned his face to the heavens. It was the first rain he had felt for months. Liz watched him from the window.

'You know what you look like?' she shouted. 'One of those monuments they put on the tops of hills – like at Rio.'

'I'm communing with nature.'

'Well, I wish you'd commune with this picnic stove. I'm starving.'

He made them one of his one-pot specialities. Boiled macaroni and onions, and when the macaroni was cooked, he tipped in corned beef and tomato puree. Liz was polite about it. She made coffee the real way with fresh ground beans in his one remaining clean pot. He had to admit he had been upstaged.

It was clear from the outset that Liz wanted things to go at her own pace with plenty of opportunity to retreat before either of them got hurt. Allan contained his soul in patience.

The following day they walked up the valley by a zig-zag path to a high lake and picnicked there. Sheltered from the wind, it was moderately warm and Allan slept in long grass while Liz took snaps and sketched. The second day was much like the first, except that it rained more heavily and they got soaked on their return to the refuge.

'Are you still keen on rain?' she said, laughing and holding up her arms to let the water run off.

'Yes,' he said and gave her a kiss. 'It reminds me of home.'

She said, 'Ouch, you're squeezing the water into me!' but she didn't resist.

The guardian was going down for his '*gasolina*' supplies and gave them a lift back to Santiago the following morning. His driving was erratic and they died a thousand deaths before he turned them out in the Calle Almirado.

At Liz's flat Allan showered before getting a taxi back to the airport. She held him at the door and gave him a long kiss.

'Thanks,' she said. 'That was a lovely weekend, and thanks for being patient with me.'

'Can I see you again?'

'Yes,' she said. 'Yes. I would like that.'

On the flight back he tried to get his thoughts back on to his counter-conspiracy plan but it wasn't easy.

'So how's it going?'

Willie Tomasco took his jacket off, revealing large damp patches in his armpits. He hung the jacket on the back of his chair and sat down.

Allan said, 'OK. I think. Yeah. Not bad at all really.'

'Would you like to give us all a talk on it?'

'Er. Yes.' It seemed years ago now that Karl Wellington, his supervisor, had asked him, a young nervous PhD student, the same thing and the floor had seemed to open beneath him, but now he took it easily. 'Yes. When do you want me to do it?'

Willie pulled a desk calendar over to him and thumbed through it. 'The heads' conference is due . . .' he said, his finger stabbing at a place on the page. 'If you could do a written report before then . . . Best if the talk coincided with publication of your report . . . say four weeks?'

Allan considered. Everything seemed to be building up to the heads' conference. The seminar, the report, Rosa and Halpern coming to the conference and Vidar, his program. He had known that a seminar had to be done sometime and he was grateful to Willie for his understanding attitude. If a report would help Willie's standing, then he would do his best for him, but he would need to ensure that there were no awkward repercussions. He wanted no whiff of controversy about his report, nothing to disturb the impression that he was a harmless boffin pursuing useless academic concerns.

Four weeks was just about the minimum he needed to finish off the work and write the report. Or it would have been before Liz began to dominate his thoughts.

'OK, Willie. I'll do it.'

After the weekend at the refuge they had talked on the phone regularly and it was Liz who suggested that she should come to Copiapo. Allan was tied up writing his report.

'I'd like to see the desert . . . but not Ocean Springs,' she said. 'I'm not interested in all that hi-tech stuff.'

He said, 'Great. I'll book a couple of rooms at the Hotel Miguel,' and waited to see if she would say 'One room will do, don't you think?' but she didn't.

Saturday, they did the town, what he knew of it and a bit more. They sat in cafés drinking harsh black coffee, eating peppery bean dishes, laughing about Allan's attempts at Spanish.

Next day he drove her out across the desert to meet Jeronimo Arostica, to see the orange grove and to talk to Theresa. Theresa told her about Allan getting roadways and trucks mixed up and Liz laughed and shoved Allan playfully. Jeronimo made Allan climb the little cliff near the ranch to show Liz.

'And you do that up mountains?' she said. 'You're mad! I'm not sure that I want to be seen with anyone so mad.'

He played down the danger, telling her about rope

technique and how impossible it was to fall and she didn't believe a word of it.

Back at the hotel, over supper, she said, 'It was right there on the noticeboard at the council, Temporary Lecturer required to teach English – Copiapo area – one month contract.' She put her fork down and looked at him. 'So I spoke to Harry – that's the guy in charge – and he said it would be OK if I wanted it – and I said I'd let him know next week – and I just thought I'd come up and case the joint – and,' she hesitated, ' – and give you the once-over too.' She blushed.

'Do we pass muster?'

'Oh, I like Copiapo,' she said. 'I'll reserve judgement on you. This mountain thing. I don't know that I could put up with someone so mad. And then there's the thing you're doing at MCI. Why don't you give that up, Allan? You know it's dangerous.'

He shuffled the food on his plate.

'I'll think about it.'

On Monday morning Liz spoke to 'Mrs Miguel' at the hotel. She wiped her hands on her apron and took Liz to the door by the main road and pointed a lot and Liz wrote some things down. On Sunday afternoon they went round a few places.

They settled on a bedsitter in a big old mansion called the Casa Rosado. Both the house and the crone who ran it had seen better days. No two square metres of floor were on the same level and the walls were riven by huge cracks, held together by iron brackets pegged by steel spikes into the masonry. But there was a back entrance and a small staircase up to the room so that it was almost self-contained, and it was cool. Allan paid for a month.

He ran her back to the airport in the Dodge, waved goodbye as she climbed the wobbling airport steps into the jet and then hurried back to Ocean Springs in a daze. The report was lying on the table by his bed and when he saw it he realised with a shock that he couldn't remember anything he had written in the last few pages.

★ ★ ★

He stood up to a few desultory claps and arranged his papers and transparencies on the desk. He looked round the audience. His abstract had been written carefully. It contained lots of obscure phrases and polysyllabic words. His hard work had paid off. Olafsen was not there. There could not have been more than ten people there and one of them was already asleep.

He put the first transparency on the projector and was pleased to see the eyes of his audience screwing up in an attempt to read it. Instead of using a laser printer, he had borrowed a portable typewriter from one of the librarians. The type-face was very small and worn. He had crammed as much as possible on to each page. He had also written squiggly symbols in free-hand, using a notation that he suspected was entirely foreign to everyone at the 'Springs'. He had photocopied each page on to a transparent acetate and satisfied himself that the result was totally illegible.

He spoke in a low monotone and watched the eyelids droop. He stood between the projector and the screen so that his shadow obliterated the display.

No one asked any questions, indeed few of his initially sparse audience were still there when he finished. Those that were had their heads slumped down on their hands and two of them were snoring.

His report was filed, unloved and, more importantly, unread in the main library. But its title appeared in the departmental report and helped Willie to fulfil his quota and get stars on his managerial effectiveness rating.

Having got rid of the seminar problem he could concentrate once more on the Vidar program, spending hours and hours among the orange trees, sitting on the tail-gate of the truck, hammering away at the keys. The weeks of exploration and library research were over. The ideas were there, they just needed to be put together.

'How about this weekend?'

'Sorry Liz, I've got to work.'

Sealed off from distractions, alone and unobserved except by the dead eyes of Bob Chalmers.

'What is it we're celebrating?'

Liz lay on her back and stretched an arm up to run a finger along the seam of the tent fabric above her head. Dappled shadows of orange trees moved on the canvas and there was a continuous quiet hum of insects.

'I've finished something I had to finish. It's ready now.'

'What was it?'

'You don't like all that hi-tech stuff, remember? It was just something I had to do.'

'Is it anything to do with the thing Peter was worried about?'

They were strict with themselves. They didn't mention Peter or Allan's work when they were in the Casa Rosado, or anywhere within the Ocean Springs complex or even when they were in the Dodge. The only time they allowed the rule to slip was when they were in the mountains.

'Yes and no.'

'You will be careful, Allan? I couldn't bear anything to happen to you too.'

She looked lovely with her long, crinkly, gingerish hair all over the pillow of the air mattress. She had green eyes and ginger eyebrows. The freckles on her nose and brow had grown in the sun.

'I'm a very careful guy, Liz.'

'You're cautious, yes, but when you get an idea in your head you stick with it. You frighten me, Allan. You're a kind of monster.'

'That's funny. Someone else once said that to me.'

'Who was that?' she rolled over to face him, suddenly interested.

'Rosa, my boss at Gairnock. She'll be coming here soon.'

'How? When?'

'There's to be a conference soon. It's an annual event. All the heads of sections come to pat each other on the back for all their so-called hard work over the past year and to plan more

megalomania for the next. Rosa's coming to it and so is
Halpern. He's the supremo in Scotland. He's a pain.'

'Is Rosa a pain?'

'No. She's nice. I like her a lot.'

'Oh! I see.' She pouted, pretending pique.

He laughed and told her a bit about their project.

'You admire her, don't you?'

'Yes, I do.'

'Is it anything more than admiration?'

Pause.

'It was, but not now. She said in her last letter that she's taking up a senior fellowship at Grenoble University and she has
met someone there she likes. She's going to get a divorce. Her
husband is obnoxious.'

'But you still have a soft spot for her.'

'Yes, I do. And I think she still has one for me. Would you
like to meet her?'

Liz looked at him carefully before she answered. 'Yes, I think
I would.'

'When will you be free? I'll ask her to come into Copiapo for
a meal some evening during the conference.'

'I don't have a class on Thursdays.'

'OK. Thursday it is. I'll phone.'

Liz liked to talk to Jeronimo and Theresa and most of all to
Jeronimo's wife Augustina. Afterwards she told Allan what they
had been talking about.

'Do you know that family gets up hours before dawn every
morning and Theresa has done a day's work before she goes to
school?'

Allan said, 'I've often wondered how they scrape a living.
Does Jeronimo own the orange grove?'

'Yes and no. He's in hock to MCI for it. MCI owns most of
the land and estates about here. And do you know what they've
done? A condition of the loan is that he doesn't grow any food
for himself on his land. He has to grow the cash crops they tell
him to grow and when the crop is ready the men come and

take it away and he has to take the price they give him. It's slav-
ery. So much for the new world order.'

Sometimes they argued about that and he found himself
using the kind of argument he had heard coming from Halpern
and Maurice.

'It's not as simple as that, Liz. Even owning a luxury yacht
creates work for the people who make luxury yachts.'

'That might work if there were no limits to anything, but
these luxury things consume resources and there *is* a limit.'

Liz was strong on the environment and he was puzzled. Was
there a right answer to anything? There was only one thing he
was sure about. People should get the government they voted
for, not one chosen by someone else, no matter how clever that
someone else might be.

They walked on a ridge of rust-brown rock. Liz wore strong
shoes but they did not protect her ankles so he was careful to
avoid scree. Sometimes she got scared by the height and he tied
her on a short rope, knotting it carefully round her waist and
taking the opportunity to kiss her.

He loved to watch her. She moved so easily. She wore wide,
baggy shorts and he was anxious lest she get sunburned so he
made her plaster on the protective cream and helped her do it.
They were long, slim legs with narrow, tapering ankles. The
slimness of them was emphasised by her chunky white socks.
As she walked along the narrow rocky edge before him, she
held out her arms with elbows inverted and hands spread in a
feminine gesture.

They stopped at a small summit and sat to eat sandwiches.
He pointed out some peaks and places he had been to.

'That's the Plaza del Toros. I'd like to take you there but it's
a bit far for a normal weekend.'

'They don't have bulls up here, surely.'

'No. It's just the shape it is. It s a great round hollow with just
a narrow entrance and huge cliffs all round like an amphitheatre. In the middle there's this great spike which is supposed
to be the bull's horn. You can see the top poking over.'

She shaded her eyes.

'What an improbable shape. You wouldn't ever try to climb a thing like that, Allan, would you?'

'Eh . . . well . . . actually, I have climbed it.'

'You're joking!'

'No. It's not that bad. It's peppered with good holds because of the way the strata lies. It is a bit airy at the top, though.'

'You're mad. Do you have a death wish or something?'

Rationalise it as he might, he knew that it was because it was dangerous that he liked to do it. Liz pressed home her point.

'You were talking about self-indulgent people at MCI and how they play computer games while people like Jeronimo slave just to stay alive. Do you not think you are being self-indulgent? What is the point of climbing and risking your neck? What good does it do anyone?'

After a while he said, 'Maybe you're right. It just seems to come naturally. I'm not properly alive unless I can climb.'

'There is something else,' Liz said as he handed her the water bottle. 'Harry, my boss, is also looking for someone to go to Argentina.'

His hand with the bottle stopped in mid-air. Then he handed it to her. She unscrewed the top and went on.

'I said I would think about it. The thing is, it's a tenured post.'

'You mean there's no time limit?'

'That's right. It means I'd have a permanent post and do some administration for the Council. I'd have jumped at the chance if it wasn't for us.'

He didn't know what to say. The sandwich had lost its taste. She handed him the bottle back and he took a swig.

'So what are you going to do?'

'I don't know. I'm thinking about it. It came up before the Copiapo thing and I'd got as far as getting my visa. But then the Copiapo job turned up and I thought I'd give it a whirl. It was only for a month and that would let me see how we worked out.'

'And have we worked out?'

'Yes. That's the trouble. So now I don't know what to do.'

'Would you marry me?' He hadn't imagined he would ever hear himself saying the words.

She smiled gently and blew him a kiss.

'Thanks for asking. But I don't want to be an Ocean Springs wife. I'd go mad there.'

'If I left MCI?'

She looked at him thoughtfully. 'Would you come to Argentina? It's not far away.'

'It's closer than you think. See that red peak?' he pointed to the East. 'Not the sharp one, the one to the right and a bit farther away? That's in Argentina. We could walk there in two days.'

'*You* could walk it in two days. You'd have to carry me.'

'Nonsense. You could do it.'

'Would you leave MCI, Allan?'

'I'm planning to leave MCI. But there's something I have to do first.'

She came over, sat on his knee and put her arms round him. The sharpness of the rocks under his buttocks cut into him painfully but he said nothing, suffering the pain stoically and gladly as he embraced her.

'It's too soon for us, Allan. We've only known each other a few weeks really. What is it you have to do?'

'It's been two months,' he protested. '. . . Nearly. It's just something important to me. But it will be finished soon.'

'Is it to do with the people who killed Peter? . . . It is, isn't it? What are you going to do, Allan?' She was suddenly alarmed.

'I think I can spoil their plans.'

'Allan!' She held his face and stared into it. Her eyes were wide and frightened. 'Don't, Allan! Stop it now! Come to Argentina now!'

She got off his knee and began packing up her knapsack. He moved to help her and stumbled.

'What's the matter with you?' she snapped.

'Nothing. I've just got pins and bloody needles that's all.'

He grabbed her by the arm. A wild plan was forming in his head.

'Listen. You go to Argentina and go soon. I'll give you some money to keep for me and you set things up there. I think I'm going to need a new passport and a whole new name. I don't speak the lingo so I stand out like a sore thumb. But you speak Spanish. They tell me people can be bribed. You set things up for me. In Argentina. So I can disappear there. And I'll walk through these mountains to reach you. They can stop me at the airports but they can't stop me in the mountains. I can run the legs off them. Stop crying!' He shook her almost roughly. 'I need your help!'

She was trembling with anger. Tears streamed down her cheeks as she stared at him and then she was shouting. Her voice was shrill.

'You're mad! Do you think Argentina is still like forty years ago? Just because some Nazis disappeared there, do you think I can spirit you away there? You think because I can speak Spanish I can work miracles?'

'We'll be all right, Liz. We'll work something out.'

The tears came again.

'You told me what you were doing was not dangerous!'

25

JULY

'It's the heads' conference,' said Marylin. 'Willie gets like that this time every year. Sprouts fangs and grows fur on his face.'

Willie Tomasco had just lost his temper – demanding action and reports finished on time.

Allan was given a plastic folder containing lists – lists of speeches, lists of visitations, lists of reports. It also had a map of the complex, the conference program and brochures about local tourist attractions. He studied the list of visitors and found Rosa's name and Halpern's too. There were even photographs. Rosa's picture was about as flattering as a photo-booth passport snap. He suspected that that was exactly what it was.

The visitors arrived, flags fluttered, the complex was alive with golf-course buggies, and then everything went flat. The visitors disappeared into the Shower Tower and absolutely nothing happened. No tours of inspection, no pompous speeches, no grillings by technical experts. They stood about and waited. Huddles formed to exchange exaggerated stories of wish fulfilment.

'Did you hear about the visit to the Halvorne? The machine went berserk and failed to do its stuff. Olafsen has egg all over his face.'

'Sam Oronsay in Documentation was torn to shreds. He'll never be the same again.'

Then, the following day, little groups of bored visitors began to trail round after liveried guides with clipboards. One or two asked questions but Allan got the impression they didn't want to hear the answers.

On the second day, Rosa and Halpern came into the department as members of a dejected bunch of visitors. Rosa lifted her hand in silent salutation when she saw Allan. Willie was there, sweating profusely in his best suit and trying to talk them through the work of his department. No one asked any serious questions. There was some complaint about the standard of the documentation but that turned out to be another department's problem. One of the visitors, a thin young man in an Italian suit, spent some time in the games suite.

Later Willie came back alone and had a hurried and bad-tempered conversation with some of the section heads. He warned them that someone was coming who would ask them about (Allan did not catch the word) and they should have (something) ready. Still later, word came that the second visiting group had been delayed by an hour. The group didn't come at all, but Rosa did. She wandered back into the lab alone and found Allan typing half-heartedly at the keys of his terminal.

'Now don't work too hard,' she said.

'Hello, Rosa. It's been a hell of a boring day.'

'You should talk.'

She pulled a brown envelope out of her crocodile handbag and said, 'Your sister Jean gave me this for you.'

He put it in his pocket.

'Jean doesn't write letters,' he said.

Rosa said she would phone him that evening after the visits were over. Perhaps they could have a meal or a coffee.

'I'd better warn you, though,' she said in a low voice. 'We may not be alone. I can't get rid of Wensley. He's sticking to me like a leech. He's a changed man.'

And at that moment Halpern put his head round the door

and saw them. He shook Allan's hand and said how glad he was to see him, and why wasn't he with Olafsen's team, and he was sorry to hear that, and so how was he getting on with Willie Tomasco's boys? The bounce was gone. The superior executive was gone and in its place was a man self-consciously acting the part. Several times he looked about anxiously without listening to the answers to his stock questions as if he was waiting for his name to be called. Then the clipboard person arrived and took them both away.

'Have you ever seen such a God-awful waste of time?' said Jake. 'I could have done something important.'

Marylin said, 'Like reaching the fifth dimension in the Alternative Reality Game?'

He walked round to the lake, found a bench under a plane tree and opened the brown envelope.

Dear Allan,

I hope you are well. Uncle Roddy has taken a turn for the worse and was admitted to the Royal on Wednesday with flu and suspected pneumonia. They say he will probably be OK but he looks and sounds very bad. I am well enough, although I find it difficult to get away to visit Roddy in the evenings and do my marking as well. He is very understanding and doesn't expect me to go in every evening.

I had a visitor the other day who was asking for you. She was a Mrs Sinclair. She said that you didn't know her but you had once saved her son from a cliff on some mountain and she wrote to you at the time. Perhaps you remember. Anyway, the reason for her visit was to ask me to send you a message from her brother – an Inspector Chalmers. It seems that he died tragically three or four months ago but she says that just before he died he was anxious to get in touch with you. She would have got in touch earlier but did not know how to until recently when she came across your name and this address in some papers of his. She said that her brother was very anxious to tell you that there was no way he could now help you and that you should (quote) look after yourself and get out of it as fast as you can (end quote). I hope this makes sense to you. It makes no sense to me at all. Mrs Sinclair was a bit hysterical. She was crying a lot about her brother. There's another bit of the message from her brother (quote) it is everywhere and it goes right to the top everywhere (end quote). That's exactly what she said. She didn't know what IT was. I hope you understand. She said it was very important. She was very insistent that I should not write to you directly but find some way of getting the message to you secretly. I don't understand what it's all about, but it sounds very alarming. I hope you haven't been getting into something you shouldn't. It would kill your uncle if you got into trouble or there was any scandal. I intend to go and see your Rosa Telman woman and see if she knows a way I can get this to you other than by post. I hope it's worth it, because I really haven't the time for all this jookery-pokery.

I think you should try to get back here to see your uncle before it's too late.

Love, Jean

He was staring at the trees across the lake and was only vaguely aware that someone had sat down on the bench beside him.

'Not bad news, I hope.'

It was Halpern. He had one leg crossed over the other, ankle on the knee, and one arm stretched along the back of the bench.

Allan shrugged. 'My uncle is ill. But he's very old. It's what you would expect.'

'Was he close?'

'Yes. He brought us up when my mother died. Like a father really. My real father died before I was born.'

'I'm sorry. Will you go back?'

'I'd like to, but there is so much to be done here. And not much time left.'

'What is it that is so important?' Halpern was smiling like an indulgent uncle.

Allan looked at him, conscious of the tears that were trying to form. Did Halpern know? Did he suspect?

'Just something. It's important to me,' he said and looked again at the trees.

'A girlfriend?'

Allan thought for a while and then said, 'There is a girl involved.'

'This is a nice spot,' said Halpern. He was looking at the trees too. 'Amazing what they can do in the middle of a desert, isn't it?' After a pause he said, 'I was intending to ask you a favour.'

'I haven't been able to get at the Labyrinth op-system yet. They've been keeping me away from it – so far.'

Halpern waved a hand dismissively. 'It doesn't matter. That problem has been overtaken anyway. I've got something else in mind . . . Rosa tells me that you've been roaming in the mountains.'

'Yes. Weekends. I couldn't exist without a break in the hills every now and then.'

'Quite so. What's it like? How well do you know the area?'

'I know little bits and there are maps, not very good ones, but I get by. It's very dry. The biggest problem is getting enough water – and shade.' He gave a little sardonic snort. 'Not problems I had much experience of in Scotland.'

'How far is the border?'

'From here? Maybe fifty miles. A bit more in some places. Chile is only about a hundred miles wide at the most.'

'And about two thousand miles long. Yes. An amazing country, isn't it? Tell me. If you had to, could you find your way over the border?'

'No bother. There are tracks.'

'How hard would it be if you were trying to avoid being seen?'

Allan looked at Halpern for a long time before he replied. The man was still staring out across the water.

'It could be done but it would be much harder. You would need to go high and on foot and that means carrying water. Quite a lot of water.'

Halpern at last looked round. His gaze was very level and

direct. He said, 'Would you be willing to take someone across the border for me?' He added, 'I'd pay you well.'

Allan puffed air between his lips like a deflating balloon. 'Who is this somebody? You?'

Halpern looked away. The fingers of the hand on the back of the bench were drumming gently on the wooden spar.

'Would you do it, Allan?'

'What's your game, Halpern? Planning to do a disappearing act?'

'Something like that.'

'Have they rumbled you? Are they going to do the same to you as they did to John Seaton?'

Halpern looked round at him very sharply.

'You know a lot more than you've been letting on. You could be in danger yourself, Allan.'

'Yes,' said Allan. 'I know that.'

'Then we're in the same boat. Why not join forces?' said Halpern.

'What's in it for me?' said Allan.

'Fifty thousand US dollars,' said Halpern slowly.

'That's just about one year's salary,' said Allan. 'If I take you over the border I have effectively resigned. Do you think that's a bargain?'

'It is if it also saves your neck,' said Halpern. 'One hundred thousand. That's as far as I can go.'

'Cash?'

'Used notes.'

'I'll think about it.'

A helicopter swung low overhead towards the local landing pad.

'Don't think too long,' said Halpern when the noise had abated. 'If you agree, then we have to act quickly. In three days' time we're due to go to the ranch at El Paso for another riding lesson. They do it every year. This time I'm going to fall off my horse and disappear – missing, presumed dead.'

'And I am supposed to be waiting somewhere nearby to collect the dead man and take him over the border.'

'You've got it,' said Halpern.

The sun was striking through a gap in the foliage above. He shaded his eyes.

'When would I get paid?'

'I'd bring it with me. A hundred grand is not a big bundle if the denominations are high.'

'Where are you heading? Paraguay or Argentina?'

'Argentina, I thought.'

Allan shuffled sideways into a more shady patch.

'There's one thing I have to know. Did you know about Jack Thornley?'

Halpern sighed.

'I suspected that you were involved with him. He was very silly. I learned about it afterwards. If I had known beforehand I would have tried to prevent it. I was just told there was a security leak somewhere on site and I had to give approval for counter measures. I didn't know what kind of leak it was. Once the person concerned is identified, the evidence is handed over to the legal department and I expected to be consulted about legal action to be taken in the local courts. Next thing Jack was dead and I was told to forget about it.'

'And you did.'

'What was the point of making a fuss after the event?'

'None, of course,' said Allan, allowing a hint of sarcasm to get into his voice. 'And making a fuss might have drawn attention to your own dabblings in the Tokyo stock exchange.'

For the first time Halpern was startled. His coolness gone for a moment.

'What . . . how do you . . .?'

'I'm not the only one who knows. I was told about your share dealings by someone else.'

'Who are you talking about? Did Dianne . . .'

Allan shook his head. 'No, not Dianne, and that's all I'm telling you. I just know you're living on borrowed time, which is why I'm taking your plan about going over the border seriously.'

Halpern was now sitting straight with his hands restless on his knees.

He said, 'Will you do it?'

'Probably.'

'When can you let me know?'

'Soon. I have to talk to someone first.'

Halpern's hand went to his inside wallet pocket and pulled out what looked like a gold-topped pen.

'I've got two of these,' he said. 'I'll lend this one to you.' He handed it to Allan.

'What is it?'

'It's for debugging a room. Just press here . . .' He demonstrated. '. . . And then sweep with the pen. If there's a bug nearby, the red light on the cap comes on. I wouldn't like you to be discussing my plan with someone where you could be overheard.'

Allan took the gadget and looked at it.

'How do I know this isn't a bug itself?'

'You don't. But it's not hidden. You can use it to sweep a room and then put it away somewhere out of range. Don't lose it. It was expensive.'

After a long pause Halpern said, 'Well, I suppose I must be going. When will I hear from you?'

'Soon.' Allan turned the pen-debugger in his hands.

Halpern was talking to the trees across the water. 'I would have suggested that you come to my room in the conference centre but you would need to show your ID card to the security guard on the door. It's probably best if we're not seen together too much.' He thought for a moment. 'There's a swimming pool in the basement which has free access. I'll go down there at midnight for a dip. I usually do. We could meet there.'

'I might not make it tonight.'

'I'll go each night until you come.'

'What's the number of your room – just in case?'

'802.'

Allan put the debugger in his pocket.

26

JULY/AUGUST

For the fifth time Liz opened the door of the oven and inspected her savoury pancakes. No amount of wishful thinking could disguise the fact that they were turning increasingly soggy and a dispiritingly darker shade of brown. Warm air from the oven swept over her. She closed the oven door, sat down by the table and mopped her brow with a cloth.

When she had agreed to play hostess to Allan and Rosa she had been genuinely interested to inspect this Rosa, but as the time drew near she became aware that it was she who was being inspected and that made her nervous and irritable. When the appointed hour came, and went, and there was still no sign of them, her irritation increased.

She had put some thought into the meal. With the primitive cooking facilities she had it was no use planning anything elegant, but it had to be impressive in a casual kind of way, so she chose savoury pancakes as the basis of the meal. She had done that before with some success. Peter had boasted about her pancakes to his friends. It gave scope for a salad with local produce and a nice but inexpensive rosé wine. Melon would start them off and peaches would bring it to a close. The most expensive item had been the coffee. She had also dressed carefully. Nothing showy, but a dress with a long skirt and a narrow bodice which would show off her slim figure. She put her hair into ringlets and tied a white bow.

As time passed her irritation turned to fear. She went to the window and leaned out into the cool night air. A radio was playing somewhere nearby – a Beatles tune with Latin American words. Thoughts of Peter came flooding back. For the thirtieth time she opened the door and stood on the verandah, listening for the sound of Allan's Dodge.

She had a fan. It had been her mother's and was almost the only thing she had that could be described as an heirloom. She used it now, like a Spanish señorita on the verandah with the white bow in her hair, her thoughts about Allan a mixture of anger, doubt and . . . yes, love. She admitted that to herself now, but not enough to make her lose her head. Allan had a kind of boyish fanaticism which alarmed her. Peter had been the same. Maybe she was just a sucker for the type, but once bitten . . .

After an hour she was reduced to taking paracetamol tablets and lying on the bed. When she heard the Dodge the anger flooded back. Footsteps on the stairs. She made no move to open the door but stood up, white-faced with anger.

'Sorry, Liz. We had car trouble,' he said.

She turned away from him angrily, expecting to feel his hands on her shoulders. She turned round again. There was a gadget in his hand which looked like a gold fountain pen. He waved it about the room, stepping up on to a chair to wave it near the hanging light fitting.

She said angrily, 'What do you think . . .'

He put a finger to his lips.

Rosa understood, but Allan was confused. They were only an hour late, after all. First the Dodge had refused to start. A mechanic from the Springs service station had traced it to a faulty plug connection. Then they had had to stop outside the complex in the desert to debug the truck with Halpern's pen-gadget. They found a bug under the dashboard and a tracer device clamped magnetically to the inside of a rear wheel arch.

They left the tracer where it was and put the bug under the bonnet so that it picked up nothing but engine noise. He had found nothing in Liz's apartment but told her about the bugs in the car to justify their lateness. To his surprise she seemed to get even more annoyed.

Liz put the food on the table and turned away quickly. The bow had come out of her hair and locks were straggling across her brow. Allan thought she looked stunning but he had enough sense to keep that thought to himself. Rosa did what she could to help but Liz resented the conspiratorial glances she detected flying between her and Allan.

'Cheers,' said Rosa cautiously, taking a sip of wine. 'Is this a local wine? It's very good.'

'At least it couldn't burn,' said Liz. She laughed wearily and let out a long sigh.

Rosa frowned and shook her head at Allan when she saw him about to say something. They ate in silence. It wasn't so spoiled really – a few blackened edges which could be pushed to the side and the melon was succulent. Liz took a second glass of wine and relaxed.

Over dessert Rosa said, 'Allan has something important he wants to tell you about, but he's frightened to open his mouth.'

'I'm glad,' said Liz. She looked straight at him. '*You* are frightening *me* to death. Do you know that?'

He nodded, contrite. 'I'm sorry.'

Liz said, 'What kind of place is this? Peter found out something at MCI and was thrown out of a window. But that's not enough for you. You've got to go poking and prying into the same thing. Why should I bother with you? Why should I care? Why should I get involved? Bugs in cars! Burglaries at my flat! I don't want it!' Rosa put her arm round her. Allan dithered.

'It is important, Liz,' said Rosa. 'Allan has found out now what it's all about. Just listen to what he has to say and then you can decide if you want to be involved. It's your choice. You can walk away from it if you want to.'

Liz shook Rosa's arm off and mumbled something.

'What, dear?' said Rosa.

'I don't want to walk away from it!' said Liz loudly. 'I don't want to be patronised. I want to know what's going on and I don't want any more deaths!'

So Allan told her about Halpern's plan. She listened to him sitting on the sofa, leaning forwards with her head buried in her hands, but she looked up when he mentioned Argentina and looked startled when he got to the bit about the hundred thousand dollars.

'When is this to happen?' She was bewildered.

'Saturday,' said Rosa. 'That's when we are supposed to go to El Paso for another horse-riding lesson. I think you should take up the offer, Allan. It's a chance to get right out of it with some money to start again.'

'I don't think I could come back,' said Allan. 'Not to MCI anyway. They'd be suspicious if two people from Gairnock disappeared at the same time.'

Rosa said, 'You could go back to Scotland with a nice nest-egg.'

Allan was dubious. 'It'd be worth it only if I can meet Liz in Argentina. What do you say, Liz?'

'No,' Liz said shaking her head. 'I'm not taking the decision for you. I'm not a part of this.'

He thought for a moment and then said, 'If I don't help him, Halpern will be killed like John Seaton.'

Liz looked at him and said coldly, 'You haven't told me about anyone called Seaton. When did he get murdered?'

Allan sat back and rubbed his hands over his face. His voice was tired.

'He was a friend of Halpern's. They were both dabbling in the stock market with inside knowledge. That's why he's rich.'

'You haven't told me everything, have you?'

'No, I haven't. You always said you didn't want to know about high-tech stuff. Well, this is high-tech and then some.'

'Tell me now.'

Allan looked at Rosa. Rosa shrugged and looked away. He

scratched his head, sucked his cheeks in, stroked his chin and then told her.

'There's a conspiracy in MCI – and elsewhere. It seems to be all over the place. MCI chips have been doctored so that they have what we call "a secret passage". It means that with a special password you can get into any MCI computer and do what you like. Lots of countries use MCI computers to run their elections and the big idea is to replace the vote-counting programs to rig the elections. Wensley Halpern was part of the conspiracy but he got greedy and used the information he had to line his own pockets. So now the conspirators are going to eliminate him if he doesn't run and fake his own death. I think he has a lot of money stashed away and he's probably carrying a fake passport.'

Liz said coldly, 'Why don't you just tell the authorities?'

Allan spoke calmly, hoping cold facts would end the argument. 'The authorities are part of the conspiracy. My friend Bob Chalmers told the authorities in Britain. I found him lying on a railway line with his head chopped off.'

Rosa looked at him wide-eyed. '*You* found him!'

He looked back at Rosa. 'The night before I flew here. I was supposed to meet him but I was late . . . I found him and then I left him there for someone else to find.'

Rosa closed her eyes and shuddered.

Liz said, 'And just what did you think you could do to stop this?'

'I've written a program – two programs. The first one is a virus. No, really it's a virus and a worm rolled into one . . .' Liz tossed her head impatiently and he hurried on. 'If I put it into the MCI network it will infect every computer on the network. But it won't print any silly messages on April the First or anything like that. It will just sit there protecting itself, preventing itself from being discovered. If they replace a machine it will be immediately reinfected by the other machines. That's the way the program works. The second program sits inside the first and is protected by it. Its job is to examine all the programs being run on the computer and if there is a program being replaced, it compares the old program with the new one and detects any nasty tricks the new one tries. It uses the theory Rosa and I developed to prove the correctness of the new program. I also gave it the formal specification of a correct vote-counting program for comparison.'

Rosa leaned over and placed a hand on his forearm. Liz saw the gesture and turned away. Allan went on.

'If it detects anything out of order it switches the programs back again. So if the conspiracy tries to rig the elections it will rig them back again and make them come out the way people really voted.'

'Have you actually done this? said Rosa.

'Not yet. I need one more bit of information. The password to the Labyrinth. My program needs it to infect new machines on the network.'

'How could you do this and get away with it?' said Liz.

'Stealing the password for the Labyrinth could be risky,' said Allan. 'But I thought I might use Halpern's computer directory name to do it. He's also got a very fancy microcomputer with a radio-transmitter. With that I could send my stuff into the network from somewhere in the mountains. I rather fancied the Plaza del Toros.'

Liz was walking about the room. She started tidying up. Putting dishes in the sink. Rosa and Allan got up to help. 'No,' she said. 'I'll do it. I know where. You go on talking.'

Rosa said, 'I'll wash.'

Liz ignored her. She said, 'And this is what Peter was on about? That's why they killed him?'

'I think so,' said Allan.

'He'd found this password thing. And wanted to stop them.'

'Yes. From what you've told me that must be it.'

Rosa handed Liz a plate and she dried it. She put it on a pile of plates.

'Would it work?' she said suddenly.

'I think so.'

'What would they do about your program? Can't they just delete it or something?'

'If it did what I want it to do they wouldn't even know it was there. They'll just get a shock when the election results are announced.' He laughed and then wished he hadn't.

She put another plate on the pile. 'You're all caught up in this, aren't you? Your own cleverness – outsmarting them. I think you should do whatever you want to do. Just don't ask me to have any part of it. I just want to get on with my life.'

Rosa looked from Liz to Allan and back again. He was still sitting at the table. He was playing with the salt cellar but his eyes were focused on infinity. He said, 'If I took a holiday now perhaps they wouldn't link it to Halpern's disappearance.'

'Could you take a holiday at such short notice?' said Rosa and then after a pause she added, 'What about your uncle? You said he was ill.'

Allan looked at her speculatively. 'Yes,' he said. 'That sounds plausible, doesn't it? You bring me news of my uncle. I catch a plane for Scotland, only when I land at Montevideo I catch another back and then head for the hills to rendezvous with Halpern. I come back a few weeks later and forget about the conspiracy. How about that, Liz?'

Liz lifted the pile of clean plates and put them in a cupboard. She didn't look at him. 'Suit yourself,' she said coldly. 'I think you two'd better go now.'

Driving back.

Rosa said, 'She'll come round, Allan.'

He drove in silence. In the gleam of the headlights the road was a broad chalk line leading them across the desert.

Later she asked, 'What are you going to do? Have you made up your mind?'

A minute later he said, 'Don't know.'

Stars, millions of them, were diamond hard points of light in the clear night sky.

'Tell me about your program.'

That was easier. Technical details. She understood at once. He got enthusiastic. They argued and threw about more ideas. It was almost like old times.

'That's brilliant, Allan. It has to work. Why have you called it Vidar?'

'Norse Sagas,' said Allan. 'Vidar was Odin's son. There was a great day of reckoning – a sort of Gotterdammerung – called the "Day of Ragnarok". Odin was killed by a wolf called Fenris, and Vidar put his foot on the wolf's lower jaw, grabbed its upper jaw in his bare hands and tore it apart. He had magic shoes, you see, which protected his feet. Then the evil god Surtur set fire to the world and to the Yggdrasil Tree with his sword. It's supposed to be a folk memory of the eruption of the volcano Hekla in Iceland. Anyway, Vidar survived . . . and my program will survive . . . no matter what they do to get rid of it . . . it's got magic shoes too . . . It leaves no footprints.'

Silence again. Engine noise and the buzz of tyres on concrete.

'One thing puzzles me though,' said Rosa. 'Wouldn't it take a while to load your program?'

A shooting star fizzed across the sky.

'Yes,' said Allan. 'About ten or fifteen minutes, I would say.'

'And if you use a radio transmitter, wouldn't they notice that, take cross bearings and home in on your location?'

He drove on for a while.

'Yes,' he said eventually. 'That is a bit of a snag. But I didn't think it was a good idea to tell Liz about that.'

Rosa said, 'She'll change her mind. You'll see. She really loves you. I can tell.'

Allan said suddenly, 'I can't leave Halpern on his own. I've got to help him.'

Rosa said, 'Yes. I understand. He really doesn't deserve your help, but I know what you mean.'

'I'm going to help Halpern escape and come back,' Allan said. His voice was too loud. 'I'll arrange a holiday like you suggested. Use Uncle Roddy as an excuse and say I'm going back to Scotland.'

A moment later.

'I'll see Halpern tonight when we get back. I can pack the truck with the gear tonight, arrange my leave tomorrow morn-

ing and drive down to Santiago tomorrow evening. Then I'll
double back . . . after I've booked on a flight to Europe.'

The road surface changed. Vibration. The tyres sang then
resumed their drone.

'After that . . . I don't know, really. I might still do the virus-
program thing. It'd be much safer to do it from a terminal
within the complex. But if I'm spotted, Rosa, I'll have to run
for Argentina. The money would be useful then.'

'They'd follow you.'

'Not if they thought I was dead.'

Midnight.

He had dropped Rosa off at the Shower Tower, gone back to
Gracewell, packed the truck and returned.

No sign of Halpern in the swimming pool. He walked back
to the truck. There was a glass-covered walk-way from the
door of the conference centre to the pool, and from the driving
seat of the truck he could see anyone using it.

Twelve-fifteen. He dug into the glove-box and found an
apple left there from a weekend trip. Thoughts jumbled in his
head. Liz. Did she really mean it? Rosa. She had kissed him
and held him tight.

Twelve twenty-five. The fountain was turned off at night
and for a few hours the complex was quiet. Most of the building was dark but there were a few windows high up which were
brightly lit. Dianne. He couldn't walk away and leave her father
to his fate.

Twelve thirty-five. He got out of the truck and walked on the
balls of his feet towards the entrance. The night-lights made it
glow yellow. He could see the security guard in his tan uniform
sitting at the desk.

The night security guard was bored. Beside his desk he had an
array of television monitors showing empty corridors and door-
ways throughout the hotel, but his attention was on another,
which was showing an episode of *Mission Impossible*. In the film
the heroes were slipping into a well-protected building under

the nose of a security guard, who was bored and watching television.

The guard shifted his eyes to the monitor showing the front
door. A man was there. The man pressed the night-attendant
button, swiped his ID card through the reader and then held it
up to the camera to show his picture. The guard did a cursory
check, pressed the admittance button and switched his attention back to the film. The guard in the film was being
amazingly lax.

Allan rode the elevator to the ninth floor. In the silence, the
hum it made seemed unnaturally loud. The indicator lights
crawled upwards towards 'nine'. As the doors opened he kept
his hand on the button as if he was going higher and waited a
second or two before putting his head out of the doors.

The corridor lights were on 'dim'. There did not seem to be
anyone there but the far end was obscured in shadow. He
stepped out and made for the 'exit' sign, trying to walk non-
chalantly. The staircase was of uncovered stone and the
stairwell had a whispering echo, no matter how gently he
placed his feet. At level eight he re-emerged into the corridor.
Again the passageway was empty.

802 was at the far end. There was a light showing under the
door and there was a noise inside as he knocked gently. Yes –
definitely a noise. The door handle turned and the door
opened a few inches. The square face of a man he had never
seen before was framed in the gap.

'Yes?'

'Dr Halpern?' Allan had prepared his reaction.

'He's not here, kid. Who wants him?'

'I had a message for Dr Halpern. Is this his room?'

'It might be. Who's the message from?'

'I don't know, Sir. I was just asked to give it to him by reception. I'm sorry to trouble you, Sir. I'll double-check at the
desk.'

He turned. His clothes didn't match the story but he reckoned he had only to fool the man behind the door for a few

seconds. As he walked towards the lift he was listening for the door closing.

'Hold it, son.'

He stopped and turned slowly. The man had opened the door a little wider so that most of his body could be seen. He was thickset and wore a grey suit and black shoes and in his right hand he had a black gun which he was pointing at Allan's chest. He flicked the gun to motion Allan back towards him.

'Nice one,' he said. 'Dr Fraser, isn't it? You nearly had me fooled for a second. Just step inside please.' He pushed the door open wider.

The room was a shambles. All the drawers had been pulled out and the contents strewn on the floor. A suitcase had been emptied on to the bed and beside it was a microcomputer in the cream and tan case of an MCI machine. There was another man in the room. He was standing in the doorway to the bathroom with one hand by his side and with the other propped on his waist.

'We got a visitor,' said the first man.

The man in the bathroom doorway held a coil of rope in his hand and beyond him Allan could see another pair of legs in grey flannel and black shoes . . . and Halpern's socks. The feet were off the floor and rotating slowly.

The windows stood wide and the curtains floated in the gentle breeze. The man with the gun waved Allan towards the window. As Allan moved he pushed him hard in the back, propelling him towards the window and the narrow balcony beyond. Allan kept his feet and his head. The Shower Tower had balconies just like the Gracewell. He stepped forwards quickly out through the window, placed a hand on the balcony rail and vaulted into space. Both men stood transfixed as Allan's body rose, pirouetted in the air and fell beyond the rail, facing inwards. As he fell Allan switched his hands and allowed them to slide down the vertical balustrades to their base. Then he gripped the rails hard and swung inwards, letting go at the last minute to propel himself feet first towards the balcony of the room below. There was a small table with a pot

plant on the balcony and he hit it with his feet, smashed it to
pieces and nearly fell backwards over the rail again.

Above him he heard the expletives. An arm appeared
through the railings above. There was a gun in the hand at the
end of the arm and it was waving about to try to get in a blind
shot. Allan lifted one of the broken table legs and swung hard
at the hand. It made contact with a satisfying crunch of breaking bones and the gun spun off into the darkness. There was a
yell and the arm withdrew. He heard someone saying 'Shit!'
several times. He put his shoulder through the louvred doors
and crashed into the room behind him. It was empty and dark.
He groped for the door.

There was still no one in the corridor but he could hear feet
on the stairs and the lift was moving. He pressed the elevator
buttons and then saw the fire-alarm button beside them. His
hand hovered over the button-push for a second . . . and then
he lowered it. The alarm would have filled the corridors with
people and made it difficult for his pursuers but it would also
have made it impossible for him to escape unseen. He was
back inside the room when he heard the corridor doors crash
open.

There was no sound from above as he stepped out once
more on to the balcony. At the right-hand end he stepped over
the rail and then, with one hand on the rail and one foot on the
balcony beyond the rail, he leaned backwards and reached a
foot out into the darkness towards the recess he knew lay in the
shadow. At full stretch his foot made contact with the wall on
the other side of the recess. His free hand groped for the near
edge and when he had it he levered himself into the straddle
position, facing outwards. There was someone in the room he
had just left. He heard a step on the balcony and a hand
appeared on the rail. Someone was bending over, looking
downwards.

A voice said 'Nothing here, Ted. Staircase,' and another
voice said 'Shit!' and the hand disappeared.

Up or down?

Safety lay downwards but what he wanted was upwards. He

shuffled, switching his weight between hands and feet, pressing hard against the opposing walls of the recess, moving upwards until he was level with the balcony of the room above. There he reversed the manoeuvre and climbed on to the balcony.

The room was empty of people except for Halpern's body dangling from the shower-rail. The contents of the wardrobe had been thrown on the floor. He found a green towelling dressing gown and stripped the draw-cord out of it to fashion a makeshift harness for the microcomputer. Halpern's jacket was lying on the bed with his brief-case. The contents had been stacked neatly on the dresser.

Passport, money, mostly dollar bills. He stuffed paper into his pockets. There had to be something else. Quick-eyed, he looked round the room.

Leather shaving bag. He had interrupted the search. They hadn't got that far yet. He tipped the contents on to the bed.

Razor, aftershave, shaving-foam, hair-brush . . . brown envelope.

He tore it open. Another passport . . . Canadian . . . name of . . . Oh my God! Wensley! How could you? More documents. They all went into his pockets. He bulged.

Once more he returned to the balcony and climbed out into the straddle position across the recess. The microcomputer was a dead weight against his chest. There was no one on the grass below him. Moving rhythmically from hand to foot like a lizard, he descended the recess until he was ten feet from the ground. Footsteps sounded and he froze. The dark figure of a man appeared round the corner of the building and stopped directly below him. The man shrank back into the shadow of the recess and waited. A faint glint of light showed on the gun he had in his hand. It had to be one of his pursuers, waiting perhaps for him to jump from one of the lower windows. Allan judged the distance and then dropped the remaining distance to land with his feet on the man's shoulders. He heard the collar-bone snapping. Then he sprinted for the Dodge.

★ ★ ★

TRANSMIT

He pressed the button.

The screen prompted him for name and password. Holding a torch between his teeth, he read the password from the twist of paper and typed it slowly.

Names on the screen. Scan. Move down through the hierarchy of directories.

No jamming signal yet. Were they watching? Would they try to fix his position?

More file names. Scan again. And again. There they were! The programs which customised the Labyrinth.

Type the TRANSFER command. The file contents were loading over the airwaves into the floppy on the micro. How long would it take? Nice machine! You always chose the best for yourself, Wensley.

Still no jamming signal. They must be trying to get a fix.

He stood up and listened. The sky above was crowded with silent stars. Across the stillness of the desert – from the direction of Ocean Springs. Helicopters? There! He heard the throb of heavy rotors starting up.

TRANSFER COMPLETE.

He stabbed at the transmit button to cut the signal and switched the machine off. Time to go. No tracer device on the back wheel arch now. It was clamped to a car in the car park by the Shower Tower. No fancy diversions or laying false trails flying to Santiago. No time to tell Liz. Or Rosa. Halpern would be found by hotel staff in the morning. Rosa would hear. She would guess he'd run. Surely she would guess. And she would tell Liz. No time to be sure. Just go like Hell for the mountains – those black wedges where the prickly stars stopped, big black mountains growing bigger by the minute as he raced towards them.

27

AUGUST

He cut the headlights and eased the truck gently through Casserone. On the road beyond the village he began to detect the first glimmerings of dawn in the sky beyond the peaks.

Jeronimo was pleased but surprised to see him at such an hour. The family were all up – God, what hours they kept! The little man soon realised that something was very seriously wrong.

Allan asked for horses and Jeronimo took him round to the corral where he lassoed a tall piebald horse and a dark fat mule. He helped Allan to saddle them up but his eyes narrowed when Allan offered him enough money to buy the animals outright and a bit more – in US dollars. He shook his head and waved a hand. Allan searched the dictionary which he had kept under the dashboard ever since his embarrassment with Theresa, and found '*prestamo*' – a loan. Jeronimo took the money doubtfully and then Allan explained with maps drawn in the sand and much flapping of hands that Jeronimo would need to come into the mountains to collect the animals later. He was deliberately vague about where he would leave them.

But the little Chilean became concerned when Allan began to press presents on to him – coils of nylon rope, his cooking

pots and pans and finally the keys and ownership documents
for his Dodge.

'*Por usted.*'

Jeronimo detected some of Allan's urgency. He chivvied
Augustina to produce food quickly then he cracked open a
bottle. Allan took the tiniest sip so as not to disappoint him.

'First time for everything,' he thought.

Allan usually left the Dodge under the orange trees but he
persuaded Jeronimo this time to put it in a shed and cover it
with straw. The rancher looked into Allan's face for a moment
and gave him an emotional embrace. He and his wife
exchanged words in low, hurried tones. Jeronimo went inside
and re-emerged with a pistol and six bullets which he handed
to Allan. Allan protested but was told that it was '*un prestamo*' –
a loan. So he accepted it with a bow and packed it away carefully in his saddle-bag.

The valley was a linear oven which the sun, imprisoned by the
steep mountain slopes on either side, kept at a searing heat
even in the southern winter. There was no wind. The Ice Age
had left no footprint on these mountains of the Central Andes.
No glacier ever bludgeoned its way down these ravines, chop-
ping off the interlocking ridges to leave wide, straightened
passages between the peaks. Instead, cut to a V by the river, the
valley dodged back and forth between the mountain spurs as
though avoiding sniper fire and each short section, from zig to
neighbouring zag, harboured a pocket of torrid, stifling air.

At its lowest point, the V was filled with rubble which
formed a flat, boulder-strewn surface. Across this, the river, a
diminutive trickle in comparison to the dimensions of the valley itself, meandered about, making a lazy way to the Pacific.
Pale pink and white, the boulders lay about, rounded like skulls
and hot enough to bake drop-scones. The place was devoid of
vegetation except for the bushes and tall blond grasses which
hugged the river bank, a ribbon of partial greenery, a narrow
haven of life-preserving shade. The huge slopes of scree, in
hues of brown and red and grey, which swept upwards on

either side to the crest of the retaining ridges, were broken by
rocky crags, of a richer red and darker brown and maroon and
purple.

The trail was just a passage of ground where the boulders
had been rolled to one side. The hooves of many horses had
trampled it and the dust was thick. It cut across the meanders
of the river repeatedly and each crossing was an excuse to
pause and dip a hand and take a mouthful. The water was
thick with silt, so it was best to let it settle in the water-bottle,
but it was fine for rinsing the mouth and dabbling the hands,
and splashing water on his neck and chest. He liked to immerse
his hat, luxuriating in the wet coolness on his head and the cold
drips landing on his shoulders and back but it was always dry
again long before the next crossing. The horses enjoyed crossing the water too. They filtered the water with their teeth and
were reluctant to move on from the gurgling ankle-deep
stream.

He had mixed feelings about the animals. On one hand they
carried the water and the food and the batteries he needed. But
on the other hand they could not go where he could go. On
foot he could cross ridges, run scree slopes, climb cliffs. On
foot he could go where the search parties could not follow.
But he needed the food and the water and the batteries, so he
had to use the horses.

He was worried by the trail of hoofprints they left behind. It
was not a problem on the main trail where his prints merged
with the multitude of others, but he was concerned that if he
tried to turn aside to find a safe spot or shake off pursuers, he
would betray himself. In cowboy films they tied the branch of
a tree to a horse and swept the hoofprints out of existence as
they moved. He tried it. It took a precious hour to hack down
the branch with his Swiss army knife. It didn't work. It did
something, but the hoof prints didn't disappear. They just
looked like hoofprints that had been swept by a branch, and the
horse didn't like it much. It whinnied and walked sideways
and generally made a nuisance of itself. The mule just stopped
and refused to budge and the only way he could get it to move

was to walk behind, flapping his arms and leaving his own footprints in the dust.

There was no way to prevent his movements being observed by people in the ranches he passed. A lone traveller eccentrically walking with two pack animals when everyone else rode was an object of interest and gossip. So speed was essential, speed and one sudden unexpected and unobserved move. He calculated he had about two days to put himself in a suitable position before they started the hunt proper. They would find the Dodge. He had no illusions that his friendship with Jeronimo was secret. They would find the Dodge and begin the search from there.

He examined the terrain carefully as he went for a suitable location for his disappearing act and found it near the head of a long narrow valley which opened out beyond into broad strath. At the narrowest point, the steep left-hand wall of the valley was pierced by a deep gully filled with massive boulders. The animals stood patiently tethered to a stone as he unloaded most of the gear and backpacked it in several trips up into the boulder-field. Some of the boulders were larger than houses and, being supported on others, they trapped between them deep tortuous clefts. Rumbling far below the surface was an audible trickle of water. Some of the gear, enough for one man-load, he left on the mule and then tried to mount the horse.

Cowboys did it all the time. Why was it that in cowboy films the horse stood still while the hero vaulted into the saddle instead of sidling away, like his perverse brute, just as he tried to step up on the stirrup? Perhaps in films the horse's feet were set in concrete. Always sensitive about inflicting pain on an animal, Allan failed to pull the girths tight enough as the horse blew its flanks out. So when he did succeed in swinging his leg across its back, the saddle slipped off and dropped him heavily on to the ground. His heart hardened and he heaved the straps tight, waiting until the animal took another breath and then giving it a further heave.

Perhaps more like Don Quixote than Roy Rodgers, he rode

into the next ranch at the far end of the broad strath and dismounted almost as though he had been doing it for years. The
ranch owner got very excited, beamed at him and introduced
his wife. They insisted on providing a meal. The wife served at
table while Allan and the rancher ate and tried to converse in
pigeon Spanish and hand signals. Allan explained that he
wanted to go further up the valley on foot. The rancher nodded
in agreement and somehow got Allan to understand that it
was too cold for horses further up the valley.

'*Muchas frio*,' he said, wrapping his arms around his chest
and shivering.

Allan paid him to look after the animals. For two weeks, he
said, and then with his pack loaded set off further up the valley.
At dusk, he turned and made his way silently back down the
trail, walking on stones to avoid leaving prints. As he passed the
ranch he kept as far from it as possible and the dogs barked
only once.

Hoping to throw pursuers off his track he had chosen the
valley because it did not run towards the Argentinian border.
From here on he would be taking a more obscure route across
the grain of the ridges.

It became very dark and he almost passed the gully without
seeing it. The cache of gear was even harder to find and he hit
his shins painfully against rocks several times. It was too dark to
find a cave so he slept in the open, stretched out in his sleeping
bag on a rock slab until dawn, but as grey light stole through
the boulder-field he found that he had several alternatives to
choose from. The deepest was the best, although it did give
him palpitations when he realised that the jumble of rock had
probably been created by an earthquake. Imprisoned down a
crevice with the crystalline underbelly of a boulder the size of
a bus just above his face, he had to fight to keep claustrophobia at bay. He tried not to think about earthquakes.

With the gear stashed underground and with a convenient
bolt-hole for himself to slide down beside it, he could work in
relatively open surroundings near the surface. He set up the
micro and laid out the batteries. One set was put aside for the

final phase, the other two would have to suffice for preparatory work. Fortunately most of the software was written so the ten or twelve hours of use which the batteries would provide, should, he reckoned, suffice.

First he dis-assembled the file he had stolen. That took an hour. Somewhere in the text was the magic string of characters – the password to the Labyrinth. He settled down to the same task he and Jack had carried out together in Burnside Cottage while Steve and Chalmers and Jocylin McCarrie kept watch. He had no print-out, however, and had to work directly from the computer screen. And he had no table on which to write so he could not spread out paper and make notes. Remembering that night at Burnside reminded him again of Chalmers and Jack.

How am I doing, Jack? I've hacked every computer in sight. I've got the password. How am I doing, Bob Chalmers? You don't need to look at me like that.

He worked in two-hour sessions, sleeping betimes.

Through a narrow chink he could observe a section of the trail in the valley below and during the first day he saw two people ride past. One of them was the man from the ranch where he had left the animals. He also heard the sound of a helicopter.

The first set of batteries gave out that evening.

On the second day a pair of riders came, riding towards the ranch further up the valley. They had gaucho gear – the full rig-out with black flat-topped wide-brimmed hats, slim waistcoats, poncho blankets, high boots and spurs like brass suns. They looked like sherry adverts. They also had guns. Six-shooters in holsters and rifles in their saddle holsters.

Two hours later they returned. They rode more slowly, looking about and examining the ground carefully. They stopped below his gully.

Allan inwardly cursed himself for not disconnecting the speaker wires in the micro. If he switched the machine off now it would emit a loud bleep. With the micro still running and clasped to his chest he slithered down his bolt-hole. The cooling fan made a low hissing noise which he prayed would merge with the sound of running water below the boulders. The click of a stone told him that the men were climbing the boulder-field. They came slowly, and he suspected they were looking into the crevices. He shrank back into the shadows of his own recess and lay still. More footsteps came to his ears and snatches of words.

They were arguing. He could tell that by the tone of voice. The words were indistinct and spoken too quickly for his dubious Spanish but he thought he heard the word 'Fraser'. There was silence for a while and then, when he looked up at the small triangle of sky which was visible above his bolt-hole, he saw a pair of spurred feet. The golden spurs glinted in the sun but the feet were pointing away from him. Stealthily he reached down, drew Jeronimo's pistol from a saddle-bag. Lying full length, he pointed it two-handed at those feet with the splendid spurs.

A shout came from lower down. The man above him shouted back. There was an electronic bleep – unexpectedly loud – some kind of call signal. The man had a two-way radio and he was gabbling into it. Then the feet turned and the man stepped past the gap and began to descend over the boulders to the valley. The footsteps grew fainter.

The episode lost him time and used up battery power. The second set of batteries gave out on the second day and he still had not completed his task. Later a helicopter flew low overhead and sailed away over the crest of the ridge above. It returned at night but deep in his crevice Allan reckoned his body heat would be masked and invisible to night-glasses.

Reluctantly he used the third and last set of batteries. At midday on the third day, he found the password and programmed it into Vidar.

He packed the micro and its batteries, hoping that there was sufficient power left.

This was not the place he had chosen for the final phase. He hid most of his gear in the bolt-hole and marked its entrance with a pattern of small stones arranged carefully to look accidental. He took a two-gallon can of water, some food, the micro and some climbing gear and heaved them on to his back. He looked at the pistol, and then with some reluctance, he picked it up and slung it on his belt.

The sun was down and darkness was falling with tropical speed. He took a bearing with his compass and set course for a march under the stars to the Plaza del Toros.

It was called 'El Toro' – The Bull – but to Allan's eyes it had more in common with a rhino. A long blunt-nosed spur thrust forwards into the centre of the rock amphitheatre and then reared upwards at its extremity into a horn-shaped pinnacle. Broad-based with a curving dorsal edge, it was exactly like a rhino's horn. There was even a secondary, smaller horn on the crest of the spur just behind it. The only things which spoiled the rhino likeness were its colour and its size. It was bright red and the major horn was at least five hundred feet high. Taken together with the height of the spur, the tip was fifteen hundred feet above the floor of the amphitheatre.

The place appealed to him. He rationalised by telling himself that a search party would be unlikely to stumble upon him while he was doing the business, a place where his stratagem could best be acted out because it was close to Argentina with a high-level route across the border where others might be reluctant to follow. But in truth it was the Wagnerian quality that attracted him.

Getting on to the crest of the spur was not difficult for a rock specialist, but the water and the micro and his gear made a heavy pack. Climbing slowly, he calculated the odds. Once he began transmission his location would be revealed. How accurately could they fix his position? Search parties, if they were close enough, might be directed into the amphitheatre, but would be unable to reach him or even see him if he was on the highest point. The real danger came from helicopters, homing in on his transmission signal. They would have difficulty landing on the tip of the horn, and if he had time he could vanish into the small but deep ravine – more of a chimney really –

which scored the dorsal side of the horn. Once in that ravine he could make his way to the crest of the spur and then, if darkness had fallen, make his way out of the amphitheatre without descending to the floor.

It was a plan, but not much of a plan. He knew the chances of success were slim. The important thing was to inject his Vidar program into the network before they jammed his transmission. He had to give them a chance of finding him. Without that chance they would jam the transmission immediately. He had to be reasonably close to Ocean Springs, close enough to give the helicopters a tantalising chance so long as his signal lasted.

On the crest of the spur he lay in shadow as the burning sun moved slowly overhead. Timing was important – daylight to tantalise the choppers, close to darkness to give himself a chance. He waited, sipping water, knowing that it might have to last a long time, for who knew what lay beyond the rim of the amphitheatre?

In mid-afternoon he judged the time to be right. He decanted some of the water into his hip-flask, strapped the micro to his back and began the ascent of the horn itself. It was desperately steep. The heels and most of the soles of his boots projected into space over that fifteen-hundred-foot drop. Moving deliberately, he found, for the very first time, a lack of confidence in his own climbing ability. He tested each foothold for friction and tapped each handhold for the tell-tale click that would betray looseness. For the first time too, on overhanging sections where the weight of the micro dragged at his shoulders and the weight of his whole body dragged at his arms, he became aware of the fallibility of his own strength. He was not used to the feeling of being alone in the mountains but he felt it now on this huge cliff. What would Hamish and Ian have made of this incredible rock structure? That was a comforting thought. He brought it to the front of his mind to banish self-doubt.

A spike under his left hand gave way unexpectedly just as he was transferring his weight to it. It released a block the size of a football which dropped away. His weight was thrown suddenly back on to his right hand. His left foot slid off its hold and he swung sideways and outwards like a flag, suspended by right foot and hand alone. In that position he watched the block falling, falling, striking the cliff face halfway down, shattering into a sun-burst of bits and a puff of smoke, watching still as the bits showered downwards, hearing the noise of the impact seemingly seconds later. Then slowly, with a straining wrist, he swung back to grab the cliff with his left hand and find another foothold.

The rock was too loose at this point. He moved upwards to the right towards the sunlit ridge. The angle eased. On the crest of the ridge, the scimitar-shaped neck behind the horn, he paused and looked round the 'Plaza del Toros'. If a party had been on the ridges opposite they would see him now silhouetted against the azure sky, but there was no one. From the crest a narrow terrace reached across the face to the ravine. He followed it.

In the ravine the climbing was easier and he could relax. It was a deep, dark chimney. In Scotland it would have been dank with slime and moss but here the rock was desert dry. He thought of Rosa and Liz and Hamish and Jack. Democracy was too abstract and too confusing a concept. MCI, the Labyrinth, the secret passage, the conspiracy were distasteful even to think about. He was climbing and he wanted to reach the summit. That was objective enough for the time being.

He slipped the combined earphones and microphone set round his head, inserted the floppy disc into the machine and pressed 'transmit'.

There was a pause.

The welcome message came up on the screen showing that the connection was made. A command typed on the keyboard started the transfer. In a corner of the screen was a small display. A tiny lightning-bolt logo flashed to show that the transfer was happening and a figure showed the percentage of the data which had already been transferred successfully.

One per cent.

He calculated that the transfer would take about fifteen to twenty minutes to get all of the data into the network.

But how long would *they* take? With the resources they had, he imagined it would not take them long to spot that he was transmitting – one, two, perhaps five minutes? Scramble the helicopters – another five. Fly fifty miles, say at two hundred miles per hour – fifteen minutes. He was cutting it fine. Not much time to ditch the computer and make for the relative safety of the ravine.

He allocated the transfer operation to background activity and began typing again to make a further connection within the network.

Five per cent.

The logo flashed at a slower rate. In background the transfer would take longer because the other things he was doing would then take precedence, but it was essential that he create a diversion, lest they jam his transmission.

Surely they had spotted him by this time? He could imagine the cavalry at work and the cowboy-style whoops of delight when they recognised his 'kiss'. Would someone blow a hunting horn? A six-shooter fired through the ceiling would be more appropriate perhaps. Would someone be calmly noting the co-ordinates of his transmission? Would they spot the background transmission and block it? He had to draw their fire – intrigue them. He made another connection. He was going through the network, working towards the main machine at Ocean Springs.

The synthesiser spoke, flat, without emotion and with a nasal metallic twang.

Voice: *Hello Allan.*

He switched from keyboard to voice input and answered.

Allan: Hello

Voice: *We were wondering how long it would be before you showed.*

They would also be wondering why he was so reckless as to remain on the air. Asking questions, even ones they would not

answer, might look like a sufficient reason. With luck they
would humour him, keep the conversation going, while they
got a fix on his position and scrambled the helicopters. So
both ends had a reason to keep the thing going. The difference
was that he had to distract them until he had loaded the stuff
from the floppy. He had to give them a plausible reason for his
behaviour. Perverse curiosity seemed the best bet.

Ten per cent.

Allan: Who's we?

Voice: *Just us. There are lots of us.*

Allan: Here at Ocean Springs or somewhere else?

Voice: *Here and there. All over. We don't recognise national
boundaries.*

Allan: Governments?

Voice: *Everyone with an interest in stability.*

That word again. Andrew Coltart's invective. Keep them
talking. Anger might add a degree of plausibility. That wasn't
difficult. He was angry. But his anger was polar cold. He had to
pretend a hot-blooded, blustering, uncontrollable anger.

Allan: Why did you have to kill my friends? They had done
nothing.

Voice: *Oh yes they had Allan. Oh yes they had. They helped you
and they also knew too much . . . Where do you think you are going
Allan? That's the third connection you've made.*

Allan: I'm coming to get you. I'm coming to your machine.

Voice: *They are all our machines Allan.*

Twenty per cent.

The helicopters would be in the air. Had they got a fix? Any
time now they could jam his signal. More questions. Quick!
More questions.

Allan: Why did you kill Halpern? Was he not one of your
people?

Voice: *He was. But he got greedy.*

Allan: And John Seaton?

Voice: *That's right. He and Halpern together. They betrayed our
trust. Tried to make themselves rich.*

Thirty per cent.

Allan: Isn't that what you are doing?

Voice: *No. We have other plans. Much more important plans. And anyway these things have to be done in an orderly way.*

Allan: It's the elections isn't it?

Voice: *Of course.*

Allan: Fitting yourselves up to be in control. What will you do with it? Buy yourselves lots of shoes like Imelda Marcos?

Voice: *Don't be childish Allan. Ensuring continuity is the most important thing. Acquiring money is no use if the value of the money collapses.*

Allan: So ensuring a strong currency is more important than democracy?

Voice: *Now you're being naive Allan. There has never been true democracy and if there ever was it would be a disaster – total anarchy.*

Allan: Why should that be?

Forty per cent.

Voice: *Because people do not have the expertise or enough information to take wise decisions.*

Allan: They don't have the information because you won't let them have it.

Voice: *That's simplistic. Digesting the information and interpreting it requires expertise and a lot of time. People could not live their own lives and do that task. There isn't enough time. They want their football or some other sport and their television. Don't ask them all to be statesmen or administrators Allan.*

Allan: They can delegate. They can vote for the general course of action they want without getting involved in the detail.

Voice: *Allan, Allan. Even choosing a course of action takes real understanding. The full facts are too complicated. Elections have always been fought and won on the basis of half-baked statistics and over-simplistic economics. We could manipulate the press and even the opinion polls but it takes a lot of time and effort and a great deal of money to dress up a manifesto to win an election. This way saves time and effort. It is more efficient.*

Fifty per cent.

It was speeding up. When they did most of the talking the transfer quickened.

Allan: What guarantee is there that the people in charge even care about the people, that they are not just stitching things up for themselves?

Was it his imagination or was that the throb of distant chopper blades?

Voice: *It is a question of trust Allan. You have to trust the people with experience.*

Allan: Power corrupts.

Voice: *And absolute power corrupts absolutely. That's an old one Allan. And again it is simplistic. What seems like corruption to an outsider will often be wise administration. It is sensible to reward the administrators. That is their incentive.*

Allan: Incentive to be corrupt. No one is immune.

Sixty per cent.

Voice: *What about you Allan? Are you immune?*

Chopper blades – definitely.

Allan: I don't have absolute power.

Voice: *But you could have had Allan. In a sense you do now. You have the password. You could control the election results if you wanted to. How would you use that power Allan? Would you be so strong-willed as to hand over all that power to the people knowing that they might choose to have a civil war and cause famine? You wouldn't Allan. The temptation to do good would be too strong. And that means you would control others.*

That disturbed him because it was true. Anyway. What the hell! Scotland was just a very small country. Did it matter so much that he had tilted the scales there ever so slightly in favour of independence? Even if he was ashamed of himself Jean would have been proud of him.

Seventy percent.

Allan: People need freedom.

Voice: *People need food, shelter and jobs.*

Allan: How do they get that by you controlling the election results?

More than one helicopter. He could hear them distinctly.

Voice: *Industry provides what people need and industry needs stability. Businessmen will not invest unless they have predictable markets.*

Allan: Is this the brave new world you are talking about? Everything controlled from the top? Everyone happy to be a gamma-delta?

Voice: *There will be a few who are unhappy. They will always be unhappy unless they are in control themselves.*

Eighty per cent.

Allan: So there are just two kinds of people: those who want to control and those who are happy to be controlled. I don't believe that.

Voice: *You are one of the ones who want to control.*

Allan: No. I want the people to control themselves.

Voice: *You may think that now. But if you were to exercise power you would do what we have done – tip the scales in favour of what you think is for the best.*

Ninety per cent.

Voice: *Why are you waiting Allan?*

He ignored the message. He did not have much time left now but he did not need much.

Voice: *Allan. What have you done?*

Allan smiled as he recognised the signs of alarm.

Ninety-five per cent.

The noise of the approaching machines was loud and he had to tilt his head to hear the click click of the disc drive.

TRANSFER COMPLETE

With an explosive roar the choppers appeared over the ridge ahead of him, three of them like hornets in tight formation.

He typed – 'Go to Hell'.

He pulled the floppy disc out of the machine and slipped it down a thin crack in the rock at his side It fell a long way, posted to the mountain's interior. He stood up.

Even from a distance the open doors were visible and he could see the elbows of men hugging long black weapons which glinted in the sun. The throb of the rotor blades merged into a continuous roar. He had the micro in his hand. Like a discus thrower he bent and swung the machine by its handle, hurling it from him and then watching as it curved over in a graceful arc, plunging, spinning, flashing as it caught the light, falling downwards into shadow to explode on the brutal rocks fifteen hundred feet below.

The roar was upon him now. He could feel the down-draught. The helicopters had moved apart and formed a semicircle round him. He watched calmly as the men took aim. He saw the first flash of fire.

The End

(nearly)

TAILPIECE

She hesitated.

The man smiled broadly and stood back with the door of the truck in his hand. He had his hat in the other hand and he used it to wave her in to take a seat beside the driver. She would be wedged, trapped between them. They were all smiles and that made her even more nervous.

Not for the first time, Liz wondered if it was worth it. A 'Gringo' travelling alone was strange enough. A 'Gringo' woman, alone, asking for a lift in a truck into the mountains, was unheard of. She glanced up at the back of the truck. Wide horned cattle with ribs and angular shoulder joints filled the open back. Nowhere to stand there. She looked at the driver, dark skinned, mustachios, wide smile with lots of irregular teeth. The cab smelled of body odour and engine oil. She smiled weakly at the driver and climbed in beside him.

If she turned back now the sense of having failed would haunt her for the rest of her life, and she knew no other way to get beyond Casserone. The old bus, with its slatted wooden seats and roof-rack with cases, boxes and crates of chickens, stopped at Casserone. She had to go further. She had to convince herself that she had done everything possible.

The driver chain-smoked, driving fast and lazily with one

hand dangling out of the window. He chatted but her answers were monosyllabic. Several times during the bumpy, dusty drive the other man slid his hand on to her knee and she, politely but firmly, lifted it off again.

As she climbed out of the cab, hands were extended to give her the help she didn't need, touching her waist and her bottom. She was exhausted, not just with the heat and jolting but with holding herself tense, waiting for the next move by the man's hand.

The men were harmless really. They had done nothing she couldn't handle and she supposed that in a way they had been kind, but she knew she would be a talking point in the bars for months to come. Stories would be told with lots of innuendo and elbow nudges and back slappings.

They handed her down her pack from the roof-rack on top of the cab and watched her walk towards the low clay-walled buildings.

'Señorita Leez!' Jeronimo was delighted and then suddenly serious when he saw the state she was in. They took her into the house and Theresa fetched a basin of water for her to wash. Augustina brought a jug of orange juice and glasses.

Later Jeronimo took her out to the shed and showed her the Dodge. He explained how the men had ransacked it and slashed the tyres. He didn't say so but she got the impression that Jeronimo had been beaten. He had a bruise on his face. But they hadn't found the money. He showed Liz where he had hidden it in one of the beehive shaped clay ovens, encased in hardened clay.

He knew where the horses were. Word had come to him from the rancher. He was dubious about taking Liz with him but she insisted and he recognised her mood of quiet desperation. Seeing the Dodge was good. It was the first positive indication she had had that her guesswork was on the right lines.

To start with they followed Allan's route up the valley. People had seen the lone man, walking with one horse and one mule and Jeronimo knew who to ask. They found the ranch where Allan had left the animals. The rancher wanted more money than Allan had given him and Jeronimo paid him with some of the American dollars. Mollified, the rancher told them about the angry men. How they had asked him about the Gringo who had brought the horses. How they had gone on past his ranch, on up the valley and then returned quickly. The men had said the rancher had deceived them. The men had said the tracks stopped a mile or so further up the valley. The rancher had protested and had been struck. The men had gone back and searched the mountains to the North and East and called up helicopters to search beyond that. The rancher spat on the ground. He hadn't liked the men and wished them to Hell. He didn't like helicopters either. They disturbed his horses and made his mare abort. He should be compensated. He looked hopefully at the pocket where Jeronimo had replaced the wad of dollars.

Jeronimo gave the rancher a few more dollars. The man then pointed North-East. He had heard the helicopters go in that direction and he had heard gunfire. He offered them wine and Jeronimo took some. They shook hands.

Liz could ride well. Jeronimo was glad of that because they could make good progress. He could not afford to be away from his orange grove for long. At night they stayed close to the river. He made a shelter by bending the branches of bushes to form a dome which he covered with blankets. It was cold at night. He made a fire and cooked slivers of tough meat on a stick. The Gringo woman was strange. She was tired and afraid but she did not complain. She urged them on when he suggested a halt. They followed trails which wound round ridges, zig-zagging and sometimes crossing tracks where Allan, on foot, had gone straight as truth.

Jeronimo raised his hand and they stopped. They were on the crest of a broad ridge between two deep valleys. Liz allowed her horse to amble up alongside Jeronimo's before she reined it in. He pointed.

'El Toros.'

Liz could see the Plaza and the great horn rising above the encircling walls. She shaded her eyes and scanned the landscape which wobbled as though melting in the heat.

'Would he have come this way?' she said in Spanish.

'No one goes to The Plaza del Toros.'

'Allan said he would.'

Jeronimo said, 'Then he would have had to pass over this ridge and this is the best place to cross it.'

'Even on foot?'

'It's on the direct line. We must go on down this trail to the right now, but Señor Fraser could have gone straight over that shoulder.'

'Can you see signs?'

Jeronimo shook his head. He did not know how he was going to persuade the woman to turn back. She would not do so easily and certainly not before they reached the Plaza. But turn back they must, eventually. In the meantime her will, fuelled by a desperate hope, drove them onwards. He would wait until that hope was gone.

He said, 'Shall we rest? Would you like to drink?'

She said, 'There's no time.'

It was late afternoon on the third day when they entered the Plaza. The sun was behind the horn as they came through the narrow entrance. The rays shafting past the peak spread outwards in a fan. The sky beyond was pink. Jeronimo stopped.

'We're here. What do you want to do?'

Liz rose in her stirrups to her full height, cupped her hands to her mouth and shouted.

'Allan!'

The sound, high-pitched and plaintive, echoed weakly around the amphitheatre and died. They waited.

Silence.

'Can you see signs?'

'There are footprints here,' said Jeronimo. 'Going in but not coming out.' He pointed at the ground. They were large footprints made by the chunky cleated rubber of climbing boots.

'Allan!'

Her throat was tighter, the sound higher pitched and the echoes less resonant.

Silence.

Jeronimo reached down and drew his rifle from its leather saddle-holster. He raised it to his shoulder and fired a single shot at the sky. The report shattered the ears, bounced around the crags and died slowly.

Silence.

Jeronimo turned to Liz.

'What do you want to do now? Where do you want to look? We must find a place to stay for the night soon.'

'I don't know,' said Liz. She was looking at the ground, dejected. 'Can we follow these foot . . .'

And at that moment they heard the pistol-shot.

They found him in among the boulders at the base of the cliff. He was lying in the dust with the pistol by his hand and surrounded by a stench of sweat and urine. There was a crevice under a boulder where he said he had sheltered from the sun. There was only a cupful left in his water-bottle. He had eaten the last of his food three days before. He had a bullet wound in his thigh which he had bound with a strip torn from his shirt.

They poured water into him. He said to Liz, 'Thanks. I'm glad you didn't go to Argentina.'

Later she said, 'I don't understand. After they shot you, why did they leave you here?'

'I wasn't here when they shot me. I was up there.' He pointed towards the summit of El Toro. She blinked and looked at him. He didn't seem to be delirious.

'How did you get down?'

'Abseiled. One leg is enough.'

Trying to be macho. Trying not to make a big deal out of it. Trying not to say how abominably his leg hurt. The descent of the horn had taken all his strength and a bit more. He had had to pick up his supplies on the shoulder of the pinnacle. The two gallons of precious water had seemed an impossible weight. When he reached the base of the cliff all he could do was crawl under the boulder.

'Why didn't they land and follow you?'

'Well, I guess they thought I was dead.'

He had chosen the red rope, hoping that the colour would be difficult to see against the red rock, and he had placed himself at the very rim of the ravine so that the rope was hidden by the edge of rock. Placing the rope had taken a long time, fixing the peg, measuring the length, judging the elasticity, everything calculated carefully, but when it came to it, he had nearly flunked it.

He had visions of the rope getting tangled round his neck as he fell. He had no way of knowing what position his body would be in when he hit the tension at the end of the rope. Even with a harness hidden below his clothing the impact could break his ribs if he had the wrong posture. And there was a worry about the length of rope. Too long and he could strike the walls of the cleft as he fell. Too short and he wouldn't swing out of sight, and would be left dangling there, an easy target. The choppers would manoeuvre round to see what had happened to him. He had to pendulum behind a big jammed chock-stone in the chimney and perch there out of sight.

He had planned a spectacular jerk backwards and then a fall, the way he had seen stunt men do it in cowboy films, but the first bullet went through the muscles of his left thigh and pulled the leg away from under him. So when he fell he wasn't acting. He hadn't known he was shot until later. He was falling into the darkness of the cleft with the noise of the choppers and the guns and the bullets ricocheting off the rocks around him.

They took a long, winding route back. He sat on Jeronimo's horse in front of the little man. He was still weak and fainted twice. Jeronimo held him and lowered him slowly to the ground. Then they rested and forced more liquid between his lips.

'Where are we going?'

They were sitting in the shade of some bushes. Jeronimo was by the river filling the water-bottles, being careful to let the silt settle out and then decanting.

'To Jeronimo's farm.'

Liz put a small water-bottle into Allan's hand.

He took a swig. 'I don't think that's a good idea,' he said. 'Someone might come.'

'Jeronimo says it will be safe. He says he'll build us a shelter not far from his house.'

'I owe him a lot,' said Allan.

Liz corrected him. 'We owe him a lot.'

She was wearing faded jeans frayed at the end and a khaki shirt worn loosely outside her pants. It was stained with perspiration and she had on the floppy wide-brimmed hat he had given her.

He said, 'Talking of us,' and looked up at her, squinting against the sun which had found gaps in the overhead foliage.

'What about us?'

Her hair was matted and straggling everywhere. She brushed it aside with her wrist.

'Are you still going to Argentina?'

'Depends.'

Her voice was tired. She sat down in the dust at his feet and hugged her knees.

'On what?'

'On whether you're going or not.'

'Oh! I see. You haven't written me off altogether then.'

She smiled. It was more of a smirk. 'Not altogether. Having gone to all this trouble to get you I think I might just hang on to you for a bit longer.'

'Long enough to marry me?'

She looked over to where Jeronimo was standing in the water, bent over the water-cans he was pushing down under the surface. She nodded slowly. 'I guess so. I might just give it a whirl.' Then she looked round at him and smiled.

'Even if I am stony broke?'

'I can earn enough for both of us until you get fit and find your way.' Jeronimo was lifting the water-cans out of the stream. 'What do you think you will be able to do?'

'Why do I have to do anything?' His voice was weak. 'Can I not just sit and watch you working?'

Her cheek dimpled. 'You planning to be a gentleman of leisure? Living off my pittance?'

'No,' he said slowly. 'I thought we might both live off these.' Painfully he put a hand in his pocket and extracted a bundle of paper. 'Halpern knew how to look after himself and he won't be needing these now.' He passed a bit of paper to her. She held it, frowning.

'What is it?'

'I think it's a Bill of Transfer to a bank in Lichtenstein. Halpern seems to have been salting money away for himself.'

'But you can't use this!'

'Why not? He can't, that's for certain.'

'But . . .'

'But it's illegal. Is that what you were going to say?'

'Yes.'

There was a long pause. One of the horses snorted.

'Well, think about this. One.' He held up a hand with one finger extended. 'Being dead, Halpern has no use for it and he probably stole it anyway. Two. How can we give it back to whoever he stole it from without giving ourselves away and getting ourselves killed in the process? Three.' The hand was getting tired. He let it fall. 'If we don't give it back and it just lies there some banker will get the benefit of it and he will not deserve it as much as we do. After all, we've just saved the world from a fate worse than death – being ruled permanently by businessmen and computer experts. Four.' The hand lifted briefly and then dropped back into the dust. 'If we do take the money we can afford to pay Jeronimo back for his kindness. We could give him a tidy sum and have plenty left over for ourselves.'

Her face broke slowly into a smile. She looked at him sideways through narrow, conspiratorial eyes. 'I see you've been giving some thought to this. How much money are we talking about?'

He smiled mischievously. 'Give or take a bit . . . without being too precise about it . . . rounding up or down . . . to the nearest whole figure . . . I would say . . . perhaps . . . it would not be stretching veracity . . . too far . . .'

'Stop that!' she said. 'How much?'

'Three million dollars.'

She looked at him with her mouth open. 'You're joking!'

'No joke. Honest. So if you were willing to marry me when you thought I was broke are you still willing to marry me if I'm rich?'

'I guess I could put up with that,' she said. 'What's the catch?'

'Well. You're quite right, of course. There is a catch. The money is all in the name of the false identity Halpern set up. He fixed himself up with a false Canadian passport.'

Allan dug slowly into another pocket, grimacing as he moved his leg. 'Here it is.' He opened it up and looked at it with eyes half shut and his head on one side.

'Actually . . . the picture is more like me than Halpern. The height is close enough and if I grew a beard . . .' He tilted his head to the other side. 'Aye. This guy could pass as me. And Canadian. That's OK. I like the Canadians. Just think. It could have been an Englishman.'

'Stop that!' she said. 'I won't have this childish xenophobia.' But she was laughing.

'OK. OK. But there is a snag. A very big snag.' He held up the passport to show her. D'you think you could bear to be married to someone who was called "Mark Thatcher"?'

She pushed her hat back on her head and folded her arms. Her lower lip pouted. 'Well now,' she said. 'I'll have to think about that one.'

Little, Brown now offers an exciting range of quality titles by both established and new authors. All of the books in this series are available by faxing, or posting your order to:

Little, Brown Books,
Cash Sales Department,
P.O. Box 11,
Falmouth,
Cornwall,
TR1O 9EN
Fax: 0326-376423

Payments can be made as follows: Cheque, postal order (payable to Little, Brown Cash Sales) or by credit cards, Visa/Access/Mastercard. Do not send cash or currency. U.K. customers and B.F.P.O.; Allow £1.00 for postage and packing for the first book, plus 50p for the second book, plus 30p for each additional book up to a maximum charge of £3.00 (7 books plus). U.K. orders over £75 free postage and packing.

Overseas customers including Ireland, please allow £2.00 for postage and packing for the first book, plus £1.00 for the second book, plus 50p for each additional book.

NAME (Block Letters) ....

ADDRESS ....

....

....

☐ I enclose my remittance for ....

☐ I wish to pay by Visa/Access/Mastercard

Number ☐☐☐☐☐☐☐☐☐☐☐☐☐☐☐☐

Card Expiry Date ☐☐☐☐